I0525448

Wolves We Feed

Vivian Catfield

CATFIELD
PRESS

Wolves We Feed

By Vivian Catfield

Published by Vivian Catfield on her imprint, Catfield Press

2692 Madison Rd.

Ste. N1-354

Cincinnati, OH 45208

www.viviancatfield.com

www.catfieldpress.com

First Edition, Published 2025.

Copyright © 2025 Vivian Catfield

All Rights Reserved

Cover Art, Internal Images, and Design Copyright © 2025 by Vivian Catfield

eBook ISBN: 9798992771572

Paperback ISBN: 9798992771565

Printed in the United States of America

This book is a work of fiction. Names, characters, places, and incidents are either the product of the author's imagination or are used fictitiously. Any resemblance to actual persons, living or dead, events, or locales is entirely coincidental and not intended by the author.

All brand names and product names used in this book are trademarks, registered trademarks, or trade names of their respective holders. Vivian Catfield and Catfield Press are not associated with any product or vendor in this book.

All rights reserved. No part of this publication may be reproduced, distributed, or transmitted in any form or by any means, including photocopying, recording, or other electronic or mechanical methods, without the prior written permission of the publisher, Catfield Press, and the author, Vivian Catfield, except in the case of brief quotation embodied in critical reviews and certain other noncommercial uses permitted by copyright law.

For permission requests, please utilize the mailing address above and the contact pages at:

www.viviancatfield.com and www.catfieldpress.com.

Reader Advisory

This novel is a work of fiction that explores mature and emotionally intense themes. The story involves a culturally different historical setting in which violence occurs and language is used that may be objectionable to today's readers.

These themes include:

- Trauma and abuse (including references to past sexual violence)
- Psychological manipulation and mental illness
- Death, grief, and brief mentions of suicide
- Substance abuse
- Violence involving people and animals
- Strong language and adult situations
- Racially and ethnically objectionable language commonly used during the era

These elements are presented in service of the characters and their stories. Great concern has been taken to balance history with avoidance of unnecessary detail.

Please take care while reading. If you are a survivor of trauma, know that your experiences matter. Your well-being is important, and you are never alone in your efforts to recover.

If you or someone you know needs support and/or wishes to report abuse or assault, confidential help is available 24/7 through the resources below.

- RAINN (Rape, Abuse & Incest National Network – U.S.): www.rainn.org | 1-800-656-HOPE
- SAMHSA (Substance Abuse and Mental Health Services Administration): www.samhsa.gov | 1-800-662-HELP
- 988 Suicide & Crisis Lifeline: www.988lifeline.org | Call or Text 988
- Crime Stoppers (U.S.): www.crimestoppersusa.org | 1-800-222-TIPS

Author's Note & Land Acknowledgement

This novel is set in the American West and its frontiers. These characters walk the lands that have been home to Native Nations, including the Apache, Arapaho, Cherokee, Cheyenne, Comanche, Crow, Lakota, Navajo, Osage, Pawnee, Ute, Wabenaki, and other peoples for thousands of years. I acknowledge with respect the enduring presence, cultures, and sovereignty of Indigenous peoples, and recognize that this story unfolds across territories originally stewarded by Native communities who continue to live, create, and thrive here. In writing about the American West, it's important to remember that the histories we tell are often incomplete. Thus, I strongly encourage readers to seek out Native voices, perspectives, and stories.

Also, I ask you to encourage Indigenous education as a meaningful step toward equity and understanding. One way to make an impact is by supporting tribal colleges and universities (TCUs). These institutions provide culturally grounded higher education to Native students across the United States. To learn more or to donate, please consider looking into the following reputable organizations for Native American education, culture, community wellness, and sovereignty:

- American Indian College Fund — Funds scholarships and supports tribal colleges and universities for Native American and Alaska Native students. Website: collegefund.org

- National Indian Education Association — A national organization focused on improving educational opportunities for Native students and preserving Native languages and culture. Website: www.niea.org

- Running Strong for American Indian Youth — Supports youth empowerment, cultural preservation, clean water access, nutrition, and education in Native American communities. Website: www.indianyouth.org

- Native Ways Federation — Promotes and supports Native-led nonprofits and increases awareness of giving to Indigenous-led organizations. Website: www.nativeways.org

For Andrew,
Who I love to the moon and back

Contents

Prologue

I n the summer of 2012, I was a newly minted English PhD without a single teaching job offer. I decided to try my hand at becoming a fiction editor. I whipped out my already heavily charged credit card and purchased tuition to attend a six-week workshop at the Publishing Institute in Denver. My hope was that it would open doors into the hallowed halls of employment at a press in New York. That hope fizzled out soon after a fruitless trip to the Big Apple, during which I went to ten interviews in five days. Finding no other opportunities there, I returned to Tennessee with my graduation cap in hand to toil through the next decade in adjunct purgatory. Although I wasn't able to secure a job after attending the Institute, I did return from Denver with three things: many delightful friends, a ton of knowledge about publishing, and a genesis of the volume that is the subject of this narrative.

My circle of bookworm roommates in Colorado included two from Michigan, one from North Carolina, and me from Tennessee. None of us had ever been West of the Mississippi, so exploring the Rockies felt like entering a foreign land. We went to Manitou Springs and sipped medicinal waters from all eight fountains. We laughed at the jokes of a blind man and his equally blind pit bull guide dog, who wore matching bandanas and sunglasses. We marveled at the view of Pike's Peak from the Devil's Head watchtower, the former outpost of Helen Dowe, Colorado's first female lookout. Normally a photophobe, I allowed my roommates to take a picture of me standing by the windows with binoculars in hand, scanning the horizon for fires as Helen must have done almost a century before.

Back on the ground, we drove out to the Garden of the Gods. I cried uncontrollably upon being surrounded by the majestic life-in-death of the desert. Having spent my entire existence up to that point in the gently rolling foothills of the Appalachians, the absence of that green ocean took my breath. The red abyss of desert swallowed me whole. Closing my eyes in hopes of stopping the tears before my friends could see, I had a vision. I was standing in that same spot, so long ago that it was past the realm of memory. Only then it was wintertime. A white blanket of snow covered the dusty red sea that swam beyond my mind's eye. I was seated on a horse, swathed in blankets, following a string of other riders to an unknown destination. One of my friends came up behind me and tapped me on the shoulder, pulling me back into reality. She asked if I was alright. I lied and replied *yes*.

We continued on through the park, pausing for all the touristy photo ops. As usual, I volunteered to take most of the pictures in order to avoid being in them. At our last stop, I had my back to Steamboat Rock, preparing to take a snap of my roommates. They waited in line for their turn beneath the Balanced Rock, mimicking the Herculean pose of countless thousands who had pretended to hold the rock steady above them. Shoaling for a better shot while I fumbled in my shoulder bag, I dropped my cell phone. Not quick enough to catch it, I watched helplessly as the most essential appliance in my life bounced down a series of rocks and fell into a hole. Seeing my plight, my roommates sighed audibly. It seemed their hopes for my documenting their turn at playing Atlas were dashed. Their dismay switched to concern as I flopped onto my stomach in the dirt and peered down into the crevice.

"Don't reach in there!" They cried out. "What if there's a rattlesnake?"

The prospect of being snake-bitten was the least of my concerns. I knew I couldn't afford to replace a $500 phone, so I plunged my hand into the darkness. As I probed in the dusty clay, I had another flash of vision in which I found something completely different. It was an old-fashioned journal, with a thin strip of leather tied around its cover. The mental image was so clear and detailed that I could almost hear the brittle cover crackle and smell the mildew of the weathered pages when I opened it. As my fingers closed around my phone, the two visions merged into one. In my imagination, the journal belonged to the woman in the winter desert.

Fortunately, my phone was unharmed, and I was able to take the photo of my friends. That night, back in my dorm room as I dozed off, I asked the woman from my vision to tell me her name and her story. It is a common part of my writing process to request that characters whom I am writing about visit me in my dreams. If you are a writer, and you've never tried it, I highly recommend you explore lucid dreaming techniques. The practice has never failed me, and it works very well if you're trying to overcome writer's block. The book you are about to read is the direct result of the dream I asked for after that first visit to the Colorado Desert.

The dream began with me holding the journal I had seen in my vision. Turning it over in my hands, I examined the once-smooth cordovan leather. I noticed the cover was strangely pierced with a triangular formation of dents, roughly in the shape of a hand with the fingers held together, but twice the size. Having grown up in the country around a number of large dogs, I couldn't shake the thought that the dents appeared to be in the shape of a massive bite mark. Carefully, I opened the front cover. The crackling of the weather-warped leather reminded me of a time in Confirmation class when I had accidentally left my Bible out in the rain while we were on a break. I dried it out at home with my hair dryer, but the cover stayed permanently bent, and my carefully highlighted and annotated pages remained forever blurred.

The writing of this journal in my dream, however, remained legible and bold. It was written in a copybook clear hand on thick, creamy ecru pages. On the overleaf was inscribed a title, *The Diary of Esmeray Ulrich—Schoolteacher*. The lines beneath it read, *My Journey from Portland, Maine to Auraria, Kansas Territory, 1858*. Intrigued by this gift from my unconscious mind, I began to read, and continued until the alarm awakened me at six the next morning. I felt so exhausted by the night's adventures, it was as if I'd never been to sleep at all.

Muddling my way through a shower and then venturing out for coffee, I pondered the possibilities of what I had just experienced. As a writer, I felt compelled to share the tale, but the problem was in contextualizing it. The story was impossible to take as fact. However, even as I knew it was deeply entrenched in the realm of fantasy, my mind trailed away to Hemingway's oft-quoted phrase, "All good books have one thing in common—they are truer than if they had really happened." I started thinking. What could I do to write a story based on this dream that preserved its historical truth, and still contained the tale's core message, as if it were a fable?

After I returned home, I researched the history of America's gold rushes, from Georgia to California. I read shelves full of books on the customs and folklore of Native American tribes. I reread Clarissa Pinkola Estes's marvelous study, *Women Who Run With the Wolves*. Then, I saw an excellent independent play called *The Man-Beast* by Joseph Zettelmaier at the Know Theater in Cincinnati, featuring the superb Jim Hopkins in the title role. Finally, I found the book *Women Teachers on the Frontier* by Polly Welts Kaufman, that introduced me to a heartbreaking fact. Almost two-thirds of women who signed contracts to teach in schools along America's Western frontier never cashed their first paychecks.

What could have happened to those women has haunted me for years.

All of them were unmarried, intelligent, highly educated, adventurous, and on the lookout for ways to make a positive difference in the world, just like I was at the beginning of my teaching career. Their hearts were full in equal parts of transcendental idealism and practical self-reliance. If I had lived a little over a century and a half ago, I could have been one of them.

Yet, two-thirds of them completely vanished from the face of the Earth. No one cared enough to find out why. I simply couldn't allow them or their perspectives to be erased. Even if, after all my research, the only narrative I could piece together was a patchwork quilt of genuine history interwoven with mythology and nightmares, I felt compelled to create it.

Because that day in the desert, someone or something chose me to tell a story.

All history of the American West is, to some degree, the stuff of fantasy. As John Wayne said in *The Man Who Shot Liberty Valance*, "when a legend becomes the truth, print the legend."

That is what I have done here. I leave determination of its veracity up to you.

July 1, 1858

Last night on the southbound train to Hartford,
I dreamt of the loup garou.

In the dream, I must have been no more than thirteen. If it were a year later, I would have been away at school by the time autumn fell. I know this because not only did I recognize the bright red leaves of the maple trees surrounding me at the edge of my grand-père's dairy pasture, but also because of what I held in my hand. It was a rabbit kit, and it was dying.

The rabbit had once been real, that I remember plainly. One always remembers her first brush with death. One of Grand-père's collies, a pup born that spring, brought it to me, seeking praise for his kill. Only, the rabbit wasn't dead. The pup dropped the poor wretch screaming at my feet. I sat down my rifle and picked up the kit, wiping some of the blood off its fur with my thumb. I could see the puncture wounds in its side from the pup's teeth. With each whistling gasp the kit took, a spray of tiny blood droplets fanned out over my palm from its ruined lungs. As it exhaled, the whistle became a scream. In vain, I attempted to cover the holes with my fingertips. This caused a shuddering tremor of fear to run down the length of the kit's tiny body, ending in the spasmodic quiver of its little white paws.

Realizing that there was nothing I could do, I began to cry. Cradling the bloody rabbit kit in my hands, I called out for my grand-père. I could hear him shuffling through the grove of flaming maple trees. The collie pup began barking, but I paid him no heed other than to shush him venomously. "Look at what you've done," I said, more to myself and the kit than the collie. "Shame on you! A baby killing a baby!"

I stroked the poor kit's head softly from the space between its eyes to the tips of its tiny ears. The kit closed its eyes and shuddered only slightly this time. I could feel it resigning itself to fate and loss of blood. It attempted one last scream, which came out with more of a choking sound. Blood trickled from its small mouth. I cupped my hands around it, bringing it close to my face and whispering as softly as I could. "I am sorry, little one. You deserved more of life. At least let your final suffering pass in this moment knowing I will never forget you."

As I stood whispering to the dying kit, the collie pup began yelping loudly. Looking up to scold him again, he turned and ran away through the woods. That was when I saw it.

The *loup garou* stood on its hind legs, watching me from the clearing.

I had only seen wolves from afar, but this was no ordinary wolf. He was more than twice the size of any wolf I'd ever seen. He stood panting and hunched over, like a man who had just sprinted a long distance. Still holding the kit in my hands, I felt every hair on my body stand on end. The *loup garou* locked eyes with me. I had only a moment to register their blazing fire before he dropped to all fours and began to charge. I could not move, even as I saw it racing toward me with astonishing speed. Too late, I began staggering backward.

In a flash, he was upon me. As I stumbled, he leapt. The impact punched the air out of my lungs. The poor kit flew from my hands, and I watched the beast sail over me to catch the rabbit in its gaping maw. I saw stars as the back of my head hit the ground. Rolling onto my side in pain, I caught a glimpse of the monster crunching its great jaws together, swallowing the rabbit whole. Straightening up to full height again, the *loup garou* stared at me once more with those furnace-like eyes. Then, with a swish of his tail, he disappeared as my world went completely black.

Of course, in real life, the day ended far differently. My grand-père came out of the woods and saw me crying, still holding the dead rabbit in my hands. Saying nothing, he took it from me and pulled out his handkerchief. Wrapping the kit in this little shroud, he laid it carefully on the ground. Grand-père asked me in French if I wanted to bury him. I nodded *oui* through my tears. We dug a small hole, placed the kit in it, and covered him with loose soil and rocks. Although we went on hunting for venison that day, I couldn't bring myself to fire a single shot.

"It is the way of the world, dear heart," Grand-père said, as we walked back toward the barns that evening. "The innocent will always suffer. There is nothing we can do. Most often by the time we become aware of their pain, it is already too late." He stopped, leaning on his walking stick with both hands. "Somewhere, always, there is a wolf waiting. Those who survive are the ones who watch for him and are ready."

The rest of the evening fades into the recesses of my memory, blended with hundreds of others like it. We had dinner in the little lodge house next to the barns. Grand-père and I played some music together. He on the fiddle, and I on the clavier. By the firelight he told me the stories of his boyhood in New France. Although I don't recall whether I asked him for a *loup garou* story that night, it seems that I must have.

Otherwise, why would I put those two thoughts together in my dreams as I have tonight?

Perhaps I am just overly tired from spending the night on the train. So much so it seems I have forgotten entirely to tell you my purpose for writing this journal. And that, dear reader, is something you should know. Later this morning, only a few hours from now, I will sign away my life. At least, for the next year or so.

I have joined the latest cohort of teachers from the National Board in Hartford. This morning, I have one final meeting before my departure. Afterward, I will be leaving on the first train for Cincinnati. Hopefully, I will be able to rest more easily, with today's business behind me. From there, I will continue by riverboat to Independence. Last, I will take a stagecoach across the Kansas Territory to a new school in a little town near Pike's Peak called Auraria.

I do not know much about the place, other than there is rumored to be gold there. Hence the reason for the school and the sudden rise in population. There are springs nearby too, which are believed to have medicinal powers. At least, that is what I have heard.

Of course, it is natural for you to wonder, dear reader, why might a woman embark upon this journey alone? Into a realm unknown not only to her, but also to most of the rest of America? Especially when she is to be the only teacher in this untamed land?

Well, to begin, I am over thirty, unmarried, childless, and generally alone in the world. Further, I am over-educated to the point of boredom, and I seek an adventure. Those, I suppose, are as good of reasons as any.

This is to be my record of the journey. Since it seems there may be no granddaughter in my hazily distant future with whom I might share this tale, I offer it instead to you.

That is... I will after I pick up my paperwork. The train is pulling into the station now, so I must pause here to say *adieu!*

July 2, 1858

I've rarely had a more condescending encounter in my life than the one I endured this morning. Although I am abundantly glad to be free of the man who runs the program (and whom I will refer to as "Mr. H" for his headmasterly, pompous air) I feel the need to record our encounter for posterity.

Mr. H felt compelled to "warn" me of the increased level of difficulty for my new soon-to-be teaching position. He completely ignored my previous decade of teaching experience, choosing instead to dictate as if I were a novice. Mr. H seemed to be under the impression I would not able to discern on my own that a farmer's child brought up to hold a plow might handle a pencil with more reluctance than his more urbanely bred peers.

Next, I found the nature of his tone regarding the native children, whom I am also to teach, most disturbing. Going through the tired and distasteful rhetoric that is more often heard among the elderly in pubs, Mr. H stressed the need for giving Native children "a firm Christian hand." He deemed this necessary "to repress their heathen superstitions and instill in them the necessary discipline to participate in polite society."

His sanctimonious comments tried my patience sorely. My reply, which I was rather proud of, given its level of sarcastic restraint, was as follows: "In other words, the intent of my instruction should be not to expand their minds, but to expel their instincts." I meant these words facetiously and they were received without humor.

In truth, I was not surprised. Based on the summer "retraining" that was required of me in order to enter to the program, it appeared one goal of establishing a school in the new territory was to erase as much of the "Nativeness" in the students as possible. This approach is completely contrary to my personal philosophy of education. My method begins with

Rousseau and concludes with the teachings of Emerson and Thoreau. All of whom found divine inspiration in natural childhood.

Fear not, I shall not indulge in a lengthy and sure-to-be tiresome digression of my educational ideals here. However, as we are still getting acquainted with one another, I do think it would be appropriate to give you a quick summation of my personal history. Perhaps then you might think me a little less mad for engaging in such an unladylike endeavor as teaching in a frontier school.

I am an only child born of the union between a common lobsterman and the daughter of a successful cheese maker in Portland, Maine. My grand-père, Émile Ulrich, the aforementioned cheese maker, was the first in his family born in America after they immigrated from France. He volunteered to serve in Washington's Army at sixteen and was rewarded with a land grant in lieu of pay. He used the land grant to open a small dairy. Out of this, he grew the large cheese company that made his fortune. His first marriage brought him five hearty sons to run the business. Upon the death of this first wife, he married a slight, pretty girl who became my grand-mére, although I never knew her. She bore Émile his only daughter, and then promptly died.

That daughter, my mother Marie, was the apple of my grand-père's eye. Although he had hoped to marry her off to a wealthy merchant, Marie had none of it. She married a lobsterman. I never knew much about my father, other than the fact he played the fiddle, a talent over which he and my grand-père bonded. The match lasted less than a year. My father died in a storm at sea while my mother still carried me in her womb. Due to his death and lack of notoriety in relation to my grand-père, I was not given my father's last name, which was Blethyn. Wanting to retire and to give my mother something to do in order to relieve her mind from mourning my father, my grand-père opened Ulrich's Tavern. The two of them worked side by side in his "retirement" that lasted thirty years.

I spent my youth as a girl of two... nay, three... worlds. One was the world of my grand-père's dairy farm north of the city. He taught me to hunt, fish, trap, take care of the animals, and welcome the pull of the wilderness into my heart. The second was the world of the tavern, in which I learned from my mother how to use a smile to obtain anything I wanted. There, I also saw first-hand what she warned me were "the worst instincts of men." Third was the world I created for myself: a fortress built of books I hoped would shield me from all of life's harsh realities I disliked within the other two.

Growing up, I had private tutors. I attended Westbrook Seminary, completing both the ladies' classical and scientific tracks in succession. I had no desire for children and no incentive to marry for money or security. Given the success of my older uncles' prolific families and our cheese business, I had plenty of both. Instead, I began teaching school in Portland shortly after graduation, primarily to occupy my mind. However, after my fifth year, I became inexplicably restless. Although the Ulrich clan as a whole was content with their "maiden aunt," the aunt herself felt stagnant.

Even so, I remained hesitant to start anything new. I blamed the reluctance on my beloved grand-père's age and declining health. My mother would have none of it. She felt she had wasted her chance for freedom with an early marriage. Mother urged me to travel and to find whatever answers were lacking in my education out in the world. Thus, on the eve of my twenty-ninth birthday, I bid farewell to the Portland girls' school where I taught, and left for a year's Grand Tour of Europe. Thanks to my age, I was permitted to go unchaperoned.

My desire to rekindle a creative fire within myself was stoked each day, first as I walked the hills of Wordsworth's *Lyrical Ballads*, and later as I roamed the streets of London, Paris, and Rome. Memories of my idyllic childhood days in the Maine woods rose with me every morning. I began again to put pen to paper, trying to reconcile man's needless desire to lose himself into the grasping smog of the industrial world, when all that he needed lay behind him in Whitmanesque *Leaves of Grass*.

Just as I had decided to return home and begin the next phase of my life as a self-styled feminine disciple of Emerson and his descendants, I received a wire that my beloved grand-père had passed away of an influenza outbreak. My mother too was gravely ill from nursing him. I took the next available ship home, but I arrived too late.

Unlocking the door of the tavern for the first time after their funerals, which had been delayed for my arrival, felt like entering a tomb. Silence rang from every corner. I could almost hear their voices and the voices of their friends, many of whom had also recently died of the pestilence. I kept the tavern closed all winter, which was just as well. Few in Portland were going out due to warnings about health and safety. By the spring thaw, I sold everything except my grand-père's dairy farm, which was already maintained by my uncles. I chose to head West, hoping to outrun their ghosts.

After reviewing the myriad of prospects that unfolded before me, I settled on the idea of teaching in a frontier school. The low pay was of no concern, as I was independently wealthy. Also, the prospect of creating something new that would be completely my own held substantial appeal. All my life, I had been known as "Émile Ulrich's granddaughter, of the Portland soft cheese Ulrichs." This was my chance to be known as Esmeray Ulrich, educator, alone.

Perhaps you can see why I bristled so much at the concerns of Mr. H regarding my suitability for teaching. Which were, I assure you, many and quite varied in their array of insinuations. These "reservations," as he called them, related to me were split into two categories: Physical and Moral. When he offered the choice of which category I would rather hear about first, I chose the former, thinking it would be quicker and less insulting.

Unfortunately, I was mistaken. Mr. H began by saying, "There is no delicate way to put this, Miss Ulrich. You are quite aged to be starting out on a venture such as this, are you not? Most of our beginning teachers are in their early twenties, and you are..."

I interrupted him there. Replying that, yes, I knew I was almost 32, but my health was sound, and I was willing to submit to a medical exam to quell any fears. Since I'd been expecting this, I added a metaphor to my reply. I explained that, contrary to popular belief, women did not spoil like milk with age. With proper cultivation we could ripen instead into something finer, like a good cheese, albeit with a tougher rind for the struggle.

Mr. H seemed to be taken aback by my retort. Clearly, he was not used to such dissension, especially from a middle-aged female whom he considered subordinate. I'm certain this hastened his launch into the second category of his many "reservations." These focused on my character. Or rather, what he perceived to be deficiencies present therein, although he preferred to shift the burden of guilt at holding such provincialism onto others.

"It's not a matter of what *I* perceive, Miss Ulrich," Mr. H said. His voice dropped an octave as he explained in secretive tones. "It's a matter of what the *parents* and *patrons* of the school at which you may be teaching might perceive. We've already established the matter of your advanced age. It is of concern not only in regards to your health, but to the fact that you remain unmarried. Plus, you are of French extraction, which can be scandalous in some circles. People in small towns tend to talk, Miss Ulrich. For a woman over thirty who is prepared to travel completely across the country alone and to accept a position working outside the home, I am afraid to say the nature of that talk is not likely to be kind. Additionally, there are the facts that not only did you travel across a large portion of Europe completely unchaperoned, but also until recently you were the proprietor of a pub. I hope you understand, Miss Ulrich, that our female educators face an uphill battle already in proving themselves morally worthy to lead their classrooms. Their personal history must be completely without reproach. If we are to take you on in this position, there must be no allusions made to your European travels, whether in the classroom or the community. Further, you are not to be seen consuming alcohol in any of their local establishments. To commit either of these two violations would result in immediate termination of your contract. Is that clear?"

To these insinuations, I replied, "Crystally." Yet, it did give me pause wondering how little a person must have to do in his or her own life to take the trouble to report such minor indiscretions to my employer halfway across the country.

Having thus ticked off his mental list before squirreling it away in some unseeable cerebral file drawer, Mr. H presented me with the papers to sign. With that task completed, he handed me a stiffly bound volume titled *Disciplinary Manual.* Finally, he shooed me out of the office without even bothering to shake my hand.

I suppose this somewhat insulting encounter was necessary in the event he might ever need to account for my shortcomings. In which case, he would doubtlessly cite these disclaimers to absolve himself from blame for my misbehavior. I read all these things and more, passing like a series of clouds on a mercurial day over Mr. H's face. As for their impact upon my personal thoughts or subsequent actions, they had little effect.

On the way back to the train station this afternoon, I stopped into a pub for a brandy. I drank it in plain view for anyone who cared to see. Upon my leave, I accidentally dropped my *Disciplinary Manual* into the gutter. Since I plan on being an exceptional teacher, at least for a year, I did not feel retrieving it was necessary.

July 3, 1858

S lept poorly on the train last night, due to having more dreams of the *loup garou*. This time; however, I was of my current age, but in a place completely unknown to me. It appeared to be a desert. There was a notable absence of flora, save for a cactus or two. As I wandered through this barren wasteland, I heard the distinct howl of a lone wolf in the distance. Thinking nothing of it, I continued to trudge along a path through an array of vast, reddish-brown boulders as tall as monuments. I was bent on reaching some unknown destination, as one often does in dreams.

The howls continued as I reached an especially large rock that appeared to be balanced precariously upon the tip of a smaller one. The sun beat down upon me. I craved a moment of rest from the heat and collapsed in exhaustion in the shade offered by the rock. While I sat panting and fanning myself with my hat, a figure began to emerge in the distance. As it came closer, I could see clearly it was a large wolf-like beast. Once again, it was much larger than any wolf I have ever seen, this *loup garou*. For some reason, I was not afraid of his approach, as I was before. I did not flee, but remained in the shade of the rock, complacently watching him.

When the creature reached the rocks, he stood up on his hind legs like a man. He began to climb the steeper side. Once he reached the flat area where I was sitting, he fell again to all fours. Nudging his massive head under my arm, he lay down beside me like an enormous dog. Strangely, I still was not disturbed by this. Instead, I ran my hands through his coarse, gray fur. It was full of red clay dust from his trip through the desert. Being this close to his dusty fur, I sneezed. In hindsight this must have been the point I first began to rouse myself from the dream. The creature stirred slightly, turning onto his side and curling into a ball. His movements were reminiscent of a domesticated animal, rather than a wild beast. As the creature drifted off into slumber, I awoke in this world to the first streams of weak sunlight shining through the train car windows.

I'm not quite sure what to make of these dreams. Perhaps they are some symbolic representation of my unconscious mind coming to grips with the fact I have committed myself to a life in the wilderness. If so, then the change in my attitude toward this creature of the unknown from fear to acceptance might signify any latent apprehension toward yet unforeseen circumstances might be abating. That would be the most welcome explanation.

On a different note, I have a layover for a night once I reach Cincinnati. Perhaps I will consult a Spiritualist there regarding the matter, if the dreams persist. Although I know many do not believe in their interpretations, I have found their guidance to be of comfort in the months since the passing of my mother and grand-père. Their passing also brought me many dreams of a most unusual nature.

However, those will have to be saved for another time. It appears the train has stopped for some reason during the course of my recollection here. Considering we pulled out of the New York station just after I finished my breakfast and sat down to write, I don't think we should be scheduled for another stop so soon. I am going to walk up to the club car to inquire about this disturbance.

July 4, 1858

S adly, it was a man. He leapt out in front of the train as we passed through the final station leaving the city.

According to some of the other passengers with whom I spoke, he was some sort of railroad financier. This would seem ironic, given the circumstances of his death. Yet, he appeared to have been intent on making a specific statement. He was overheard shouting, "This is the last time you shall ever have the chance to run over me," by several bystanders in the seconds before he made the fatal jump.

This I learned after my fellow passengers and I were asked to disembark from the train. We waited a few hours on the nearby platform for another, so that an official inspection could be made of the site and the pieces of the man's body recovered. I say *pieces* because the man was dragged a considerable distance from the platform after the point of impact, resulting in the severing of his body at the pelvis. Although the coroner and his team attempted to be discreet about the collection and retrieval of his parts, I am positive I saw one of his legs being extracted and carried away wrapped in white cloth. His shoe was sticking out. The sight of it made sick to my stomach. I had to sit down to prevent myself from vomiting.

While I waited sitting on my trunk for the next train to arrive, I found this sort of thing has become disturbingly common along the route from New York to Ohio. I was away in Europe for the majority of 1857, ascribed "the panic year." Little of its impact lingered in Maine upon my return. However, the desperation it inspired in this part of the country seems to have been more acute and enduring.

From what I have gathered through conversation, the Panic began last year with the failure of Ohio Life and Trust. That failure was the first in a chain of dominos. Eventually, it overtook much of the East Coast banking industry, which in recent years has become inextricably inter-twined with the new railroads being built throughout the West. Together, their investments facilitated expansion of settlement into newer regions of the country. As several railroad companies floundered and declared bankruptcy, commercial credit began to dry up. This made it more difficult for Western merchants to purchase grain and other goods from farmers. In turn, it destabilized and then deflated the cost of grain. The ultimate result was that hundreds of farmers lost their lands. Abandoning all hope of recovery along with their farms, many chose to push even further West. Those desperate men discovered a new goal of striking it rich in the gold and silver fields.

Normally, I do not follow the financial news. I couldn't care less what happens to the greedy financiers of the American railroad industry. Nevertheless, I find this particular series of events troubling. From these unfortunate farmers, it is likely many of my future students will have sprung. To me, it is always useful to know the backgrounds of my students, so that I might choose readings best suited to gain their attention and interest. I must take some time to consider what works might appeal to children whose lives have been uprooted in hopes of finding their family fortunes by chance in a foreign land. At present, all that comes to mind when I try to recall treasure hunting tales are pirate stories, none of which I think are particularly likely to promote the proper types of aspirations to instill in the minds of the young.

However, upon further reflection, pirate stories might suit our current social climate after all. America is a nation built on the work of pirates, each of one kind or another. Their mythologies of purloined gold leading to sudden glory would certainly hold undeniable appeal for the budding industrialist. In today's society, the pirates wear top hats and tails rather than tricorns and doublets, and terrorize the stock markets instead of the high seas.

My apologies for expressing such cynicism on the anniversary of our nation's birth. It's just that, given today's events and their cause, I find less to celebrate than usual this year.

July 5, 1858

We've managed to make our way through Pennsylvania and most of Ohio without further incident, Thank God!

The smoke from the steel mills hung over Pittsburgh like a malignant miasma. Even though the heat was over ninety degrees, the attendants kept the windows tightly shut so the passenger cars remained free of the poisonous vapors. I pity those who live there all year round. They must have lungs of iron to endure it.

Columbus was no better. Factory upon factory belching voluminous clouds of black coal smoke. The poor workers swarmed to and fro like bees among hives. Their relentless busyness brought to my mind a contradictory passage from Thoreau, in which he opined "idleness was the most attractive and productive industry." Given the eagerness with which these Midwesterners so quickly lash the heavy yoke of labor to their shoulders, I would wager Thoreau's wisdom is not popular here.

Nor does the art of casual conversation between strangers seem to have reached this portion of the nation. At the Pittsburgh stop, I attempted to engage a gentleman on the subject of the headlines in his newspaper, only to have him rise and move to another seat. Once removed, he began chatting immediately with another fellow regarding steel prices. When we stopped in Columbus, an extended family consisting of two mothers and a number of children boarded. Thinking I could possibly start a conversation at the very least about their schooling, I inquired as to how far along each was in his or her studies. The replies of the mothers were terse to say the least. While they did not get up from their seats to actively move away from me, I had the distinct feeling they would rather not be in my company.

This made me self-conscious, which is a circumstance of exceeding rarity. I am almost never so. After enduring half an hour of their stony silence and harsh sidelong glances, I removed myself to sit upon a stool at the bar. I could feel the harsh judgment of their tightly drawn faces as they studied me while I paid for and sipped my glass of brandy. Tapping my fingers in time to a happy tune I hummed out of nervousness, I saw out of the corner of my eye one lean over to the other and whisper something. Looking down at my left hand, it dawned on me what they were gossiping about. There was no ring on my finger. Yet there I was, an unmarried woman of their age, daring to drink alone at a bar on a train!

The ridiculousness of it gave me the giggles. I couldn't help myself. I turned and looked straight at them. Then, I downed the remaining contents of my glass in the largest single gulp I could manage. Catching me grinning at them over the empty rim, they gasped in unison. One even clapped her hands over the eyes of the little girl seated in her lap, which made me laugh even harder as the girl pushed them down.

Although this encounter was most amusing, it makes me wonder. Was the insufferable Mr. H correct in warning me of the proclivity toward gossip of the populace I intend to serve? Regardless, I intend to change for no one. Like my treasured brother in thought, dear Walt Whitman, "I choose to celebrate myself, no matter what anyone else chooses to assume."

July 6, 1858

A rrived at last in Cincinnati on the noon train. After almost six full days with the rails rumbling beneath my feet, walking on *terra firma* again felt slightly unsteady at first. It was as if I were regaining my land legs after many days at sea.

After taking a carriage to the hotel, I decided to have a walk downtown. Whereas Pittsburgh and Columbus seem to have laid their stock in fortune in coal and steel, Cincinnati appears to be a city content to live off the literal fatback of the land. By that, I mean hogs. The change of industry appears to be better for the texture of the air, which is far less foggy, if not for the smell. The odor is distinctly that of an enormous barnyard. Given the proliferation of pork in the metropolis, I was surprised to learn they have not adopted the customs of their Southern brethren. There is no barbecue to be found anywhere.

This was a shame, since my hopes had been high for a good barbecue plate upon seeing this Porkopolis firsthand. While dining instead at the little German restaurant on the ground floor of the hotel, which was quite good, I learned that pulled pork is generally frowned upon by locals. They feel it is food for colored people only. I found this sentiment most unfortunate, but said nothing to refute it. Though I have enjoyed and seen many other white people enjoying a good barbecue on my travels through the Carolina coastal region on several occasions. From my travels, I have learned it is almost impossible to change culturally ingrained culinary tastes.

The matter of social relations between Cincinnatians and their neighbors across the river in Kentucky is even more peculiar than their arbitrary classification of barbecue. Although I have gleaned they are content to trade with them in business, they do not socialize with their Southern counterparts willingly. This is true whether the Southerners in question are white or colored, German or English, in their lineage.

Even though I have only been in town for one day, I have already observed several instances in which the local businessmen disparaged the accents and intellect of the Kentuckians whom they had recently encountered immediately after said Kentuckians were out of earshot. Also, I have noticed the jobs worked by freed men and women of color are of the most undesirable occupations. For example, all the difficult and dirty work of butchering hogs and processing their flesh into consumables is done by black men. In contrast, the final product is bought and sold by merchants and customers who are primarily white. The end results of keeping people of color pushed down into the lower links of this food chain, so to speak, are clear. By keeping them in heavy labor and at low wages, there is never any danger of their rising up in society to become legitimate rivals for the German and other European immigrants who dominate the merchant classes here.

These circumstances are made even more puzzling considering this is the city which gave birth to Harriet Beecher Stowe's great book, *Uncle Tom's Cabin*. How is it possible to express such poignant written sympathy from afar for those who are enslaved, only to subject them to a different sort of slavery by low wages, limited employment prospects, and social ostracism when they arrive upon the north shore of the Ohio River, seeking asylum?

Hopefully, I will have some resolution to this puzzling question soon, as I am invited to attend a benefit dinner for a Catholic orphans' society tonight. I will save off the rest of today's entry until then, in hopes of being able to provide a more satisfactory answer.

***

Alas, my hope of reconciling the boldness with which Midwesterners advocate for the abolishment of slavery in print with their reluctance to openly offer genuine assistance to those who have fled its bonds have been dashed. It appears there is only a small contingency of citizens here who are actually true to the cause of abolition. In the cocktail hour after dinner, there were many whispers of this person or that who was a participant in what they call the Underground Railroad. These brave souls, some white and others free persons of color, offer safe harbor in their basements, barns, and what have you to escapees who are freshly fled across the river. Then, I am told, they also give fugitives advice on the best routes to follow in order to continue their journey into the more complete safety of Canada.

It came as somewhat of a shock to me that, even if an escaped slave is able to reach Ohio, which is a free state, he or she might still be apprehended and forced back into enslavement. Previously, I had assumed merely crossing the Mason-Dixon Line all but assured their freedom. However, tonight I learned that whites unsympathetic to the cause, and in fact, even some of the more unscrupulous members of the colored community seeking to make quick money as a finder's fee, often turn in tips to "slave catchers" who troll the riverfront communities hoping to kidnap runaways and return them to their owners for a bounty. How devastating it must be, to risk one's life in an attempt to make it to a free state, only to find it is not truly free! I am afraid that America will never be rid of the abominable institution of slavery without war.

Regardless, other than these small whisperings and rumors, there was little said about the plight of the enslaved. The focus of the evening was on raising money for children recently orphaned by epidemics of cholera, typhoid, influenza, and tuberculosis. All of which, I learned, have left their long scars upon this young city. The number of orphans' homes in the area are many. Most are run by the fathers and sisters of the Catholic Church. These institutions provide food, clothing, and education to these unfortunate children until the age of fourteen. After that time, they are given the choice of going to work full-time, usually in some sort of factory or vocational employment, or continuing their high school studies part-time and working part-time, until they reach the age of eighteen. It seems to be the best possible option for them. Otherwise, they would remain untrained beggars on the streets with no skills they might hope to utilize to improve their condition.

My only quibble with the orphans' homes is that they are only open to white children, not to those of any color, whether black, native, or otherwise. When I inquired as to what was being done to assist these other portions of the community, my questions were completely ignored. Thus, I am to assume the response would be "nothing." Yet again, I must wonder to myself, since I seem to be unable to find anyone to answer, what do these people of color think they are running toward as they risk their lives to flee

Southern enslavement? Are they so truly blinded by hopeful desperation as to believe they will be embraced with open arms as soon as they set foot on the Northern side of the river? For their sakes, I hope not. Such a naive misplacement of faith would be too tragic to bear thought of.

July 7, 1858

A s I waited to board the noon steamer today, for the last leg of my journey along the routes of civilized transportation, I read a most sorrowful tale in the local paper. Whilst I was at the orphans' benefit dinner, a mother and child were killed right here, near the Cincinnati docks. In light of my ponderings last night, I feel it is necessary to recount the story of their wretched demise.

The mother had been an enslaved woman in Kentucky. Her child, a boy of six or seven, was the product of an extramarital union between the woman and her master. Neither of their names were mentioned. Although the paper did not state whether the woman was coerced or not, I assume that was the case, since so many of these terrible situations often are. By the time the boy reached walking age, it was clear he bore a strong resemblance to his father, the owner. Understandably, that caused trouble within the household. The father in question, probably trying to erase the visible evidence of his guilt, made plans to steal the boy from his mother and sell him downriver to another planter in Memphis.

Upon learning her son was to be snatched from her, the mother fled, taking the boy with her. Being summertime, the river was slower and at a shallower depth than usual. She was able to swim it while carrying the boy on her back. Her floatation was assisted by a piece of driftwood. Nevertheless, as she neared the other side, a bounty hunter who had been notified by her master to be on the lookout attempted to arrest her at gunpoint. According to several eyewitnesses, who had secreted themselves behind trees and underbrush to gawk at her recapture, the mother rose half out of the water and slung the piece of driftwood at the slave hunter. She knocked the rifle from his hands. As he fell back in surprise, several of the onlookers rose from their places of concealment and opened fire.

The woman was shot numerous times. Yet, she staggered on. The boy, who was also shot but remained alive after this initial volley, grabbed her up under the arms and attempted to drag her back toward the river. Alas, she was too heavy. When the original catcher regained his feet, he beat the boy down and tied him up. The article concluded by saying the boy was to be transported to the sale in Memphis on Friday.

Another article in the same newspaper, which I only had time to skim before being directed to board the steamer, warned of the "dangerous history" regarding unrest between whites and the colored population in southwestern Ohio. The article stressed this latest incident was "yet another reason for white citizens to continue to go about their daily business with an abundance of vigilance and caution when dealing with Negroes," whom the paper claimed, "had a tendency to become violent when provoked." The first example cited was in 1829, when over a thousand of what were then called "Aboriginal Americans" were driven out of town and their homes burned. Then, another series of riots took place over the course of two months in the spring of 1836. These resulted in many casualties among the Aboriginal American community, along with the burning of the *Cincinnati Weekly* and *Abolitionist* newspaper offices. Edited by New York transplant James Birney, the paper admonished Southern slaveholders. This angered many Cincinnati businessmen, whose trades depended on the purchasing power of plantation owners. Last, in the Riots of 1841, a cannon was fired down Sixth Street as whites attempted to drive these so-called Aboriginal Americans, who by then were armed and more ready to defend themselves, out of the "Little Africa" neighborhood near the pork slaughterhouses, where they worked. Many were killed, three hundred colored people were arrested, and almost the entire neighborhood was burned to the ground.

As far as I can tell, the colored people of whom the article urges whites to be wary were, in every account, the defenders and not the aggressors. They also sustained much heavier casualties. Thus, I feel strongly the warnings of the editors are grossly misdirected. Clearly, it is the colored population who has the most to fear from riots here in Ohio.

Surprisingly absent from this article, I noticed, were two more riots of more recent history that had nothing to do with colored people. However, I remembered hearing of them as a young teacher back East in Maine. In both 1853 and 1855, large scale riots, the latter of which also involved the use of a cannon in city streets, broke out between white German immigrants and "nativists" or non-German whites, in Cincinnati. I suppose this information was left unmentioned because three years later, it became apparent the influx of German immigrants actually brought a great deal of economic prosperity to the city. Therefore, to disparage them has become passé.

The only thing that remains constant in America, it seems, is the ability of money to purchase social acceptance. With it, entrance to any social circle is thrown open. Without it, all circles remain closed.

July 8, 1858

S ettling into my cabin here on the steamer for what promises to be
nine days of work and quiet reflection. According to the schedule,
we should arrive in St. Louis on Monday morning, which is about
twice as long as it took to cover a similar distance by rail from Hartford
to Cincinnati. After a night's layover in St. Louis, I am to board another, smaller boat to take the Missouri River upstream to Independence.
Although I have been abroad on a large ocean liner, I've never been on a
river steamer before, save for your typical ferry boat. Traveling on these
two should be just enough time for the novelty to remain pleasant.

Since this is a mixed cargo steamer, our hold is filled with flour, sugar,
and salt. For this I am thankful, since I've heard horror stories from
my fellow passengers regarding their previous voyages traveling in the
decks above smellier wares. As for the passengers, I have been met with
mostly businessmen. However, these are much more loquacious and
engaging than the dour ones I met on the train through Ohio. Perhaps
it is the anticipation of heading towards new opportunities in the West
that has them in high spirits. Whatever the reason, I am glad to be in
more jovial company.

The cabin itself is cozy enough, with a single bed, washstand, small desk
and chair, which is really all I need. Meals for passengers are given above
decks, so as to take advantage of the summer breeze enhanced by the swift
movement of the boat. If today is of any indication, the food should be
satisfactory if not indulgent. Eggs and toast for breakfast with a mug of
coffee, which I brought back to my cabin so I could begin work on lesson
plans for the school. Dinner tonight was roasted chicken with potatoes and
carrots, along with strawberry pie, which was quite good. I am very fond

of strawberries. The season is so short in Maine, I do not get them as often as I would like.

Having so much time to myself has given me the rare chance to ponder at length what kind of home that I will make. This opportunity is unique to my experience. Having never decorated a home of my own, I'm quite excited. It is my understanding my living quarters will be in a sort of loft apartment above the schoolhouse, which is currently being built in anticipation of my arrival. Furniture was not specified in the terms of the contract, so I will have to wait until I arrive to know what might be provided.

Before leaving Portland, I ordered several books on the cultivation of home gardens appropriate for the climate, as well as some on cooking, medicine, sewing, and crafting. I grew up in a household in which the vast majority of daily chores were conducted by staff. We ate before opening and after closing in the kitchen at the pub and had a maid who saw to the other domestic needs. Thus, I really had no desire or opportunity to learn the various womanly arts, as some call them. However, now is as good a time as any to begin to fend for myself, so to speak. I feel that, after perusing these volumes along the journey, I should be more than up for the challenge.

My greater concern is what awaits me in terms of my students. Mr. H warned, as I have mentioned already, about the probability they would be unsophisticated. That is not the part that worries me. Instead, I wonder whether I have brought the right sorts of materials to provide them with a useful and suitable education, given their unusual background. Since I was given no clue as to how many students I might have, or what their level of literacy might be, I ordered three dozen sets of McGuffey's Readers for grades one through six to accommodate the younger children, as well as the students who might be behind the standard level for their age.

Considering most students finish Grade Six at some point between eleven and thirteen, I don't suppose I will have very many students older than that age group. Since the community is small, it is likely their working lives will begin early. Most of those coming from more affluent families will send their older children back East to boarding schools so they can spend their teen years preparing to enter college or some type of professional field. Of course, if there are native children in addition to whites, there is absolutely no way of telling what their abilities or needs might be. Regardless, I like to be prepared for every eventuality. I ordered a second set of all the standard college preparatory texts in subjects such as classical rhetoric, history, literature, languages, and mathematics, so I could tutor any more advanced students who might be interested on an individual basis.

At the moment, I have my typical teaching day scheduled as follows:

9am: Reading
10am: Grammar
11am: Rhetoric
Noon: Lunch and Recess
2pm: Arithmetic
3pm: Geography
4pm: History
5pm: Music and/or Sketching (optional)

My thinking is that by doing the reading first, we will be modeling an example for the remainder of the morning during the grammar and rhetoric lessons, which will in turn assist them on writing their own compositions. Having read a great number of essays on how physical exercise enhances intellectual development, I have packed supplies for many types of outdoor games in addition to books and slates. In particular, I hope to start a little baseball team, which I think will foster a sense of healthy competition. After lunch and recess, we will begin with the most difficult subject first, arithmetic, and follow through with geography and history, tying those lessons back in some way to our readings from that morning to close the day. Although some educators frown on ending the day with art, or really having art at all, I feel it will be essential for my students. They will likely have no other outlet for gaining appreciation of culture. Still, I understand more practically-minded parents might deem this completely unnecessary, so I tacked it onto the end of the day as an optional activity.

My smallest concern is whether or not my students will like me. Despite the fact all my training has emphasized the necessity, especially in a frontier school, of a teacher being seen as a stern, authoritative figure, that has never been my natural inclination as an educator. In fact, I have observed it is much more difficult to maintain an environment that is conducive to learning when the children fear their teacher. That type of attitude is likely to incite rebellion among more mischievous students.

Rather than demanding the respect of my students, I prefer to earn it. The question remains as to what might be the best approach to do so. At my girls' school in Portland, this was achieved by affecting a certain level of erudition and sophistication to which they might aspire if they wished to become educated young ladies. I have my doubts as to whether this type of appeal would work in the very different surroundings of a frontier town, in which all knowledge seems to beg practical application. Perhaps that will be my approach... to provide every lesson not as knowledge to be gained simply for its own sake, but instead for the actual improvement of their daily lives.

We shall see. I will think upon the matter further, and record any additional revelations.

But for now, the candle burns low, so I must bid you *adieu*!

July 11, 1858

W hat a night! After the relative peace of the last few days, during which I have been undisturbed enough to plan every lesson for the Fall Term, I was awakened to a deafening boom. It shook the cabin so hard the looking glass hanging above the washbasin fell from the wall and shattered into pieces on the floor. Scrambling into my dressing gown, I met the steward in the hallway. He informed me one of the steamer's three boilers had blown, and the paddle wheel was incapacitated. Then, he darted off, calling back to me to dress and pack my things since it was highly probable we would have to evacuate.

Turns out, he needn't have been in such a rush. Although the boat was completely immobilized due to the broken wheel, the fact the other two boilers did not also explode in a chain reaction meant we were not taking on water in such a way that was unmanageable. After the boatmen smartly and swiftly contained the fire, all that remained was for us to wait for the tow boats, which arrived before noon. Hooking up one to each side with a series of ropes each as big around as a man's torso, the plan is to pull us the last of the way, and then complete repairs in the docks.

Thus, we are now progressing toward St. Louis at a much slower pace. This means I will probably not have a layover at all. Instead, I will need to get onto the next boat immediately upon landing. I had been hoping to use that layover night to consult with a Spiritualist about these dreams I've been having. I will address that later in this entry, after I've explained the incident at hand further. At the moment, I feel very fortunate the explosion wasn't worse, and that no one was harmed except for the man who may have been our saboteur.

The matter of this boilerman's apparent suicide is most curious. From what I have heard, he was half native/half white and had worked for the steamer line without incident since it first opened in 1854. According to all accounts, he was a hardworking and level-headed individual, who was generally liked by his fellow crew members. Regardless, by what I've gleaned third hand after first being filtered through other crew members and second through my fellow passengers, this boilerman was mumbling strangely out of his head about insensible things when he went to relieve his crewman as scheduled at midnight. The man who was leaving the shift was worried enough to stop him and ask if he was running a fever. The troubled man snarled that he was fine in such an off-putting manner that his crewman backed away, thinking he'd received some bad news, but not wanting to press for details.

Being the only person in the boiler room at the time of the explosion, no one actually saw what happened. The other boiler man said everything was running perfectly and that he'd just finished refueling them before the shift change. The only other indication something was about to happen was that a boy who worked in the stockroom above heard the man screaming and cursing just before the blast. Thinking the man had hurt himself and attempting to rush to his aid by the front stairs, the boy ran out the door of the room opposite the rear of the vessel. This likely saved his life. The floor under the shelves where he had been counting stores was blown away, sending a searing fire draft up through the chimney.

According to investigators, the man was cursing not because he was hurt, but because he knew he was somewhat thwarted in his efforts to do even more damage to the steamer. A small wooden box filled with almost two dozen sticks of wet dynamite was found wedged into a crevice near the coal bins. Some type of leak in the boiler room allowed the first few layers in the box to become soggy. The bottom of the box was pried off, and the last layer of sticks removed.

The current consensus from what was left of the scene was that the boilerman had put two sticks of the dynamite under each boiler. Then, he lit them at the same time, while standing as close to the center boiler as possible. If his intention was indeed to kill himself, he was somewhat lucky. One of the two placed under the central boiler blew, tearing him apart from the knees upward. However, since the remaining five were still too soggy to catch, it seems the rest of us enjoyed the greater piece of luck. An explosion of all three boilers simultaneously could have resulted in the demise of everyone aboard.

I've been very shaken by this incident. Not only, as you might imagine, because of the immediate threat to my personal safety, but also because of the nature of the series of dreams that I've been having nightly since leaving Portland. Looking back over my journal here, I see I've made note of only two so far. It was my intention that if I didn't dwell on them during my waking hours, perhaps they would cease. Yet, they have not. Instead, the dream in which I was engaged just before the explosion last night makes me most uncomfortable. It now seems prophetic, when viewed in hindsight.

In the dream, I was underground. At first, I thought it was some sort of natural cavern. During my previous travels abroad in France, I've visited several caves I found fascinating. That would have been a very normal mental picture to revisit. However, as my eyes adjusted to the dimness of the light in the dream (which is yet another strange phenomenon, because even though my dream life has always been quite active, it usually doesn't include such visceral sensations) I found it was not the typical cave filled with stalactites that had so piqued my curiosity before. Instead, I could tell it was not a natural cave, but rather a man-made mine. Waving the lantern in my hand to the left and right, the walls gleamed with a luminescence that I recognized must be gold. Why I knew this, I haven't the foggiest idea. I've never been inside a gold mine. Moving closer to the gilded walls, I reached out to run my hands over their surface. I could feel the contrast between the rough granite and the smoothly cleaved breaks of golden nuggets as big as my fist protruding among them.

Slowly, as I marveled at this discovery, I became aware of footsteps echoing in the distance down into the blackness of the mineshaft. The sharp, crunching rapidity of these footfalls told me the person was running as fast as his feet would fly. Distracted, I swung my lantern toward the darkness, just as I heard a man's voice cry out in panic. "Ruuuuuuunnnnnnn!!!"

Instinctively, I dropped the lantern and fled toward the entrance. As I ran, I could hear something that began as a low, dull growl, growing progressively louder. It was about a hundred yards behind me. In a few seconds, I could no longer hear the flight of the man whose warning I heeded. Within fifty yards of the mouth, a whoosh of dark gray dust hit me in the back like the hot blast of a furnace. I stumbled but did not fall, and continued, coughing and panting as I ran.

Finally reaching the mine's entrance, I broke off to the side amidst a grove of scrub pine. Bent over with hands on knees and gasping for breath,

I noticed I was wearing men's trousers. The fact had only a second to register before I saw my creature, the *loup garou* of my dreams, come shooting out of the mine. His fur sparkled with flecks of embers under a layer of grime. He fell immediately to the ground, rolling back and forth in the red clay soil. Extinguishing the sparks, he lay whimpering in the dust.

As has become the bizarre normalcy of these dreams, I felt no fear of the enormous wolf-like creature. Approaching cautiously, I could smell the acrid scent of burnt fur. The beast lay completely still, the slight movement of his side and his labored wheezing the only indication he remained alive. I will never know how the dream should have ended. At that point, I was jerked awake by the explosion aboard this steamer in real life.

I'm aware most are skeptical of reading too much into dreams, but after over a week in which this creature has made his presence known to me with increasing frequency, I cannot help but wonder if there is some knowledge I am meant to gain. His appearance last night clearly was some sort of warning that danger was very near.

I'm also aware many believe Spiritualism is complete nonsense. However, as I've mentioned before, I found great comfort after my mother and grand-père passed, knowing they weren't completely absent from my life. Rather, they existed in a different realm, veiled from human comprehension. How I wish I would be allowed time for the layover in St. Louis. I have heard it is a great city for mediums. I could do with the comfort now, given the series of strange deaths that have plagued my journey so far. I feel very strongly there is some omen in them that I must heed.

Perhaps I will relate this story as to the source of my confidence in Spiritualism at a later time, when news in my present life is slower. For now, my hand grows weary. I would prefer not to open another bottle of ink, lest it spill in my trunk during the transition between ships.

July 12, 1858

I begin today with two kinds of news: Good and Bad. However, the bad news might not be that terrible after all. It gives me ample time between now and my departure from St. Louis to find and consult with a Spiritualist about the concerns articulated in my previous entry.

The somewhat poor news is that, upon our late arrival in St. Louis, we were informed we must give a statement to the local inspector before leaving the vessel. This is allegedly the standard procedure the steamboat company must follow in order to successfully apply for insurance benefits and attempt to recover the cost of repairs. I have my doubts though. Not about the fact the company plans to use insurance for the repairs, but that this is "standard procedure." I think the company is worried someone else on board might have additional insights as to why the boilerman chose to commit suicide by dynamite. Perhaps their coming forward later might result in a prolonged investigation, or another lawsuit related to person or property. That could cause further damage to the company and its reputation. *Sigh.* This is an unfortunate consequence of living in increasingly litigious times. How I loathe lawyers!

Due to the delay caused by this inquisition, I will not be able to jump from boat to boat without a layover, as I had originally supposed. Instead, I will have to wait for the next available steamer heading West to Independence. It doesn't leave until Thursday at noon. Rather than being disconcerted, I actually welcome this news. Spending a few days in the last major city I will see for a while gives me the time to steady myself and clear my mind of all that has transpired since leaving Hartford. Hopefully, I might regain the sense of optimism with which I first embarked upon this endeavor.

I've got some time on my hands to hover in the cabin until I am called up to give my statement. While I wait, I might as well relate to you the circumstances of my previous encounters with Spiritualists. They have given me reason to believe their work is not the hokum some are quick to judge it to be.

First, lest you think I am a witch or some other sort of pagan convert, allow me to assure you that Sundays of my girlhood were spent in attendance at the First Parish Church of Portland. Although the Ulrich family was not of sufficiently august personage to warrant the dedication of a family pew, as the Longfellow's have, we engaged in the fellowship of the Unitarian community regularly enough for me to inoculate myself against spiritual sickness with all that I felt was necessary from the Bible, accompanied by healthy doses of tolerance and acceptance for which Unitarians are known. This opened the door early to my interest in spiritual inquiry.

The summer after my graduation from Westbrook was when I first learned of the Fox sisters. Probably everyone in New England heard of them that summer, since their claims they contacted the ghost of a peddler who was murdered in their basement caused quite a sensation. Overnight, it became very fashionable among the young set in which I moved to gather in one parlor or another by candlelight, hold hands in a circle, and attempt to communicate with the dead. Then, it was just a game—and an excellent reason to be in close contact with handsome gentlemen in the dark without causing a scandal. It's always been more of a girl's thing than a man's. My girlfriends and I would take turns leading the sessions. As they married off, I gradually became the only one left. The interest our social circle had in the fad lost its intensity. When the story broke in 1851 that their cousin signed a statement swearing the Foxes were frauds, our group had largely moved into the domestic sphere. For our set, the Fox sisters' fall from grace went unheard as a lonely tree tumbling in the forest.

Perhaps because I remained solo, without the yoke of wifely duties across my shoulders, I had time to continue to pursue my explorations within the spiritual realm. During my summer breaks from school, it became sort of a sport. As soon as I read of some new phenomenon, I had to seek out one or more of its practitioners and see for myself whether their attempts to communicate with the spirits was real or fantasy. First, I ventured South through the Carolinas, where I encountered all kinds of hoodoo and voodoo magic. Alas, it always turned out to be some sort of sham or another. These faux voodooers played on the obvious exotic appeal of possessing rare spiritual knowledge known only to fellow Africans. They were mostly former female slaves who purchased their freedom after years of selling themselves to the night. Their presence was abundant in the Coastal regions. I was never mean-spirited enough to expose these women in front of their paying customers and thereby deprive them of their liveli-hood. Many times though, I walked out of a séance overcome by a fit of giggles induced by catching a glimpse of a helper behind a curtain or an ill-concealed string used to fake a levitation.

Later, in my travels across Europe, I encountered more down-on-their-luck Greeks and Italians attempting to take advantage of their olive complexions and dark curls by posing as gypsy fortune tellers. These individuals were a peg down from their Southern voodoo coun-terparts in my book, mostly because they didn't only employ assistants to help with their illusions, but also to pick the pockets of their patrons while they wishfully pretended to be under hypnotic trance. I allowed myself more liberties in poking fun at them. At one such gathering, after catching a glimpse from the corner of my supposed-to-be shut eyes at the fortune teller's assistant creeping behind a heavy curtain around the perimeter of the room, I volunteered to be the next one hypnotized. Then, I turned the tables on them by pretending to be a long-dead aristocratic lady from whom some jewelry had been stolen. At the peak of my alleged possession by this lady, I flung my hand dramatically to point at the creeper behind the curtain. He dropped the purse he had been rifling through and fell forward, crashing onto the table. A dwarf came out from under it, screeching. His beard was singed by the candle he'd held up under a hole in the table for the crystal ball, so as to give it the ethereal appearance of being lit from within. Even now, as I think about it, I cannot help but chuckle.

Edinburgh was scheduled to be my next-to-last stop before returning home to Maine. I missed Dublin due to news of my family's illness. There I finally encountered something worth my interest. The first clue this spiritual experience was to be different from those previous was the fact I did not have to pay for an invitation. Instead, I heard about the proposed séance at a public lecture on the works of Emanuel Swedenborg. I was invited to join the host and a group of mostly intellectuals for a round of experiments on what they termed "theosophy." Specifically, their goal was not to go rapping around the edges of tables in an attempt to mimic the knocks of stray ghosts on some sort of spiritual door, but rather to use meditation to throw the door wide open and walk through themselves, by means of something they called astral projection.

When the main lecture concluded, a group of a half dozen or so of us regathered at eleven that evening. After we were briefed on what was to transpire, we went into a room in which there were a number of couches and chaise lounges. Each of us chose one and lay down. We were instructed to relax, and allow ourselves to be guided through a series of meditation techniques, intended on allowing us to release all thoughts of our day and clear a path for journey into the astral plane. At some point, I fell asleep, only to sensorially awaken into a dream in which I was flying over very steep mountains covered in snow. Sailing above tall evergreens, I was struck by how absolutely quiet everything was. Only the sound of my dress flapping in my wake let me know I was moving at all. I did not recognize the land over which I flew. This did not bother me. At last, I began to tire. I found that by lowering my feet back to what would be a normal walking position, it felt like I was pulling a horse to a stop. Slowly, I descended to the ground.

Touching down felt a bit like leaping from the top step of a carriage. A bit too hard, but not enough to throw me off balance. As I stood gazing around this crystal wonderland, tiny flakes of snow started to fall from the sky. Sticking out my tongue like a child to catch one, I felt something brush my shoulder. Thinking it was a piece of snow fallen from the cedar tree that towered over me, I gave it a brush. I found out instead it was the tassel at the end of a cord. The cord was made of soft silver silk. When I instinctively wrapped my fingers around it, there was a little tug upward. It felt like a fish on a line, something moving and alive.

Oh, I heard myself wonder aloud. I turned around and looked up into the tree, from whence it appeared the cord had come. I tugged back on it gently. As I did, I had the sensation my feet were slipping. Thinking I had stepped on a patch of ice, I attempted to regain my footing. The second step I took slid right out from under me too. Feeling myself begin to fall backward, I grabbed onto the cord with my left hand as well. In a rush, the snowy world disappeared. It seemed for a fraction of a second the cord was the only solid piece of matter in the universe.

I awoke on the chaise lounge with the length of silver cord still grasped firmly in both hands, my arms outstretched. The other members of the group sat in straight-backed wooden chairs. Each one had a pleasant look of curiosity on his or her face. They watched me as one might watch a bird in an aviary. Behind them, I could see the morning sun was just beginning to rise. Its golden light stretched like long fingers down the curved streets of the city.

"How was your rest?" the leader asked.

I hesitated a moment, yawning deeply before I replied, "I hate to admit it, but not very rejuvenating at all. I'm actually quite exhausted."

The whole room laughed softly, but not in a menacing way. More like a knowing way.

"Then it was as it should be," the leader replied. "Souls travel fast. Sometimes it's hard for the body to catch up. Why don't you share your experience with us. Then we will do the same. I hated to wake you," he gestured to the silver cord. "But we were already up and about, ready to exchange ideas."

I started to apologize. He waved me off. "Please, there is no need for apologies here. All of us have traveled before. We know it is hard sometimes to leave those worlds of beauty and comfort to return to this one. You'll get used to controlling it in time."

We took turns sharing and discussing our journeys. Most had been enjoyable to some degree like mine. One man had felt as if he were back at school. Then, he had been the head boy. In the projection, he flew unrecognized above the heads of pupils decades his junior. A lady recalled a forest she had seen one happy summer in her youth on a trip to visit her mother's family in Bavaria. Another elderly man, who was a sailor in his early years, had felt the sensation of swirling around among the masts. Only when he attempted to settle down near the stern, he missed. He fell into the water, terrified as he saw the boat sailing away without him.

Each of these accounts was examined like a piece of literature for symbolic significance. The older gentleman was judged to have unresolved issues, feeling that he had somehow missed the boat of opportunity for a different life he might have led after his time as a seaman. The former head boy and Bavarian woman were seen to be searching for safe places of happiness and comfort from their youth. Whilst I, who had dreamed of a place I'd never been, albeit in a climate similar to the snowy winters of Maine, seemed to them to be looking for a new sanctuary that reminded me of my old life, but with the option for more independence. In hindsight, this reading appears accurate, as only a few days later I received the news to return home. And here I am, on my way to the snow-capped Rocky Mountains.

Long story short, I must be wrapping up. I have been informed I am next to give a statement before disembarking. I returned to Maine upon hearing of my family's illness with a renewed interest in supernatural communication, and a strong sense of foreboding that I would not find them alive. Sadly, as I have recalled here, that turns out to have been the case.

Nevertheless, in the many weeks of restless nights while I wrestled with the decision to either remain in Portland and take up proprietorship of the pub alone or to chart another course, I put what I had learned about spiritual travel while abroad into practice. At the risk of seeming mad, would you believe it if I told you I spoke to both my mother and my grand-père during these nocturnal wanderings? And in both cases, they told me that it was time to move on?

Of course, one might believe these were the product of my traumatized brain. Simply working out what I wanted to say to them, and anticipating their replies back to me. The dreams of wishful thinking. Though the dreams were so vivid and so comforting, they were hard to ignore. I began thinking that some of my other dreams might offer insights into the possible future direction of my life. I wrote them down, with the intention of seeking out a medium whom I thought had at least some credibility and could assist in their interpretation. Perhaps I will find one in St. Louis over the next few days. Hopefully through them I will gain some perspective on why the first part of my trip has been so ominous.

July 16, 1858

St. Louis, it turns out, has been a most interesting city. It has all the amenities of her sisters back East. Great playhouses, wonderful restaurants (including barbecue!), and lively company to fill all of them. In hindsight, I'm glad I've had this extended stopover to enjoy before I head into the hinterlands. Although I am the kind of person who is completely able to make her own amusements if need be, I consider myself to be more of an amiable person than I have been lately. It is my sincerest hope I get along with my soon-to-be students and whatever kinds of families to whom they belong. Otherwise, I am beginning to worry the life of a frontier teacher who knows no one might be lonely.

Today's entry shall be quick. The most interesting part of these last few days is happening tonight. I am going to a mummy unwrapping party, followed by a séance. Kind of a two for one. Found out about it through an advertisement in the local paper. Although I've seen plenty of mummies both domestically and abroad (anything Egyptian is always in vogue for its mysterious beauty), I've never witnessed an unwrapping before. Heard about it, and wanted to go, but the circumstances just never presented themselves.

As for the séance, I've heard the medium is very good. A "real" one, as opposed to a "fake", although that judgment I will hold in reserve for now. The timing is certainly right. We are to begin at midnight, about an hour after the mummy-only crowd has departed.

Updates tomorrow after I've boarded the last boat and have time to write. *Adieu.*

July 17, 1858

All settled into my cabin. It is considerably smaller than on the previous steamer—no desk or washstand. Just a bed and shelves for luggage, but I digress. Last night was both intriguing and discomforting in equal parts. Still trying to make sense of it all.

The unwrapping was by far the most intellectually stimulating portion of the evening. A physician, Dr. Ernest Wheeler, performed the examination and dissection. His credentials were given at the beginning of the cocktail hour before the event began. Upon reflection regarding the events I will describe, it seems necessary to relate in support of his mental soundness. Dr. Wheeler graduated with honors among the first classes from St. Louis University's Medical School, years before it bent to the pressures of those dreadful Know Nothings.

An aside: Apparently the terribly misnamed American Party goes around fomenting rebellion even in these parts of the country. Not only were they responsible for the anti-Catholic riots in Cincinnati I mentioned in my account a few days ago, but they also caused a Great Schism here. They forced the Medical School here to break off association with what is reputed to be a highly distinguished Catholic university or risk closure.

Regardless, Dr. Wheeler built a solid medical practice, mostly in the general line, for the benefit of the Old City Hospital. Since then, he has more or less switched his research studies over to focus on ailments of the mind and the possible connection of spiritual sickness with emotional illness. In fact, there was talk during the cocktail hour that the Catholic Church may be looking to build a hospital here in St. Louis specifically for ailments of that type, which would be a first in America. More on that later... I must not get ahead. I will force myself to begin at the beginning of this most unusual evening.

Both entertainments were held at the Varieties Theater as fundraisers for the new Lutheran Hospital, which is organizing to take the place of the old City Hospital that burnt down last year. It is a most remarkable space. The main hall has a movable floor built in a style I've seen in Paris. It can be utilized either to seat an audience on an incline, so as to view performances on the stage more advantageously, or converted into a completely flat space for balls and the like.

At seven o'clock, doors opened in the main hall for cocktails. The floor was in its flattened ballroom state, to accommodate both the inner ring of chairs surrounding the wooden sarcophagus and the outer ring of Egyptian curiosities. Those lined the walls for the perusal of guests before the unwrapping. I had a brandy and mingled among the several dozen audience members while viewing the artifacts. According to the placards posted around the perimeter, the mummy whom we were about to meet was a female noble woman who may have been the wife of a court physician. Given the substantial amount of jewelry and number of mummified babies that were part of the display, I surmised that in life, she must have been abundantly rich in earthly adornments, but woefully poor in producing healthy progeny.

Taking my seat in the ring along the left side of the sarcophagus, I listened to Dr. Wheeler's lecture about how the mummies were preserved. Apparently, their brains were pulled out from their noses and then their bodies embalmed in oils and spices, wrapped, and set out in the desert heat to dry like pieces of jerky! Can you imagine the smell! And the flies! Then, Dr. Wheeler and two assistants carefully employed several chisels and a bar to loosen and remove the lid of the sarcophagus, setting it down onto a cloth beside the table on which it lay. Next the doctor produced a very long, thin pair of surgical scissors. He removed his jacket and rolled up his shirt sleeves, revealing his very freckled forearms. Beginning at the mummy's feet, Dr. Wheeler cut apart her bindings. Each snip was accompanied by a little puff of dust, which had doubtlessly gathered over the millennia.

However, when Dr. Wheeler reached the abdomen, he let out a pained, *Oh!* Dropping the shears, he stepped back from the mummy. Even though I was seated directly across from this part of the corpse, I could not see what caused him such alarm, due to the stiffness of the bandages that were peeled back into a fan surrounding her. I leaned forward, but Dr. Wheeler, observing my curiosity, waved me back. "No, no, miss. Please, I must make an announcement. I was not expecting this. You may want to listen first, and then decide whether you still choose to view the body." Since there was nothing else he could have said which would have possibly intrigued me more, I hung on his every word.

"Ladies and gentlemen. I know we have all been looking forward to gazing into the face of this woman who has not been seen for over a thousand years. Nevertheless, before I continue with the unveiling of her body before you, I must declare an important fact, in the interest of decency. The woman who lies before you passed away while she was with child. From the extent of her condition, it appears the child may have been very close to full term, given the outline of its form is clearly visible beneath the skin. Thus, she may have died while in the process of giving birth. If you are squeamish about such matters, or have any religious reservations, I urge you to withhold your interest until after the other patrons have had the opportunity to observe the body in full, so that my assistants might obscure the indecent portions from your more sensitive view. Thank you."

As the doctor resumed his removal of the bandages, the crowd around me crackled with whispers and speculation. Some politely indicated the shrouded infants among the artifacts, while others pointed to them outright. All were wondering what must have happened to this poor woman, who had lost so many children, only to perish herself while trying to bring another into the world. One young woman seated directly across the circle from me began to cry softly onto the shoulder of a slight man in a brown tweed suit, whom I assumed must be her husband.

I kept my eyes on Dr. Wheeler. He had begun to sweat profusely at the temples. I noticed the hand with which he pulled back the bandages shook. Progressing at last to the top of the woman's head, he placed the scissors on a small tray and slowly pushed back the bandages surrounding the woman's face. They fell to pieces under the gentle pressure of his caress. For a long moment, he stood staring intently into the woman's face. Then, he turned his back and indicated by gesture alone for his assistants to fold back the remaining wrappings along the length of her body. Removing his spectacles, which were fogged with perspiration, Dr. Wheeler began to walk the perimeter of the circle, addressing each of us closely.

"I invite you to begin the viewing now, starting with the lady in black here at the six o'clock position and continuing clockwise around the circle. It tends to progress most smoothly if we begin at the feet, and then go around in turns, rather than all crowding up at once. I will stand near the head of the corpse to respond to any questions you might have. Insofar as I can tell from my brief examination so far, the woman appears to have been in her late twenties, and succumbed during childbirth. The evidence of her difficulties with pregnancies are all around us." Here he gestured to the infant mummies. "It is possible some childhood disease may have threatened Egypt during her lifetime. Until further examination is conducted and methods of diagnosis among the medical community improve for bodies that have been so long postmortem, we may never know for sure. Regardless, I invite you to come up as indicated, unless you prefer to wait until the second round, for reasons I mentioned before."

The lady in black popped up immediately from her seat. She advanced toward the body with a magnifying glass in her hand. Clearly, she was undisturbed by Dr. Wheeler's warnings and had come fully prepared to make the most of the evening. The swiftness of her movements was surprising, given she otherwise appeared to be of advanced age and walked with the aid of a silver-headed cane. Looking self-consciously amongst one another, as if to decide whether or not decorum would prefer if they waited for the second round of shielded viewing, the rest of the crowd rose one by one and took their turns. Not one of them held back.

When it came time for the sobbing woman to view the body, I noticed she spent only the briefest of moments glancing at it. Dragging her husband around in a quick circle, she then half-pulled him out the back door of the auditorium. Outside, I could hear her being sick. I attributed this to the fact her stomach was easily upset, because she was heavy with child.

When my turn came to view the corpse, I lingered, trying to study every inch of her leathered skin carefully so as to make mental notes. Although I had briefly considered applying to the new medical school for women in Pennsylvania in 1850, I didn't think it was fair at the time to do so. I had only just accepted my first teaching post in Portland a couple of years prior. Thus, I was still in that early stage of euphoria young teachers have in which they believe they can make a difference in the lives of their charges. However, I've always been interested in medicine. Whenever I can, I try to take advantage as opportunities present themselves to engage in studious inquiry of that sort.

Dr. Wheeler must have observed my high degree of interest. He accompanied me in my trip around the body, answering my questions thoroughly, and with more technical specificity than most. As I completed my viewing, he asked if I planned to stay for the séance afterward. To my surprise, his countenance brightened a bit when I replied affirmatively. This gave me the initial impression, which I was to find out soon after was correct, that he was keenly interested in keeping my company.

There was an hour's interlude between the unwrapping and the séance. I lingered in the lobby of the theater with the others who intended to remain for the entire evening. By this time, the young wife had recovered from her upset stomach and was able to engage in conversation. She told me her name was Vera Loren, and her husband, Karl, was a banker there in St. Louis. Having heard about the séance from a friend in her book club, she was determined to go. Ever since her young son, Robbie, died of cholera a few years before, she had been plagued by dreams of him running lost through the woods and calling out to her. Her hope was that she would be able to help Robbie cross over into peace before the arrival of their new baby, by reassuring him that he would not be forgotten.

The woman in black, Mrs. O'Malley, as she asked to be called, informed me she went to as many of these proceedings as she could find. She and her husband, the late Bill O'Malley, had owned a number of apartment buildings in the city. Unfortunately, in his later years, Mr. O'Malley began to grow senile and distrustful of others, including his wife and the local financial institutions. Rather than putting the rents as he collected them into the bank, Mr. O'Malley developed an eccentric habit. He put each month's collections into a tobacco tin, sealed it with wax, and then buried it somewhere near the building from whence it was collected. Mrs. O'Malley learned of this circumstance only a few months before her husband's death. A lady from her church had seen Bill digging a hole while she was on her way home from midnight mass. Knowing Bill was a sleepwalker, and concerned about what he might have been up to, the two friends returned to the spot. There, they dug up the first box of money.

In a moment of deathbed clarity a few months later, Bill O'Malley informed his wife he had been "securing" money that way for years. He died before divulging any actual whereabouts. Then, her handyman found one more tin by chance in the backyard of another building where she had directed a new fence to be built. After discovering her husband hadn't made any new deposits to their business account in almost two years before his death, Mrs. O'Malley put two and two together. She determined all of that money must be hidden on their other properties. Rather than aimlessly searching "like a squirrel for lost nuts," as she put it, and randomly digging up the lawns of her other buildings, Mrs. O'Malley staked her faith on mediums. She hoped to gain insights as to a pattern of where the remaining money was hidden.

I was so intrigued by Mrs. O'Malley's tale, I didn't notice as our medium came up behind me to invite us back into the theater for the séance portion of the evening. When she tapped me lightly on the shoulder, I jumped. She laughed, not meanly, but the tinkling bell type of laugh one might expect from a little girl. Although it was clear that the medium was a grown woman, somewhere in that broad expanse of indeterminate middle age between myself and Mrs. O'Malley, she was slight of stature. Barely the size I was at twelve. However, I was more surprised by the fact she was Chinese, and her English was as clearly articulated as mine.

Introducing herself as Miss Jilpa, the lady laughed again. I told her my name was Mae, and that I was a teacher. She replied, "Ah, Mei, a beautiful flower, yes. I can see that clearly. But a teacher? That I am not so sure of, unless you mean you are a teacher as I am. A teacher of life."

By the challenging look with which she accompanied this statement, I felt sure Miss Jilpa meant the same thing as several other mediums I have encountered. They believed I was among those who possessed the gift of second sight. I have a strong suspicion this assumption is made on the basis of my eyes. They are a somewhat startling shade of green. I have often been told by my students that their intensity is somewhat disturbing when I make eye contact for too long. Therefore, I usually try to avoid it, unless they are being unruly and need to be disciplined. At those times, an unsettling glance can be most useful.

But I must not digress here into idle classroom talk. It is late, and I want to get the rest down before I go to sleep.

Miss Jilpa led the Lorens, Mrs. O'Malley, and me back into the theater. The gurney that held the mummy had been moved somewhere out of sight. The circle was now much smaller, with only six chairs drawn tightly around a wooden table covered with a simple white cloth. I noticed with my trained skeptic's eye that it was not long enough to conceal anyone beneath. Also noteworthy were the absence of a crystal ball, teacups, or any other common tools of divination and spiritual communication. Instead, there were several small incense burners on brass stands spaced out a few paces behind the circle of chairs. They gave off a pleasant odor which I could not quite identify. Amber or sandalwood. Perhaps opium. As I pondered what method Miss Jilpa planned to use in order to put us in contact with the other realms, Dr. Wheeler returned and took a seat at the table. He immediately addressed my unspoken curiosities.

"Thank you for returning for this more intimate portion of the evening. We certainly appreciate your generosity in making the additional donation to the building fund for our new hospital. We are also grateful Miss Jilpa has chosen once again to share her time and talents without compensation as a gift to all of us." They exchanged smiles and nods as he continued. "If you have a question, it will be answered here. Or, as they say in Chinese..." he nodded again toward Miss Jilpa. She stated simply, *you qiu bi ying*, which I took as a translation of his words.

"Miss Jilpa is a Chinese spirit medium, or *jitong*," explained Dr. Wheeler. He pronounced the last word very carefully. "Since she was a young girl, the gods of her country have made her a vessel for communication with the dead. She moved here to America with her family so her father and brothers can work with the railroads. Miss Jilpa has been graciously willing to share her gifts with us. We first met after she responded to an advertisement in which I was soliciting interviews with those who believed they had clairvoyant powers for a medical study. So far, she is the clearest case of clairvoyance I have ever encountered. Tonight, for the benefit of our new hospital, she hopes to offer each of you peace through serving as a channel for your loved ones who have passed on. Please remember anything said by Miss Jilpa once she goes into her meditative trance will not be words of her own volition. Instead, they are the voices of spirits who may choose to speak through her to each of us. Do each of you understand?"

We nodded slowly in unison.

"Good. We will begin then with Mrs. O'Malley."

"Age before beauty, hmm?" she smirked. Miss Jilpa stretched out her open palms across the table to the older lady. Mrs. O'Malley laid her crooked, wrinkled hands on top of the medium's smooth ones. Miss Jilpa laughed again, much more softly this time. She looked Mrs. O'Malley squarely in the eyes. After a minute or two of watching the odd lock of their intense gaze, Miss Jilpa's eyelids began to flutter softly, and finally closed. Her hands dropped to her sides.

Slowly, Miss Jilpa rose from her chair. Mrs. O'Malley studied her, with her hand over her mouth. Miss Jilpa tottered unsteadily to a far corner of the room. Reaching into a nonexistent pocket on her dress, Miss Jilpa pulled out an object only she could see. Turning around and around several times, finally she stopped. She raised a finger in the air, and said, "Aha! Southeast! Here it is!" Making gestures as if she were digging with a spade, Miss Jilpa rummaged through an unseen bag on her shoulder. Pulling out another object invisible to us, she placed it carefully down into the imaginary hole. After filling in the hole with the spade, she looked down at her shoes and produced an imaginary handkerchief from a breast pocket. Sitting down heavily on the window sill behind her, Miss Jilpa meticulously wiped her shoes clean. Then she trudged back to her seat at the table. She stretched out her hands again to Mrs. O'Malley, whose gnarled fingers were trembling. When Miss Jilpa spoke, her voice was curiously too deep, and with a decided Irish lilt to it.

"Margaret, old girl, doncha member anythin' I tell ye? Course not! Yer allus a' jabbrin! Any'ow, look to the so'eas' marker o' each piece o' land. Tha's the money corner!" Punctuating this last exclamation with a wink, Miss Jilpa's hands fell to the table once more. She opened her eyes to see Mrs. O'Malley gazing at her—stunned speechless.

Miss Jilpa spoke in her own voice. "You wanted to know where your husband buried the money you thought he had lost. Did his answer mean anything to you?"

"Yes," the older lady replied. I could almost see the gears turning in her mind. "In one of our last conversations, Bill was rambling on about deeds. How I needed to bring him the files with all of the land deeds for the company because he wanted to show me something. I didn't think anything about it. By then Bill was asking for all sorts of things that made absolutely no sense. He'd get hung up talking about details that were completely insane. Like his shoe shine box, when he'd been in bed for weeks with no shoes on. He was always particular about the appearance of his shoes. Had to be able to see himself in them every day before he left for work. Even when he started forgetting everything else, his shoes were always immaculate."

"Did you ever look in his shoe shine box?" asked Dr. Wheeler.

"Well, no," replied Mrs. O'Malley, somewhat indignant. "I mean, I kept hold of the deeds, of course, because they are of value. But who goes poking about in someone's old shoe shine box? I had the valet toss it into the pile of things going to the charity sale."

"Someone who might be looking for clues as to where her husband hid his money, when he knew he was becoming forgetful. Did you ever stop to think that if Bill had his wits about him enough to know shining his shoes was the only thing he'd remember to do every day, no matter what, he might have left a reminder there for himself? So he'd be able to find it and show it to someone else for help?" Dr. Wheeler asked.

At this, Mrs. O'Malley made no reply, but her thin lips formed a round "O" shape.

Picking up on what Dr. Wheeler was suggesting, Miss Jilpa smiled thoughtfully and said, "Perhaps all is not lost with the shoe shine box. Did he not say, through me, any other directions? It seems as if I remember it just as I was awakening."

"Southeast," I replied. "He, or you, said the southeast marker on each piece of land is the money corner." Mrs. O'Malley stared at me.

"That makes very good sense," said Miss Jilpa. "In my country, the southeast corner of any home is known as the money corner." Then, Miss Jilpa asked Mrs. O'Malley, "Did your husband know anything about *feng shui*, by chance?"

"I'm not sure," said Mrs. O'Malley, shaking her head. "He may have. When he was a young man and in the merchant marine, he sailed several trips to China. But that was a very long time ago. Before I knew him, and before either of us came to America. He did tend to go on about it every now and then though, when he'd had too much to drink. I couldn't stand him when he was blustering drunk like that. I always got up and left the room."

"Perhaps you should have stayed to listen," said Mr. Loren, who had been so quiet through the whole exchange I'd completely forgotten he and his wife were even there. "Men say a lot of important things their wives never hear because they're not listening." At this, Mrs. Loren gave him a pointed look. Karl stopped speaking abruptly.

Mrs. O'Malley pressed her lips tightly together in a thin line. "Perhaps you're right," she said primly to herself, more than to anyone else in particular. "Nevertheless, I thank you Miss. Jilpa, for your insights. I will look into the matter as soon as I get home."

We all sat regarding Mrs. O'Malley's awkward attempts to appear nonchalant for a few moments, knowing full well the old woman was absolutely dying to get home and scramble through her files for land surveys. In my mind's eye, I could see her racing out, spade in hand, to dig for the money in the southeastern corner of every lot she owned as soon as it was daybreak.

"Well, I think it's time to pause here so Miss Jilpa can rest a moment," said Dr. Wheeler. "Let us recess until eleven. We shall reconvene with the Lorens next, if that is alright with everyone?" He nodded in my direction, silently asking whether I minded going last, to which I responded that would be fine.

During the next half hour, Mrs. O'Malley summoned her driver and went home. While Mrs. Jilpa rested in the green room of the theater, I had time to chat with the Lorens and Dr. Wheeler. On its face, the Lorens' reason for being there was very simple. Vera was still distraught several years after having lost her firstborn son to cholera. She hadn't carried another child to term after Robbie's birth. When he passed, Vera worried she would die childless. However, now she was almost full term with her first viable pregnancy since Robbie's death. Mrs. Loren wanted to know if she could expect that this child would survive, or if it would be stillborn like the rest. Yet, as I will relate soon, there was certainly more to their story.

As for Dr. Wheeler, his initial interest in consulting with Miss Jilpa, and then in convincing her to share her abilities here in her new home of St. Louis, started when she responded to his ad. As Dr. Wheeler interviewed her, Miss Jilpa stopped him. She took his hand lightly and told him she was sorry for the great pain and loss he had suffered. She warned him he was still a haunted man, and that if he did not overcome such feelings of guilt, the symptoms of that haunting would destroy him. Startled, Dr. Wheeler asked Miss Jilpa for more details. Miss Jilpa told him straight away she knew his fiancée died by her own hand, and that she blamed him for it.

According to Dr. Wheeler, his fiancée Rebecca, a former childhood sweetheart, became distressed when he asked her to delay their wedding for a year so he could go East. He wanted to go to Washington, DC, for a year's residency at Georgetown. On the day he was scheduled to leave, Rebecca went to the site on which their home was being built, slit her wrists, and then set herself on fire. Although the unfinished house was burned to cinders, there was enough left of Rebecca for the autopsy to find she had been at least six months pregnant. The problem with this was he and Rebecca had not consummated their relationship. On account of his Catholic faith, Ernest had wanted to wait until they were married.

Almost immediately after Rebecca's suicide, Dr. Wheeler began having nightmares in which she screamed at him for leaving and causing her to have no choice but to hide the shame of her affair by killing herself. Unable to sleep or barely function, Dr. Wheeler declined the residency that had caused so much trouble. Over the course of the next year until he encountered Miss Jilpa, Ernest became dependent on laudanum. After their initial meeting, Miss Jilpa began counseling the doctor spiritually. She instructed him to confront Rebecca in his dreams with the fact it was she who had brought about her own demise, and that he had nothing to be sorry for. Once he did this, Dr. Wheeler claimed the nightmares ceased. He was able to wean himself off the laudanum. Since then, he continued his regular medical practice, and began scholarly exploration into the powers of mental and spiritual healing.

By the time Dr. Wheeler finished telling this story, Miss Jilpa returned from the green room refreshed from her previous session. However, as my eyes grow heavy, I am afraid I will have to continue this story in the morning. I got almost no sleep last night, the reasons for which I will relate tomorrow, when I am myself renewed by the restorative effects of slumber.

July 18, 1858

S uch a dismal day! Ceaseless torrents of rain and heavy winds are beating down mercilessly upon us, causing the boat to rock a great deal. Thus, you must forgive my poor penmanship. At any moment I may have to make a diving catch to save either my coffee or my inkwell from sliding onto the floor.

Regardless, after the rest of us, less Mrs. O'Malley, settled back into the chairs around the table, Miss Jilpa took one hand each of Vera and Karl into her own. Closing her eyes to enter her trance, almost instantly she jumped back from them. She put her fingers into her mouth like a child who had burnt her hand on a stove. Miss Jilpa gazed longingly at Vera for a few moments. Then she dashed around the table, collapsing onto the floor and grabbing hold of her knee. She pressed the side of her face against Vera's leg. At this, Vera gave a small exclamation of surprise, then instinctively began smoothing Miss Jilpa's hair as one would a frightened child.

"Karl!" Vera whispered. "Don't you see she's acting..."

Stiffly, Karl interrupted her. "Yes, I see perfectly." His icy tone caused Miss Jilpa to turn and narrow her eyes at him. Sitting just behind Karl's left shoulder, I could see Miss Jilpa's soft brown eyes harden into hateful slits. I swear their color turned darker as she leapt at him. Before I had time to register what was happening, she was upon Karl, clawing and biting at his neck!

As I learned later, Dr. Wheeler was prepared for this. He sprang into action. Grabbing Miss Jilpa by the arms and pulling her back, he screamed at her in Chinese. Gradually, Miss Jilpa ceased to struggle and went limp in Dr. Wheeler's arms. Walking her back over to her chair, Dr. Wheeler sat Miss Jilpa down gently. He arranged her hands in her lap and gave her a few more instructions in Chinese, softly this time. Miss Jilpa began to awaken.

We watched her warily. None more so than Karl, who dabbed at the blood dripping onto his collar with a handkerchief.

"What was that?" asked Vera, in a trembling voice. "What happened to her?"

Dr. Wheeler put his finger to his lips to indicate we should remain silent. "Miss Jilpa will tell us herself when she is fully awake."

True to the doctor's prediction, when Miss Jilpa awakened, she informed us there had been two spirits working through her. One was indeed the spirit of the Lorens' lost son, Robbie. It was he who had caused her to run and attach herself to Vera's leg. However, upon hearing his father's voice, the channel through which Miss Jilpa was receiving Robbie's sense of longing for his mother's protection closed. Another presence made itself known to her. Whereas Miss Jilpa felt the strength of connection between mother and child strongly enough to know from our earlier conversations this was Robbie, the more sinister spirit had not made his name known.

"All I felt," Miss Jilpa told Karl, "was an extreme and intense hatred for you. That it wanted you dead. Do you have any idea who or what might want to cause you such great harm?"

Karl took a deep breath and cleared his throat, looking extremely uncomfortable. "Yes, I have some idea. But it's..." Karl paused, as if searching for the correct word. "Not... logical. Not rationally possible."

"If you can share with us, it might provide me the ability to interpret some of the other things I saw as well. Through the mind's eye of this other entity, I saw the death of another man. He looked somewhat like you, Karl, but older. I could feel my hands around his neck, strangling him. He was trying to speak but could not. It was just in a flash. As you spoke, it's like I could hear the victim's voice coming from you."

Karl's clear blue eyes grew wide. "My father," he whispered. "You saw the death of my father. My older brother, Otto, strangled him to death. He did not know I was watching until after it was done. I had gone out to play and returned to the house to sneak a slice of pie before dinner. My mother and sisters were at the market. I was not quite seven, but Otto was grown. Otto, he... he had not been right for a long time. Not himself. He'd never been a good student. Always a big joker. The kind of fellow others give things to just for the pleasure of having him around." Here, Karl stopped again. I could see confusion clouding his face as he tried to make sense of what he was telling us, even as he spoke the words.

He went on, "They had dismissed Otto from the university. He was home doing nothing except drinking and fighting with my father over money. Things had been getting worse. Otto was violent when he drank, but my father was a big man—bigger than me—and strong. Father didn't want to embarrass the family by seeking professional help. He thought he could handle it. That he could make Otto come around on his own. But he couldn't. He just couldn't." Karl's eyes rimmed with red. Vera moved closer to her husband and took his hand.

"Father overestimated his strength at his age. Otto was as strong as Father had been as a young man. He strangled him to death. Right there in the kitchen, with his bare hands. Then he kicked and stamped his face into pulp. I couldn't do anything. I've always been so ashamed that I stayed hidden away like a frightened rabbit. I was too small to stop Otto, but I could have distracted him. Perhaps Father could have escaped. Anyway, after it was done, Otto ran away. Father had tried to take Otto into business with him. He put his name on all of the accounts. Thought that by showing him trust and giving him a few responsibilities, Otto would grow out of whatever had a hold on him with the drinking. But he was wrong. Otto cleared out all the family accounts and left."

"What happened then?" I asked. "Was Otto ever caught?"

"Yes," Karl said. "He was caught and tried after running through Father's money. He was living on the streets in Berlin. Seven years later, Otto was picked up again for beating a woman to death. A prostitute. We received word from the police Otto had been caught. I was called to testify against him. By then, I was of an age when my testimony would count for something. I will never forget his face. Thin and gaunt. No teeth. A walking disease. He'd always been big and muscular, but all of that was wasted away. I was glad my mother had not lived to see it. She grieved herself to death over Father's murder, mostly by refusing to eat. My oldest sister, Lina, had been nineteen and engaged to a banker at the time. Her fiancé, Anselm, agreed to take my other sister, Frieda, and I in when mother passed. Otto was tried and convicted of Father's murder. He was sentenced to hang, but died in an attempted escape from prison. The last time I saw Otto alive was in court on the day I gave my testimony. Otto said he would come for me and kill me with his bare hands just as he had Father. There's never been any doubt in my mind that if his escape had been successful, Otto would have made good on that promise."

Miss Jilpa nodded, "Yes, that makes sense. I could feel the rage Otto had against you." Then to Vera, "I know this is difficult for you to hear, Mrs. Loren, but it is best that your son, Robbie, passed of cholera when he did. It was a merciful killing by the gods."

Vera looked confused. She asked Miss Jilpa to explain further. "Your son, Robbie, would have grown up to be a very bad man. Worse, I am afraid, than his uncle Otto. He would have killed his father, and you too. I believe that is why you had such difficulty conceiving after him when he was alive. Children, by their nature, are innocent. However, there is a malevolent presence that follows this family's sons. The eldest son, in particular. I am not sure what it is, but I'm certain I do not want to attempt to contact it again. It is hungry, and it is looking for another soul to latch onto. So much so that it is dangerous, even for me, to encounter. Robbie, as he came of age, was to be its new vessel. It poisoned your womb, Vera, so you would cling only to Robbie, no matter how wrong it seemed he was turning. It sought to destroy the trust between you and your husband, so that by the time it started to became violent with Karl, you would think he deserved it. Whatever that thing is, it had already started the progress of taking over the boy's will when he contracted cholera. He would not have remained the sweet child you knew for much longer. It is a blessing for Robbie's soul he succumbed to the disease, and to yours as well. Sometimes, the innocent must suffer from the sins of the wicked, even if they occurred long ago."

Karl looked as if he wanted to say something here, but caught himself. Miss Jilpa studied him for a moment, and then continued to speak to Vera. "Despite this, you will be happy to know the child you are expecting is a girl. She will be your last and only, but she will fill both of your lives with such light and happiness that you will not wish for more. A delightful girl. This will be the end of your family line. It is best to end in this way. Focus all your energy on her. And know that, although Robbie is lonely and misses you, it is not right for you to attempt to contact him again. You will see him, as he is supposed to be, in the next life."

Both Vera and Karl seemed relieved to hear this. They thanked Miss Jilpa for her interpretation and departed.

After bidding them goodbye, Miss Jilpa turned to me. "I am very weary. Is it necessary for me to tell you about your wolf, or do you think you can just accept its message through me on your own?"

Her question stunned me. Until that moment, I had said nothing to anyone about my intentions of inquiring about the *loup garou*. Apparently, there was no need. When we locked eyes, I knew the answer. Miss Jilpa had intuited my questions simply through holding my arm as we walked into the room.

I was relieved to hear her little tinkling laugh as Miss Jilpa watched the realization of this dawn on me. "The energy of your thoughts is very strong, Mae Ulrich. Stronger than I am sure you realize. If you were to train that energy, it would be as strong as mine. You have to learn to trust yourself first, before it can come through." Miss Jilpa took both of my hands in hers, and stood facing me. "I can feel the spirit of your wolf standing behind you even now. It is so close, that it is almost a part of you. Soon, it will be. Close your eyes, and I will show you who he is."

Obediently, I closed my eyes. Feeling a gentle pressure, as if someone was pushing me backward lightly on each shoulder, I had a quick sensation of falling. I heard the click of my boot heel on the floor as I took a step to brace myself. Otherwise, I felt disconnected from the present world. Looking about me in this new realm, I saw the wolf. My *loup garou*. He was running by my side, but there was something different. I was running too, as fast as he, but on all four limbs! The forest sped by in a blur as we raced. The wolf glanced over at me, and the look on his face—I swear it was like a smile. The way a happy dog might smile at a person. Thin-lipped, with the tips of his canines barely visible. His bright green eyes twinkled with it. Then, I felt the familiar pull of coming back into this world. It was just like what I had experienced in Edinburgh. Once again, I realized I was standing there in the present, holding Miss Jilpa's hands.

"What did you see?" she asked dreamily, swaying a bit on her feet from exhaustion.

"I saw my wolf. We were running through the forest. It was strange, almost like he was smiling at me."

"That's because he *was* smiling at you," Miss Jilpa said. "When you meet him, you will know him by his smile. He is happy you are among friends now. That you are learning to sense his presence, even though he is still very far away. Like our friend Mrs. O'Malley this evening, you should learn to talk less and listen more."

"So... he's a protective spirit? Someone from my past? My grand-père perhaps?"

"No, not him. And not from the past—from the future." Miss Jilpa let go of my hands, and gave me somewhat of an impatient look. "Just listen! You have the power to understand from your dreams, if you will truly *listen*. I know precisely who and what he is. It would do no good to tell you. At this time, you would not believe me. You are too practical—too eager to be skeptical. What this is, you will only begin to believe after you see it with your own eyes. Even then, you won't believe fully until *it becomes you*."

Dr. Wheeler returned from seeing the Loren's off, and offered us a ride in his carriage. Chatting about the evening's events and her impressions regarding my dreams, although I could tell she was tired and winding down, Miss Jilpa nevertheless made sure to instruct us to stay in contact. As she explained mysteriously to Dr. Wheeler, "because Mae is in need of your study and guidance."

Continuing onto my hotel, I asked Dr. Wheeler what Miss Jilpa meant. "She gets a little frustrated at times with Westerners. How unwilling we are to accept communication with the spiritual world. From what I have read and she has told me, it is very different in China and other parts of the world." He took a pad out of the interior pocket of his jacket and scribbled an address. "Write to me, once you reach Auraria. It's my office address. For the time being, I still live in the rooms above it. Haven't really been eager to look for new accommodations since, well... you know."

Here, Dr. Wheeler caught my eye. Just for a moment, I felt it. A profound sadness. He was extremely lonely and wanted to leave this place, but had no idea where to go. He turned his head to the side, watching me watch him. Then he cleared his throat and continued. "I agree with Miss Jilpa. It would be very interesting to me, professionally speaking, if we could continue our communication. And if you would permit me to educate you on some of the possibilities you might explore related to your gifts."

I started to object, but Dr. Wheeler raised his hand. "No, no. If Miss Jilpa thinks you have the gifts of perception, then you do. Whether you choose to learn to use them or not is up to you. Again, if you have an interest, please contact me once you've reached your destination. That way, I'll know where to write back to you. *My* interest," he leaned heavily on the word *my*, "is genuine."

I studied him again, taking in his thick red hair sprinkled with gray at the temples, and his inquisitive blue eyes, I raised an eyebrow. "Genuinely professional?"

His reply was only one word as he assisted me out of the carriage. "Genuine."

Damn this storm! The boat rolls like an apple in a tub. Ink bottle fell and broke. Need to clean it up before it sticks. I'll have to open a new one and finish later.

July 19, 1858

W ill this deluge ever cease? I've never seen so much rain from a summer storm! It's like some sort of Biblical plague! I continue to hear the crew fret about our primary cargo, which is a load of salted pork in barrels, getting damp. I can see why. Once this rain stops and the summer heat returns, the probability of mold ruining it is high. Moldy bacon is unsellable and inedible.

The other passengers I've seen in my treks back and forth to the galley to pick up my meals all seem slightly green at the gills. At present I am fine. Not moving about much, which helps. Just staying in my cabin reading. Not only are the other passengers quite wan looking, but they are less in number. Far fewer people seem to travel from St. Louis to Independence than from Cincinnati to St. Louis. After finally having some interesting people to talk to on my last night in the city, this part seems even more lonely.

The bright spot in all of it, I suppose, is that I've completed my lesson planning. Also, I've had ample time to dig into the trunk of books I've brought along. I'm trying to sift some meaning out of these mysterious dreams I keep having. Before I left Portland, I collected all of the volumes I could find with any mention of wolf or *loup garou* stories. I ordered a few more of the latest texts on dreams too. Even though I am learning a great deal about werewolves and the myriad of superstitions surrounding them through history, I have yet to run across a single werewolf that not only appears in dreams, but also seems both friendly and protective.

Quite to the contrary, every werewolf and *loup garou* legend I have read so far portrays them as savage beasts, all the way back to ancient times. Although I know it's fiction, you may remember the werewolf King Lycaon from Arcadia? He was the one who came into the palace under disguise and took hostages. After that, Lycaon attempted to test whether Zeus was a god by killing and roasting one captive, Epirus, then seeing if Zeus would eat him. Of course, Zeus, being a god, refused and unleashed his wrath upon the crazy tyrant. Zeus killed his fifty sons, burned his palace, and banished Lycaon into the wilderness. According to the footnotes, Zeus did so because Lycaon behaved like a wild wolf, preying on the flesh of humans. It is from him we get the word *lycanthrope*, which was the Greeks' term for *werewolf*.

Not to be outdone, the Romans had their own werewolf myths. One, recorded in Virgil's *Eclogues*, tells of a man named Moeris, who could use herbs and potions to turn himself into a werewolf. Then, he called ghosts from their graves. I remembered these from my Classics classes at Westbrook. However, I had forgotten about them, as one does with things studied long ago. I would think these ancient accounts, which were sort of tucked away in the recesses of my memory, could be one possible origin of my dreams. Except for the fact they're all depicted as sinister, which is not at all the feeling I have been getting from my wolf dreams.

Then, there are of course the dozens of stories my grand-père told me about French and Indian werewolves. I've been trying to jot them down from memory for comparison. The Wabenaki tribe, Grand-père told me, had a series of stories about a sort of wolfman creature named Malsumis. He was the brother of Glooscap, their Creator figure. Glooscap taught the tribes how to live properly in harmony with nature, and avoid such evils as over-hunting, which weakened the land and the community. In contrast, Malsumis, Glooscap's twin brother, represented everything predatory, including the violent and indiscriminate pillaging of game to excess, due to his ravenous and insatiable wolf-like appetites.

I can somewhat see the connection of Malsumis tales to my dreams. My greatest fears about my new teaching position are in regards to the intentions of the miners taking up residence in the Auraria region. From my grand-père, who traded and developed relationships with many natives in his younger days as a trapper before buying into the dairy business, I grew up with a greater respect for their cultures than most people. In fact, curiosity about the different tribes in the West was one thing that drew me to my present occupation in the first place. Logically, it is only natural my dreaming mind might manifest concern that the newly discovered veins of wealth in these lands might be stripped from their native people like a wolf strips meat from the bones of a deer. Interpreted this way, the wolf is a metaphor for predator.

However, this theory is still missing the reason why the wolf is such an inviting character to me. In fact, every European folktale would suggest the exact opposite—I should definitely fear the wolf. Every little girl has heard the tale of Little Red Riding Hood and the Big Bad Wolf. I've of course brought a copy of the Brothers Grimm's tales for children. Several actually, so my students may share them. That was actually the very first possible source I thought of in my quest to find the meaning of my wolf dreams. Considering I am a teacher of young children, it is highly possible the heightened imagination of children's stories might work their way into my life asleep as well as when I'm awake. Yet, the wolf who threatened Red Riding Hood appeared initially under the guise of her grandmother, only to later cast that identity off and reveal his predatory nature. There has been no similar pattern of devious secrecy and unveiling with my dream wolf. He, or *it*, since I'm not sure it's a *he*, has always appeared as a wolf in plain view.

Last are the stories about the *loup garou*. Being a woodsman in his early life, and a Frenchman always, my grand-père physically collected these stories. Kept newspaper accounts and pasted them into a sort of scrapbook. All the way back to the 1760s, from when he was a young boy in France during the first flush of *loup garou* panic. I brought this cut-and-pasted collection with me too. As you might imagine, the stories alone were simultaneously fascinating and horrifying as a child. Grand-père only made them more intriguing by retelling them in dramatic fashion from the old news reports. Looking back on them now, these stories had a very practical function. Growing up, I was the type of child prone to wandering off by myself to explore. Given increasing issues with mobility as he aged, I'm certain Grand-père used these stories as a sort of extra insurance against my ramblings. A child who is afraid of some beast in the woods will not stray off there alone.

Perhaps that may be the answer then. In some way, I equate my grand-père's attempts to protect me by using his wolf stories with the sense of security that knowing he was close by always provided. Maybe now that Grand-père is gone, and I am traveling into an unknown land, I have somehow tamed this ferocious beast into the kind of guardian I understood him to be. Grand-père was always open about the things that he had done. He never denied the fact he killed other men during the Revolution, or any of the other cruel acts he committed while he "carved a life out of the wilderness," as he used to put it.

Thinking about it that way, weren't all the founders of America were-wolves in some fashion? Genteel enough by the light of day, or as we choose to recall them now, but ruthless when no one was looking, in a time far back enough no one really remembers?

July 21, 1858

A rrived at last in Independence. So glad once again to be on *terra firma*!

The town here is bustling, but far less culturally advanced than St. Louis. Most of the activity seems to center around the impending gold rush, which promises to bring hordes of settlers from now through Spring. Apparently, some man named Cantrell arrived a few days ago with news of a big gold strike near Pike's Peak. The strike was made by a Georgian who goes by the curious name of William "Green" Russell. He's a well-known prospector who's been in the area for years, accompanied by his group of white and mixed-race Cherokee miners. The confidence in this strike being "the next big one" seems to stem from the fact that not only is Russell involved, but that many others are rushing over from less fruitful strikes nearby.

There's even an investment firm already. It's headed by a fellow named William Russell too. He's a different one from Vermont though. I don't believe they're related. This one plans to start an Express Stagecoach Line within the next few weeks from Leavenworth, a few miles northwest of Independence, due West to the gold territory. The hope is to transport all the new people who are predicted to swarm West like locusts. Word is they're trying to buy out some mail company that already exists along the route, so they can win a federal mail contract and have a steady income stream by May.

It appears my worries about being lonely and isolated from the rest of the world, at least for very long, were unfounded. There is no doubt in my mind now that my school will grow in swiftly. I feel certain I will not be the only teacher for long. If I can just make it through this first year, it's highly possible the population boom will make Auraria the size of St. Louis, or at least Independence, by next summer.

Although all this news is certainly exciting for the future, it doesn't really solve my present travel issues. According to the information I researched before beginning my trip, and what I have gleaned upon my arrival in Independence, I have two options when it comes to transportation along this final leg of my journey.

First, I can either pay a good bit more to carry my two trunks and ride in a test coach driven by Russell's company along the Northern way. The cost to transport my clothes is almost the same value as the clothes inside! They call that path the "Smoky Hill Route." Alternatively, I can pay a bit less and find an independent driver to take me along the "old Santa Fe Route" to the South. This route is more established and less expensive.

The second option would add almost two days to my trip, since the trail ends at Manitou Springs then requires a turn north to get to Auraria. Of the two, I'm inclined to take the more scenic Southern Route if I can find someone to take me. Not only does it pass through Manitou Springs, about which I've heard some fantastic local legends, but also the tribes who live along it are rumored to be more friendly. They're more likely to allow me to engage them in conversation, if I have the good fortune to meet some who speak English. Since I'm hoping that at least half, if not more, of my school will be children from local tribes, I'd like to start learning as much as I can about their cultures before school begins. That way, I will know best how to reach out to them.

I'm heading out for dinner now. With luck, I'll meet a few of the locals. Perhaps I can pick up the trail, if you'll pardon the pun, of someone who looks safe and is willing to accept payment to drive me along the old Santa Fe Route.

Fingers crossed!

July 22, 1858

L uck must be on my side at last on this trip. I not only found a driver for the Santa Fe Route after dinner last night, but she's the mother of one of my soon-to-be students! We leave at noon today. I am writing this while sitting on my trunk, awaiting her arrival.

Penny, the girl's name, is twelve going on thirteen, and seems to be surprisingly sharp for a girl who's never been formally schooled. She's quite outgoing too. Penny came right up to my table where I was eating alone and asked if I would like to join the group of friends with whom she and her mother were dining. I think the girl was bored by their conversation and scanned the room for something more interesting. Penny's pretty too, in a very unusual way, with brown eyes bright like polished chestnuts and a cloud of curly red hair that many girls would die for. Although I don't think she knows it. She's sprightly and outspoken as a boy, albeit one in a frilly dress and with ribbons in her hair. If all my students are as quick-witted and congenial as Penny though, teaching them should be a breeze.

Her mother, Brandy, is a very attractive woman. She has dark brown hair and a personality more charming than perky. Upon first meeting her, I would never have guessed her trade, other than by her dress. Brandy was showing a bit more cleavage than most would deem appropriate, although not openly advertising of her occupation. There is no delicate way of putting it, especially since I am sure I'll have to address it at some point. Miss Brandy Stockbridge is a madam and the proprietress of the only saloon in Auraria at present. Neither Brandy's occupation nor what others might think of it bothers me. However, I believe it bothered her to have to admit it when we met. I think she tries to shield Penny from it as much as possible. From what I know of her so far, Brandy had a surprisingly conservative upbringing. Somehow or other she ended up here doing what she does. She parents Penny on her own. I'm sure I will hear the rest of the story along our ride.

Regardless of how Brandy earns her money, it's apparent she has already made quite a lot of it. She has ample business savvy to keep it flowing. Her trip to Independence was to pick up a load of custom-sewn silk sheets, velvet draperies, hand-painted wallpapers, new china settings and silverware, to redecorate her saloon and its private upstairs rooms. She also selected an array of fresh dresses for her girls to wear in the new musical numbers she has planned. Brandy anticipates the arrival of hundreds, possibly thousands, of new men coming to the area over the next year. Her intention, as she expressed it to me, is to make Stockbridge's, not only the first saloon in Auraria, but the best, even as competition begins to arise.

Brandy's intellect and ambition seem to be first rate, even if directed in an unusual manner. I am happy to have the opportunity to travel with her. Normally, I would feel a bit uneasy at the thought of traveling in the company of only two other females alone through a strange land. However, Brandy and Penny have a definite air of knowing how to handle themselves in any situation, which makes me feel more at ease. Judging from the multitude of well-wishers who stopped by our table as we dined together last night, Brandy must know everyone and everything that goes on in the territory of which I am soon to be a resident.

Hopefully, we will become friends. Although I know it would not be considered a prudent decision by my employer Mr. H, for my first friend in the area to be engaged in Brandy's line of work. What Mr. H does not know will not hurt him. Growing up the way I did, I've never been one to judge people for such things anyway.

I'm sure if Penny has her way, this will happen. The poor thing hung on my every word last night. Despite her mother's popularity, Penny is clearly dying for attention. Penny will certainly make an eager and engaging pupil. As she matures, she might become a friend as well in her own right, of which I am most glad. Though letters are always wonderful to receive, the welcome of friends nearby has always been dearer to me.

Oh, I've almost forgotten to include the second most important part of my day! I had been expecting a telegram from my employer regarding the official start date for school, but none has arrived. Perhaps it will be waiting for me in Auraria. At any rate, a different telegram was waiting for me at breakfast this morning from Dr. Wheeler, of whom I've written about from St. Louis. He was checking to see if I'd made it to Independence, and whether I had safely secured passage onto Auraria. Such a thoughtful man! He must be an excellent doctor, and very attentive to his patients. It's really a shame what happened to him with his fiancée. Someone who cares so deeply about others should have someone to care about him in return.

July 23, 1858

A nd away we go!

Brandy, Penny, and I set out this morning for Auraria by way of Manitou Springs. It was amazing how quickly all signs of humanity disappeared once we were outside of the city. It's like we are on a transatlantic voyage, with no one else but us on our little ship of the prairie. The tall grasses wave and ripple in an endless undulation that is quite hypnotically beautiful. If the weather holds like it is, with a constant wind keeping the summer heat at bay, our journey should be more pleasant than I'd imagined.

Penny continues to hang on my every word, particularly any that involve "what fashionable girls do back East." As in, what they wear, how they interact with one another, what they read, what they eat, etc. My understanding is that Penny has designs on going East herself, if not for boarding school in a year or two, then definitely to attend college. She speaks of it quite openly. I have not heard Brandy say a single word against it. In fact, Brandy speaks strangely little at all when Penny and I are conversing, or when I am reading to her.

Penny drove her own wagon most of the day today, because she wanted to hear me read aloud. I noticed that once I began, Brandy tried to keep her wagon right along beside us. Every time I looked up to take notice of her though, she dropped back. It's like she's listening to Penny ask questions she wishes she could ask, but does not want to appear foolish or that she is grasping for lost youthfulness. Brandy is a very young woman in spirit, though I can tell she's seen much by the wrinkles of hardship around her eyes.

Today, we traveled from sun-up to sun down. At the first glimmer of dusk, Brandy informed me we were near a campsite she had used often in her travels. Our first stop in an actual town will be Council Grove, which we should reach by the evening of our fourth day. After that, we will pass through Forts Zarah, Larned, Dodge, and Lyon, before coming at last to Bent's Fort on about day sixteen or so. Each of these, as I have heard from Brandy, are decent enough small towns in which to spend the night and pick up food or supplies. All of them are built up around original military forts, but contain nothing else really of note for travelers. Brandy seemed to think I would be very intrigued by the folklore surrounding Manitou Springs, though she wouldn't tell me much about it yet. I get the feeling she wants me to experience it first-hand so she can compare her own impressions of it with another rational, like-minded woman. She doesn't want to spoil the interaction by filling my head with preconceived notions.

Dinner around the campfire was roasted sausages and potatoes. Brandy and I each handled a skillet so both parts of the meal could come together at approximately the same time. Penny made little apple fritters that she toasted expertly with a sort of little wire basket contraption. It had a snap to hold it shut and kept the dough tightly packed around the filling. She claimed to have made it herself after getting tired of too many fritters falling apart into the fire. As Penny was explaining how she came up with the idea, I watched Brandy beam at her daughter's cleverness. Apparently, there are all sorts of other handy domestic mechanisms Penny has invented that I will have to see when we arrive in town.

Brandy and Penny must have made this trip together numerous times, because they have the daily routine down pat. I was very impressed to find that not only had they planned every day's breakfast and dinner along the route, with breaks for us to eat in town when such accommodations were available, but they had outfitted the wagons with narrow beds in the middle to keep us off the ground at night. This prevents the lost time of pitching and taking down a tent each day we are between accommodations. When I joined the trip, they moved both of their little pallets to Brandy's wagon to give me the privacy of my own space. That was very thoughtful. It's tight— because of my two trunks I have to sleep sort of curled into a ball so my legs don't dangle out the back. I tend to sleep that way anyhow, so it isn't much of a bother.

After dinner, Brandy and Penny have a tradition of telling stories. Some they have read over the years and others they have heard locally from natives. Not surprisingly for a girl of her age, Penny loves a good ghost story. I'm sure I will be hearing quite a few new ones—an experience I welcome. Over dinner it came out that I had never heard of the Donner Party, which drew a big "Oooooh, Mother!" from Penny. "You have to tell her that one first," she exclaimed. "Since Old Mr. Russell kind of started it all. It's so scary!"

Brandy told the story. I will record it here because I feel the tragedy is significant. If you are reading this just after supper, then I encourage you to pause an hour or two and digest your meal before proceeding.

Penny knew the tale by heart. Her chestnut eyes sparkled in the firelight as her mother began. "About twelve winters ago, when Penny was still just a baby, there was a group of settlers heading west. The country was different then. There weren't easy roads to follow, or towns along the way to pick up supplies and have a good night's sleep in a real bed, as there are now."

"Because they were the first," interjected Penny, in a whisper that could have been heard in a saw mill. "And they were cannibals!"

"Well, there you go," replied Brandy, throwing up her hands in exasperation and picking up the poker to jab at the fire. "Settlers turned cannibals. Abridged version, courtesy of Miss Penelope Stockbridge. End of tale."

"No, no! I'm sorry!" Penny wailed. "Mama please, tell us the whole thing! It's better when you tell it. I promise I'll be quiet and not say another word."

"Doubtful. You might suffocate." replied Brandy, who set the poker down and resumed her story.

"Originally, they left from Independence, just as we did. Only they had much farther to go. All the way to California."

"Mama and I went all the way to California when I was three, but I don't remember it," Penny whispered to me, this time at a lower volume. "She was smarter though. We sailed."

"So much for promises," said Brandy, rolling her eyes. "Who's telling this story again?"

Penny made a motion like she was buttoning her lips. Brandy resumed a second time.

"*As I was saying*, they left Independence. Five hundred wagons in all, running like a great river over these plains." Brandy made a sweeping motion with her arm to indicate their vastness. To me she added, "Initially, they were led by William Russell. Not the one with the gold mine in Auraria, but the other one who's about to open the stagecoach line. I'm not exactly sure at which point they parted ways, or why, but it was sometime around when they left Fort Laramie. By the time they reached Fort Bridger, they had decided to change their original plan to follow the Oregon Trail out past Fort Hall and along the Snake River. That was the usual way. Instead, they chose to follow the advice of a rider whom they'd met as he was advertising a new way that he claimed to be shorter. It was called the Hastings Cutoff. Trying that new route was what caused the trouble. First, they lost a couple of weeks going through some of the most treacherous parts of the Rocky Mountains. Then, they had to cross an enormous expanse of desert, for which they were not prepared. There was no way to gather water, because the big lake they finally came to was as salty as the ocean. People and cattle began to go crazy with hunger and thirst. Many died. Finally, in late September, they made it out of this desert territory and to the foothills of the Sierra Nevada. By then, it was too late in the season to safely cross a second set of mountains, especially with their weary men and tired oxen." Here, Brandy's voice began to take on a huskier sound than her usual velvety alto. It had a bit of rough accent to it that I struggled to place as she continued the story.

"What was left of the five hundred wagon loads of families began to quarrel. They split off from one another into several smaller groups. The ones who decided to press on against all odds were the smartest. They followed a cranky old Irishman named Reed whom nobody liked. That group made it through to civilization and over to Sutter's Fort by late October. However, about eighty or so others, the ones who chose to stay back with a personable fellow from North Carolina named Donner and take their time getting across, almost all died. An early blizzard came the first week of November and trapped them in the mountains. They became so desperately hungry for food, that some tried to go out and hunt. Most of those who did froze to death. A small group finally straggled on snowshoes to a Miwok encampment thirty miles away, looking so much like death themselves that the Indians ran away initially. However, eventually they were able to convince the Miwok they were looking to find help for those still stranded. The ones who stayed back at camp, well... as Penny told you... they chose to find food in other ways. They ate the sick who naturally died first. Men, women, children, it didn't matter. At last, some say they began killing each other off, one by one. Anyone who appeared weak was a target. Only the strongest and best able to withstand starvation survived until a rescue group was able to come through in March. But at what price? Not one any of us would be willing to pay, I'd wager. Half of them were dead and had been worked through the innards of their companions by then. Other explorers kept finding their bones for years afterward, strewn through that area around the Fremont Pass where they perished. The ones who lived have spent their lives lying about it to cover up their guilt, but inside they know."

By this point the fire had died down to embers. Penny, despite her initial enthusiasm, had grown heavy-lidded during the retelling of the tale that she'd heard many times. However, since these atrocities were new to me, I was wide awake. As Penny dismissed herself and crawled into the wagon for sleep, I asked Brandy whether she didn't worry about telling such ghastly stories before bedtime to a young girl.

"I hope they scare her into her wits," replied Brandy, to which I asked whether she meant "out of her wits" instead?

"No," Brandy replied, somewhat snippily, for she was exhausted too. "I always say what I mean and mean what I say. I want her scared *into* using her wits, and her *own* wits alone. *Always.* That is why I tell the story as I do. To emphasize the outcast Irishman Reed who everyone thought was wrong was, in fact, one of the few who survived without becoming some kind of savage animal. I want Penny to know a person in this world must use her wits to take care of herself, and to not care what anyone else thinks. Because if they are the sort who always follows the path just as they're told to, mindlessly like sheep, then they're the first ones the wolves will devour when times become tough."

As Brandy said this, she picked up the sausage pan and studied it closely in the light of the lantern. Until that moment, the thought hadn't registered with me that she still had her gloves on. They were clearly expensive, custom-made. The leather was thicker than one might suppose for a lady. Her face squinching up in dismay at the sticky state of the skillet, Brandy pulled off first her right glove and then her left with her teeth.

That's when I first noticed it. Brandy's left hand only had two fingers. A thumb and pinky. The middle three were gone.

Stunned at their absence marring the otherwise delicate appearance of her slender, tapered hands, Brandy caught me looking at her.

"Sewing machine accident. I was sixteen. If you'd like to hear that story, ride in my wagon tomorrow and leave little Miss Chatterbox with her own thoughts for a while."

I did not protest or offer any apology. To do so would have seemed insincere. I can already tell Brandy Stockbridge is not a woman who cottons to those who are disingenuous.

I write this by a candle that I now extinguish. Hopefully in the morning, I shall be more enlightened.

July 24, 1858

After breakfast at daybreak of biscuits, bacon, and fried eggs, we hit the trail again.

As soon as we were on the road, I told Brandy a quick summary of my background, from growing up around my French grandpère's enterprises in Maine to my travels abroad. I hoped that sharing this information would make me seem more worldly and accepting than was expected of an average schoolteacher, and encourage her to open up. It worked. Brandy spared me the awkwardness of having to inquire about last night's promised account of her life by beginning it just after we pulled ahead of Penny's wagon early this morning. I will recount it here, as faithfully as I can muster.

Brandy was born sometime just before Christmas Eve, 1826, which makes me about four months older than her. I say "sometime" because she was placed on the steps of St. Patrick's Cathedral during midnight Mass. She was found by a priest as he locked up. The thick swaddling of blankets in which she was bundled sat inside a handmade holly wreath. A tiny knitted rabbit that looked to have been made out of an old glove was tucked inside with her. The priest immediately took her to the nearby Sisters of Charity. The group of nuns had begun a series of fundraising concerts that year which helped them found the first Asylum for abandoned Catholic girls in New York City. Wasting no time, the Sisters had her baptized the next morning under the name "Holly Hare," no doubt to honor the wreath and the stuffed rabbit that had accompanied her.

Holly, as she was then known, grew up amongst the nuns. She was tutored by them in reading, mathematics, and the like, along with the two dozen or so other girls who would form the first cohort at the new Asylum. The Sisters worked diligently to provide the girls with the education and environment necessary for them to become good citizens, even

going without food and beds themselves so their charges might want
for less. Patronage of the Asylum was solicited from many of the New
York merchants and traders there on Wall Street, as well as from the
owners of textile mills along the New England coast. Many of these
mill owners took on the girls as garment workers as soon as they were
deemed old and responsible enough to work. Holly was placed with one
of these such garment manufacturers in Lowell, where she began work
carding wool at twelve. By fourteen, she was promoted to running her
own loom. Having lived her entire life in a room full of women, shoulder to shoulder, both sleeping and waking, mill life had not bothered
Holly as it did others. She had planned to make a career of it.

However, one day, as she was chatting with a coworker in the line,
Holly carelessly allowed a piece of cloth to get jammed in the works,
stopping the whole machine. Scared of the reprimand that would come
from her supervisor, Holly attempted to reach into the machine and
pull out the tangled piece of fabric. As she was working the fabric
free, the weaving mechanism collapsed on her left hand, crushing three
of her fingers. Trapped, all Holly could do was scream for help until
the dreaded supervisor arrived with an engineer. Although they took
her to the doctor immediately, he was unable to save Holly's fingers.
They had been completely flattened and almost severed from her hand.
The doctor finished the job, amputating her mutilated fingers. On the
day she left the hospital, Holly attempted to return to work. She was
immediately fired for her previous negligence and endangerment of the
machines by attempting to unjam them herself, rather than ringing for
the supervisor. Her belongings were packed up, and she was turned out
of the dorm within hours.

Thus, at sixteen, Holly found herself homeless and jobless. Intending
to return to New York, in hopes of asking the Sisters for help in finding
other employment, she had a stopover in Amherst that would change
her life. As she was sitting in the train station eating a hotdog, a group
of college boys passed by her. One made a lewd comment about her
ability to take such large bites of it. Then, he alluded to her potential
to take other things into her mouth.

"It must have been a bit of the devil who possessed me then," Brandy
explained to me. "Because I replied saucily, *Well... wouldn't you like to
find out?*"

This apparently intrigued the cheekiest boy, who sat down beside her and struck up a conversation. Within a few minutes, she managed to pull the three of them into thrall. By the time the train arrived, the brash boy got on with her, leaving his friends behind.

When I asked her what happened next, Brandy giggled and said, "I guess he enjoyed what happened in the sleeper car that evening. When we got off in New York, he asked me to turn right around and follow him back to Amherst. Which I did, after he bought me dinner and gave me ten dollars. I used it to buy a room there for a week. During which time he must have told every friend he had. I met all of *them* very soon, if you catch my drift."

Here, she paused, winking at me to make sure I knew what she meant.

Over the next few years, the woman who would become known as Brandy Stockbridge made quite a bit of money from servicing the young gentleman scholars of Amherst, during which time she learned what she called a number of "truths" about men.

"First, they're always kinder when they're younger. Second, the chubby ones and those who are most socially awkward are usually the sweetest and most gentle. And third, all are nicest to you the first time they see you, and then again at the last. So, you have to make yourself always seem on the verge of leaving forever to keep them interested."

For the next three years of her life, she kept a small apartment near the college, well-furnished by her encounters with the boys. Because of her frugal upbringing, she managed to save several thousand dollars. The young men became part of her "extracurricular education" as she called it. Many enjoyed talking about their travels and studies with her after their visits, finding her the most sympathetic ear in their lives. Alas, all of this came to an end when she found out she was pregnant at nineteen.

"It couldn't have gone on forever," she said, resolutely popping the reins on the horse's back, as they had slowed while she was talking. "In the beginning, I was the girl they had longed for back home, but would never have. However, being almost twenty, and definitely a girl no longer, I was already losing some of that innocent appeal. Perhaps it was for the best." Her clientele dwindled after Penelope's birth. She found taking in washing and picking up piecework sewing paid the bills, but was far more tiresome than her previously frivolous employment. Then, she had nothing to do but bolster the egos of young men, and watch the money rain down upon her.

"Why Penelope?" I asked, regarding her curiously classical name choice.

Brandy smiled, "Because she was a weaver of tales. Deceiving all the other men while she waited for her own. Odysseus. The man of twists and turns. Kind of symbolic of a woman avoiding fate, I thought. I could empathize."

I told her, considering the circumstances, I thought she'd made an appropriate choice.

By 1848, the few boys who still came to see her began talking with excitement about going West for a Great Adventure in California. Gold had been found near San Francisco. Many fantasized about ditching their college plans to take their chances at striking it rich before settling down into the domestic life of commercial farming, for which they were being trained. Seeing this as her next great opportunity, possibly to grow up with the country and the young men who had provided her living as they all moved into the next phases of their lives, the young mother Holly Hare and her daughter Penelope departed on a long voyage "round the horn" to California. For the trip, she chose to use a different name.

"Boys nicknamed me Brandy at the start. The first time they asked me what I drank, I said *brandy* without knowing what any of the drinks were. I hadn't ever touched a drop in my life until then. And Stockbridge... well, I thought it sounded classier than Hare. There was a professor all the boys admired by that name at Amherst. I thought it had sort of a sophisticated Old English air about it, so I took it for my own."

Making it to San Francisco, the freshly renamed Brandy Stockbridge had the good looks and fortune to meet up with an esteemable old madam, whom she called Ms. Lillie. Appreciated for her level head and lack of bad habits, Ms. Lillie took Brandy under her wing. She showed Brandy how to select the best and safest clients, and advised her on how to save money.

"Miss Lillie knew I would leave and strike out on my own one day. She was fine with that," explained Brandy. "So long as I promised to do it far away from her and her business! As I was heading down the back side of my twenties, I thought it was time. My looks were holding up, but the thirties are when they usually start to slide. I wanted to get out with my pride intact. So I could say *I* left the boys, rather than the boys left *me*," she cackled.

Brandy started hearing news of a place in the Colorado Mountains that everyone thought would be the next big gold strike. She gathered up her money, furniture, clothes, and Penny, who was by then about ten, and left for Bent's Fort. It seemed to be the jumping off spot for prospectors. When the Green Russell party set up camp near what came to be called Auraria, Brandy was one of the first in line, with a wagonload of lumber to build her saloon. That Spring, Brandy hired out the miners who were taking their week off in their field rotations to build a large, eight-bedroom boarding house. It had an owners' suite out back, past the dining room for her and Penny. Four rooms downstairs for legitimate guests, and four rooms upstairs for those who would stay only a portion of the night. To these, she added a great room with a piano and a small stage for dancing.

"Lillie sent out the first girls in May. Hand-picked them herself. She gets so many who apply to her that she can't keep them all. She sent me her four best who were willing to take their chances on something new. They all came from someplace else, so it doesn't matter to them, so long as the money is good. They're already there, settling in, and eager to have all these new things. It'll be the showiest place in town, and I plan to keep it that way."

I had no doubt she would.

Regardless, Brandy's plan was to continue to expand her business by adding more girls and better entertainment as the town grew with the gold boom. She'd seen it happen in San Francisco. How a city could explode almost overnight from the hills, like Athena sprung from the head of Zeus. Yet, Brandy had different dreams for her daughter, Penny.

"She's a pretty girl, and far too cunning for her own good," Brandy sighed, shaking her head. "She'd do well in this business, but she could be so much more. Penny has…" Brandy tapped the side of her head, "a brain. And I want to give her the best chance to use it. I'm sending her back East in the Fall after she turns fourteen. To the best schools money can buy so she can see what she can make of herself." Brandy slowed the horses to a trot as she spotted our campsite for the evening. It was then I realized she'd talked all day. I'd just sat silent, absorbing it all. Hopping down from the wagon, Brandy motioned for Penny to stop too.

"Maybe once she finishes school, her poor old mother can finally retire," she sighed.

"You'll never retire," called Penny, pulling up behind us. "You'll die with the men all standing around hanging on your every word, because that's how you want to be remembered. As the center of their world."

"Perhaps you're right," replied Brandy, half to me, and half to her daughter. "Perhaps that's all I want. To be the center of someone's world. Is that too much to ask?" They erupted in gales of laughter at the question and hugged one another before setting up the campfire.

As I lay here writing this tonight, I find their life so unusual. Brandy, as I have been instructed to call her, since only a privileged few are allowed to know her whole story, and Penny have every reason to be completely embittered with the world. Yet somehow, they find it within themselves to keep cutting up and making the best of it. I don't know if I could. I'm so fretful nine mornings of ten, when I have no reason for it at all. I have nothing truly to complain of, save for lack of companionship. Perhaps that's why I've befriended them.

A woman who is wily enough to weave her way through life's many twists and turns is the best kind to count as a friend, in my book.

July 25, 1858

Tonight, we've made it to Council Grove, where I was surprised to find a sizeable town and an excellent hotel with a restaurant called Hayes House. It just opened last year.

According to Penny, she and her mother have already stopped here several times on their trips back and forth to better outfit her place. They've always found it welcoming and well-appointed. Once again, it gives me hope my choice to go West to a township that is for now undeveloped will only be without the usual comforts for a year or two.

As for the rest of town, Council Grove is quite a fascinating place. Along the lines of Plymouth Rock, I think, but in the West. Many years ago, in the 1820s, the original settlers and Osage tribesmen came together at a particular tree, aptly named Council Oak. They agreed this place would be a respite along a path of safe passage, and no hostility between the races should be perpetuated here. Five hundred dollars was given to the Osage tribe for this privilege, under the direction of then President John Quincy Adams. An interesting concept for sure. It is the first place I have seen natives and whites milling about together, frequenting the same places of business, since I left the small towns of Maine.

Brandy spent a great deal of time after dinner speaking with the proprietor about menus, budgets, and such. She plans to make her establishment as posh as possible. Penny took the opportunity to show me something truly unique. A real Native American story circle! Encouraged to look for her own amusement while her mother talked business, Penny heard about other native children going to this weekly gathering and invited herself in. Probably seeing Penny as all others do, a harmless and bored girl, they allowed her to stay. In turn, I was permitted to sit and listen as well.

The storytelling circle took place in a swept lot behind the native-run trading post where buffalo and elk hides are bought and sold. Much to my delight, all the children sat quietly and respectfully as the elders, both male and female, took turns telling stories. This experience was quite the contrary to what I had been trained for by Mr. H back in Hartford. There, it seemed every other word out of the instructors' mouths was a sermon preached on the need to uphold discipline amongst native children who had been raised with what they offensively referred to as "wild tendencies."

As with much else I heard in this "training," their warnings about the behavior of native children was to be taken with a grain of salt. In my view, a good educator simply must find something a child is interested in, and his or her attention will be no problem to hold. Since these tales clearly had them enraptured, I will summarize them here to refer to later on when I need a way to reach out to them.

Given in chronological order, it seemed, the first tale told by the most aged elder was the Osage creation story. Surprisingly, I found it to be much like our Christian creation story. For the Osage, there is a Great Spirit in the sky whom they call Wakonda. Before there was an Earth, all living things were also spirits that flowed in and out of the greater and all-encompassing spirit he represented. These spirits went first to the sun, but they found it too hot and bright. Then, they went to the moon, but it was too dark and cold. At last, they came to the Earth. Yet, it was covered with water. Despite flying in all directions, to the North, South, East, and West, they could find no place on which to land and rest. Their hearts became filled with sorrow.

At last, seeing their predicament, and wanting to provide a place for them, Wakonda began to speak the world into existence. From the middle of the waters rose a great white rock, which burst into flames, causing much of the water to evaporate and dry land to appear. It was soon covered with new waves of grasses, as the plains are now. Trees grew, and the floating spirits descended to the new Earth as beings of flesh and blood. They ate the grains of the fields and the fruits of the trees. There was great rejoicing and giving of thanks to Wakonda for providing them with this abundant life.

Soon after, Wakonda began to speak the animals into existence. First the crane, who flew across the sky, proclaiming the red children of Wakonda had come. Next, the wolf was made. He caused others to tremble at the strength of red peoples' legions who were warriors of the earth. Last, the buzzard, who is the seer of all life and death. He is spoken of by wise elders who know that from Wakonda they come, and to him they will return. The series of events described was very similar in sequence to the story of Noah's Flood, and the order in which the Christian God created the heavens and the earth. I think this tale will be most useful when trying to bridge the gap between cultures. I suppose many of my native students will be hearing the Christian creation story for the first time while in my classroom, so it will provide contrast.

This story was followed by another, in which the Osage learned how to manage life in their new world. Awakening to the fact they were naked among the animals, they desired clothing, and made it from weeds and grass woven together. Until they learned to create and use weapons like the bow and arrow, they used clubs to hunt deer. After that, they learned to chip tools from flint, to make fire by rubbing elm twigs together, to warm themselves and to roast their food. Last, they taught themselves to build houses of grasses harvested from the plains with scythes made from the shoulder-bones of deer, and to make pottery, with which they could cook and store things.

It's worth noting that during each of these important cultural developments, the Osage began by asking among themselves what was to be done, rather than merely praying to Wakonda for help. This sense of self-reliance, I think, is similar to Emerson's writings and our modern Transcendentalist movement, where finding solutions to live simply are more important than complaining about the lack of intervention from Providence. As such, I think it will be a good lesson to teach my white students, who tend to rely too much on prayer for solace. For even as our Christian parable goes, God helps those who help themselves.

After these initial anecdotes, the elders went around the circle again. The stories told in the second round related in some way to a lesson personal to each child present. Most involved what I've heard called Trickster Tales. Many involved a fox outwitting, or attempting to outwit, some other kind of creature for its own gain. The results of the foxes' efforts were mixed, showing the children that being shrewd and cunning, while a desirable mental ability, did not always equal success. Instead, creatures that worked diligently and patiently were rewarded with the best results. In many ways, these tales reminded me very much of Aesop's Fables. I made a mental note to look back through my books and to compare the details of what I heard in the Osage story circle with the Greek stories I knew by heart. They could be another way to encourage the native and white children to reach out and understand one another.

I was somewhat surprised that a tale near the end of the circle was addressed directly to me by an elder woman of the tribe. Even more surprising, it was a wolf story. She seemed to study me deeply, looking into my eyes before selecting it, as if she were reading in my soul what kind of animal should be drawn out. Here is the story she told for me:

A grandfather decided to teach his grandson about life. He told the boy, "Every evening when I go to sleep, and every morning when I wake up, there is a fight going on inside me. It is a terrible fight between two wolves. The dark wolf is every imaginable evil: anger, arrogance, ego, envy, false pride, greed, guilt, lies, resentment, self-doubt, self-pity, and sorrow. The light wolf is every possible good: compassion, empathy, faith, generosity, hope, humility, joy, kindness, love, peace, serenity, and truth. Yet, I am not alone in having this war between two wolves inside me. Within the soul of every person on earth, the same war is being fought every day of their lives." The grandson thought for a moment, and then asked anxiously, "But grandfather, which wolf will win?" The grandfather replied simply, "The wolf you feed."

At the conclusion of this story, each of the older Osage nodded in silent agreement with the truth of the tale.

Thinking back over the evening, I still wonder how the elderly woman knew a wolf story was the one for me? I have told no one here about my wolf dreams, except you, reader. I wonder whether the wolf was just a coincidence that caused me to take notice of her message, rather than clairvoyance on her part. How many traits of the darker wolf do I harbor? I admit there are a few. Although I try diligently not to tell any lies that matter, I have been told I am both arrogant and prideful. Yet, I can be paradoxically self-doubting. In my defense, I possess some of the lighter wolf's characteristics as well. I have never been willfully cruel to anyone who didn't deserve it, and I can be very kind and loving. Sometimes, I give too much, to my own detriment. To quote my dearest Whitman, *I contradict myself, I am large, I contain multitudes.*

Perhaps that is why the wolf of my dreams is a solid shade of gray.

The wolf that I feed is an emotional omnivore.

But if my spiritual wolf's diet is indeed balanced, then why did the Osage woman feel the need to tell me *that* particular story?

July 26, 1858

B ack on the trail again this morning. According to what Brandy told me, the territory we have to go through next week between here and Bent's Fort will not be as hospitable as what we enjoyed in Council Grove. Despite the long-ago treaty between the Osage and the earliest settlers, relations between whites and natives in the area have deteriorated over the years. Mostly because white Americans continue to break every treaty they make with the local tribes. As they push each one off their native lands in an expansion westward that seems to have no end, they cause not only resistance to their imposition of authority, but also in-fighting among different tribes. Our invasion disturbs many settled boundaries of where they felt comfortable and had a rightful sense of belonging.

Brandy said different tribes coped with this encroachment in different ways. Some, such as the Comanche and Apache, chose to stand their ground and fight, refusing to be pushed back any further. Others, like the Utes and Navaho, kept conceding small amounts of land and retreating farther and farther into the desert or mountains. Finally, some like the Pawnee and Arapaho, tried to bridge between the two worlds by trading, with marginal levels of success. Regardless of whichever method they choose, from what Brandy has told me, it was almost always the Indians who ended up getting the short end of the deal.

"Though, I think the Utes are going to get the upper hand in Auraria at least." Brandy smirked, as she completed her assessment of the situation. I asked her why.

"Because of that gold vein that Green Russell found. It's right in the middle of Ute territory now. Land that wasn't even theirs, but the government backed the Utes up onto it because no one else wanted it. Now gold's been found, I bet the Utes are going to give them a hell of a time negotiating how to get it out. I hope the Utes dig in and really stick it to them. Poor folks deserve something decent after being run all over the country."

"So, do you really think Green Russell's going to buy the Utes out? Maybe split the profits of what they are able to mine there?" I asked.

"Not if he can help it," Brandy replied. "Russell's just like all the rest of those wildcatters. Shrewd. Doesn't trust anyone as far as he can throw them. He'll try his best to cheat the Utes out of it, by hook or by crook. Best chance they've got is Just Cawdor negotiating for them. He's got a real ax to grind with Russell. And it's old and rusty—the worst kind."

"Just who?"

"Cawdor," Brandy explained. "I'm sure you'll meet him when we get to Auraria. He's the kind of fellow who seems to be everywhere all the time, once you know him. Kind of spooky that way. He's a cousin of Green Russell's, only Cawdor doesn't count him as family anymore. Not after Russell left him to die on his first trip out to California during the Rush."

"Wait, what?" I was confused. "Why would Russell have abandoned him?"

"It's a long story. I don't know all the history behind it. For that, you'll have to ask Cawdor himself. Here's the part I do know." Brandy leaned over to me, preparing to share a particularly juicy piece of gossip. "Cawdor was among the first party Green Russell led to California back in '49. At some point, Cawdor took ill. Tuberculosis, I heard, because everyone who knew him then said he was coughing up blood. By the time they made it just north of Bent's Fort, out to that place with the big red stone formations, Cawdor was falling off his horse. So, Russell and the rest of his bunch just left him there. Only he didn't die."

"How could they do that? Especially to someone who was family?"

"Because Russell was in charge, that's why. Man's got gold fever. He's been back and forth to Georgia where he's from half a dozen times. Always with a bunch of Cherokee he's related to somehow through his wife. They do all the grunt work of digging and panning for him, hoping to get their share whenever they finally make a strike, I guess. I wouldn't be holding my breath if I were them though." Brandy raised her eyebrows skeptically, "But I haven't finished Cawdor's story." She paused for effect, clearly enjoying how much I was hanging onto the tale. I nodded emphatically for her to continue.

"Cawdor didn't die because he was saved by wolves." Brandy stated.

Again, I was confused. "Wolves! How? What kind of wolves?"

"Just your basic gray wolves, the way Cawdor told it to me. Last thing he remembered before losing consciousness was Russell directing his men to set him up by some tree and then riding off with his horse. Cawdor tried to yell at them to come back, but he was too weak. When he woke up, he was completely healed. Sleeping in this cave up in those sandstone formations, huddled up among a pack of wolves. Then here's the best part... he was naked! Pretty good-looking fella too, in the face. Body's a little rangy though. Still, wish I..."

I interrupted Brandy's fantasy. "What happened to his clothes?"

Brandy grinned, pleased with this titillating detail. "Cawdor didn't know. Maybe the wolves took them. Maybe he stripped them off somewhere and forgot about them when he was high with fever. Who knows? And that isn't all. Not only was he mysteriously well again, but for some reason, one of the wolves had found a Pawnee trading woman passing by on the way back to Bent's Fort. The wolf somehow enticed her to follow it to the cave. There, the she found Cawdor, hungry and naked, but healed of the tuberculosis. She took him to the tribal gathering where she was headed. When Cawdor told them all what happened to him, her fellow Pawnee took it as a sign he was chosen by the gods for some reason, to be their emissary in negotiations with the white settlers and miners."

"Why did they believe him?" I pressed. "Didn't they think his story was far-fetched?"

Brandy looked at me like I was dumb. "Cawdor's half Cherokee, and he looks it. Natives trust almost any bad thing another native says about a white man. Doesn't matter what tribe he's from. And the Pawnee worship wolves. They have all sorts of legends about how a man can take on the strength and cunning of a wolf for protection in battle just by putting on his skin. A man randomly showing up and lying about being so favored by wolves would be like someone showing up in Notre Dame Cathedral and lying about being a false saint. It's just not done. However, there was some resistance to Cawdor's presence, because not all tribes believe the same thing about men who have such close ties to wolves. The Navajo, for example, have a whole lot of crazy stories about these things they call skinwalkers. Men who are turned into wolf-like creatures for committing terrible acts, like murdering their family members. They're the very incarnation of evil. Which is why until Green Russell and his men came back through the area the next year after the Bust of the California Rush, the Navajo would have nothing to do with Cawdor in negotiations of any kind. Or with the Pawnee for a while, because they sheltered him. The Navajo were afraid that Cawdor was a lying skinwalker who had killed his family and was cast out for it. Now though, I guess you could say they've accepted he must be a good wolf after all, and a sign meant for the Pawnee. They've left him alone."

"Oh," I breathed, digesting all this information. I felt like I had a lot more to learn before I would be prepared to understand this complex web of native customs and spirituality.

Seeing me mentally working through this information, Brandy finished her story. "Since then, Cawdor has earned the respect of several tribes. He has made his living helping to facilitate trade and other negotiations among the whites and natives. He has a pretty good head for it. Speaks English, Cherokee, and half a dozen languages of the other tribes around here. They all trust him, too. Not just because of the wolf thing, but because Cawdor's a genuinely honest man. Something *very* rare around these parts." From the way Brandy leaned heavily on the *very*, I was inclined to believe her. "And, for reasons I'm sure I don't have to explain further, Cawdor hates Russell. He'll do everything he can to get the Utes the best deal on this whole mining enterprise."

I told her I had no doubt that Cawdor would do that very thing.

My curiosity is definitely piqued about this Cawdor person, for a number of reasons. First, he seems like a mythical figure, saved by wolves and all. Second, if anyone can help me sort out relations among the doubtlessly diverse and possibly hostile native students I will be teaching soon, he sounds like the man to do it. Third, if he's actually good-looking enough to turn Brandy's head when she's so sick of men in general, he must be quite a sight to behold. Last, I wonder... if Cawdor was saved by wolves, could it also be possible that sees the *loup garou* as I do? And if so, could he help me to better interpret my own dreams?

Unfortunately, I'll have to wait at least a week until we get to Bent's Fort to find out.

July 28, 1858

Writing this entry in the small hours of the morning, under very strange conditions. Rather than taking our usual night's rest, we're forging straight on for the sake of safety.

Yesterday, we came upon the shocking scene of a completely burnt hunting camp. Piles of ashes from several dozen tipis were squashed flat by a wave of summer rains. The bloated and rotting corpses of dead native men, women, and children were still strewn all over the hillside. Buzzards had picked out their eyes, and what other of their remains that predators hadn't gnawed away lay putrefying into jelly amid the tall grasses. Even though it was clear from the amount of decay they had been killed many days, possibly even weeks ago, the lingering smell was worse than the offal pit behind a summer slaughterhouse.

Stopping the wagons, Brandy, Penny, and I got down to examine the scene more closely. Every one of the victims had been shot. Mostly in the back, so far as I could tell. They appeared to have fallen face down in mid-run.

"Must have been an Army raid," Brandy said, kneeling next to the corpse of a young woman. The poor lady had a bloodied hole almost the size of an egg caved into the back of her head, right along the center part of her two braids. The skull was exposed and it was apparent some animal had been feasting on the soft meat of her brain. "If it were a rival tribe, they likely would have taken a young girl like this for ransom, or for a war bride." Brandy straightened up and surveyed the ground. Seeing a baby lying a few yards away with its chest caved in around the perfect shape of a horse's hoof print, Brandy pointed it out to me. "Yep. Definitely Army."

"Oh, Mama, that baby!" Penny breathed, seeing what Brandy pointed at as she walked up slowly behind us. Penny's voice quivered. "It's just like

Chipeta told me. What happened to her when... only this little one didn't make it."

Brandy pulled her daughter to her side. Penny buried her head into her mother's shoulder. To me, Brandy explained, "Penny has a friend, older, who lives with the Utes in their village near Auraria. Chipeta. She's Apache. Her whole village was wiped out in an Army raid years ago. The Utes found her crawling around the ruins and adopted her." Brandy smoothed Penny's unruly copper hair.

The girl stepped back, sniffling and trying to gather herself. "We should look around, Mama. See if there's anybody left."

"Okay, pumpkin. You do that. We'll see too. Just to make sure." Brandy glanced over to me. Without saying a word, I could tell she knew we'd find no survivors.

Stepping closer, Brandy whispered in my ear, "We came this same route the first week of July. Could see the smoke of the camp to the South of here but didn't think anything of it. Summer is prime hunting season. They were probably too busy to give anyone trouble. If this is the same tribe, and it very well could be, they may have been laying out for a week or more."

As we picked our way carefully through the blackened grass, trying not to step on anyone's remains, I heard horses approaching in the distance. Brandy instructed Penny and me to go stand by the wagons and hold our teams so they didn't startle. As the riders came closer, I could see they were two native men. Brandy raised her hands in the air and called out to them several times in Spanish. "*Paz, mi amigos! Paz! ¡Lo siento que estén muertos!*" Or, in English, "Peace, my friends! Peace! I am sorry they are dead!" They slowed their cantering horses to a walk and dismounted about ten feet away from us.

The taller one looked around and narrowed his eyes, saying "*No hay person en Apache. Solo que no debe hacerse.*" Since this was beyond the limits of my Spanish, I looked over to Brandy for a translation. She shook her head, *no*. I took that to mean I should remain silent, which I did. Brandy continued to converse with the two men in Spanish, slowly allowing her hands to drop to her sides. Although I strained to hear, I didn't understand a single word besides the name Chipeta, which I had heard Brandy say in reference to Penny's friend earlier. Hearing the name, and seeing Brandy gesture toward Penny, they nodded. After they walked around the remains of the village together, Brandy came back over to where Penny and I stood.

"Everything is okay, or as much as it can be, considering," she said. "These men are Apache. They have been watching the campsite from afar since it burned. The dead Indians were a Comanche hunting party. The Army was ordered to kill any Comanche they saw along this route. They're planning to come through soon and build a few more forts to expand the route for the new stagecoach and post line that opens in the Spring. A rail line will follow. Comanche have been giving the Army trouble for years, since this was their original land."

Brandy paused and inclined her head to the West. "There is a large group of Apache hunting about a day's ride that way, on the other side of the river. Originally, they planned to follow the same route North as these poor folks. However, after the raid, they were afraid they'd be mistaken for Comanche and changed course. They went just over to the other side instead. These two were left behind to watch along the river and make sure the Army had not seen them and weren't following behind to ambush. They've been here about a week, and were about to head back to join the main party when they saw us ride up. I've explained to them who we are. They've agreed to ride slowly, so we can follow along with them. That way, we're sure not to run into any more trouble."

As Brandy explained, the two Apache trotted up on horseback. I smiled hesitantly at them, and they frowned in unison. The older one asked Brandy of me, "*Ella habla espanol*?" To which I knew just enough Spanish to reply, "*No. Hablo Francais.*" He turned to his friend, and mumbled something, which I took to mean "say something to her in French." Only he was speaking in Apache. His friend looked much younger, probably about sixteen or so. He was lighter skinned, with a thin crooked nose that looked as if it had been broken at least once. The friend shrugged his skinny shoulders, as if to ask "What should I say?" To which he received a stern look, and quickly blurted out "*Hola Francesca!*" I couldn't help but laugh at his garbled greeting of Spanish and French. Then, I asked him, "*Tu crois que je suis francais?*" His close-set eyes narrowed. He looked down at the ground, apparently thinking hard. It was clear he knew enough French to understand that I was speaking it, but not how to reply. Finally, he said, "*Si*," slowly and thoughtfully. To which I nodded and smiled, unconvincingly I'm afraid, and carefully corrected, "*Oui.*"

To Brandy, I whispered, "He thinks I'm French."

"It's better that way," she whispered back. "Always best among Indians you don't know to have them think you are Spanish or French. Anything but regular American. None of them trust Americans. Or Englishmen. I told him I am from California, but I live over in Auraria now, and run a restaurant, which they are welcome to come and eat at any time. I always say that when I meet new Indians. They like to hear it, although almost none of them ever take me up on it. Probably because few others think to invite them anywhere, so it makes them suspicious. Also, I told them you are my French-speaking cousin who has come to teach French to Indians at the new school. Our traveling together makes more sense if we're related. They think French is useful because all the Frenchmen they know are the ones they trade with. They see those men as rich, so they'll be more respectful of you."

Here, Brandy stopped and turned to say something to the men again in Spanish. It must have been something along the lines of *let's go*, because they circled around on their horses so one of them was on the outside flank of each wagon. We climbed up, with Brandy taking the reins of Penny's wagon. She indicated that I should guide my own team. The skinny Apache with the broken nose remained by my wagon, while the tall one rode beside Brandy. He murmured another question to her, and she smiled over at me.

"He says you should teach the young one more French while we're riding so he can make his family rich. Give it a try. You may get some more students from it."

So, that's how we left the village of the dead Comanche. With me trying to teach French to the young Apache. I will grant he seemed eager to learn, which was certainly surprising, given all we had just witnessed. Considering how much enthusiasm these Indians have for learning French, I will have to make sure I add some elementary lessons to my plans for the older students.

From there, we rode all night and the rest of today, coming up on the Apache encampment just before nightfall. Our guards took leave of us to wade their horses across the river, and to explain our presence to the rest of their tribesmen. Brandy said they would send word in the morning from their night watch as to whether there was anything on the day's ride ahead of us before we departed. Although it's comforting to know this particular group of Apache is friendly, I'm concerned about what other tribes might think of us as we go along.

I'm not *really* afraid of them though. They seem to be reasonable enough people who don't go looking for trouble unless someone else behaves aggressively toward them first. Still, I couldn't help but notice how the young fellow with whom I was attempting to speak French was so standoffish and shy. He even jumped in his saddle a bit every time I raised a hand to make a gesture in hopes of clarifying a word. As if he were afraid of me. I'm one of the least intimidating people I know. I didn't like it at all. Hopefully, before school begins, I'll have the opportunity to meet more native youth from different tribes and see what I can do to make them feel more at ease in my presence.

Having people behave as if they're afraid of you, when you've done nothing to them at all, is probably the most unsettling feeling I've ever had in my life.

The last thing I ever want to be is a monster.

July 30, 1858

I'm so exhausted I can barely hold up this pen, but I feel I absolutely must record what we saw last night. It was after we left the company of the Apache men and reached an abandoned Army camp a day's ride over. After witnessing it, the three of us agreed it was imperative we put as much distance between us and whatever happened back there as possible.

Coming up to the Army camp, it looked not much different than any other. An earth works dug out of a hillside for a makeshift fort, enough to accommodate up to a dozen men. Yet, the most noticeable thing about it as we got closer was the silence. No sentry accosted us, nor did he make any announcement of our arrival. He couldn't, because he no longer had any throat.

The gutted remains of the sentry's body were propped up against the flagpole. Having no skin or musculature to support it, his head flopped forward. I could see he had been scalped. The flesh of his chest was ripped to ribbons, with his rib cage open and the ribs all sticking out at twisted angles. His heart, lungs, and other entrails were missing, hollowed out like the inside of a gourd. Vermin had taken his eyes. The spookiest part was his rifle. It was still loaded, with his withered finger twisted over the trigger like a claw. Whatever killed the sentry had been so fast it had not given him enough time to fire his weapon.

The contrast between the relatively clean-cut incisions that allowed his attacker to tear his hair away and the gnawed mauling of his guts was bizarre. It was impossible to discern whether he had been mauled first, then scalped, or vice versa. As I bent in for a closer examination, I heard Penny cry out. "They're in here!"

Brandy and I hurried up and over the hill, around the dugout, and came to the front door. The air was thick with flies. "Shut the door!" Brandy yelled at her daughter. Penny complied, coming over to us.

"They're all in there. Dead soldiers laid out in a row side by side. It's too dreadful! I don't want to go in there again. Mama, we shouldn't be in this place!"

"I agree, darlin'," said Brandy softly. "I'm sorry you had to see them first. Why don't you walk back around the hill and hold onto the horses? If you see anything else, holler out to us immediately, but don't wait. Jump on one of them and go. We'll catch up." It was strange to see Penny timid. She's such a bold girl most of the time. The soldiers' remains in the dugout had shaken her up. Obediently, Penny began to trudge up and around the hill, away from us.

Brandy took a couple of handkerchiefs from among the pockets of her skirts, handed me one, and put the other over her mouth. "For the flies," she said, opening the door. The black swarm hit us all at once.

Inside the dugout was intensely dark. There were no windows or any source of light. Bending down, I could barely make out Brandy taking hold of something that looked like a man's boot. "Get the other one," she said, motioning a foot or so to her right, where I could see the boots were attached to the legs of a man. Under her instruction, we staggered backward out of the dugout. Each of us held her handkerchief over her mouth with one hand, and dragged the dead soldier by a foot with the other.

Once we had him in the sunlight and out of the main cloud of flies, we could see he had been eviscerated in the same gruesome manner as the sentry. Scalp removed, throat torn out, chest and rib cage ripped open. The heart and organs were gnawed away. "I think they all must be like that," Brandy said, still muffled through the handkerchief.

"But why?" I asked. "Is it some kind of revenge ritual? For murdering everyone in the hunting camp back there?" I motioned back the way we'd come. "Some other Comanche, or maybe the Apache?"

Brandy shook her head and folded the handkerchief back into her pocket. "I don't think so. The scalping, yes, that looks Indian. Or French," she turned her head slightly to the side, as if making the comment pointedly in my direction. "Since the Indians learned that particular skill from Frenchmen, after all." She walked around the corpse of the soldier, studying it closely. "However, I can't think of any Indian who would do *that*. I mean, what *did* they do? Whack them each in the chest with a sledge-hammer, and then pry their ribs open? That would have been extremely difficult. And require an uncanny amount of strength. Plus, look at this." Brandy knelt and pointed into the poor soldier's empty internal cavity. "That scraped pattern on the bones. It's like his insides have been licked clean. I've heard of bears or cougars mauling a man to death, but this..." she shook her head.

I knelt beside her, studying the body more closely. "It definitely looks like the work of some kind of animal. But," I motioned in the direction of the dugout, and then to the flagpole on top of the hill, "What animal would lay them all out in a row like that? And with the sentry backed up to the pole, as if he's still on watch." I stood, taking a few steps back and glancing around the swept yard in front of the dugout. No tracks. Although that wasn't surprising, the wind blew constantly here. Any trace of tracks would soon be wiped clean by the elements. "No, I don't think it was an animal. I think it was a man, and he was mocking them. A revenge killing with a message. Putting them back into their apple pie order as if nothing had happened, because they killed those Comanche and walked in their blood like they were nothing. It's symbolic. The Army was heartless, in taking their land, so whomever this was took *their* hearts. Gutless in killing women and children, so he tore out *their* guts. Without conscience about any of it, so he ripped off the tops of their heads. And then," I scanned the ground, "he even cleaned up after himself. Just like the government always comes in to wipe the slate clean of anything the Army ever does wrong. That has to be it. It's a message. Because the wind and rain might have erased their tracks, but do you see any blood trails anywhere? Other than right around the bodies?"

Brandy rose and looked slowly around the campsite. For the first time, I could hear a tremor in her normally low, steady voice. "No. No, there isn't any blood. You're right. Something did this, and then cleaned it up. And I think you're right to say it isn't just an animal, but I don't think it's just a man either."

"Well then, what was it?"

Brandy turned to face me. "Something unnatural. It sounds crazy, but could it have been," she paused, considering. "A skinwalker? No, that just doesn't make any sense."

As we dragged the soldier we had removed back to his comrades, and then hauled the sentry down too, beside them, Brandy explained what she meant.

"To the Navajo, a tribe Southwest of here, and a few others, there is a legend of creature that used to be a man, or a woman sometimes, but who has transformed into a beast. The most common way is for a medicine person to start working in black magic, so they become a witch first, and then a monster. Other legends say anyone who kills another person without justification can become one, or even a normal person can be possessed by the spirit of a skinwalker and coerced to do evil things merely after locking eyes with them. Regardless, the one thing that skinwalkers have in common is that they are extremely vicious, always hungry for human flesh, and they can transform from human form to beast whenever they wish."

Something clicked in my mind. Like gears in a very precise clock that had become jammed, but just started running again.

"So, they are like the *loup garou*?"

Since Brandy was unfamiliar, I explained to her that in French culture, there is a similar creature, which can be created under similar circumstances. Through unjust murder, blasphemy, and other means, but the result was the same—a man-beast with a murderous thirst for human blood. As quickly as I could, I summarized my grand-père's tale of the Beast of Geauvdan, and a few others that came to mind.

By the time I finished this explanation, we had all thirteen bodies stacked side by side again in the Army dugout. Brandy suggested we dab up the cracks around the door with mud, to create a kind of crypt for the soldiers. That way, their bodies wouldn't be desecrated further until the Army sent out someone to see what had become of them. Last, we should leave a note, explaining the situation as best we could. I agreed, and returned to the wagon for pen and paper. I wrote two copies of the same letter, describing what we had found and our theories about what might have happened to the men. Brandy and I signed our names, and I sealed both letters with wax using the stamp from my trunk. I slid one copy under the door so it could easily be found when it opened, and wrapped the other in oilcloth to protect it from rain before using a piece of waxed twine to tie it securely to the door handle.

Walking back up the hill to the wagons, Brandy said, "There's just one big problem with this whole explanation."

"That our theory is just a coincidence of two legends from two different worlds about two creatures that don't actually exist, and it's much more likely there's some kind of crazy person on the loose?" I asked.

"Actually, no," Brandy said, swinging up into her wagon seat. "I completely believe your *loup garou* and the Navajo skinwalker are both real." She paused, seeing the incredulity written across my face. "Even if you don't. Believe me, I've witnessed enough human monsters in my lifetime to know the aftermath of one that isn't human at all when I see one. No, my problem is that if the *loup garou* and the skinwalker are both evil, then why would either one do a justifiable thing like killing an outpost full of Army men? Men who most likely murdered that entire Comanche party we saw. It doesn't make sense. Who's the real monster here?"

"The one you feed," piped up Penny, who had been silent this whole time. Glancing back and forth between us, Penny repeated what we had heard from the old storyteller in Council Bluffs. "The wolf that grows strongest is the one you feed."

"Well," her mother said, picking up the reins of her team and coaxing them onward. "Whatever that was back there has been fed the bread of wickedness..."

"And drank the wine of violence," I said, finishing the Proverb, slightly surprised to hear Brandy quote it. Picking up my own reins, I noticed something in the wagon seat between Penny and me.

"I had to bring the flag with us," Penny explained. She smoothed the fabric she'd folded so neatly into a triangle and placed it on her lap. "I took it down while you two were in the dugout. Whatever happened, they lost. There was no one there to guard it anymore, so it didn't seem right to leave it. It's not a very old flag. I thought maybe we could put it up at the school. Unless you already have a flag?"

"No," I replied, somewhat surprised at myself. "Out of all the things I packed, I didn't think to bring one."

July 31, 1858

Looking back over what I wrote last night, I know I must have nodded off, but it doesn't matter. After we made camp and had a bite to eat, we were all out like candles in a sharp wind. I was moving slower this morning too, and don't feel quite as well as usual. I'm sure it's the lack of sleep. Even though I fell asleep easily enough, I awakened half a dozen times in the night from the same nightmare.

It's that wolf again, only this time, he doesn't lie contentedly at my side. Surely, it must be some sort of trauma associated with the wretched Army camp and the discussion that Brandy and I had about what might have attacked it. In the nightmare, I am lying on my belly in the tall grass, which in and of itself is a most curious thing. I'm terrified of snakes and would never do so in real life.

Regardless, there I lay, arms stretched in front of me, as I watched the whole ghastly scene unfold. The beast charged up from over the far side of the hill, swift as the wind, and tore out the sentry's throat before he could even scream. As the sentry's blood spewed, the creature clawed his chest open, crunching into his ribs like a large dog clamping onto a goose. Having slopped his entrails onto the ground, he took off again. I followed him, crawling through the grass on all fours, so as not to be seen. The door of the dugout was jammed shut behind him. I heard the men scream for God and mercy as he mauled them, one by one. Slowly, their cries died down. I saw the creature lope out of the door, as nonchalantly as a hunting dog let out for the morning. There was no blood on his fur. I remember thinking he must have licked himself clean. As he came closer to where I lay in the grass, I became anxious he would see me too. Not that I had any sense he would attack me too, as I still strangely had no fear of him. I only wanted not to be seen, for whatever reason.

At that point, I woke up. When I dozed off again, the beast was gone. Instead, I saw a man in a long gray duster coat that flapped out away from his body in the wind like a cape. His back was to me. I had just enough time to register how odd it was he should be wearing such a coat in the summertime when he began to turn in my direction. He cocked his ear as if he heard something. I shrank down in the dry grass, cursing silently as it crackled around me.

Fortunately, the man didn't notice me. I couldn't see his face, because I was looking directly into the afternoon sun, which was very bright. He turned his back to me again, and strode resolutely over to the body of the sentry. I heard a tearing sound, which I knew must be the man in the gray coat cutting the sentry's scalp from his skull. Peering through the grass, I saw him stuff the scalp with its bloody clot of matted blonde hair into one of two bags he had slung across his body, *bandolero* style. The two of them together formed an *X* shape over his chest.

He removed both the bags and coat. Then, he proceeded to take off the rest of his clothes, folded them carefully, and placed them into the other bag. I felt slightly self-conscious, and averted my eyes at his nakedness by curling up in the grass. When I looked back, he was gone. Although I trotted over to where he had stood, near the body of the sentry, I saw no sign of his ever having been there. Only the hollowed-out body of the sentry remained, propped against the flagpole as we found him in real life.

Yet, I know it must have been many days before, because the sentry still had eyes.

At this point in the dream, I awakened a second time. When I closed my eyes again, the whole scene started over.

I've spent all day mulling over this man and beast, and can come to no other conclusion that they must be one in the same. That he is the *loup garou* of my earlier dreams, only now turned into a savage man. Yet, for what purpose, I know not. Perhaps, if the wolf is a sort of spiritual and emotional guardian of my psyche, then it is possible that within the context of my fevered brain, he has been transformed in a manner which I would understand. A metaphorical story symbolized in human form. My mind's self-preservative effort during sleep to make sense of the aftermath from horrific deaths I have encountered recently, but attempted to push out of my waking thoughts.

All of this makes perfect logical sense. Especially when I consider it within the context of the similar stories Brandy told me about the Navajo and their skinwalker creature. Yet, it still concerns me. Both of these creatures are associated with evil. Does that mean that, by comforting myself with dreams of them, there is some darkness that lurks inside me? A darkness of which I was previously unaware, that has somehow been awakened now I have left the carefully defined mental spaces and habits of my youth?

Could it be, now that both my body and my spirit have complete freedom to roam at will, unfettered with the structures imposed by modern society, I am becoming some sort of beast myself? Or is it all just a series of signs I'm losing my mind?

August 1, 1858

M y apologies, dear reader, for the bizarre, self-doubting questions with which I concluded my last entry. I'm feeling more myself again this morning. Brandy, seeing my owl-like countenance, took the reins and let me sleep in the back of the wagon most of the day. Curiously, I had no more disturbing dreams. Perhaps it is the security of sleeping in the daylight, while I know those I trust are watching, that keep the terrors away.

This evening, as we set about making camp, an Indian scout rode up. Speaking to him in Spanish, as I have learned is her custom when encountering new Indians, Brandy found the Cheyenne are about a day away. A hunting party under the leadership of Chief Black Kettle should be here by morning. They move during either the night or at the height of the noonday sun, so as not to disturb the buffalo. According to him, buffalo move in a manner similar to deer, stirring at dawn and dusk. Their scout wanted to know how long we would be in the area. He asked if it would be too much trouble for us to wait and travel again tomorrow evening. Waiting would give the Cheyenne their best advantage to kill as many of them as possible.

Of course, wanting to promote a positive relationship with Cheyenne in the area, Brandy agreed, with a caveat. She asked the scout if we could ride along with the evening hunting party. To my surprise, he agreed. Before bidding us farewell, he looked Brandy up and down with an unmistakable air of respect.

"The Cheyenne are a matrilineal society," Brandy explained to me after he disappeared over the horizon. "It's unusual for them to ignore any reasonable request from someone who is clearly a mother. They have too much regard for them. Something white men could learn from, surely."

She snorted a little half-laugh to herself at this joke and continued. "Although it isn't common for the women to hunt, they do take care of horses. Sometimes they ride along the flanks to help herd the buffalo. I thought you might want to have a taste of what it meant to be a real Indian while you can. Something to help you relate more to your students and their experiences. We can ask to help set up the tipis afterward too, and maybe cook a little. This tribe is good for welcoming whites who are willing to be welcomed. Black Kettle is a very unusual sort of leader too. I wouldn't have asked if he hadn't been the one in charge. A lot of Indians say he goes too far and gives too much. I think he sees plainly what the situation is that's coming. Whether they want to or not, Indians have to try to find a way to live near the whites that keep pouring into their lands."

Here Brandy paused again, looking thoughtfully down at the ground. I could see she'd traced a silhouette of a buffalo in the dust with her toe. Seeing me looking at this childlike motion, she self-consciously swiped it away.

"I think you're excited about tomorrow," I said to her, reading into the image.

"Well, of course I am!" Brandy replied. "Like I said, who knows how long this kind of thing will even go on. Once the stagecoach and then the railroad come through in the next year or so, the least that will happen is the buffalo will change their migration patterns. That will make it harder for hunters to follow them. Also, how long do you think the fur traders will continue to tolerate having to trade with local tribes once they have easier access and rail transportation? My guess is not long. They'll overhunt the buffalo like they do every other valuable animal everywhere else, until there are none left. So, yes. I'm excited. I've only done it once before, but believe me, you're in for the thrill of your life." Brandy gave me a mischievous look, and kicked a clod of dirt my way. "That is, if you can hang onto your horse and your bloomers, Frenchy."

I kicked dust back at her. "I can as well as you can, Yankee. Bet you don't even have any bloomers and have to ride side-saddle." We proceeded to playfully kick dirt at one another, hurling insults like two mean little girls, until Penny returned with some firewood. She asked what in the world we were doing, stirring up all that cloud.

"Acting silly," I said, pushing hair back from my sweaty forehead. Saying this, I realized I hadn't been as happy as I was at that single moment since I'd returned from Europe almost a year ago. I watched Brandy try to draw Penny into our dust-storm. Penny squealed and dodged away. She's always fussy about her appearance, even out here when there's no one to see. Putting her hair up in curious formations of braids and curls. She's so pretty, but in a way different from her mother. Brandy's is a wild, dangerous sort of beauty. Penny is simply lovely. Their personalities are the same though. There's more than a bit of the devil in both of them.

What would Penny's life be like, I wonder, if Brandy paid for her to go to a fancy boarding school back East? Would she miss her mother's brashness, in a world where everyone and everything is so reserved? Or would Penny push herself down into a box of what she was supposed to be, and forget all about this other sort of existence?

Seeing them as happy as they always are together, I can't help but think of my own mother, Marie. How different we were! I loved her, but it wasn't in the way that Penny and Brandy do. Like they're sisters who happen to be different ages. I loved Marie because she was my mother, and that was enough. My mother was always proper. In many ways, it's hard to believe she made such a reckless marriage outside of her social circle and then ran a pub. However, the pub was always Grand-père's enterprise more than Mother's. Other than when she "turned it on" as she would say, for the sake of male customers, Mother was a sighing cipher.

For my mother, everything revolved around "what people would think" of her as a young widow raising a daughter. When Grand-père would take me up to the dairy farm, teaching me how to milk cows or to track animals, I would always return to some shamefaced lecture on how I should not discuss such things in public, especially if I ever wanted to catch a husband. Which is doubly strange, considering she never remarried and had a general disdain for the habits and manners of our predominantly male clientele at the pub. She seemed to want to erase everything about my father after his death, including his name.

Which was, by the way, Blethyn. I don't remember if I've mentioned that properly. Gareth Blethyn. I never get a chance to say my father's name, since I've always been constantly reminded of his unimportance. Who was he? This Gareth Blethyn. Did he enjoy catching lobster? Was he happy to know he had fathered a daughter?

Or did Mother even tell him she was pregnant with me? I will never know.

For that matter, I'll also never know what Marie actually wanted out of life. I'm sure she regretted her early marriage, and wished she'd taken time to travel beforehand. But if the marriage to my father had not happened, would she have chosen something different instead? Would she have had the courage to do as I have done?

From everything that I remember about my mother, I seriously doubt it. Although she pushed me to get out and see the world, I never once remember her even going to Boston or New York to see a play or to shop as other women who had our kind of money did. What held her back? Fear of what someone might say about her? That they still judged her hasty match decades after my father's death?

Resting here tonight, out under the vast openness of the prairie sky, my mind wanders. Do my uncles back in Maine still miss their baby sister? If not, I may be the only person alive in the entire world who even cares that Marie Ulrich ever existed.

So much for what people think, if perhaps less than a year after your death, no one thinks about you at all.

August 2, 1858

This morning, an hour before daybreak, Brandy and I dressed in bloomers and went to meet the Cheyenne at their encampment. Because she begged and pleaded so much to be able to see what was going on, Brandy allowed her to follow behind us, leading both packed wagons to the crest of a ridge that provided a better vantage point. From there, Penny could see the camp on the opposite side, as well as the buffalo grazing in the valley.

The village hummed with activity and anticipation. Men and boys were getting ready for the early morning rush of the hunt, while women and girls cleaned tools and prepared to harvest the kills. Even the children were helping to set up square mechanisms made of wooden poles, which were used to pull and stretch the hides out flat to dry. Every member of the village, it seemed, had a role in the hunt.

What amazed me most was how all of this activity happened soundlessly. The whole community was a breathing giant of divided labor. The quiet, I suppose, was necessitated by the large herd of buffalo I could see down in the valley near the edge of a low ridge. The location was a strategic choice. The Cheyenne had a perfectly clear vantage point for viewing the herd below, without fear that the animals would be able to see them.

I didn't have to guess who Black Kettle was. It was apparent from the ring of men standing encircling him as we rode up. The Cheyenne scout from the day before had announced our impending arrival. When we walked up to the ring, it parted soundlessly for us to join. Seeing the two of us, Black Kettle nodded in acknowledgment. He proceeded to give his instructions. The scout translated them into Spanish for Brandy, and she relayed them to me.

The plan was simple to execute. A group of younger, experienced hunters would come down the sides of the ridge and proceed straight forward, pushing the buffalo toward the river. There, they would ride among them with spears to lance as many as possible from the sides. To prevent the herd from scattering, two other groups of mostly boys, plus Brandy and myself, were to ride inward from the left and right, hollering as loudly as we could to scare the buffalo forward. Last, a group of older hunters stood across the river, ready to shoot the buffalo straight on with arrows as they plunged into the water. A dozen or so of the heartier women were positioned downstream with nets strung on ropes to snag any wounded buffalo that fell into the water so they wouldn't be carried away by the current. However, the majority of the women would arrive shortly afterward to skin and section the carcasses, which would then be carried back to the village for further processing.

Black Kettle gave the signal to start by raising both hands to the sky and crying out to the heavens. Then, we took off! I was with a group of boys who, if they were my pupils, I would have guessed from middle grades and above. The looks spread across their faces were of pure exhilaration as they swooped into action from our position along the right flank of the herd. Caught up in it, I whooped too as I flew by beside them, my long braids straight out behind me in a burst of speed. The only other feeling that compared was the time I went sleigh riding in Switzerland. Then, the world whizzed by in a silent wall of white. Here, it was so much faster and more exhilarating! The energetic roar from the men as they pursued the fleeing buffalo made the hot summer air pulsate. It seemed we all breathed and rode as one in a dizzying herd of life and death together.

Watching the smoothness of execution, exactly as planned, was like witnessing some kind of brutal ballet. Every hunter hit his mark, felling his buffalo then circling back and away to clear room for his comrades. As we came to the river, and heard the call to turn about, I could see the older hunters sitting resolutely on their horses as the massive wave of terrified beasts surged forward, plunging into the river. Some scurried to the side and out again, as the rain of arrows fell upon them. A great many buffalo were stabbed full as pincushions, bellowing their last as their lungs filled with blood and burst. None made it all the way across.

Following the lead of my fellow flankers, we continued down to the riverside, where all buffalo still breathing were quickly put out of their misery with quick swipes of long blades. Then, we heard the swift approach of the women coming down from the ridge to begin butchering the fallen animals. Trotting over to Brandy, who was beaming from ear to ear just as much as the boys, I pulled out my little rose gold pocket watch to check the time. The entire rush had taken less than a quarter of an hour, yet the valley was littered with dozens of dead buffalo.

"Pretty great haul, huh?" Brandy called, surveying the territory as I approached. "Must be nice to make a year's living in a matter of minutes."

"You mean this is enough meat to feed the tribe for a year?"

Brandy laughed. "Not quite. I was exaggerating, but only just a little. They'll hunt like this during peak season for a few months. But not every day, and not to this magnitude. We just happened to get lucky enough to take part in a big rush on a herd they'd been watching for a while. I know they'd hoped to make another pass at them this evening, but now I don't know." She put her hand to her brow to shield her eyes from the rising sun. "The rest of the herd scattered and took off pretty fast. It may be another few days before they regroup."

Brandy turned her attention to the women working in pairs on the ground, stripping hides. "I kind of want to try my hand at that too, you know, but I don't want to butcher one badly and cost them the meat. Still... wanna get down and see if they'll let us watch?"

Equally intrigued, I nodded, and followed Brandy to where a pair of younger women were just beginning to peel an animal. Greeting them in Spanish, I could tell by their gestures to come forward that we were welcome. While they did the cutting, Brandy and I were allowed to stand on either side, helping to slowly and steadily pull the hide off in one whole piece. The buffalo's skin was still warm as I took hold of his hide. I spread both arms out wide, one up near his snout and the other by his shoulder.

With my torso pressed against his bloody side for balance, I pulled with all my strength straight backward. My fingertips dug into the slippery fat layer under the edge of his skin, and my thumbs wrapped underneath in his wooly fur. Neither Brandy nor I were as smooth as the Cheyenne women. They giggled as we sweated and struggled when we got stuck on a sinew or the turn of a leg. By the time we had it off and lying fur-side down in the grass, my arms were greasy with fat and bloody up to the elbows. The whole front of my bloomer costume was slick with it as well. Brandy was worse. She even had a big glob of fat stuck to the side of her face, which I staggered over and picked off.

The two Cheyenne women laughed at us, making motions about how messy we were. I noticed that even though they had done the bloody job of cutting, they were mostly clean except for the blood on their hands and the buckskin aprons on which they wiped their knives. Brandy spoke to some of them in Spanish again. I could tell without understanding every word that they were saying we should roll up the hide and get on with helping them piece out the animal. So we did, enabling them to work much faster with four as we helped position and hold the buffalo while they did the butchering. All in all, we had it dissected in about an hour. The pair of Cheyenne women moved onto the next body. I suggested to Brandy it would be best if we went back to our camp to change and wash off before the fat set into a crust, and she agreed.

That evening, our scout rode out again to state that Black Kettle and the other elders had decided to wait and allow the herd to regroup for a day or two before pursuing another hunting expedition. However, he also said we were welcome to come to dinner with the tribe that night to celebrate the successful hunt, and to hear stories told in the Cheyenne tradition.

Naturally, although I'm fairly worn out from today's activities, I'm eager to go and hear their tales. I want to contrast them with the other stories we heard back in Council Bluff. I'm beginning to realize there is a great study to be made of native mythology, if one only takes the time to listen and compare. From what I have seen so far, I believe that, to paraphrase Hamlet, "There are more things in the native Heavens and Earth, than we Americans have dreamt of in all our philosophy."

August 3, 1858

D inner last night was like nothing I have ever experienced. I tasted my first buffalo, which reminded me a lot in flavor of deer, a dark meat with a kind of wild spiciness to it. And I heard many interesting stories I hope to have time to write down over the next few days, before we get to Bent's Fort. Also, we are now traveling with an intriguing half-Pawnee, half-French woman named Nascha Le Pont, but more on her later.

First, the food! The buffalo meat was roasted and spiced with several kinds of peppers. There was also corn roasted in its shucks and then covered in herbs, and pots of beans. It was all quite piquant, and seasoned with bits of buffalo meat. Their bread was not leavened, but instead cooked in a frying pan over the fire, which can be rolled around the meat to make a kind of sandwich. All of it was good, very flavorful, and reminded me a lot of the weeks I spent touring Spain. Brandy told me many of the trade routes for the tribes in this area run all the way from Canada to Mexico. They got a lot of their seasonings from the Spanish, which explained the peppers.

After we finished eating, the tribe gathered in a circle. Black Kettle began the evening of storytelling by praising the bravery of his hunters and the diligence of the women. He gave thanks to their Creator spirit for blessing them with this bounty from the Earth. Then, he became more somber, and spoke about the necessity of finding ways to use the harvest of this hunting season to increase their trade and communication with whites. This provoked half nods of assent and half whispers to the contrary from the crowd. He ended with a warning to the naysayers that failing to improve relations with whites would ultimately prove to be the end of the tribe. He made it clear he felt they were coming, whether they wanted them to or not.

Although I hate to say it, I believe the great chief is only partially correct. Even if natives cooperate with whites, this way of life, in which one does each according to kind, and shares alike, is simply not compatible with the methods pushed by modern captains of industry. Despite what my beloved Henry David Thoreau advocates for in *Walden*, few Americans are willing to go to the woods to "live deliberately." Instead, they go deliberately to exploit as many resources as they can to carry back East. The native tribes might buy themselves some time to figure out how to assimilate by appeasing these early settlers and white traders. Once the railroad comes in though, their way of life is in serious peril.

The heavy mood left by Black Kettle's speech was lifted afterward, through a round of dancing and drumming. I had no idea what I was doing, but I joined in with the other women anyway. It seemed to be the right thing to do. The dance had some type of symbolic meaning, with the motions of our arms reaching to the sky in praise, and then mimicking the work of everyday tasks, while our feet stamped in time with the music. My impression was it was meant to signify the compact between the Creator and his people. If he bestowed them with the gifts of successful hunts and good harvests, then they would honor those gifts by working to use them to their greatest extent.

Post-dancing, the littlest children were taken off to bed by some of the women, but the rest of us gathered again for stories. Not surprisingly, given the high spirits of the evening, many of them were about money.

The man who had been our guide told the first story. It was a funny one, about a coyote trickster and his money tree. In it, Coyote tied some money loosely by strings up in a walnut tree, and waited for some dumb white men to come by. When they did, he told them this was a special money tree. They could buy it from him cheaply, because he already had all the money he wanted and was ready to move on. Skeptical, the white men tried to tell Coyote money doesn't grow on trees. To prove them wrong, Coyote shook the tree. Lo and behold, the money he had tied up in there came out. The white men were impressed! But when they shook the tree, only walnuts fell out. Coyote explained they had to be patient. The magic of this tree took a while. Eventually the walnuts would ripen into more money. The dumb white men bought the tale, and paid Coyote a great sum of money for the tree. Coyote left with a big basket of his original money and their money combined. Though the white men tried to be patient enough to let the walnuts ripen into money, eventually their patience ran out and they shook the tree. Only plain walnuts fell out. One of them climbed up in the tree, examining the leaves, but found no money. One of them got the idea the money must be stuck inside the tree, so they cut it down, chopping the trunk and every branch in half. Still no money. Last, they could hear Coyote howling with laughter way off in the distance.

The moral to the story, to paraphrase the tale's ending, was that white men are always out to get something for nothing from Indians. However, if the Indians were sly enough, they could use the white man's greed and laziness to take advantage of him, and end up even richer themselves for doing so.

This tale was followed by several others about Coyotes getting the upper hand over whites, all for similar reasons. The white men underestimated the craftiness of Indians, and lost money to them due to their ignorance. Each one garnered huge rounds of laughter, which in turn seemed to encourage every teller's rendition to get wilder and louder. One even involved a Coyote putting the money up a burro's rear end, and then telling the white men that by kicking the animal in its stomach, it would defecate money. As the tales became more bawdy, Black Kettle rose and requested that a new line of tales be started. I think his choice was in deference to us, because we were female guests of the tribe that night.

That was when I first noticed Nascha. It must have been because everyone else was so boisterous that I hadn't beforehand. Her round gray eyes were huge and striking. As she turned her gaze to each person around the circle, each one immediately fell silent. Nascha wore a robe made of a wolf's pelt, with the animal's head on top of hers like a hood. Unlike the other native women around me who were very tan, Nascha's skin tone was sallow. Though her cheekbones were high and beautiful, the dark circles under her eyes made her appear wraith-like. I had the immediate impression she was not entirely Indian. When she recited her story in English with a slight French accent, I knew I was correct.

Before beginning, Nascha explained she heard this story from a group of Lakota with whom she traded, and it had special meaning to her. She was a half-Pawnee who married into the Navajo. I will try to put Nascha's words down as faithfully as I can here, because I believe it has some meaning in it for me too, given my dreams. Here is the story:

"Once there was a Lakota woman who married into the Crow tribe. However, her marriage was unhappy. She missed her family. Some of the Crow women took pity on her. They told her to go and hide from her husband and the other Crow men down by the creek. While she was hiding, a pair of wolves came upon her. At first, she was afraid they would try to kill her, because they circled around and around, growling. However, the wolves comforted her and treated her kindly. They led her on a path away from the Crow men who pursued her. Eventually, the woman and her two wolf friends were caught in a blizzard on the open prairie. Out of nowhere, two more wolves came up to help shield her from the harsh winds and cold. After traveling through this blizzard, they came to a cave in the mountains. Inside were many wolves, tearing apart a deer for meat. The cave smelled horrible. Again the woman was afraid, but when one of these new wolves came and dropped a piece of deer meat at her feet, she realized the wolves meant her no harm. She learned to live among these wolves, drying deer meat to eat and learning the wolf language. Becoming one of their own, she learned each wolf had a role to play in the pack. Some were hunters, some cared for the young, but all depended on one another. Soon, she came to smell like the wolves, and not like a human. Mostly, the wolves stayed away from humans, because they did not like their smell. One day that fall, some of the hunter wolves saw the Lakota woman's mother out digging turnips and crying, because she thought her daughter was dead. The wolves went back and told the woman, who felt sad for her mother. She told the wolves she wanted to return to her mother and her people. The wolves understood. They told her they would take her to her mother, and she could signal them by waving a blanket whether she wanted to stay or return with the wolves. If she waved the blanket twice, that meant she wanted to stay with her mother and the wolves would leave. However, if she waved once, the wolves would come and take her back. When the woman saw her mother, the mother burst into tears. She welcomed her daughter back with open arms. The woman waved her blanket twice, and so the wolves knew. They went away and left the woman back with her Lakota family."

The circle was silent for a moment. Before I knew words were even coming out of my mouth, I had asked a question. "What would have happened if the woman's family had not embraced her, and she had returned with the wolves?"

Nascha turned her sad, gray eyes to me, and smiled in an oddly knowing way. "She would have become a wolf forever."

There were many other stories told during the evening, but that was the one which resonated with me the most. Have I been dreaming about a wolf because I, like the woman in the story, am away from my family? Does the wolf represent my desire to once again be part of a pack? Perhaps. But if that is so, it is an impossible dream. Although I have several uncles back in Maine who would surely welcome me, the members of my family to whom I was closest—my grand-père and my mother—are no longer part of this world.

So, is this the path I have chosen in essence? To become a wolf forever?

I will have to speak with Nascha about it tomorrow.

Brandy knew Nascha already. No surprise there, as I am beginning to understand Brandy knows everyone along this route. When we set out this morning, Brandy asked her to join our little group, so we are now all traveling together. I am glad of it. Nascha's reason for being in the circle last night is that she trades in furs and hides. It seems unusual a woman would have such an occupation out here all alone, carrying so much money by herself through dangerous territory. I'm sure there is a story behind it. I hope to find out soon what it is. From the way the Cheyenne fell silent under her gaze last night as Nascha began to speak, I get the sense she is a woman not to be interfered with.

And that, I am learning, is an excellent thing to be in this part of the country.

August 4, 1858

The stories from our night among the Cheyenne have clearly stirred something within me. Last night, I did something I have not done since I was a child. I went sleepwalking. Not just around the campsite, but out into the prairie alone. If it had not been for Nascha's following and waking me, who knows what might have happened?

After we made camp, I was so exhausted I don't even remember falling asleep. However, I do remember dreaming I heard a wolf howl, way off to the West across the rolling hills. At some point during the dream, I rose without waking. I began to run, still in my nightgown and in a stumbling sort of fashion, away from the camp and along the riverside.

Nascha saw me go, and she followed. I remember little else from the dream, other than hearing the mournful wailing of the wolf, calling me so I could not help but follow. The full moon was like a golden ball hanging crisp and clear in the cloudless summer sky. When I had gone as far as I could in following the sound without crossing a bend in the river, I stopped and stood gazing blankly across. A wolf was face-to-face in front of me, whispering things in wolf-language that somehow I knew the meaning of. I felt strangely comforted.

The next thing I knew, I was awake and staring into the face of what I thought was a real wolf. I jumped back in surprise, only to realize it was Nascha. She was wearing her wolf headdress, with the fur of the great gray beast cascading down over her shoulders and back. She held my face in her hands and whispered soothing things, hoping I would wake gradually of my own accord.

Nascha led me back to camp. We sat talking for a long time. Or rather, she asked me questions and I answered them. Nascha sat mostly quiet as I responded to her inquiries about the call that had caused me to rush out into the prairie. Upon mention of my thought it was somehow related to my dreams about the friendly wolf, I noted an uptick in the frequency and vigorousness of her nodding as she listened. Finally, when I finished my explanation, Nascha asked how many other people I had told about my dreams.

"Nothing to Brandy or Penny," I said, wondering what she was getting at. "A little bit to this doctor and his friend, a medium whom I met at a séance back in St. Louis. I haven't gotten around to the whole story with them yet. There hasn't been an opportunity for me to even get a letter in the mail since we left Council Bluff. Dr. Wheeler wired ahead to make sure I had arrived safely, which I thought was very sweet of him, and..."

Here Nascha cut me off. She held up her forefinger, as if scolding a child. "Tell no one else of your dreams. I know exactly what they mean, for I used to have them too." Quickly, she glanced to see if Penny or Brandy were awake or listening. Not seeing them, she continued, leaning close to whisper in my ear. "Would you like me to show you what I see right now?"

I responded affirmatively. Nascha raised her right hand. With index and middle fingers spread into a V, she touched them lightly to the side of her right ear and motioned forward, touching my left ear in a similar fashion. The world as I knew it was gone in a flash. Instead, I could see the mouth of what first appeared to be a huge cave. As the vision became clearer, I could tell it was the same mine shaft from my earlier dream, in which I had narrowly escaped a cave-in after hearing a voice calling out for me to run.

Then, I saw a makeshift gallows. The bodies of several Indian men hung from it, their stiff corpses twisting in the wind. The wooden beam creaked and groaned under their weight. Slowly, I became aware of a low, pleading moan that evolved into a howl. I realized this was the same howl I had followed into the night. And then, I saw *it*. The great gray wolf of my dreams, head raised and nose pointed to the moon. The vision was clear enough that I could see the dampness welling up around his eyes, as if he were crying. He circled the poor men, rubbing his side against them and nudging against their bare feet with his nose, but to no avail. Finally, the wolf lay down underneath them with his back to me, put his head on his forelegs, and began once again to whimper softly.

This vision cleared away as Nascha removed her hand from my temple. When she asked what I had seen, I described it to her. She smiled her sad smile in assent. "Yes, you are seeing what I see. What we are all seeing, those who are people of the wolf." When I asked her what she meant by this, Nascha explained.

"On my mother's side, I am Skidi Pawnee. We are known as the People of the Wolf. The French traders who came, like my father, named the river I was born near the Loup River, because in French *loup* means..."

I interrupted. "Wolf. I am French too, by way of Maine. My grand-père spoke French all his life. He taught me."

"We should speak it together then. I could use the practice, as I hardly ever see any Frenchmen in my travels," Nascha replied, continuing. "The Pawnee take our courage, our cunning, even our directions from the Wolf Spirit." She pointed up toward the star Sirius, which was just beginning to come visible as the morning lightened to gray. "He is our guide and protector in all things. I wear this headdress to honor him, but also to take on his spirit and his strength. Some believe there are those among us who can truly hear the call of the wolf from many miles away, signaling when the Pawnee should be aware they are in danger. Tonight, I too heard the cry you heard. Only I knew it to be one of my brothers. I could feel he was mourning. I wanted to rush to him, but he was very far away. It will take us at least two more weeks to get there. To the place where those men were hung. However, I am in no hurry. If they have been killed by the man whom I think must be responsible, they will still be hanging there when we arrive. He'll leave them as a sign to scare all the other Indians who work for him."

"So, you know who killed those men and where they are?" I asked.

"I believe so. That mine is near Auraria, where you are going to teach school, no?"

I nodded, and Nascha continued. "Well, then the only man who could possibly have had the authority to judge them guilty and have them hanged must be the same man who drives them to work like slaves. Green Russell."

The name clicked in my memory. "The man who found the gold."

"The same," Nascha replied. "Since he is a Southerner and used to pressing work out of the enslaved, but there are no black slaves out West to do it for him, he has brought a whole band of his Cherokee relatives to take their place. Made them all kinds of promises, I'm sure. But like the promises of most white men to Indians, they are lies. Green Russell would sacrifice all of them, if need be, to keep the gold for himself. Even though his wife is Indian. Cherokee. From Georgia, like him. I pity that woman.

My guess is she married him to keep from being removed out West like her brothers. Still, that was a devil's bargain to make. And now," Nascha said, throwing up her hands, "Here they are anyway. Together again out West, about to make Green Russell rich."

"And the wolf?" I pressed, even more mystified by this hint of an explanation. "What does my," I stopped, correcting myself, "*our* Wolf have to do with all of it?"

Nascha's sad gray eyes met mine. "You were more correct the second time. *Our* Wolf. You started to say *my* but he is not yours alone. He belongs to all of us. He is the truest extension of the Great One on Earth. Even though he was not born Pawnee, he is still Indian. The Wolf Spirit lives fuller in him than any I have known. If not, he would have died long ago, and I would not have found him a living man. Because the protective spirit of the Wolf is strong with him, he in turn lives to protect us."

"So, you see him too then?" I continued eagerly. "Why do you think I can see him in my dreams? I am not the slightest bit Indian."

"You don't have to be Indian by blood to be moved by the spirits," Nascha replied. "Anyone who truly chooses to listen can hear the call. You hear because your ears are tuned for the truth and your heart is open to respond to the sound of suffering. My father was one such as you, but he is long gone now. A story for another time." Here, Nascha trailed off. She studied the ascent of Sirius that heralded the progression of the sun across the morning sky.

I didn't want pry into the story at which she had hinted, but I still had one more question. "What do you call him? This wolf of ours."

"He is called by many names. Waya by his Cherokee kin. Witch by the Navajo, like my husband. But if you want to call him as the whites do, it's Cawdor."

I recognized the name. "Just Cawdor. Like Brandy told me." Then, I realized her connection. "*You* were the trader who found him in the desert!"

"Yes," Nascha replied, a smile crinkling the corners of her gray eyes at last. "I've always been told I am good at finding things. And now," she said, offering me a hand up as she rose, "I have found you."

The rest of the morning went by in its usual flurry of packing and stowing to get onto the trail. I cannot wait to speak to Nascha again later tonight. She seems reluctant to tell me any more about Cawdor or why we are all connected by this Wolf Spirit symbol when we are within earshot of Brandy and Penny. I can understand her reluctance, since this seems to be a deeply private secret shared only among Indians. Yet, she is half French, and I am an Old French Mainer, but we still share the same visions. What is to be made of that?

Can it really be as Nascha said, that one can hear native spirits without being Indian?

If that's true, what in God's name has given me the ability to do so?

August 5, 1858

Today's journey has been one filled with revelations. Not so much about my wolf dreams, although I mean to ask her about those tomorrow, but about Nascha herself. I've never met anyone who was so unlikely to be alive. As we sat a bit away from the camp after dinner, watching the red-gold sun set across the rippling waves of grass, Nascha explained her history.

She was born near the Loup River in the Nebraska territory, as I mentioned in the previous entry. Her mother was Pawnee and her father was a French fur trader. Among her mother's family were many wise women and shamans. It was thought an alliance with the first such French gentleman to come into their area would prove to be fruitful. And indeed, it had been. Pierre Le Pont, according to his daughter, was a jolly man who loved the outdoors, wine, and conversation in any language he could learn. He adored his Pawnee wife and family, which grew to six children like stair steps in rapid succession. He showered them with any riches he could obtain that would be meaningful in either his country or among her people. This helped him build relationships with his Pawnee family. Nascha was the eldest and her father's favorite. He took her along on his trade routes from the time she was old enough to walk and talk. Soon, she was known at all posts too. On the long trips, he taught her to speak and read French and English, as well as her native Pawnee. He stressed the importance of being able to relate to others in their own language as a method of making people relax enough to make trades. It was this early association with Pierre's business and learning how to negotiate within his world that would later provide Nascha with a livelihood, effectively changing her life.

Pierre's fortune grew quickly. Descended from a family of boatmen, who ferried travelers back and forth across the Seine for generations, he was a natural when it came to trading. His jovial demeanor quickly earned the trust of several tribes. In turn, Pierre earned the Pawnee a lot of profit from his skillful sales negotiations of their wares. Unfortunately, Le Pont was also something of a free spender, who loved to boast he would soon be the richest man in the territory. At that time, there was still a significant population of Spanish traders in the area. They were jealous this stray Frenchman had so thoroughly ingratiated himself into what they regarded as their domain.

One evening, as they were making the return trip from Bent's Fort, Nascha and her father Pierre were ambushed by a group of Spanish bandits. Overwhelmed by their onslaught, the Spanish bound them hand and foot. They promised not to kill them if Pierre would lead them to the Pawnee village and then act as their negotiator. These Spanish wanted Pierre to make the Pawnee agree to hand over the majority of profits from their trade and keep it ongoing. Pierre, thinking he could outwit them once he was among the protection of his own village again, decided to play along, relying on his faith in being rescued.

"Papa kept telling me in French I had nothing to fear. That the Pawnee were strong and would take care of us, if only we could get home," Nascha explained sadly. "But Papa was a fool." As they neared sight of the Pawnee village, Pierre asked the Spaniards to unbind him, so he would appear to ride up as if among friends. However, seeing him flanked by a band of heavily armed Spanish highwaymen whom they had long feared, the Pawnee leaders suspected a double-cross. Despite almost two decades of a mutually beneficial relationship, there were more than Pierre realized who still did not trust the laughing Frenchman.

Instead of the extortion negotiations going as planned, a brawl ensued between the dozen or so mounted and armed Spanish marauders and the mostly unarmed Pawnee. They had been going about their daily tasks when the ambush occurred, and were unprepared. Mistakenly interpreting the Pawnees' hostility as having been signaled somehow by Pierre, the Spanish leader shot him in the back of the head first. He died instantly. The rest of the fight was quick and bloody. By the end of it, Nascha's village of almost a hundred Pawnee were dead or had fled for their lives. The killers left one small group of women alive. They were tied up and kidnapped, for purposes obvious to anyone familiar with what my mother used to call, "the worst instincts of men."

Nascha was among these women taken as slaves to their lascivious desires. After being beaten savagely several times, she found it easier to give in to them than to endure any more pain. Nascha's mother took poison and committed suicide rather than allow herself to become further violated. Waking to see her mother's dead face, bloated by poison and mouth dripping with bloody foam, Nascha searched her body. Tucked carefully inside a hidden pocket sewn into her mother's skirt at the small of her back, Nascha found the tiny bag. It was still stuffed with enough poison to fill her palm. Wriggling out of her own skirt, with her hands and feet still bound, Nascha switched skirts with her mother.

"In some languages," Nascha told me, "the word for *poison* and the word for *gift* come from the same root. For me, this was true. The poison my mother left me was the gift that granted me my freedom."

Though she had to endure another day of abuse, Nascha used it to her advantage. Pretending to submit willingly this time to their disgusting advances, Nascha was able to persuade her captors to untie her so she could engage more fully. When they were done, Nascha forced herself to smile, as she had seen true whores do, even though she was in such terrible pain she could barely walk. She offered to cook dinner for them as they proceeded to their second evening of drunken celebration.

"They were so happy with their little *squaw*," Nascha spat. "Bastards never realized they were rutting over their own death. I tricked them into eating the poison hidden in their supper." Her gray eyes glittered with the hardness of diamonds, "And they loved it."

Gulping down their food, the Spaniards passed out almost immediately where they sat around the campfire. They awakened half an hour later blindly staggering and began vomiting blood. Nascha used the time in between to unbind the other women, who stood around the circle armed with the Spaniards' guns. A few tried to run off, but they moved slowly due to the poison. The women shot them down. Some lay pleading for mercy in the dirt, coughing up blood and pieces of entrails.

"Every one of them, when it became certain he was going to die, cursed us. We got tired of listening to it and watching them squirm. Poured kerosene over them and burnt them to crisps. Their bodies looked like hunks of buffalo meat that fell into the fire. We took back our horses and wagons and went to a Navajo settlement that I knew from my trading with Papa to be honest and friendly. They took us in. Most of us were able to marry, after a time, including me. That's where I live now, when I'm not on the trade route."

When I asked her whether she'd had a chance to bury her mother or father, Nascha's expression grew harder. "No. Neither one. I couldn't make myself go back to the village where Papa lay, and Mama, well..." her mouth drew into a thin line. "I've always wondered why she could not do what I had done. Why had she taken the poison herself, but left me there alone to endure it? What was so special about her pain that she felt only she deserved to be delivered from it, without even telling me she was going? If I had not thought to search her body, we all would have died. She pays for it now, I am sure. For if a Pawnee, especially a woman as gifted and wise as she, turns her back on her family and kills herself, she becomes a Wendigo. I am sure she walks these hills still, cursed with the craving to consume human flesh and make herself whole again. Desperate to reconnect her spirit with the Earth she abandoned."

I did not press Nascha any further after this. We sat for a long time in silence. The sun had set, causing a sudden chill to come over the prairie. Finally, she offered a conclusion.

"That was a long, long time ago. As you can see now, I am getting old." Nascha traced the corners of her large, down-turned gray eyes along their creases. For the first time I noticed the wrinkles extended over her cheekbones. She must have been at least in her fifties, which was somewhat startling. I had not noticed her age before. Given her lithe figure and straight posture, I would have guessed her no older than I. "My fat Navajo husband is older still. We have no children. If we did, perhaps I would allow them to go to your school. Do you think there is anything you could teach them that I could not?" The hardness in Nascha's gray eyes softened again to mischievousness.

"I'm certain there isn't much I could contribute in the way of character training, but there might be a few academic points I could add to their education." Nascha seemed pleased with my response. We walked back to the campsite together.

As we did so, I could not help but study this tall woman whose owl-like gaze remained fixed steadily on the stars coming up over the horizon. What other horrors had she witnessed, I wondered, in addition to those she had told me this evening? How had she managed to go from survivor to someone who was respected, or perhaps feared, enough to travel alone along the trade routes on which her own father had been ambushed and killed?

A story for another time, perhaps, if I can get her to talk about it. I am beginning to understand no one makes Nascha Le Pont do anything she doesn't want to do. At least, not for long, and not without paying dearly for it.

August 6, 1858

Tonight, I am perplexed as to what I should believe regarding the conflicting histories I have been given. Although I have not yet made up my mind about the matter totally, I have always thought whenever one is told two completely different versions of the same story, the truth lies somewhere in the middle. In this case, the existence of a potential middle ground is questionable.

Despite the fact we were a good distance from camp last night when Nascha told me her story, Brandy somehow overheard us. Whether her eavesdropping was intentional or not, I do not know. I tend to think it was. Brandy, although she welcomes the idea of our traveling with Nascha, does not seem to trust her as willingly as I do. Or... I did, until this afternoon, when Brandy told me a somewhat different version of Nascha's story.

The parts about Nascha's parentage and the ravaging of her family and village by the greedy Spanish marauders seem to be in concordance between both tales. Yet, the two accounts diverge in regards to Nascha's revenge.

"Did she say anything about what her husband's people, the Navajo, call her?" Brandy asked, not long after were back on the trail. I knew something was on her mind when she pulled me aside after breakfast and made sure I would be riding with her that day. I answered no, but replied Nascha did say her mother had become something dreadful called a Wendigo after committing suicide.

At this, Brandy took a deep breath and sighed. "No. She's telling it wrong. According to Navajo legend, it's not the fact a person commits suicide that causes them to become a Wendigo. It's that they have eaten human flesh, which is an abomination. The perpetual hunger for it afterward turns them into monsters."

"Nascha didn't mention anything about her mother eating anyone." I replied.

"Of course she didn't," answered Brandy, popping the reins lightly over the horses' backs to get them to move faster. This put even more distance between our wagon and Nascha's, who was just behind. Brandy leaned over close and whispered into my ear. "Nascha's mother was just a sad case of a victim desiring relief from disgrace and suffering. The dead are easy targets for blame. As the sailors say, they tell no tales to defend themselves. Nascha started telling that story about her mother being a Wendigo to scare people who came looking for her. Not long after she and the other Pawnee women arrived at the Navajo village, more white men began to disappear. Nascha and the other women at the Spanish massacre are the Wendigos. They didn't just burn those men who attacked them. They cut off and ate pieces of them too. Although, I'm sure Nascha skipped that part."

Brandy continued before I could ask why. "Some of the plains tribes, including the Pawnee, are descended from the Aztecs. Hundreds of years ago, before the white settlers came, the Aztecs engaged in human sacrifice to their gods. Most of the legends I have heard about it involve the sacrifice of virgins. Even though the tribes officially abandoned the practice long ago as barbaric, there are still a few among them, shamans mostly, who believe a reclaiming of power can come from human sacrifice. I have been told the line of Pawnee shamans from whom Nascha is descended on her mother's side was one of these groups. Nascha is very spiritual and very severe, as I am sure you have noticed. She believes in some of the more obscure, ancient ways. When the time came for her revenge, she did it in the oldest way she could think of. By burning and eating those men. But not too much," Brandy cocked an eyebrow at me, "because they were poisoned. I've heard it was just their fingers. Gnawed them clean like little roasted chicken bones."

"From whom did you hear this?" I asked, incredulous.

Brandy scoffed. "From the best source of all. Nascha's husband, Gad. Give Gad enough to drink, and he'll tell you anything. Likeable enough fellow though. You'll meet him when we get to Bent's Fort. He's one of those people I call *charmed*. Gad always seems to be in the right place, at the right time, to say just the right thing to the right person. Probably why Nascha chose him. Gad isn't much to look at, but he's congenial, which helps. Nascha's not usually much of a talker unless she's working out a deal of some kind. Gad isn't her first husband though. Nascha told him that too, and Gad told me. One thing no one knows for sure is Nascha's real age. Even Gad. She'll tell you she's old, but not *how* old. Same with the other survivors. Everyone who's known them for a long time says they all look the same as the day they first rode into town decades ago. Which is part of the whole curse, if I understand it correctly."

Brandy acted as if I should know. When I shrugged, she explained. "The curse of being a Wendigo. They never age. Evil keeps them young or some such nonsense. Normally, the Navajo would have become wary of them and pushed Nascha and her women out of the community. But right now, they're nervous about the white men coming in to settle who want this gold. The Navajo are the most established tribe in the area. It's been their home for generations. They don't want to do anything to kick up sand and call attention to themselves. However, if their appeasement tactics fail, having a group of Wendigo to back up the tribe can't hurt. So as long as they are docile otherwise, the Navajo leave them alone. Plus, Nascha brings in a lot of money for Gad. He does a lot of things for the tribe. Gad's not a chief, but he might as well be. He controls the tribe's finances, and that controls the tribe."

I couldn't believe what I was hearing. "So, you're saying the Navajo are so afraid of white men, and so in need of money, that they're willing to accept the protection of what they believe to be a group of some kind of flesh-eating monsters?"

"Yes," Brandy affirmed, summing up as we heard hoofbeats approaching. "One thing you'll learn quickly about the frontier is that there are only two rules that govern it. One—he who makes the money makes the rules. And two—he who makes the rules has only one thing to fear. Nature. Whether human nature or on a much grander scale," she swept her left arm across to indicate the horizon, "Otherwise."

The rider was Penny. One of her horses was limping. She wanted her mother to have a look at its foot before we went any further. We all stopped so Brandy could dig out the sharp stone that had become wedged into the soft meaty part of the animal's hoof. Brandy had him walk round on it a bit. The horse took mincing steps, and he shied away from her when she tried to pick up his leg again. Seeing the horse was still in pain, and that Brandy was having trouble, Nascha got down to help. Pulling out a small box of salt, a bottle of iodine, a thick piece of cotton wadding, and some heavy waxed canvas, Nascha set to work cleaning and packing the horse's hoof securely. When she finished an hour or so later, the horse walked with a bit of a wobble, due to the conglomeration of bandaging attached to its hoof, but more confidently.

"I still wouldn't let him pull that wagon or carry riders," Nascha said to Brandy. She wiped her hands clean on a rag after she'd put away her supplies. "But he should be fine enough to walk along beside. We can redistribute some of the weight off that wagon among the two of us, so it will be less of a burden for the other fellow."

As we unloaded Penny's wagon, I noticed Nascha eyeing my two trunks full of books and clothes. "What's all that?"

"Things that I need for school," I answered, more defensively than I intended. Her tone implied my extra cargo was an unnecessary burden. "Books, mostly, and supplies. And my teaching wardrobe."

Nascha grinned at me sort of sideways, but said nothing more than, "Humph. Dead weight then. Are you sure you need all of it?"

"Yes, she's sure," Penny piped up, in my defense. "We have to have books for school."

"Ah, yes... books are needed if one is to have school. The bigger question is whether or not school itself is needed at all. We were just getting to that last night, weren't we?" Nascha's gray eyes glittered. Somehow, though I couldn't figure out why, I felt Nascha knew Brandy and I had been talking about her.

Brandy spared my having to reply. She shielded her eyes with her hand, gazing up at the sun, which was well past noon. "Ladies, if everything is wrapped up, we need to get back on the trail. I'd like to be pulling up at Bent's Fort by Sunday evening. All this sweating and sleeping in wagons is starting to wear on me." Penny nodded in agreement. She bounded obediently back up into her wagon.

For an awkward moment, I stood looking back and forth between the two women. Brandy had already turned to walk back to her own wagon. Nascha remained immobile. She was sizing me up for some reason, perhaps to see if she could detect some hint of betrayal or disbelief from the slightest twitch of muscle. I could feel the intensity of her silver gaze, but I looked away. It made me uncomfortable. I turned and followed Brandy.

After we got back into the wagon and had pulled out to a bit of a lead, I asked Brandy why she thought Nascha and Gad had never had children.

"How can a dead thing give birth to a living child?" Brandy replied.

"You can't really think those stories about the Wendigo being undead are true?" I asked.

Brandy thought for a few seconds. "I think there is definitely some reason every person, white and Indian, walks a wider path around Nascha and those other women. What that reason is exactly, I'm not sure. What I do know is the Navajo believe it, and that is a good enough reason for me to treat her as they do. Respectfully, but kept at arm's length. You'd be wise to do the same."

Seemingly eager to change the subject, Brandy requested I pull out one of my books from the trunk and read to her to help the time go faster. I did. We spoke no more of Nascha or any other strange matters for the rest of the day as I read aloud from Emerson's *Self-Reliance*.

As I write this, I continue to wonder which account I am to believe. If I choose to believe Brandy, and what she claims to have seen and heard from the Navajo, then Nascha is not just a victim who heroically overcame terrible abuse and what could have been death. Instead, she is a woman who did so, but from the strain of her suffering has become a sort of mythical monster. Whether natural or supernatural, it is impossible to discern at present. By believing in Nascha, I choose to stand behind a woman who has avenged her victimhood, but paradoxically blames her mother for being a weaker victim. As I puzzle over this question, I cannot help but find the answer in favor of Brandy's account. The most logical answer is that Nascha is an emotionally damaged woman. Someone who has earned the grudging respect of others who initially feared her. The part that troubles me most is the conclusion that line of thought leads to.

If the Navajos' fears about Nascha are legitimate, then the fact remains I am now partially under the protection of a cannibal. A cannibal who evaluated me this afternoon with unnerving suspicion in her gray eyes. My greatest comfort is that I did not meet her gaze. At this moment, I'd feel safer looking straight into an eclipse.

August 7, 1858

By tomorrow night, we will have completed the most arduous part of our journey. According to both Brandy and Nascha we will arrive at Bent's Fort by supper time. Although I am sure every crevice of my body is filled with hot dust and I will be gladder than ever in my life to take a proper bath, I cannot help but note the journey has not been as difficult as some I have read about. We haven't even had any substantial rain. Yet that could be simply because we've timed it just right. There isn't ever much rain on the prairies in August.

Nevertheless, during what I hope to be my final night of sleeping in a wagon, I have been presented with one more mystery to solve. That being, of course, the mystery of the origins and nature of Just Cawdor. Both Nascha and Brandy have told me different accounts about him. I am comforted by the fact that, unlike some of the other mysteries that this trip has brought to my attention, at least this one purports to have an ending. I am highly likely to meet this Mr. Cawdor in person shortly after we reach town. That is one of the few details Brandy and Nascha agree on. Just Cawdor is the sort of man who seems to be everywhere, all of the time.

I'll begin with Nascha's account first, since it is the more bizarre of the pair. Several years ago, while on one of her trading trips heading North out of Bent's Fort along the old Ute Indian trail, Nascha passed through an area of curious red rock formations near Manitou Springs. She said we would pass it again on the way to Auraria and to be on the lookout for them.

"Those rocks are sacred to the Utes," Nascha explained. "Much as the wolf is sacred to the Pawnee. For it is from those red rocks the Utes came. Because of that, they believe their people will stand forever like mountains."

I replied I looked forward to seeing them, but was unsure I would know what to look for, because I had heard the desert parts of Colorado were filled with red rock formations. Nascha's reply was intriguing. "How do white people know a church is a church? You will know them when you see them, if your eyes are open at all. It's always easy to know when one is on sacred ground."

Regardless, when Nascha came upon these great red rocks, she saw two wolves passing in and out of a cave among them. As she stopped to watch, it was as if the wolves were in conversation with one another. It was late fall and already chilly. Nascha was wearing her wolf headdress. As she approached the wolves, they made no effort to attack or flee. Instead, they carried on as if she was just another wolf passing by. Looking into the crevice in the rocks from whence the wolves came and went, she saw many other wolves huddled up inside, sleeping in one huge pile. In the middle of this wolf pile was a naked man. Not wanting to startle the wolves, Nascha made whimpering sounds to wake them gently, like those a lonely pup would make. As the wolves stirred their way out of lazy slumber, the man moved as one of them. Stretching out his arms long in front, he pulled back into a crouching position, like a wolf does. When he saw her, the man jumped up, banged his head on the ceiling of the cave, and rolled over to the side wall where he had stowed his clothes. He struggled with his back to her to put them on. Nascha stepped away from the entry to give him some privacy and waited for him to emerge.

"Weren't you scared?" I asked. "What if he were some kind of crazy person? He could have attacked you."

At this, Nascha rolled her eyes. "Not very many men are dangerous when they're both naked and unarmed, if you're holding a gun."

Once the man was dressed, he came out and spoke to Nascha. His white shirt and denim trousers were stained red with dust and ripped out at the seams. He told her he had been part of a group of prospectors traveling West from Georgia. When it became apparent from his coughing up blood that his tuberculosis, thought to be in remission when they left, had returned and was getting worse, his companions abandoned him there by the side of the road to die. At that point, he was so weak from fever and thirst he could not even rise to walk for help or search for food. So, he crawled over to the cave seeking shelter from the wind, and fell fast asleep.

Cawdor explained to Nascha that during his slumber, he had the most incredible dreams. In them, he fantasized he was running much faster than he normally ran. Surrounding him on every side were a pack of wolves. Together, they bounded across the open prairie, wheeling in unison like birds on the wind. Wherever one went, the other followed. "It was the greatest freedom I have ever known," Cawdor said.

When he awoke, it was nighttime. Cawdor found himself surrounded again by wolves. Dozens of them. Only this time, they were real. He was strangely unafraid in their presence. Cawdor reached out to touch one, just to be sure. His caress was met by a thick coat of coarse gray fur. Blinking into awareness and disbelief, he glanced around the interior of the small cave. A few of the younger wolves had brought apples they'd found somewhere to gnaw on. One of them, seeing him awake, rolled an apple over to him playfully. Ravenously hungry, Cawdor ate the apple, dust and all. Seeing this signal of hunger, the other young wolves rolled their apples to him as well. By the time he had eaten three or four of them, Cawdor felt well enough to sit upright.

That was when he noticed it. His chest no longer felt tight. As he rose cautiously to his feet, he didn't erupt in a fit of coughing. Glancing down at his body, Cawdor could see not only had his old musculature returned from where the tuberculosis wasted it away, but his muscles were twice the size as they had been before. Just to be certain, he forced a cough. He felt no pain and saw no blood. Something had cured him during his sleep.

Cawdor asked Nascha what day it was. She surprised him by saying it was early November. Claiming he had been abandoned in May, Cawdor had no recollection of how he had spent the intervening months. Since his miraculous recovery, he had felt little desire to rejoin the company of men. He preferred instead to live among the wolves. During the days, he knew he slept, but at night, Cawdor continued to have elaborate dreams of running with the pack.

Sensing his grip on sanity was tenuous, and that other spiritual factors might be at work, Nascha persuaded Cawdor to leave the cave and follow her on to Manitou Springs. At first, he was reluctant, but eventually he relented. Along the route, Cawdor became increasingly talkative, as if speaking with another person revived his memory of having once been fully human.

"From the experiences he spoke of," Nascha said definitively, "I knew I had found a Wolf-Man. A protector of the people, just like the Old Pawnee legends believed would come for us, to save us from the whites. It was said the Wolf-Man would appear just before a Great Battle. We should pay him heed, because his word was the word of the Wolf. Also, his arrival signaled we should be cautious. Because when the Wolf-Man came, the white man and his tricks were soon to follow."

"Well, that turned out to be true, didn't it?" I inquired. "Wasn't Cawdor abandoned by Green Russell? The man who now has struck gold in Auraria?"

"For that, you will have to ask Miss Stockbridge," Nascha replied curtly. "I do not trouble myself with the business of white men and the burden of their history, except where it concerns my own. Nor am I concerned with their money. The parts of life I am interested in trade in no currency. Their values are ancient and taken on faith." Nascha seemed resolved to cut me off here as usual, having had the last word. I would have none of it, and pressed her further.

"If you have no concern for white men's money, then why are you a trader in furs?"

Nascha's eyes flashed cold. "My only concern with their money is to see them parted from it. *I* do not care for it, but I know *they* care for it a great deal. *They* would do anything for it. Me, I give all that I do not need to the people of my village and others. They need it more. The roots of their family trees have been broken and twisted beyond recognition. Look at me," she said. "A half-Pawnee woman married to a Navajo man. A plains runner and a cliff dweller. It is not a natural pairing. We are opposites, thrown together by necessity of survival. That is what the white man does. He takes and he takes. So I take back from him, then I give it away to those he has taken from."

"Like Robin Hood," I said.

Nascha smiled a wicked smile. "Not quite. From what I understand, this Robin Hood of yours desired only to take money. When I can, I take back what is truly ours. Life itself!"

Having gotten the last word as she desired, Nascha turned away. I knew what her back to me meant. *Go to the white woman for the rest.* So, I asked Brandy.

"Just Cawdor?" Brandy replied. She tried to wipe a smudge of charcoal off her face, but only succeeded in smearing it down her sleeve. "Where did he come from? Hell, I've already told you all I know. There are tons of stories. If you've spoken to Nascha, you've probably gotten the most entertaining one. That he's a Wolf-Man who was sent to save the Indians. Filled with the natural spirit for native vengeance or some such." Brandy stabbed at the fire, which was struggling to heat up under the frying pan rack, as she continued.

"From what I know, he's a very decent sort of fellow. A trader too, but a different sort than Nascha. She'll shaft any white man she gets near any chance she gets. She always has the best furs because she's not afraid to go out and get them directly from the Indians first-hand, so they keep trading with her. Cawdor is a bit different, but successful in his own way. He's more of what you might call a mediator. He tries to make sure that everyone stays on good relations with one another. He takes a small cut from both sides to handle the negotiations. He's got a knack for it, that's sure. I would say it's from being half-Indian and half-white, but that wouldn't explain why he's so much easier to deal with than Nascha. Maybe it's because his Indian half is Cherokee. They seem to have been able to get along with us," she gestured to indicate our whiteness, "better than most. Or maybe it's because he's Southern. He's used to everyone being treated like a second-class citizen if they aren't part of some plantation owner's family." Brandy flipped the metal poker in a circle to cool it off before laying it down in the grass, wiped her hands again, and shrugged.

"Who knows? The only thing I do know about Cawdor is that he's the only white man I've met who has never shown any interest in my girls. Drinks plenty when he comes in, and he'll flirt with them, but no put away. He could be funny, maybe." Brandy wavered her hand back and forth. "He kind of looks it. You'll know what I mean when you see his face. Almost pretty, rather than handsome. He might have been an actor at some time too. I always hear him talking about plays and such to anyone he thinks will listen when he gets a snoot full. And you know what they say about *show people*." Brandy raised an eyebrow to make sure I understood her insinuation. "Is he a *spiritual being* though? Eh, my guess is *no*. But is he a decent fellow who gives both the Indians and whites he trades with a fair deal? Who hasn't ever caused me any trouble, even when I've had to physically set him on the street because he was too drunk to stand? Yeah, I could attest to that."

Here again, I couldn't resist pushing to see if I could get a bit more information. "About his name, though. It isn't his real name. You know that's in a play, right? *Macbeth*? Do you think he cribbed it from there?"

"I don't have the foggiest clue," Brandy replied, pulling the last slices of bacon out of their wrapping. She smiled at herself for having kept our nightly rations perfectly portioned. "That's exactly the kind of question I'm sure he'd love to answer. If you'll get him a little drunk first, of course. Like I said, he'll talk your ear off about the theater once he's about three sheets to the wind. 'Til then, he's quiet as a mouse." Brandy prodded at the bacon with a wooden fork, and then waved at me with it. "I would point him out to you when we get to Bent's Fort, but you'll know him when you see him. Tall, rangy fella. Arms are kind of too long for his body, but muscular. Like a boxer. Odd eyes too. Wrong color for an Indian. The Indian shows strong in the rest of his face."

"How do you know he'll be there?" I asked.

"Cawdor?" Brandy said, her attention once again trained to the bacon. "Cawdor's like Fate. He's always turning up where you least expect him."

August 8, 1858

Wouldn't you know we've ridden hundreds of miles for weeks without seeing a drop of rain, yet the moment we pull up in town and start to unload, it pours?

Brandy wants to stay a few days here at Bent's Fort, to see if she can drum up a little excitement for the improvements she's making at her saloon. So, we each took our clothes trunks off the wagon and hauled them upstairs to our rooms at the hotel. Nary a porter to be found in this deluge, so we had to struggle and sweat with everything up to the second floor. By the time we'd finished carrying our trunks, I was completely soaked to the bone. As we unloaded, I noticed Nascha doesn't travel with a trunk. She keeps all her things in multiple soft bags made of waterproof canvas. After this fiasco, I think she is wise.

As soon as she'd gotten settled in, bathed, and changed, Brandy was out again, working her way through the crowds. She left Penny with me, which I really don't mind at all. Penny is a bright girl, and we get along well. Strangely, we didn't spend as much quality time together on the trip as I had hoped. Penny tends to be quieter around her mother. Perhaps it's as my mother once said, about being around my grand-père and his old man friends. "There are some people who take up all the air in the room." Ironic to think about it in this situation though, considering the surrounding air in question was the entire prairie.

After Penny and I had refreshed our clothes, we went in search of dinner. Finding what looked to be a decent restaurant only a short walk from our hotel, we went in and ordered some tamales, rice and beans. The clientele was mixed. Equal parts traders, Indians, and Mexicans. Nothing out of the ordinary. Until I noticed a group of somewhat well-to-do white folks who had staked their claim on several tables at the north end of the bar.

One woman in the center of the group, dressed in bloomers, seemed to be holding court. The rest of the party milled about laughing at her every quip. I asked the waitress who she was.

"Oh, that's Mrs. Julia Holmes!" The waitress exclaimed, growing wide-eyed at the surprise of someone not recognizing a local celebrity. "She's the lady who just came down from climbing Pike's Peak. First one! You just missed that newspaper fella. She told him the whole story. Maybe she'll tell it to you if you go over and ask her nicely. She's really friendly."

I needn't have worried I would miss out on hearing Mrs. Holmes's tale. It was retold at least half a dozen times as different groups of people shoaled in and out of the restaurant, congratulating her. Apparently, Mrs. Holmes was a semi-newlywed. She and her husband James had only married the year before. Penny was enthralled with the tale on the first and second cycles, but by the third, she was batting her eyes sleepily. I walked Penny back over to our hotel and tucked her in. We chatted for a few minutes about this and that, and she was out quick as a candle caught in a breeze.

Still wide awake myself, I went back over to the restaurant and took a seat at the corner of the bar. I've always liked sitting at the corner, because it gives me the opportunity to evaluate the entire room, and to speak—or refuse to speak—to just about anyone. Since it was a Sunday night, most everyone had already eaten and left. The bar was empty save for one tall, thin man sitting with his hat pulled far down over his eyes. He was leaning against the wall by his left shoulder and seemed almost drunk enough to fall asleep. I paid him little mind.

By this time, the conversation among Holmes's party had changed to the more sobering subject of emancipation. It became clear to me immediately Holmes and her husband were abolitionists. As the drinks kept coming and the conversation got louder, I could also tell a different group sitting at the corner table opposite the Holmes party was beginning to get irritated. Their conversation became gradually louder too; only, their side of the argument was in favor of maintaining slavery. From their accents, they were Southern, so their viewpoints were of no surprise. Economic self-interest primarily, I thought, was their motivation. The powers who control the factors of production rarely want to yield to paying their workers any more, or even compensating them at all, if they don't have to.

Holmes's party steadily became aware of the increase in volume from the opposing group's conversation. I saw Julia lean over to her husband and whisper something, to which he shook his head vigorously. All of a sudden, Julia Holmes stood up. Her husband grabbed her by the wrist and tugged at her, trying to get her to sit down. She shook off his grasp. Striding round the table, she addressed the party of men.

"Gentlemen, we can hear you talking about politics from across the room. Why not come over and we will have a lively debate? You seem to be primed for it, and I am more than game. I think the merit of our side can hold its own."

Well, after that, you could have heard a pin drop! After a collective sharp intake of breath pulled all the air from the room, no one from either party said a word for several tense moments. Then, hot and sweet behind my ear, came a soft, whiskey-soaked whisper. "Ma'am, you had better slide over here closer to me. Things 'bout to get ugly."

As I turned to face the man, I had just enough time to glimpse the sharp outline of his jaw. I realized he was the thin man with the hat. Then, I heard the crash of glasses behind me.

"Down," the man whispered tersely. The next thing I knew, his long, muscular arm was around my shoulders. He pushed me under the bar and hovered over me, covering my head and upper back with his body. I could feel his warm breath over the small of my back, and felt his fast heartbeat through the fabric of my dress.

Moments later, I heard two women shriek. A rain of beer mugs and shot glasses came flying across the room like a crazy indoor hail storm. Mrs. Holmes fled back over to her side of the room. As I slid down with my back to the underside of the bar and peeped around the corner, I could see her do the same beneath the table where she and her friends sat. The owner of the bar, a fat Indian man in denim trousers and a white shirt, began swearing in a mixture of English and his native language. From what little I knew of their manner of speaking, he sounded like a Navajo. The rowdy men at the other table laughed at him. I took as a sign the onslaught was over, so I crawled out from my hiding place and around the corner of the bar.

Imagine my surprise when I saw Brandy, under the Southern men's table, doing exactly the same thing as I was! Our eyes caught for a second. She gave me one little head shake side to side. If she thought I might want to go over and check on her, her answer was definitely *no*.

The Navajo bar owner was attempting to get the Southerners to leave peacefully. They were having none of it. Especially after Mr. Holmes stepped up to defend his wife's request.

"I don't give a damn about what that big-mouthed Yankee woman over yonder has to say about nothin," the man in the green jacket shouted. He appeared to be the leader of the group. His words slurred with drunkenness. "*And* I don't care to hear nothin' from no coon defenders tonight. 'Specially if she's some kinda mountain climber. If'n you's a doin' yer duty, young feller, she'd be off climbin' you, and her mouth full of somethin' else!" The green jacketed man gestured rudely to punctuate this comment. Mr. Holmes lunged for him, fist drawn. The heavyset Navajo barman wedged his way between the two of them, arms raised trying to maintain distance. The man in the green jacket reached back under his coat for his pistol. Mr. Holmes froze in mid-swing. His eyes fixed on the weapon.

Quick as a flash, the thin man who had pushed me to safety under the bar darted around its edge and past Holmes. With a smack, the pistol went flying into the air. Hitting the ground, it discharged a shot into the ceiling. The thin man wrapped his long fingers around the hand of the man in the green jacket and squeezed. Even from across the room, I heard the bones in his hand crack under the pressure. He let out a roar of pain and jerked his hand away.

"Goddamn you, Cawdor! You done broke my hand!" The original argument forgotten, the man cradled his crushed hand in the crook of his other arm. His face, already red with drink, turned purple.

Calm as a midnight pond, Cawdor replied. "Not that much. Maybe just a couple little bones. You's about to get in worse trouble. Pullin' a gun on a fella like that." He gestured toward the door. "It ain't becomin' to a man of your stature to be actin' like some kinda white trash, pickin' fights with women that way neither. Now, jus' go'on back to yer room and get straightened up fer awhile. Ain't no bad harm been done yet that can't be fixed if you quit."

The man in the green jacket stood sulkily for a few seconds. Brandy crawled out from under the table and tiptoed over, whispering something into his ear. He grimaced, then nodded. Brandy led him out by his good arm. The rest of his group followed, with several taking time to spit wads of tobacco onto the floor along with insults partially under their breath that were still meant to be heard. "Coon lovers" and other hateful things. I was glad to see them go, but ashamed that Brandy went with them without offering me so much as a backward glance.

Mr. Holmes and the Navajo barman thanked Cawdor profusely. As the Holmes party invited me over to sit at their table, Cawdor sat down with us.

"I take it sir... madam..." Julia said once we'd all settled in and somewhat recovered, "the two of you are sympathizers with the cause of abolition." I replied I was. For I am, even though I hate to say I've never done much to support it. Frankly because I've had little opportunity. Where I'm from in Maine, there simply weren't many Africans, enslaved or free. Plus, I'd never seen an enslaved black person until I was in college and took my first trip down the Coast to the Carolinas. Even then, their plight hadn't registered very strongly with me. The ones I'd seen were all waiters and domestic servants in the restaurants where I'd dined and hotels where I'd stayed. They were all well-groomed and attired in the style of any other servant I'd ever met. Perhaps that's why I never really thought much about their situations. Still, like every other person of care and feeling in America, I had read *Uncle Tom's Cabin*. More recently, the terrible incident I witnessed with the mother and child killed by the slave catchers in Cincinnati haunted me, even if I didn't know what to do about it. So, yes... I felt I was speaking honestly when I said I was a supporter of abolition, albeit an inert and ineffectual one. Cawdor had an alternate opinion.

"No ma'am, I don't reckon' I am," he told her. "Though I don't blame people who are. It's just that my Daddy was a Cherokee. We've already lost all the battles there are to fight with fellas of that kind. Don't know if I'm ready to take up another. Sad to say I know that sorry ol' dog who was just in here though. His name's William Russell. People call him Green Russell. It fits him, considerin' he's a real snake in the grass. He's my uncle on my Momma's side. Mean as a snake too, and twice as quick to snap. But he's smart and purty rich. Sad to say he's about to get richer soon, with that new gold mine of his, and that'll only make him more ornery."

Here, Cawdor paused and stared at a knot hole in the pine floor. "But as for supportin' a cause? Naw, I don't reckon I'm for anybody's cause 'cept my own at this point in life. Can't stand to watch decent people get talked down to like that though. Y'all seem like decent people. It's not that I don't care 'bout the black man, or what he goes through. I do. I just that I don't see how much good it's gonna do to make him free, when he keeps on livin' in a place that hates him so much. He'd have to leave to have any kind of life. And most of 'em ain't got a pot to piss in or a window to throw it out of to make that happen either. Their masters keep 'em that way. Out of cash and beat down, feelin' like they don't amount to much. Keeps 'em from running away. I figure someday, they'll find a way to get out of it, if they're strong enough. Either that or they'll die like the Indians. White people been doin' the same thing to us for even longer'n there've been black slaves in America. Difference is, don't nobody care 'bout us Indians at all. Not now, an' probably not never. So, we got to take care of ourselves, and our own business. If'n you want to take up for slaves though, go right ahead. It's a free country, and somebody sure as hell needs to do it. It just can't be me. I got too many problems of my own."

Cawdor tipped his hat to the Holmes party in farewell, and then to the Navajo barman. On the way out, he handed him a few silver coins that he pulled out of his pocket with a bandana. Pointing up at the hole in the roof where the bullet had gone through, he said, "Nascha ain't gonna be happy when she sees that, is she? Make sure you tell her it warn't my fault." The fat Navajo barman managed a snort that was almost a laugh, as I realized he was Nascha's husband, Gad. Nascha... whom I hadn't seen since we'd come into town. I wondered where she was.

"You like to walk in the evenin'?" Cawdor asked. His question caught me off-guard, as I pondered Nascha's whereabouts. I replied affirmatively. "Good. I'll be out there walkin' then. Jus' come out whenever yer done with them." He gestured toward Holmes's party. Then, he staggered outside, bumping into the door jamb as he went.

"What an oddly interesting fellow," said Mrs. Holmes, as Gad brought out the final round for the last call. Setting it down on the table, he announced it was on the house and took one himself. We toasted Julia's success a final time before parting ways. I wish I'd had the courage to ask for Mrs. Holmes's address so we could keep in touch, but I've always been terrible at that sort of thing. Who knows how many people have slipped in and out of my life anonymously simply because I'm not the sort of person to trouble them by asking for a second meeting?

I had scarcely stepped off the boardwalk to cross the dusty street to my hotel when Cawdor appeared by my side.

"Where did you come from?" I asked playfully, pinching his sleeve.

"There!" Cawdor pointed up as high as he could into the clear, star-filled sky.

"Mmm hmm," I replied. He was drunk. Drunker than he had seemed at the bar. Having grown up in a bar and seen every type of man in every kind of mood, I could tell Cawdor was a happy drunk. At least, for the moment.

"Were you waiting for me to come and walk with you?" I asked sweetly.

"Mmm hmm," he hummed back, mocking me, his eyes dancing. Brandy was right. Cawdor's eyes were truly remarkable. Their color seemed to change from green to blue like a wave as he stared dreamily at me.

"Are we staying in the same hotel?" I prompted, when he said nothing more.

"Nuh-unh," Cawdor grunted, shaking his head vigorously. The drinks must have hit him all at once, I thought. Or perhaps he'd gotten another snoot full from a flask while he waited. He just stood there swaying, waiting for me to continue.

I gestured to a bench nearby. "Would you like to sit down?"

"Nuh-unh," Cawdor garbled again, mimicking me by casting his arm in a wide arc to indicate the rolling hills in the darkness beyond the edge of town. "I'm okay. I stay out there. With the stars."

"I see," I said, in a reassuring tone I normally reserved for my students. "Well, thank you for walking me across the street. This is my hotel. I will leave you here. Okay?"

"Okay," Cawdor said, grinning sleepily. "Tomorrow then." He paused and tilted his head to the side. Wrapping his long arm around one of the posts supporting the balcony of the hotel's second floor, he swung around it like a boy. Then, looking me square in the eye as he spoke, his speech pattern changed from the slurred Southern drawl I had heard all evening to a shockingly crisp English accent:

Tomorrow, and tomorrow, and tomorrow.
Creeps in this petty pace from day to day,
To the last syllable of recorded time;
And all our yesterdays have lighted fools
The way to dusty death. Out, out, brief candle!
Life's but a walking shadow, a poor player,
That struts and frets his hour upon the stage,
And then is heard no more.

Automatically, I capped his lines, matching his assumed English accent:
It is a tale told by an idiot,
Full of sound and fury,
Signifying nothing.

"That's from Macbeth," I said. Remembering what Brandy had mentioned during our last night on the trail, I eyed him curiously. "But you're not an idiot."

"I know," he replied, a little too loudly, before shushing himself back into his natural voice. "I'm Cawdor," he slurred. Pointing to himself, he spun around the pole again. "Just... Cawdor. That's *all* that I am."

"Well, that's plenty," I said, smiling at his childish self-satisfaction. I mimicked his hesitated delivery. "I'm Mae... Ulrich. That's all that *I* am."

"That's *moooooooore* than enough," said Cawdor, spinning around the pole one final time as he staggered out into the street.

"Tomorrow, then?" I asked.

"Tomorrow," he mumbled.

As Cawdor stumbled away down the street, I wondered if he really was camping outside of town, and if so why. He didn't look as if he were too poor to afford a room. His clothes were well-made, if a bit worn and dusty. He had paid for his drinks immediately, rather than charging a tab, which I knew was the habit of most broke men. But then, this Cawdor was nothing like any man I'd ever met. Especially when he was drunk. Any other man would have tried to take advantage of the situation of having saved me at the very least from taking a beer mug to the face, to try to force a kiss or to push to be invited up to my room.

Cawdor had done neither. He had recited Shakespeare like it was some sort of out of body experience, and then walked away randomly into the night. Now that I have met this unusual fellow at last, he remains even more of a mystery. And a bit of a handsome train wreck.

What am I to make of him?

I guess I will find out... tomorrow.

August 9, 1858

Today, I received a letter from Dr. Ernest Wheeler of St. Louis, the physician I had met at the mummy unwrapping. The bellman said it had arrived some days before, but he'd forgotten to give it to me the previous evening. In it, Dr. Wheeler seemed very distraught that some ill had befallen me. He claimed to be worried, since I had not responded after the telegram he sent about the time I was in Council Grove. Truth be told, I hadn't given it much thought. Dr. Wheeler was a nice man, but I could tell he was struggling with a lot emotionally. Both from the death of his fiancée and from something else I still can't quite put a finger on. After I had my coffee, I trotted down to the telegraph office and sent him a wire that said:

ARRIVED SAFELY IN BENT'S FORT. ALL'S WELL. SORRY TO CAUSE WORRY. WILL POST LONGER RESPONSE TO LETTER NEXT WEEK FROM NEW ADDRESS IN AURARIA. BEST, MAE.

I felt the need to respond quickly, because this was what Dr. Wheeler's letter said:

Dear Mae,

I hope this letter finds you well, but it is my most urgent fear it will not. An ominous thing has happened so many times since we have met that I am compelled to tell you about it. Although we have only spent one evening in each other's company, I feel we made a strong connection, which I hope will grow into friendship over time. Regardless, although I like to think of myself as a man of science and not superstition, perhaps you will understand the nature of my concern from what I am about to relate to you here.

First, if you recall, I told you about the tragedy of my fiancée, Rebecca. How she burnt herself in the house I was building for us because I had delayed the wedding. Unbeknownst to me then, she was pregnant with another man's child. As you might imagine, my sleep was disturbed for many months after this horrible loss. Eventually, I came back around to myself. Regardless, the night after you left, poor Rebecca appeared to me again in a dream. At least, I thought it was her. As I rushed forward hoping to pull her from the fire, I saw it was not Rebecca who stood in a burning building, but you. When I reached the threshold, the whole thing came crashing down. I could hear your screams as you were engulfed in flames. What is even more disturbing is I continue to have this dream. Night after night, I wake up in a cold sweat, watching you burn.

I hope you don't think me morbid, or worse, completely insane, for saying these things. Please do not think I do so lightly. After several nights of having this nightmare, I consulted with Miss Jilpa, the medium who was at the mummy unwrapping. She told me these were not ordinary nightmares, but a premonition you were in danger. Miss Jilpa urged me to warn you immediately. This is the source of my grave concern!

Miss Jilpa, as we have discussed, has a true gift and is rarely mistaken. I almost took off after you myself, but I thought it would be better to try to send a wire first. I knew you would pass through Council Grove, everyone going West these days does, so I tried there first. When you did not respond, I remembered you were following the old Santa Fe Route, which would take you through Bent's Fort. Thus, I sent this letter. If I get no response from it, then I will make one more attempt to wire you again in Auraria. If I receive no response a third time, I will begin the trek out there myself.

I'm sure you are wondering by now why, if I am so worried you are to perish in a fire, I would wait so long to come to your aid. The reason is this—when I have the dream, the fire always happens when there is snow on the ground. Not just a dusting, but a thick, heavy blanket. I've consulted the almanac and dozens of other sources on weather in the territory. From what I understand, the first snowfall is not usually until late September or early October. Thus, if you are to arrive before the school year begins in late August, you should know if the scene there looks like the one in my nightmare. If it does, please tell me, and I will come immediately. I am not sure what I can do to prevent this from happening, other than to escort you away from there personally. If that is the only solution, I am willing to do so. It would be easy enough to find another teaching appointment for you here in St. Louis. The city is growing in leaps and bounds. I would not expect anything in return for directing your safe passage. It would be comforting enough for me to know, within my plagued brain, that at least I have been able to set something right.

All that is left now, if you are still reading and do not regard me as a total madman, is to share with you the vision I have had of the building in which I see you burning, so you will know when you come to it, and hopefully contact me.

I feel very strongly it is a schoolhouse. It may be the school house where you have been assigned to teach. The last structure on the edge of town, it is two stories high and built of wide pine boards. The outside is whitewashed and there is a wood burning stove in the center of the classroom, between two long aisles of students' benches. There is a porch covered by an overhang, and a woodpile to the right of the door outside. There is also an upstairs, which I feel must be an attic of some kind, or maybe a living-quarters, since I can't imagine where a teacher living alone might be housed otherwise to avoid gossip. When I see you in the dream, it is always through this upstairs window, which you are looking out of and crying for help. There are children too, whom I cannot help but surmise to be your students.

Miss Jilpa claims the reason I can see your expression and the rest of the scene so clearly is that I am having an out of body experience during this dream. She thinks I am actually floating outside the window in spirit form, watching you when it happens. I know we have spoken before about the strange nature of your wolf dreams, and of our mutual experiences with travel along the spiritual plane. Because of this shared confidence, I pray you will heed my warning and consider the possibility that leaving will save you from grave peril.

Once again, please let me stress I do not mean to frighten you, but to warn you. I believe you are a woman who is of strong will and a good judge of character, so I trust you will find that my intentions are genuine. To close, I implore you to write to me in reassurance as soon as you receive this or any of my other correspondences.

Last, know that if you need me, I am prepared to depart at a moment's notice. There is nothing more precious in this life, I have learned, than honest communication.

Your Faithful Friend,
Dr. Ernest Wheeler

I read the letter over several times, but could detect no treachery in it. After I returned from sending the wire, Brandy was downstairs with Penny. Both were having breakfast and coffee, although Penny's was fortified with substantially more cream. Willing to forget her snub of the previous evening in hopes of gaining a friend's wisdom, I let Brandy read the letter.

"There are only two general possibilities," Brandy said, folding the letter over and handing it back to me. "Either the fellow is honestly some kind of clairvoyant and you're really in for some trouble, or he's like every other man in the world, and just trying to find the right angle to get under your skirts by invading your mind."

"That's exactly what I'm trying to figure out," I said, putting the letter into my purse. "Which do you think it is?"

"I think that's a pretty poor way to try to catch a girlfriend," Penny piped up, unbidden. "It isn't like anything in a novel."

"Hate to burst your bubble, my dear, but men rarely behave like those in novels," Brandy said to her daughter, somewhat snippishly. "However, if you want my opinion," she continued, pausing to slurp the last of her coffee. "I think the truth may be a bit more complicated. You say this doctor has had a history of emotional trauma? Well, what if he really is having these dreams, and he really does think you're in danger, but it's not clairvoyance? What if it's just some sick contrivance because he's having the same feelings for you that he had for his now-dead fiancée, and has conflated the two? So he now associates love with fire and death?"

As usual, Brandy had a good point, but not the one I wanted to hear. It would almost be more comforting to know Ernest had envisioned my demise through some feat of clairvoyance than to suppose I was just a stand-in for his long-departed fiancée within the tortured confines of his overheated brain. The first is a magical possibility, but the second is a sad absurdity.

While we sat pondering these options, we saw Gad strolling up the boardwalk. I waved to him, but Brandy regarded him coolly. Nevertheless, Gad approached the window next to our table. I was happy that Gad addressed the previous evening's events so I didn't have to. Once Gad established he had no animosity toward Brandy, since he knew she had been doing her best to generate business for her place in Auraria by chatting up the richest men in town, she softened a little. At that moment, I could see why someone as austere as Nascha would have married a man like Gad. Even though he was quite plump, with a round face that most would not normally regard as handsome, Gad had a warm way about him that could unthaw even the frostiest of social situations. The kind of man it was impossible to hate.

"So, no hard feelings then, eh?" Gad concluded, patting Brandy on the shoulder, leaving his meaty paw to rest lightly there until she issued her verdict.

"No, no. None at all. We proprietors of drinking establishments have to stick together, and set standards of good behavior for all." Brandy's smile was mostly sincere, with just a hint of force behind it. The same smile I felt she must have given her paying gentlemen—half filled with genuine pleasure she was being admired, and half left with the realization she'd rather by cared for by someone else. A truly professional smile.

As soon as Gad left, I asked Brandy whether she had decided what time we were to depart tomorrow for Auraria, the last leg of our journey.

"Why would I leave for Auraria now, when I have the opportunity to build more business by staying here for a few more days?" Brandy asked, raising an eyebrow.

"I understand that," I replied, "but I'm eager to get going. I have no idea what state my schoolhouse is going to be in, and I'd like to have at least a week or two to prepare before my students arrive."

"Well, no one's stopping you from taking a horse and riding up there. We're not far away. This part of the route is safe enough and well-traveled. Don't tell me you're afraid of going alone? I've done it myself many times. Haven't you traveled all over Europe alone? I'm sure there are far more evils that might befall an unescorted woman in the Old Country than out here on the New Frontier."

I was about to continue my protest, but I caught myself, knowing it would fall on deaf ears. I was foolish to suppose that Brandy and I would be close friends forever. It was sheer luck we'd crossed paths leaving St. Louis. Her life was built around enjoying fortuitous circumstances as long as they lasted, and building quick intimacies, while always looking out for self-preservation first. She was correct I shouldn't be concerned about the distance. Four days' ride on an established road wasn't the danger to end all dangers. However, perhaps you'll think me weak and foolish for saying so, but I was afraid to go alone. Maybe because Ernest's letter spooked me,

I don't know. I just had a strange sense about it, which I covered up by making an excuse.

"But I have no horse of my own. I had thought I'd wait to buy one when we got to Auraria, since I was traveling with you and Penny the whole way."

"That was a silly thought," Brandy quipped. She turned to see a group of men coming down the stairs, clearly the worse for the wear and in need of breakfast. "You'll have far better selection here in Bent's Fort with so many traders coming and going. In fact," Brandy paused to wave at the last of the men, whom I recognized from the night before as Green Russell. This morning, he was without his green jacket and his hand was bandaged. "If you hurry," she finished, "you might just catch the noon sale. I heard from the boys last night a drive was coming in with a fresh selection for the miners to choose from as they head back to camp."

Dismissing me with a wave of her hand, Brandy put on her best professional smile. The men sat down, surrounding us at the tables nearby in the cafe. Green Russell himself stood hovering expectantly behind my chair, waiting for me to get up. From the way he cleared his throat, I got the distinct impression he would have dumped me out on the floor if I tarried too long.

Sensing a long day of her mother's uninteresting banter about to commence, Penny caught my eye. "I'll go with you. Help you pick out a horse," she offered. Poor girl. Even though I know Brandy wants the best for her daughter, it seems Penny spends her entire life looking for ways to distract herself. She tries so hard to be out of her mother's way.

After going upstairs to get some money, Penny and I went out onto the street. It was only a few blocks walk to the auction stand. I could see dozens of men were already gathering in anticipation of the sale. Pulling my hat down over my eyes, I squinted in the already sweltering heat. Seeing me surveying the territory, Penny said, "Looks like it'll be a while before the auction starts. Drivers aren't here yet. Probably won't be until noon. Don't you need a cart too, for your trunks? There's a carter's shop over there." She indicated the path down another street. "If you're not superstitious, we can put the cart before the horse." Penny's face lit up in a grin, clearly pleased with her joke.

"Quick you are, young one," I returned, smiling at her. "Lead on!" Winding our way two streets over to the carter's, I noticed Penny waved at every merchant along the way. To my surprise, many waved back, and shouted her name, "Penny!" To some she called, "For your thoughts!" It seemed to be an inside joke between them.

"How did you come up with that?" I asked.

"Oh, the greeting?" Penny answered. "When Mama first started coming here a couple of years ago, there wasn't a cafe yet. But every morning I woke up hungry as a bear. I'd come out here and walk among the stalls, to get an apple or a roll and some cheese. When they'd ask me for money, I'd tell them I didn't have any. They'd have to ask my mother later. Since my name was Penny, I'd tell her to give them an extra penny for their thoughtfulness. A penny for their thoughts. It was just a cute little thing we said. Mama always paid later, so it worked out."

Once again, I could not help but marvel at the girl's independence and resourcefulness. Surely, she'd inherited this boundless confidence from her mother. Yet, it hadn't served Brandy much good, other than making her the best loved madam in town. I could see why Brandy felt confident about leaving Penny alone for the day, but also insistent she be sent back East to school. A girl with Penny's personality and looks, combined with the education and money her mother had never enjoyed, would move like a hurricane through the staid New England social circles, bewitching everyone whom she met.

Unsurprisingly, Penny knew the carter. In a matter of minutes, we were touring his lot, looking at ready-to-sell two-wheeled gigs that could be pulled by a single horse. Settling on a lightweight number with steel-re-inforced rims, painted a jaunty shade of light blue. I paid him cash. He wheeled it inside the shop to be oiled down and made ready for the journey. I could pick it up that afternoon, he said, if I was able to buy a horse.

Also on Penny's suggestion, we visited the saddler a few shops down for some tack. Since he was friends with the carter, the two collaborated on measurements. He had a harness and bridle already made for the style of gig I'd selected. "This saddle ought to look right nice with it as well," he said, pulling out a light tan, calfskin saddle from the series skirting the outside wall. "Extra padded seat and adjustable stirrups too. Ought to be comfortable for a lady, if she's used to riding astride?"

"Yes, I am," I replied. He resettled the saddle onto a pommel sitting in the middle of the room and motioned for me to get on. I did so, with as much grace as one could muster when slinging a leg over such a thing in a full skirt. It was very comfortable, and it had a pretty floral detail burned into the leather. Buying it, along with some matching saddlebags and a blanket for my still unbought horse, I told the saddler I would pick it up that afternoon after the sale.

"You've got an awful lot of riding gear for a woman with no horse," Penny observed.

I agreed. It was beginning to make me uneasy, spending all that money on a cart and tack with no horse to put it on. "Let's go over the sale yard and wait for them to come in."

Standing on the platform, I quickly became uncomfortable with the number of men staring at Penny and me. They looked us up and down as if we were the horseflesh on sale. However, I didn't have to endure it long. By half past noon, we began to hear calls and yips from over the rise at the edge of town. The drivers came clattering in with a herd of about two dozen horses. The men who had been milling about ogling us crowded to the rail, and began whistling for the auctioneer's attention. "What'll ya give, gentlemen? What'll ya give? Let me see those fists full of dollars in the air!" I dug into my purse for all the remaining money I had on my person. Penny pulled me forward, and urged me up to the rail.

"You'll not get nothin' if you don't toe the line for it! Push on in!" Penny insisted. She wormed around me and sat down, her legs swinging over the edge of the platform.

The auctioneer ordered the drivers to corral the horses up, and then let them out, one by one, to trot around the sale yard. The horses were of all breeds, colors, and ages. I had no idea where they might have acquired such a random assortment. The one that caught my eye most was a young mare, not far past filly age, with a lot of spring in her step. She was a great big girl, a bay paint, and had a white mask on her face. She looked strong, with huge feet and thick legs. Her eyes were calm and large, like bright chestnuts. While some of the fillies close to her kicked and started, the mare trotted calmly around the yard as if it had been her own pasture. Pointing her out to Penny, I asked what she thought.

"Yep, that's just what you need. A big ol' girl like that won't have any trouble with that light cart. Even with two trunks, she'll pull it in jiffy." Penny stood up, dusting herself off from where the horses had kicked up dust onto the platform. "She's already shod too, which is always good. Dunno how she ended up here. Looks like somebody's farm horse. Maybe they died. Should be able to get her at a good price though with so many fillies. All these clowns will want something younger that they can breed."

I agreed, and put part of the money back in my purse. The bay mare was a solid horse, but given the number of younger competitors, the price shouldn't be too high. Or so I thought.

The starting bid for each animal was $100. Most sold for between $150 and $200, with a big black stallion going for the most at $250. As the bidding went on, I became more anxious. Men kept trying to push Penny and me aside. We kept needing to elbow our way back to the rail. Several made a point to shoulder their way in right at my breast level, and then wriggle around there for a second, grinning like catfish until I pushed them back. The smell of their sweat was disgusting. I began to feel sorry for their wives or whoever else had to deal with them on a regular basis.

When the time came for my bay paint mare to be bid, I figured I'd save myself the trouble of the back and forth, not to mention the risk of losing her, and make a high opening bid. "One hundred and fifty dollars!" I called out loudly, brandishing my cash in the air like a sword, as the bay mare made her second calm circumnavigation of the yard.

The auctioneer gave me a quizzical look, then looked back off to the side of the platform. From somewhere in that general direction, I heard a gruff voice call, "One hunnert e'en!"

"One hundred dollars even, from the whiskered gentleman in the bowler to my left!" The auctioneer called, still looking in the direction of the other voice. Thinking he hadn't heard me, I called out my bid for one-fifty again. Yet once more, I heard another male voice. This time a man standing at the rail on the other side of me called "One-twenty." The auctioneer echoed his bid. "One hundred and twenty dollars from the man in the blue tie to my left. Do I hear one hundred and thirty?" I exchanged glances with Penny. She sensed what was going on too. The men were deliberately ignoring my bid. On the count of three we both cried out in unison at the top of our lungs, waving our arms in the air. "*One hundred and fifty dollars!*" The auctioneer looked straight through us. He acknowledged a different bid for a hundred and thirty, then another for a hundred and forty.

Penny elbowed me hard in the ribs. "You're going to lose her!"

"Naw she ain't," came a voice I recognized from right behind me. "A hundred and fifty, boss! Right over here in the middle! J. Cawdor!"

"Good to hear from you, Mr. Cawdor," called the auctioneer, looking right over my shoulder as if I were still invisible. "Can anyone top that bid for this mare?" No comment arose from the crowd.

"Don't say nothin'," Cawdor whispered in my ear. The auctioneer called for bids twice more before declaring Cawdor the winner.

When the driver led the bay paint mare over to Cawdor on her rope, he pointed at me. "Hand it to her, she's the one with the money." The driver looked confused. He turned back to look at the auctioneer. The auctioneer shook his head vigorously and shuffled over. "Mr. Cawdor, I'm afraid we have to take the money from your hand. You can give it to her afterward if you want to. Women are not allowed to buy horses at this sale."

I could see Cawdor was about to get wound up. Not wanting to make a scene, I thrust the money into his hand. "Just pay the man. I'm ready to get the hell out of here." Cawdor stared at the money for a second, then he looked at me and sighed. Smoothing the crumpled bills, he extended them to the auctioneer at the furthest reach of his long, outstretched arm. To the driver, he said stonily, "Hand her the rope."

As we walked away from the platform, Cawdor chastised me for not standing my ground. I told him I was hot and tired of being groped. It didn't matter to me who paid for the horse so long as I ended up with her.

"Besides, I'm used to it," I said. "No one back East takes a woman seriously when she wants to buy anything big. Why should I expect it to be any different here?"

Cawdor stopped and turned to me. "You're right. Ain't nothin' ever gonna be any different for you, nor any woman, until you *make* it so." He spat on the ground. "I thought you might be the type, but maybe I was wrong. When are you leavin'?"

Thinking I had made him angry enough that I had broken the fragile beginning of our friendship from the previous night already, I told him the next morning. I added I planned to go by myself, in a bit more of a sullen tone than I probably should have.

"Well, I'm leavin' tonight," Cawdor spat again at the ground. "If you want me to accompany you, I'd suggest you go back and pack up your things. I figure you got a lot of 'em. Do you have a wagon?"

"No, I plan to balance my trunks on my head like an Egyptian woman fetching water," I replied indignantly.

"Folks, don't argue!" Penny pleaded. "There's no reason for it. Yes, Mr. Cawdor. Miss Ulrich has a gig and tack. Bought it this morning."

"Well, nice to see there's hope for guidance from the next generation," Cawdor smirked.

"Anyone new in town might need to be directed to the proper place to purchase things," I replied haughtily. "But I will have you know I selected and paid for them myself."

"With your father's money, no doubt. I'll meet you at Gad's at sunset," Cawdor said, walking away without waiting for my reply.

"My father is dead," I said. He stopped, but did not turn back around. "My grand-père and mother too. So, the money and whatever happens to it are mine and mine alone."

Cawdor scratched at a clod of dirt with the tip of his boot. He began walking away again, kicking small puffs of dust with his shuffling steps. "Sunset," he replied, never looking back. "And wear somethin' suitable for ridin'."

I looked at Penny. "What's his problem?"

She wrinkled her nose and shrugged. "That's Just Cawdor. He can't do anything nice without saying something nasty about it."

August 10, 1858

After saying goodbye to Penny and repacking my trunk, I picked up my wagon and headed over to Gad's saloon for some dinner as I waited for Cawdor. Gad was in fine spirits and made me hash browns with cheese and an omelet with peppers, onions, and salsa on top. I never realized how much I missed cheese until I'd gone a week without it! Gad seemed happy to talk, and he was glad I planned to travel the last part of my journey with Cawdor.

"If any man can give you the lay of the land and the people in it around here, it's Cawdor," Gad said, polishing the glassware. "He's a square one. Good friend to have."

We passed the time in casual conversation about the people I'd likely meet in Auraria, and what kinds of students their children might be. However, when I attempted to turn the conversation in the direction of his wife, Nascha, and why I hadn't seen her since we'd arrived in town, Gad suddenly remembered something urgent in the kitchen he had to attend to. He left me to finish my meal alone at the empty bar. Even to her husband, it seems, Nascha is somewhat of an enigma.

I didn't have long to wait though. Cawdor came riding up on his horse at sunset. It was a dappled gray gelding with streaks in his mane. The kind of horse more suited for an old farmer, I thought, than a man who traveled all the time. He saw me sizing up the horse and commented, "He might not look like it, but Troy here is the smoothest riding horse you've ever seen."

Patting his horse's neck, Cawdor smiled. His eyes were enchanting, and his profile was so sharp, it was as if cut from marble. His lips though, were a bit too thin for his angular face to be considered truly handsome. And his teeth... there was something about his teeth... They were so perfect it was disconcerting. Not only were they dazzlingly straight and white, unlike the teeth of any other outdoorsman I'd ever met, but the canines were very long and pointed, like those of a large dog. His smile wasn't unpleasant, just not quite... natural somehow. His voice was different too. At Gad's bar when he'd been drinking, his Southern accent was very thick. Then at the auction after he'd sobered up, it had smoothed out some. Now that we were alone, it was barely noticeable. I wondered if the change was deliberate. Catching me staring curiously at him, he resumed his usual stoic expression. Cawdor seemed to be the sort of person who was content to stay silent until someone else started a conversation.

"Brandy told me you were a big lover of the theater," I offered.

"Yeah, that comes from my Momma," Cawdor said, beckoning me outside. "She was an actress. We lived in Savannah for most of my childhood. She worked in a stock company of actors there. It's sort of a sad story from a long time ago." He swung himself up onto Troy's back in one smooth motion.

I climbed up into my own little blue cart, taking the reins of my bay mare. "Well, we've got almost four days between here and Auraria, and as you can probably tell," I pointed the tip of my new leather crop toward my trunk of books in the back, "I love a good story."

Cawdor smiled again. This one was longer, I think, because he felt more secure looking away from me. Having been around a lot of men with bad teeth in my lifetime, I got the impression he was ashamed to let me see him smile.

Waiting until we were out of both sight and earshot of town, Cawdor began telling me his history. It went something like this:

"I was born on Christmas Day, 1829. My mother, Charlotte, as I'm sure you know, if you've been talking to Brandy on the way over here, was Green Russell's eldest sister. She was about twenty or so when I was born, and Uncle Green was about ten. Anyway, they'd just struck gold that summer in Georgia. Near the original Auraria and Dahlonega and half a dozen other places, all on Cherokee lands. Up until that point, the whites and Cherokee had gotten along better than most in North Georgia—better than they had in North Carolina, anyway—and many had married one another, including my parents. All that changed after the gold was found. North Georgia mountain country wasn't any good for growing cotton like down in the Delta. When something was finally found of value, all the poor white folks thought it was finally their turn to lay claim to a piece of it. They wanted to get rich like all their slave-owning cousins on the plantations.

Trouble was, the land wasn't theirs to take. It belonged to the Cherokee. The State of Georgia didn't care. They let white settlers go in and stake claims to whatever they wanted. The Cherokee tried to fight it the proper way. They took their case all the way to the Supreme Court, but they lost. The State of Georgia swooped in and took their land, and the gold along with it. They gave it to whichever poor white folks could get there first. Then, things got violent. When many of the Cherokee refused to leave, President Jackson sent the Army in to make them go. Rounded them up like cattle and pushed them West. Killed all who refused. My father was one of them. Shot dead standing unarmed in his own front yard. Momma found him lying there when she got home that evening. She'd been up at her father's place that day, ironically they were arguing over what to do with me. As a white woman with a half-Cherokee son, it was likely that she'd be forced out West too.

Her father and brothers wanted to stake their claim for gold. Ultimately, they did. Made a bundle off of it too. Momma would have none of it. She always said it was blood money. I reckon it's true. Blood money stolen from the Cherokee who were forced off their land in the mountains built North Georgia just as much as the blood beaten out of the backs of African slaves built the cotton country down south in the Delta. It don't seem that nobody really gives a damn about either one. The State of Georgia still stands. America too. Someday I wouldn't be surprised if they put a gold dome on the capitol, just to show off what they stole. They keep talking like there'll be a war of some sort about it, but I still say it won't fix nothin'. There's always been a lot of high-minded talk about how America was founded for religious freedom, but that's all bullshit. The only temple that America's ever worshiped at was the Temple of the Almighty Dollar. Might be a good idea to start putting that on all the money. In Gold We Trust."

Cawdor paused, chuckling bitterly to himself, then began again. "Anyway, nobody wants to hear a philosophical lecture from a cowboy. What happened next is Momma and Granddaddy had a big fight. He told her she was a traitor to the family if she didn't go along with their move onto Cherokee land. If she tried to run away, he refused to allow her to use the family name for me. Everyone knew she couldn't use my real father's name if she wanted to stay in Georgia, because of the Cherokee removal. Not having a white American-sounding name could have been a death sentence for me. So, Momma, who always had a big theatrical streak, even before she became a real actress, told her father that if she couldn't use his name and she couldn't use her husband's name, she would give me the name of a traitor and teach me to be proud of it. Hence, she changed my name on the spot to Cawdor."

"The traitor who was killed at the beginning of Macbeth," I said, making the connection.

"Yep," he replied. "Then when Granddaddy asked what my first name would be. Momma told him that was it. Just Cawdor. Because there was no justice in this world but the fact she and I had each other, and that was enough. So, the name stuck. I've been Just Cawdor all my life. Momma ran away to Savannah and joined a theatrical company there. She was pretty and talented, so she made a fine career out of it. Enough to send me to a good school there in the city where I learned all the things boys going to college are supposed to learn. Languages, maths, sciences, the usual subjects. None of that interested me as much as being on the stage. Growing up sitting in the wings of a theater, you kind of catch the fever of it. By the time I'd turned fourteen or so, the summer she first got sick, I thought I'd made up my mind that's what I would do. Be an actor. Then Momma came down with tuberculosis. Over the next few months, she kept getting sicker and sicker, until she couldn't act anymore. I wasn't quite old enough to take up serious parts yet to earn any real money. She insisted I keep going to school until I finished. She died in January, just after I'd turned sixteen. By that time, she had been in the hospital for months. We'd lost our apartment. Her stage manager was letting me sleep in the basement of the theater, so long as I'd keep it clean. My school tuition was paid through the end of the year. I'd taken enough courses to graduate, so I got my diploma and left."

"Where did you go?" I asked.

"The number one place I shouldn't have—back to my Momma's family. I had heard they'd done very well in the gold rush there and thought maybe they'd be willing to share a bit of it. Enough for me to go to college so I could teach school in a few years maybe, or at least pay me to do some kind of work while I put on enough age to play paying roles in another theater. Sounds stupid, I know. Why would they ever hand over money to the kid whose mother had run away and named him after a fictional traitor? By that time, Uncle Green had grown up. He was tired of being outshined by his father and older brothers. Itching to strike out on his own for this new gold country in the West, Uncle Green convinced me and a bunch of our Cherokee relatives to come along, promising us each a share of whatever we found. Stupidly, I believed him. A lot of us did, mostly because we were tired of hiding and ready to get out of Georgia. Maybe it was the romantic in me too, thinking I'd come out here and have some great adventure and get rich enough to buy my own theater. But of course, that never happened. I never made it to California. By the time we'd gotten to about where we are now, I was really sick. Having watched Momma go downhill for so long, I knew what it was. The tuberculosis. Uncle Green could tell too, and it scared him. When I got too sick to ride on my own, he set me out to die. Right here in this desert. Don't know where exactly. I was too delirious by then. It was somewhere between here and the cave we'll come up on tomorrow."

Here Cawdor stopped again, though I could see his mind still churning. The lines on his angular face pulled tight. I could tell he was working through old thoughts. I kept waiting for him to go on. To tell the part of the story I knew was coming next. About how he woke up in a cave surrounded by the wolves that saved his life in some mysterious way. However, he didn't, and I didn't want to push him. I checked my pocket watch. It was five in the morning. We had ridden all night as he'd told his story. The sun would be coming up soon. I wondered if we'd stop and make camp at last and sleep during the day. I hoped so. I was completely worn out. Finally, Cawdor turned toward me with that wolfish grin.

"That old bastard didn't kill me though. Not yet! The irony of it all is that, here I am, one more time, on the other side of the country. Me, the half Cherokee boy, who's Daddy died trying to keep the gold for his people. Nothin's changed. I'm still trying to make sure the white men like Green Russell don't push all the other tribes off their land and steal their gold too!"

Cawdor's grin erupted into a defiant cackle. "It's like that part in Ezekiel... a circle within a circle, a wheel within a wheel. Over and over and over again. And in every rotation of it, people like me keep getting run over." Then, he muttered under his breath. "But not this time, goddamn it. This time, the wheel stops where I say it should."

Pulling his horse up, Cawdor hopped down abruptly. He started untying the bundles for his bedroll and tent. He pointed to a flat spot on the ground under a few scrubby trees nearby.

"Shade will be on that side when the sun comes up. You'll want to pitch your tent facing West so that it isn't in your eyes when you're sleeping. We'll set out again at sunset. I prefer traveling at night. It's..." he seemed to search for the right word, settling on, "*quieter.* Alright with you?"

I agreed. We spoke no more as we pitched our tents and settled in. He made no mention of food, so I ate the cornbread, cheese, and leftover bacon I'd saved from my breakfast at Gad's. I'd brought tinned food and biscuits for the remainder of our travels, but no cookware. For some reason, I hadn't considered at all what Cawdor might eat, or if we'd be sharing meals at all.

Thinking back over the night as I lie here writing this entry, I find many oddities about Cawdor and our journey so far. The strangest one to me is the fact he travels at night. For a man who talks all night about himself, he goes to great lengths to maintain quiet around him otherwise. He might be a great tradesman and negotiator, but I've seen enough plays and been around enough actors to know when I've seen one desperately in need of an audience. Cawdor's truly a man who's missed his calling if he doesn't go back to the theater. Because out here, it's clear his only audience is me.

August 11, 1858

For the first time today, I saw the red rock desert of Colorado. I cried uncontrollably. I don't know whether it was the barrenness of the landscape, which stands in such stark contrast to the lush rolling green of the upper Appalachians and its crystal-clear glacial lakes, or just the sheer aloneness of not seeing or sensing any living creature other than myself for miles and miles. Nevertheless, I wept.

"I felt the same way when I finally saw it," said Cawdor. "The vast nothingness." He looked up at the sky, which was beginning to lighten after our second night of traveling. "After a while though, you start to look at it as a canvas. A blank slate on which nothing has ever been drawn. It's up to you to give it life."

"Is that how you see it?" I asked him.

Cawdor shrugged. "That's how I try to see it. It's getting harder though, with more people coming in and erasing what I've sketched in my mind. About how things ought to be. I reckon it's that way anywhere. People ruin everything."

He waited for me to stop sniffling without looking at me, and then asked, "We're about to that cave, if you want to see it? Might make camp there today if it's empty."

I nodded. He hadn't said another word about his past or his time with the wolves during our second night of traveling. Instead, he'd filled me in on all the details he thought I "ought to know" about Auraria in order to "get along with people better." More on that in a bit.

The cave was inside an enormous red stone monolith that looked like it had been carved by the hand of some ancient god. Stepping inside the narrow crevice of its opening, the height of its interior took my breath away. Almost the entire thing was hollow, stretching up what would have been several stories high to an eclipse in the darkness. Shining my lantern around, I could see that all of the interior walls were covered with names and pictures. The names were in many languages—English, Spanish, French, and probably countless native dialects I couldn't understand. Many were scrawled right over older writing and drawings. I could see one clearly depicted a buffalo hunt, but the others were harder to discern. As I bent forward to examine them, Cawdor motioned toward what looked at first like a dotted line that went straight around the room, at about the height of a normal man's topmost reach. Upon closer inspection at the part where Cawdor was pointing, the line wasn't just random dots, but instead looked more like...

"Paw prints?" I asked

"That's what it looked like to me too," Cawdor answered. "I knew the Pawnee worshiped the wolf, and that some of their lands weren't very far from here. I figured that part must be theirs." He looked back and forth from the prints to me, as if expecting me to come up with some further interpretation on my own.

"That seems possible," I said, squinting. Looking at them closer was difficult, because they were so high up. "They're much too big to be made by a real wolf though. Besides, where would they get the blacking?"

Cawdor's thick eyebrows, strangely heavy-looking on his angular face, knit together as he motioned toward the fire pit at the center of the cave with his lantern.

"It's possible someone could have left enough charcoal remnants from a fire that wolves could walk through it and then put their paws on the wall. But all in a straight line like that?" I wondered aloud.

"No, no... I agree. Normal wolves wouldn't have never done nothin' like that." The expectant expression on Cawdor's face drifted away. He went back outside.

As I heard him shuffling around, untying his bedroll and collecting starter twigs for the fire, it occurred to me he seemed disappointed I hadn't made some kind of connection about the wolf markings. Then, it dawned on me. My dreams. Cawdor wanted me to make a connection between my wolf dreams and the markings.

There was only one problem with that theory. I hadn't told him about my dreams at all.

When Cawdor returned with arms full of supplies, I asked, "Did Nascha tell you about my dreams?"

"No," he said, looking away. "Why would Nascha and I be discussing your dreams?"

"Well, because they..." I trailed off, as I saw the muscles contract in his back under the thin cotton of his shirt. He was waiting on me to say something about the dreams now, I was sure of it. But why would he lie?

"Because they were very interesting, is all. About mining and the desert, and all that."

"And all what?" Cawdor whispered, his voice still tense as a coiled spring. "What else?"

I faked a gigantic yawn. "Oh, nothing. It can wait until tomorrow. I'm really worn out." The tension in his back released. Cawdor continued making his pallet on the ground. After we'd both finished assembling our beds, I lay down on my side of the cave. I sat my lantern down beside my journal to write. I could feel him watching me.

"What's that you're writing there?"

"My journal," I said, seeing no reason not to be forthright about this mundane detail. "I try to write down everything important that's happened to me on my way out West here." I cleared my throat. "For, you know, posterity."

Cawdor cackled and rolled over to look at me across the dwindling fire. "Who do you think is going to read the memoirs of a frontier schoolteacher?"

"You never know," I said, bristling a little. "Someone might. Lots of people read Melville's *Typee* and Cooper's *Last of the Mohicans*. They were frontiersmen of different kinds. I've got several copies in my trunk. Just in case any of my students want to write about their own experiences on the frontier before it's gone."

"*Humph!* Before it's gone. Hell." Cawdor rotated onto his back, still glancing sideways at me. "There's so many damn things already gone about this country. Who's gonna care about people like us?"

"You might be surprised," I replied in my most teacherly tone.

Cawdor was silent for several minutes. He stared at the lantern light licking up the walls. It danced in and out among the hundreds of years' worth of writing.

"I would tell you about what happened when I first woke up here, but I can't now that I know you're a liar."

I put my journal down, indignant. "What do you think I'm lying about?"

"I know you dream about wolves. About seeing a wolf, and running with a wolf, and being a wolf yourself. And when I asked you about your dreams, you only told me half the truth. So that makes you a liar."

"Well then, you're a liar too. Because you said you didn't talk to Nascha about my dreams. You obviously did, because she's the only person I've told."

Cawdor sat up. "Another lie! You told that medium and the doctor in St. Louis too! I know it, because I heard you! You never should have said anything to him, because he'll only come out here and get his fool self killed somehow. His kind always does."

"How on earth could you..."

He interrupted me. "For a smart woman, you can be really dim—or maybe just stubborn. Probably the latter. Lots of women are, and smart ones are often the worst. I know about your damn dreams because I have them too! I saw you in them! I *hear* you *all* the damn time!" He turned in a huff to face the wall.

What could I say to this? Cawdor must have been telling the truth, but how? I'd never second-guessed why he'd been so protective of me from the beginning, or why he'd asked me to accompany him to Auraria. I'd assumed it was out of some generic sense of male chivalry. What if it was something else? An urge to get me alone and talk about the strangeness of our mutual dreams in a place so alien that perhaps it wouldn't sound crazy after all?

I've always accepted Miss Jilpa could have visions, and that all sorts of communications with the supernatural through mediums could be true. I had even sought out interpretation of my dreams through their guidance. Why then, was I so resistant to the possibility that Cawdor could actually hold the key to interpreting all of it? It was easy to believe in a theory, but hard to understand that such a thing was actually happening *to me*.

"Cawdor, I'm very sorry," I said. "I don't know why I didn't tell you the truth before. I guess I was just scared."

"Of what? Me?" His voice went up an octave, as if he'd already been concerned.

"No, of me," I replied into the air. "I've spent much of my life being skeptical and smug about everything. Even things I wanted to believe in. Perhaps that's my way of feeling superior over life. That I feel like I am the only keeper of my truth."

Cawdor thought for a moment, then relaxed onto his back. "So, I was right. You are stubborn."

"Yes, I am."

"*Humph*," he said again, smoothing his dark, straight hair away from his face. "Are you ready to tell the truth now?"

"Maybe," I replied, hesitantly. "I'll try."

"Okay, shoot then."

So, I told him, from beginning to end, all the different dreams I'd had. About the *loup garou* on my grand-père's dairy farm. About running across the fields faster and faster in the night. About the wolf who had run out of the collapsing mine. Cawdor lay there quietly, listening. When I'd finished, he asked if that was all.

"That's all I can think of right now."

He *humphed* once more, sleepily this time. He smiled his strange, toothy grin to himself. "Perhaps the rest will come after you've had some more sleep. Or when we see those rocks tomorrow."

Cawdor put his back to me and faced the wall again, curling up into a ball and letting me know without saying so that the conversation had ended. As I fell asleep, I kept going over in my mind how it might be possible. Even if his knowledge of my dreams were by some sort of spiritualist phenomenon, an interconnectedness of souls, that still didn't explain why he'd known I'd told Miss Jilpa and Dr. Wheeler, unless...

"I can hear you," Cawdor had said. Then it clicked. That smile.

"*Do I have to even tell you?*" Miss Jilpa had asked. "*You will know him by his smile.*"

I stared at the curved shape of Cawdor's back under the gray wool blanket, wishing I could wake him one more time to be sure. At the same time, if my suspicions are correct, I'm scared to find out what on God's earth all of it might mean.

August 12, 1858

A nother revelation this morning! Cawdor showed me the very red rocks from my dreams of the wolf! One was huge, shaped like the prow of a ship. The others were balanced precariously one on top of the other. I could see that he understood from my excitement I recognized them, and he was glad. Still though, Cawdor waits to tell his own story in bits and pieces. He seems to be hoping I will somehow divine it on my own from interpreting my dreams. Which is difficult, because even though the dreams were quite vivid out on the prairie, for some reason they've stopped since I came to Bent's Fort. Perhaps they will begin again when I am settled in Auraria.

We had another visitor today as well. Just at dawn, as we were making camp for our usual "day of rest." It was Nascha. She seemed very intent on speaking to Cawdor outside of my hearing. They rode away over a ridge while I was making my breakfast for dinner, such as it is. I will be so glad to get to town again tomorrow and have a "real" meal again! Cawdor eats almost nothing. I have no idea how he keeps going. When he returned, Nascha didn't come with him, which didn't surprise me. She doesn't go in for exchanging pleasantries much, and I hadn't seen her otherwise since our arrival at Bent's Fort.

Her mission was to request Cawdor join her hunting party on a hunt the following night. It would continue for several days. "She wanted me to leave immediately, but I told her I had to make sure you were safe in Auraria before I left," Cawdor explained. "She wasn't very happy about it, but she knows as well as I do that this last little stretch here past the mines is the most dangerous to travel alone."

When I asked him if it was because of robbers, he replied yes, that was certainly part of it. Also, he claimed, "a lot of the men who come out here to prospect are wildcatters. And like animals, they're capable of anything. Attacking a woman on her own to satisfy themselves would mean nothing to them. If they thought you'd cause them any trouble, they'd just slit your throat first and let the buzzards clean it up afterward."

As you might imagine, I was very troubled by this information. Brandy had implied the route was safe. I pressed further, to figure out why he felt more secure with leaving me alone in town. I told him it was likely the same potentially dangerous men would be there as well. Cawdor *humphed* in the manner to which I'd become accustomed, and said, "Too many people would notice you in town. The more people who would recognize you and care if you went missing, the safer you'll be. Murder's a hanging offense, but only if you're caught. In town, the likelihood of getting caught is greater, whereas out here," Cawdor gestured to the wide-open wasteland of the red rock desert. "Who is there to hear you scream?"

We spent the rest of the evening's travels more quietly than usual. Cawdor seemed to be deeply engrossed in thought. As we rode, I kept trying to think of what to name my horse. None of the typical bay horse names seemed special enough for the creature that was likely to be my constant companion. Wildfire was out, because her temperament was too steady. Ginger seemed too precious, like a horse who would mince around as she walked.

"I'm surprised you haven't considered Cressida," said Cawdor, as he slowed his own horse to a walk. He smiled again, with that sly, toothy grin. "It fits. After all, we're in the gold country. There's a good bit of discussion about gold and what's a human's worth in that play."

"How did you..." I asked, but Cawdor interrupted me.

"Well, I figured sooner or later you'd come round to notice you're riding an unnamed horse. You usually chatter on like a squirrel. When you were quiet at last, that seemed like the most natural thing you should be thinking of." Noticing but choosing not to comment on the fact that it was he who often chattered on when we were alone, I decided instead to try the name out on my mare.

"Cressida, what do you think?" I asked her. "Or Cressie. Is that your name?" The horse's ears pricked up and turned round to me as if on swivels. She whinnied, and gave a little jump.

"She likes it!"

"Thought she would," Cawdor said, grinning to himself as he clicked to his own dappled gray, urging him forward again. "C'mon Troy, old boy! Let's get a move on!"

"Oh, *Troy*!" I replied, as it dawned on me. As in the play *Troilus and Cressida*, of course! How could I have missed it, especially coming from a theater man? I'd heard him calling that horse Troy for days. I thought it was just a dumb joke of some kind—the Trojan Horse—*ha ha*. If Troy hadn't responded to it so well for the whole trip, I would think that Cawdor might have changed it after seeing my bay, so the names would match. He's that way, I've noticed. Constantly trying to create a connection or point at little hints that could tie us together in some way, waiting to see if I'll notice. To what purpose, I have no idea, other than the fact he seems to be a fairly lonely person. He must be, if he is out here by himself in this desert with only his horse and people such as Nascha for company.

As we made camp for our last day of sleep, I thought I'd try once more to get the details about Nascha out of him. She continued to puzzle me even more since her sudden reappearance and departure.

"I wouldn't be too concerned with her," Cawdor replied brusquely. "Or with Brandy. They're both fine enough ladies, I guess. But you have to hold them each at arms-length for similar reasons."

"What reasons?" I wondered.

Cawdor scratched his head and gave me a look to which I had become so accustomed over the last few days. "Isn't it obvious? Because either of them will do whatever it takes to survive. I don't blame them really. They've both had very hard lives, exploited in similar ways, but coped with it differently. Nascha's constantly on her own, even though she's married, while Brandy is a slave to the company of others. However, they both seem to be of the mindset it's harder for fate to hit a moving target, so they're always going—changing alliances, traveling to different places—with one purpose. Self-preservation at any cost. Even though neither is too bad off, monetarily speaking, maintaining any friendship, especially with another woman, is something that they're not willing to afford."

"Why especially with a woman?" I asked. "I would think they'd want an alliance. A sort of sisterhood of struggle."

"Nope, that ain't the way it works," Cawdor said. "Not out here anyway. I can see why you might think that, coming from back East. Out here, every other woman is competition."

"Women in the East compete too," I persisted. "For husbands, for atten-tion."

Cawdor disagreed. "That's not the same thing. Those were small com-petitions for social positions. Petty rivalries. At the end of the day, all you knew you had a home to go to and men to take care of you, whether they were fathers, brothers, husbands, or fiancés. Women in the East have more value because their culture has advanced to the point in which Culture, with a capital C, is a desirable luxury. But here... the only things of value are gold, timber, meat, fur, and the blood and bone it takes to pull it out of the ground or yank it off some dead animal. Colorado doesn't have time for Culture. Not yet, anyway. Ten, twenty, fifty years from now, maybe, but not now. It's that way amongst men too. All of us scrapping and fighting to find our place and establish some kind of order here in the wilderness."

I began to wonder if this was one of those times in which Cawdor was waiting for me to come around to some conclusion. "So, are you saying I'd be better off trying to make friends with men out here in the West?"

"God no!" Cawdor replied, more forcefully than I'd anticipated. "Men are even worse. They want other favors nine tenths of the time. No, what I'm trying to tell you is you shouldn't trust anyone but yourself. That goes for out here, or anywhere."

I looked at him, pointedly. "Then why should I trust you?"

Cawdor stopped and squinted at me, with that *shouldn't it be obvious* look again. "Because we can't..." he touched his right hand to his temple and motioned back and forth between us. "We can't keep sec... oh, God damn it! *Figure it out!* I'm going to get something to start the fire with." He trudged off in a huff.

I knew what he almost said—we couldn't keep secrets from each other. I assume it's because of the shared dreams. But if that's the case, and we are literally of the same mind somehow, then why in the world does he have such a hard time saying so?

August 13, 1858

Finally reached Auraria today. Given what was there when we arrived, I wished to God we hadn't. Another vision from my dreams, but one I'd hoped wasn't reality.

Hanging on the gallows in the middle of the road, so you'd have no choice but to pass by, were five men. All Indians by their clothes, and long dead. Most of their flesh had been ripped from their bodies by animals, and what was left hung in torn ribbons, black and putrefying in the August heat. Their remains were wrapped in lengths of chain, out of which protruded shards of ribcage and other bones. Clouds of flies as big as hornets swirled in tornados around them. The smell was so wretched I had to dig my heels in and force Cressida to walk forward. The horse's instincts were the same as mine, to turn around and never return.

"Found stealing gold from the mine—allegedly," said Cawdor, pulling a bandanna up over his face. "About a month ago. They were supposed to await trial by the territorial governor. Russell pushed for it early. Tried to testify for them, but I wasn't allowed. Nobody ever believes an Indian trying to vouch for another Indian anyway. They were hung same day they were found guilty, and been left here ever since." He pointed to a series of nails sticking out of the front of the gallows platform. "Used to be a sign there that said you weren't allowed to cut them down. Looks like somebody took it. *Humph.*" Cawdor looked back over his shoulder at me as he steered Troy around the gruesome spectacle. "You know that saying about how some people will steal anything that ain't nailed down? Well, this ain't that kind of place. It's worse!"

"Did you think they actually stole anything?" I said through my fingers, hand over my mouth. Pinching my nose shut wasn't enough. The smell was reeking into my body. Walking past them, I could see their skulls had been used for target practice. All the tops blown were blown off except for pieces of bone sticking up here and there like the points of hideous crowns.

"Dunno for sure, but probably not," Cawdor said. He urged Troy into a trot to get past the miasma. "Russell doesn't pay any of his workers their shares like he promised. No big surprise. I never figured he would. Conned them into doing all the hard labor of pulling the gold out of the ground, and then accused them of stealing it. That way he could execute them rather than paying up. Free labor. Even freer than bringing black slaves out here. He'd had to have bought slaves. That would make them too expensive to kill. But free Cherokees? Ha! Nothing is more expendable than a poor working man. No investment, all return."

Past the gallows, the town was laid out in one long, steady curve to the left in a row of single and double-story wooden buildings. The usual assortment of main street businesses had sprung up. There was a general store, post office, small bank, church, blacksmith, tannery, lumber yard, and what must be Brandy's saloon. From its brightly painted pink false front and ornately carved wooden curlicues around the eaves, the saloon looked like a building masquerading as a birthday cake. At the exact opposite end, past the blacksmith shop on the edge of town, was a large, unpainted building made of wide pine boards with a steep, pitched roof. I asked Cawdor if that was the school.

"Yep, that's it," said Cawdor. "Built it a couple of months ago, after the governor sent money for it. Should have painted it, but claimed they ran out of money, which I doubt." He walked Troy up to the hitching rail out front of the post office and tied him on. "We can ask in here to see if we need keys. Council made it clear nobody was to go inside, so they might have it locked." Agreeing, I hopped off Cressie's back and secured her to the rail beside Troy.

Inside, the post office was a simple, bright room with white walls and a counter painted blue. A washed out looking, heavyset old man with a drooping mustache lay propped up on one arm. He was asleep at the cash register, with a cold mug of coffee beside him. A sign on the desk announced him as the Postmaster.

"Excuse me, sir," I said softly, trying in vain not to startle him. He jumped like a prairie dog out of a hole. Cawdor chuckled behind me. "My name is Esmeray Ulrich. I'm to be the teacher for the new school over there," I pointed out the window. "Might there be a key I need?"

"Oh, certainly, certainly!" The Postmaster chortled. He sucked a tuft of unkempt and over-long mustache into his mouth, then pulled it out to hang in gray, slimy strands that trailed down his jowls like a sad walrus. "I have keys and paint, and several large boxes that have been here for weeks. And also...," he stumbled around behind the counter, patting numerous crates as if touching them would help him remember who they were for. "Two letters... let me see, let me see. Oh, wait!" he paused, as it came to him. "They're out back. One moment, and I'll have it all together for you to sign for. Then you can be on your way!"

The Postmaster waddled duck-footed out the rear door. I watched through the window as he toddled to the outhouse and back with a small, white canvas sack that was stamped *U.S. Mail.*

"Why does the Postmaster keep the letter bag in the outhouse?" I asked.

"He probably ran out of catalog pages. Christmas ones don't come out for a couple more months," Cawdor replied. "Wiping material."

Dumping the contents on the blue counter, the Postmaster shuffled through the pile. "Ah, here we are!" he said, holding up two letters triumphantly, one fat and the other thin. "One from the Teachers' Board in Hartford and another from a Doctor..." he cocked his head to the side and pushed his pince nez glasses further up his nose to squint at the name. "Ernest Wheeler, of St. Louis." Not used to having the senders of my mail announced, I took possession of the letters hesitantly. A few cautious glances reassured me there were no brown markings on either envelope, despite their questionable storage.

Opening the one from Hartford, I peered inside. "Not going to check the one from your beau first?" Asked the Postmaster, winking at me and twisting the soggy ends of his mustache into points.

"He's not my beau." I said briskly, ignoring his overly assuming *mmm hmming* that followed. I figured it was directed more at Cawdor than me anyway. The contents of the Hartford letter appeared to be information about school procedures and instruction. I decided to read it later, along with the letter from Dr. Wheeler, when I was without an audience.

"All this is yours too," continued the Postmaster, pushing one of the crates out from behind the counter. "Looks like books and school supplies to me. Pretty heavy. That other one over there is tools and such, you can hear the nails rattling around inside. This one," he got up off the package he'd been sitting on, "is paint, I think. It sloshes. Do you have help?" He motioned to Cawdor, with another overly assuming *hmm*.

"Yeah, she does," Cawdor sighed. He peered over the counter at the four crates. "We'll have to take a couple of trips. Probably carry two at a time, once we get her trunks off the gig. Are you gonna be open all day?"

"Only 'til noon" the fat Postmaster replied. "Then I take an hour for lunch, and come back 'til five."

"That'll work," said Cawdor, glancing at the grandfather clock behind the counter. "We should have it all out of your hair within an hour."

Since it was only about a hundred yards to the school house, Cawdor and I walked the horses down. The lock, I noticed, turning the skeleton key for the first time, was a simple affair. One strong jerk could pull it off the door entirely. "I'm guessing they didn't think there'd be much need for security in keeping people out?"

"Probably not. Biggest problem with school's always been keeping folks *in*, not *out*," Cawdor joked, as we walked through the door.

"Oh!" I exclaimed, seeing the lumber piled up around the walls. "Oh, I didn't know all the desks would be unassembled." In fact, the only thing in the entire room that had been fully installed was a wood-burning heater in the center. Its long chimney went up through the ceiling and out the roof. Even the chalkboard was leaned up against its spot on the wall, rather than hanging. I tried lifting one side up to the level where it should be, and could, but there was no way I would ever be able to affix it to the wall on my own.

"How in the world am I supposed to get this up here?" I asked Cawdor, throwing up my hands. "I can drive a nail, sure, but I'm no carpenter! Is my first day's lesson going to be, *Dear students, welcome to school! Here's how to build your own desk!*"

"I *told* you," Cawdor said impatiently, "I would help you." He surveyed the room. "You've got plenty of materials. More than enough, really. If they've sent you a saw and a few hammers, we can set it to rights in a week or so. I helped build whole sets for my Momma's theater in Savannah. I think I can manage a few rows of desks and benches."

"Well, okay, thank you," I stammered, not knowing how to properly accept his offer. "But what about up there?" I pointed to the ceiling. "I suppose my living quarters doesn't have any furniture either?"

"Then, I'm guessing that's what all this extra lumber is for," he replied coolly.

I went over to the steep, ladder-like staircase next to the wall and walked up far enough to peer into the loft. Sure enough, it was completely bare, save for the stovepipe going straight up through the center of the room. "You must be right," I called back, coming down. "There isn't any stove up there either. Doesn't it get really cold here in the winter?"

"Yep, pretty snowy too," Cawdor said, glancing up at the ceiling and pointing. "Surprised they didn't put any grates in the ceiling to let the heat from the stove rise. But we can do that too. Once you figure out where you're going to put the bed, we can cut out some spaces. I'd go ahead and order a few now though, while you can. Mail is slow all the time. It stops running entirely for months once the hard part of winter sets in."

I didn't know what to say. Cawdor was volunteering so much of his time. It would take weeks for us to get everything built. We'd be lucky to have it finished in time for school to start. Thank you didn't seem to be enough.

"Don't worry about it," he shrugged. "Besides, once you see my half-assed carpentry, you might not be so grateful. I've only ever built anything for people to *pretend* to live in, not to *actually* live in."

We spent the rest of the morning unloading my trunks from the gig, and then going back and forth to retrieve the other two loads from the post office. By the end of it, I was dripping with sweat and completely worn out. Cawdor announced he had to leave because he'd promised to catch up with Nascha and her hunting party by dusk.

"Can I at least change and offer you a beer from the saloon before you go?"

Cawdor glanced up at the sun. I noticed for the first time he didn't carry a watch. "Naw, I better get going. It's a good half day's ride back."

Exchanging goodbyes, I locked the door behind me. Dragging out my bedroll to have a cushiony spot to sit down, I reopened my school letter from Hartford. Not only did it include very detailed instructions and a day-by-day schedule of the year's required curriculum, but also other information about classroom discipline (the second longest section), expectations of teacher behavior (the longest section by far), and pay schedules (the last day of every month). It also contained a smaller packet of plans for constructing the school furniture. "How thoughtful," I muttered to myself, rolling my eyes. "Too bad they couldn't send a couple of carpenters along to make it happen."

Next, I looked at the letter from Dr. Wheeler. At first, I was hesitant to open it. What could it possibly say that I wanted to hear, or that would be productive? Not "I've been having more nightmares and fear for your safety," certainly. That would only make me anxious, which was the last thing I wanted, given all the work ahead of me.

What if it's an invitation, though? I thought to myself, turning the slim, surprisingly crisp envelope over in my hands. An invitation to what, I wondered? To chuck all this mess and high-tail it back to St. Louis, where I could marry him and live like a normal human being, instead of out here in the wilderness? *Don't be silly,* I thought. *You don't even know if he fancies you. Or if he did, what then?* What if, as I had suspected from our first and only meeting, and the concerned telegrams that followed, Dr. Wheeler *did* fancy me? Did I want to become a doctor's wife in St. Louis? Before I'd even given the freedom of making a living on my own a chance?

"Not today," I said aloud to the air, setting the letter aside unopened and checking my tiny rose gold pocket watch. It was almost two. I'd been up now for eighteen hours without eating a bite, and I was starving. What I really needed was food, maybe some beer, and to pick up a couple of days of supplies from the general store before I came back to collapse early. The last thing I needed was to think about being rescued by some doctor from St. Louis.

August 14, 1858

L ast night, the wolf dreams returned. Only this time, it wasn't just my wolf. Others were with him. I was back at the entrance to the mine, the same place from my previous dream where I had narrowly escaped a cave in. From my position, I could see a ring of creatures hiding in the underbrush. At first, their eyes looked like wolf eyes, but the shapes of their faces were all wrong. Not a wolf's long snout, but broader and flatter, like a bear. They also seemed to have some kind of antlers, which made no sense at all.

For a long time, I just watched. They appeared to be waiting on something. It seemed they were communicating softly through a series of clicking and whistling sounds. Then, my wolf, for somehow I could feel his wolfishness different from the others as he moved, came out of the underbrush and trotted toward the mouth of the cave. When he had been inside for a few minutes, I could hear men's voices but could not make out what they were saying. Then, the wolf loped back out of the mine and away into the desert. A short, fat-faced man in a broad-brimmed hat followed him.

That's when I heard it. The clicks and whines coming from the creatures in the underbrush crescendoed in pitch and volume to a deafening multi-tonal screech as they rushed ahead. They ran partially upright, propelling themselves forward like gorillas on their muscled haunches and swinging through on their extraordinarily long arms, which ended in sharp-nailed fingers like claws. The man shrieked and turned to run, but it was too late. They were upon him in only two or three bounds. Ripping him apart with their powerful bear-like jaws full of long, crooked teeth, they dismembered him in a matter of seconds.

The creatures sat crunching on the man's bones and cracking horns as they butted each other out of the way for scraps. I heard more voices from inside the cave. One of the creatures looked up and sniffed the air. I could see its gray eyes flash silver. Making another series of clicking and whining noises, all the creatures—there must have been at least half a dozen—clamped down on the remnants of the man they'd just devoured and slunk slowly back into the underbrush.

Moments later, three more men emerged. All miners, I guessed, from their clothing. Each was carrying a shotgun. Standing at the entrance to the mine, the tallest one in the middle fired a shot into the air. The creatures made not a sound. Peering into the darkness, one spied the poor chubby fellow's hat lying on the ground. He went over and bent as if to pick it up. That's when the creatures rushed again. No screech this time, just a great press of forward motion, like a wild herd being let out. One leapt right for his head. In a single bite, the beast tore it clean off his body. I heard this second man's skull crack and saw his brains burst out like a squashed fruit between the beast's teeth.

The tall man did not flinch. He shot directly at the beast and hit his mark. The creature fell backward into the dirt, but two others set upon him. Wrestling right and left, each soon had an arm pulled off his torso. While he still writhed in the dirt, the others were already digging their snouts into the organ meat of his midsection.

The remaining man, a short, stout fellow with a bloated gin blossom nose and dark curly hair, screamed and fled towards the perspective from where I was witnessing the whole nightmare unfold. Just before he ran straight into me, another creature landed square on his back. He fell to the earth with a hard smack. His head wrenched to the side, and I heard a loud crack. I knew his neck was broken. Rather than digging in, this last beast leapt off and ran away a few paces after making his kill.

Watching him flick his tail impatiently from side to side as the others rushed forward, I could see it was my wolf who had broken the man's neck. Standing so close, I could discern the differences between the two types of beasts easily. Mine was more wolf-like, albeit an absolutely enormous one with piercing green eyes, whereas with the other creatures, it was hard to say what they were. Their bodies, for the most part, were wolfish, but their heads were definitely more bearlike, with much thinner fur. Their snaggle-toothed jaws were like nothing for which I had any comparison. And their horns! Those were the most curious of all. They were like great elk antlers spread as wide as a man was tall.

Once they'd rendered the four men to nothing but piles of bone and gristle, the horned beasts lay down lazily in the dust. My wolf made a sort of whining sound. One silver-eyed beast rose, stretched, and ambled slowly over to him. After having some sort of conversation in their differing languages, my wolf trotted off. The scene went dark as I awakened.

It's been hard to maintain focus on the myriad of things that need to get done around the school today after the dream. After jerking awake, I sat and watched the sunrise from my window overlooking the street. Deciding the saloon probably wouldn't open for meals until lunchtime, I went downstairs to fire up the stove for coffee, thinking that working on my lesson plans—normally a great way for me to kill a few hours—would be enough of a distraction. However, I've been completely unable to concentrate on anything all morning. Ultimately decided just to sit here and write it all down in a list, hoping to make some logical sense of the dream and thereby put it to rest.

Here are the facts I know to be true so far:

1. There is a massive gray wolf, about whom Cawdor and I seem to share dreams.

2. That wolf is always friendly to me, sometimes even protective, in these dreams.

3. However, that wolf also helped to lure four miners to their deaths in my most recent nightmare. And that same wolf killed one of the miners himself.

4. Although my wolf did not eat the flesh of the men, those other horned beasts did.

5. I cannot say for certain what those other beasts are, but they're terrifying.

Now here is my attempt at deductive reasoning, based on the facts above:

1. Wolves, in my unconscious dream universe, appear to be protective figures. They appear when I feel apprehensive and uncertain.

2. This employment of wolf-as-symbol may be tied to associations of my grand-père as a protective figure, since he often told me stories of the *loup garou*.

3. Cawdor, most likely, has a similar subliminal association, and/or we share some kind of yet-to-be-determined psychic bond.

4. Yet, if that is the case, then what is to be made of the wolf figure in my most recent dreams being presented as a betrayer and killer of men? Does that mean I am losing faith in the old mechanisms on which I relied for self-comfort now that I am away from civilization?

5. Does the emergence of these new horned creatures—unidentifiable as any specific kind of beast, but definitely more dreadful and dangerous—signify an essential change in my psyche? The emergence of some alternative self-preservation instinct?

This line of reasoning makes sense when considered in the context of my feelings about why I could never completely trust Brandy or Nascha. If I am feeling *more* anxious about this new adventure than previously, and less willing to trust those around me, it makes sense the visual symbol my mind used represent this shift would change too. My tortured brain may have abandoned the imagery of a wolf from my grand-père's stories because it was only sufficient protection from lower levels of danger. In its place, my psyche seems to have conjured up more fearsome beasts to match my rising level of fear. I think this rationale is plausible.

Although I wish I had someone to consult with about it. Someone who familiar with the mind's workings and open enough in their thoughts toward Spiritualism to be willing to talk it out with me. Of course, Dr. Wheeler could be such a person, but then I would have to answer his letter. He's already highly concerned about the dangers of my situation. However, I am afraid Cawdor is right. Ernest is just the sort of person to be impulsive enough to rush out here and accidentally get himself killed.

Perhaps it's best if I wait for Cawdor to come back from his hunting trip and consult with him about it. That's probably the most sensible thing to do, instead of getting everyone else stirred up about my strange dreams. Lord knows, I have plenty enough work to keep me occupied, what with school beginning in just over a fortnight! I just have to steel my nerves and put my nose to the grindstone.

August 15, 1858

I've never been a willingly regular churchgoer, especially since my family passed. This morning though, I thought I might make an exception and show up. Initially, my thinking was that, if there were any mothers with school-aged children in the area, then they would most likely be found in highest concentration at church. Therefore, it could help my school's recruitment efforts to make an appearance and invite them to stop by and enroll on Monday. Not to mention I might be able to find some women my age to at least have a cup of coffee with. That would help my feelings immensely. As it turned out, attending church was an excellent idea for recruiting efforts, but a poor one for finding friends.

I wore what I thought was a smart, conservative dress of bright grass-green knobby silk and a slimmer line, pleated skirt with just a slip. I hate those blasted crinolines! They're so impractical and always getting stuck in the door. I added a matching hat; small-brimmed and tasteful, with one dark green bow in back. Stepping into the church quietly, I took a seat near the end of the second pew. Within a few minutes, as the church began to fill, I found myself continuously being prompted to move time and time again. It appeared I was consistently sitting in someone else's favorite spot. As I moved, I could see the women's hot eyes judging my outfit negatively. This was likely because wearing a slim-line skirt is generally only seen as fashionable for city women who work.

At last, I gave up and stood in the back corner. Only two or three women in their crinolines could fit on each pew with their companions. This meant that by the time the minister walked in from the side door, every pew was full to overflowing. Not having a hymnal, I hummed along as best I could in the corner, trying to participate without drawing attention to myself. Alas, my efforts were unsuccessful. When the minister motioned for the congregation to be seated following the hymn, I found myself without a place. Rather than ask if anyone could make room, the minister cleared his throat loudly and pointed at the back door. Not wanting to make a scene, I obediently moved out the door as directed. Every adult eye in the place focused on me, full of disapproval, as if I were an unruly child.

There were benches outside for the purpose of seating latecomers , facing back through the windows toward the pulpit. With these windows open, I had a clear view of the minister. When he next expelled a boy, for shuffling his legs and accidentally kicking the back of the pew in front of him, I was happy to have a companion outside. I say *boy*, but as he straightened to full height, I reconsidered my assumption.

He was enormous! He was over six feet tall, and had a broad, strong-featured face that, if it weren't covered in freckles, would easily pass for a grown man's. He was heavy-set and muscular for his age too, even though he still seemed young. His skin was unusually pale, and he had an unruly mop of thick, dark curly hair that stuck out in every direction. On his way out of the sanctuary, he stepped on at least half a dozen feet. When he sat down, I judged his boots to be almost twice the size of mine. Although he tried to act as if he were paying attention to the sermon, I could see him studying me from the corner of his eye. Finally, he couldn't stand it anymore, and whispered, "What did you do to get put out here?"

Seeing the minister watching me through the window, I carefully held the boy's gaze while I pulled a small notebook out of my bag. I pretended to be copying down the words of his sermon. In reality, I was writing the boy a note, which said, "I'm not sure. Perhaps it's because I don't fit into any of the pews. I'm the new teacher at the school down the street. Would you like to come? I start enrolling students tomorrow."

As soon as the minister's gaze was averted, I passed it to the boy. He took it eagerly. When he opened it in his lap, below the viewing level of the windowsill, I could tell he was pretending. He held the note upside down. I should have known better than to assume he could read. Regardless, he seemed eager to gain my favor. He refolded my note and put it into the back pocket of his britches. Then, he beamed at me so emphatically the minister called to him from the pulpit.

"A bit more reverence, Master Mooney. I can still see you out there on the porch!"

From the second pew where I had initially sat, I saw an entire family of faces turn in our direction. They were all sandier-haired variants of young Mooney beside me. The woman, in my former seat, was extremely tall as well, but rail-thin with a severe aquiline nose. She pursed her lips together in a hard line, and made as if to rise. Her husband motioned her down. I could see their children, seated in a row like stair steps. Their eyes sparkled with mischief as to what might happen to their brother next. Slowly, other congregants turned, until every eye in the place was fixed on the boy who sat on the pew to the right of the porch entrance. At first, he resolutely stared at the whitewashed wooden walls of the church's exterior. As the seconds ticked away, he ultimately lowered his gaze to the floor and closed his eyes as if meditating. This action seemed to have satisfied the minister, who continued his sermon. Ironically enough, the message was about Jesus suffering the little children to come unto him.

Not wanting to cause the boy any more trouble, I made no attempts to divert his attention further. Instead, I studied him as he had studied me. Even though his facial features were similar to those of his equally pale-but-freckled siblings, his hair and eyes set him apart. His eyes were round and so black you couldn't tell where iris ended and pupil began. They were set rather deep into his face too, under thick black brows that were very heavy for his age, on either side of a wide, pug nose. He would grow up to be a very stout man with that bone structure, I thought. Eventually, he opened his eyes, which though dark glowed with hatred. Not just at the minister himself, but also at the backs of his family in the second pew. The darkness bothered me. Having spent a lifetime observing children, I only know of one source from whence it comes, and it is never from the child himself.

Hours later, long after my legs had gone to sleep and so had I, sitting there in the warm sun like a cat, I awakened from my daze as the congregation began to file out. Stationing myself by the bottom of the stairs and digging out the leaflets we'd been given to advertise the school out of my bag, I motioned for the boy to stand beside me. He stumbled over, tripping on a loose board, and I held out a handful of leaflets to him. He looked at them warily. "What are they for?"

I had to make him admit it, even though I hated to. I needed to get it out of the way. "They're for the new school opening down the street in a couple of weeks. I'm Mae Ulrich, and I'm going to be the teacher there."

Stepping closer to him, I stood on tiptoe to whisper in his ear, "It's okay. I know you can't read them yet. But you will, soon enough. That's what the school is for, to teach you." He looked skeptical, but took the leaflets I offered him anyway. They looked extremely small in his massive, thick fingered paws.

As the families passed us, I began to notice the mothers, fathers, and even the children would accept the leaflets from me, but not from young Mooney. His face returned to its former hard look. Time after time, he extended his hand with a leaflet to someone, and they turned away from him to take one from me. Although I was heartened by how many families were interested in signing their children up for school, it disturbed me how they ignored the boy. It seemed especially ridiculous, because at his size it was like ignoring an elephant.

The boy's family were among the last to leave. I thought I'd see if I could get it out of them why he was treated so. However, they did the same, walking right past his outstretched hand as if he weren't there. The father, plump, pink, and round when standing, led the rest of the family. His walk was labored and waddling. The rest of their tow-headed brood followed behind like ducklings. The mother lingered to speak with me about her other children. She seemed interested in the prospect of their attending, but when I asked if Mooney would be joining us, she shook her head.

"No, no... I don't think so. Not Jonah," she murmured, acknowledging his presence at last. Then softly, although not quiet enough for him not to overhear, she said, "Not too bright, that one. He was my poor sister's boy. We've tried to teach him, but he gets everything all jumbled up. Clumsy too. He'll turn out alright, with a bit of discipline. Strong build, like his father. Shouldn't have any trouble finding labor work. Hopefully," she glanced back, where Jonah remained stony-faced, sensing we were discussing him, "he doesn't have the same temperament."

Seeing the boy disguising his shame again, I couldn't resist pressing on with a lie. "We've been given special training at the Institute for more challenging pupils. Could you perhaps think about letting me have a try with Jonah? Some of the new methods might help."

"Perhaps," she said, dismissively. "If you'd like an experiment. Certainly nothing to lose there." Jonah's aunt laughed a high, false laugh, and excused herself to scurry after her husband. Jonah faced me, once again with his eyes closed. I decided the direct approach would be best.

"Well, Jonah, I've heard what your aunt thinks. Now what about you?"

He opened his dark eyes and stared at me, clearly puzzled. "About what?"

"About *school?*" I said, leaning on the word. "You *do* want to learn how to read, don't you? I can teach you. I've never failed to teach any of my students. A lot of them looked far dumber than you. Some smarter, but *many* dumber." I puffed out my cheeks and went cross-eyed as I said *dumber* a second time. "I mean, can you imagine? Some even look like this!" Bowing my legs, I waddled, duck-like, as I'd seen Jonah's uncle do only moments before. He caught the reference, and started giggling, then clamped a hand over his mouth. I got closer and elbowed him in the ribs. "C'mon... what do you say?"

"Like, now?"

"Well, I was thinking about in two weeks, but if you want a little head start, maybe yes... now. What other pressing appointments do you have this afternoon?"

"None," Jonah said. "I usually just go out and kick around by myself on Sunday afternoons. Ride my horse. Stuff like that."

"Well, I have a horse. Perhaps we could ride together. Why don't you run home and tell your aunt I'm asking her permission to start tutoring you ahead of time, so you'll be up to speed. Do you see that building down there at the end of the street?" Jonah looked where I was pointing and nodded. "Ride down there and knock when you're ready. I'll be inside pulling some things out of the stacks for you."

Jonah stared at me in disbelief until I shooed him away. Walking back to the school, it occurred to me Jonah was probably so eager for my company because he was like Penny. A child constantly around adults, but remained virtually invisible to them.

I'd barely had time to get back to the schoolhouse and open my book trunk when Jonah came galloping up on an enormous black horse with great, shaggy feet. Its mane was so shiny, the animal positively glistened in the sunlight.

"That's some horse you have there," I said, sitting down next to the stack I'd pulled out.

Jonah beamed. "Sir Gawain is the best horse ever! Isn't his coat fantastic? He knows his name too. Comes right to me the moment I call him, every time, no matter what. And you should see me make him jump!" He wheeled the young stallion around in a circle so I could see the horse's powerful legs at full advantage.

"Can't wait!" I said, trying to match his level of excitement. Actually, I was curious about seeing the two of them jump. It would probably cause an earthquake! Still, I was almost as happy as he was to have someone enthusiastic to talk to. Almost but, not quite.

Turning back to my trunk, I pulled out a book. "Should we begin with *Sir Gawain and the Green Knight* first then?"

A cloud passed briefly over Jonah's face, like rain through a summer day. Then he brightened. "Sure. I know that one by heart. It's my favorite."

"Have you read all the King Arthur tales?" I asked, only realizing I'd misspoken after the words came out of my mouth.

"Well, um... not exactly. But I *know* them. My Mom read them to me."

"I see," I said, wanting to ask the next natural question, but hesitant. Jonah saved me by volunteering the information.

"It's okay to ask. Everyone here in town already knows, but they don't talk about it. She's dead. My Pop killed her. He was drunk, and they were arguing over his leaving the bank with my uncle and going out to the mine. She didn't want him to go."

"Oh, Jonah, I am so sorry!"

"It's okay. I mean," Jonah stammered around, "it is and it isn't. It happened a few months ago. I saw it happen, but like I said, I'm not supposed to talk about it with anybody. He backhanded her real hard and she hit her head. They'd fought like cats that way for years and years. He was a pretty mean drunk always. Mom stayed with him because he had money. He and my uncle were—are—partners at the bank here in town. The thinking is that if Pop can be in on the mine from the very beginning, they can make a fortune off it. He's a pretty tough guy, so he stays down there, watching so that no gold gets skimmed before it's brought in. Uncle Sam stays here to mind the bank in town. Nobody says anything about Mom. Everyone knows, but..." Jonah shrugged resignedly, "everybody wants to get rich. They know Pop and Uncle Sam can make it happen. Only reason I told you is 'cause you'd find out anyway. I didn't want you to think I was touched in the head or anything, because my Aunt Ida and Uncle Sam don't like me."

I winced at the matter-of-fact tone with which Jonah admitted he knew his aunt and uncle didn't care for him. Then, I asked Jonah if his own father had ever hit him.

"When I was little, before I learned how to get out of the way, yeah," Jonah replied. "I learned pretty quickly to stay gone when Pop was drunk. It's easier than you'd think, especially because Mom was always willing to duke it out with him. She didn't drink at all. Aunt Ida doesn't either. Pop would come home from the bank drunk. Mama would start preaching at him, and they'd have a row. She was a good mother otherwise and I miss her tons, but..." Jonah paused here again searching for the right way to say it without seeming disrespectful, "she could have saved herself maybe if she'd spent less time on the Bible and more like I did. Finding ways to stay out of Pop's way."

I'd been putting my saddle on Cressida as Jonah explained all this. Partly it was my effort to let him tell his story without being stared at. He seemed to have the most to say when left to talk to the air, and I could tell he needed to get it out. Having already changed into my bloomers and riding jumper, I swung up onto Cressida's back. As we turned the horses toward the path out of town, I changed the subject. "So, how did you get Sir Gawain?"

"Oh," Jonah said, patting the stallion reassuringly on the side of its neck. He came back into conversational consciousness and made eye contact. "Uncle Sam and Aunt Ida gave him to me when I came to live with them a few months ago. Like I said, they're really good people. It's not that they don't dislike me that badly. It's just that... well... they're scared."

"Of your father?"

"Yeah, I guess. That as I get older, I'll be like Pop. I look like him, before he got really fat and sick, I mean. From drinking too much. I'm taller than he was though, like Mom. Everyone says I'll end up really big." Jonah stretched out his arms. I had to steer Cressida away a few steps. He mumbled sorry for bumping into her, and slouched back down.

Jonah slouches *a lot*, which I realized as I slowly began to notice other things about him. I couldn't help it. I had been trying so hard not to stare at Jonah so he wouldn't feel self-conscious as he was getting his history off his chest. At last, I knew why he looked so familiar, even though I hadn't met him before. His stocky frame. The dark curly hair. That pug nose. I studied Jonah's nose and thought about what it might look like after a lifetime of heavy drinking. I had to ask. "Jonah, does your father have a big nose? Red and bulbous looking, the kind people call gin blossoms?"

"Yeah, how did you know?" Jonah said, puzzled. "Did you see him on the way into town?"

"You could say so," I replied, already lost in thought. "Why don't you narrate the story of Sir Gawain for me as we ride around a bit. When we stop, I want to show you a little technique we call a read-along to see if we can figure out what's holding you up in progressing with literacy. Okay?" Jonah agreed. As we began our loop of town, I only half listened to his near-perfect word-for-word recitation of Sir Gawain's tale, complete with alliterative verse.

All I could think about was how sure I was the big-nosed man I had seen my wolf kill last night must have been Jonah's father.

I have a hard time believing it to be true. Because that would mean my wolf isn't just a symbol in a dream at all. It would mean he's a real wolf. Or a wolf man. A *loup garou*.

However, if *that* is true too, then what in the name of Hell were those other creatures?

August 16, 1858

I 'm so glad that Cawdor came back into town from hunting today. He really helped to put my mind at ease about the connection between Jonah's appearance and his coincidental resemblance to one of the men killed in my dream. Turns out, I might be a bit more clairvoyant than I've previously realized, but there don't seem to be any strange beasts roaming the mountains. At least, not of the inhuman kind. More on that in a few moments.

When we got back to the schoolhouse Sunday evening after our ride, it took me all of fifteen minutes to figure out what was wrong with Jonah's reading. The poor boy needs glasses. He's so nearsighted he can't see the type in a book unless it's about three inches from his face. His word recognition is poor for his age, which is to be expected considering he can't see without practically resting his nose on the page. But as soon as I give him a magnifying glass or write a word enormously large on the chalkboard, he grasps it right away. It'll be a struggle for a few months, maybe a year, as he gets up to speed. He's eager to learn, and I feel confident he'll catch up quickly.

"Why didn't you tell anyone you couldn't see the words?" I asked.

Jonah looked confused, "How could I? Mom read to me when I was little. When it was my turn to follow along, I couldn't see anything but little squiggles on the page. If I tried to get closer, she'd push me back and say that wasn't the way people were supposed to read. I was supposed to sit up straight, not all hunched over. I just gave up and listened closely, so that I could pretend I'd learned to read by just holding the book and reciting it back. She didn't catch on until later. She just thought I was slow. I didn't want to cause her any more problems. I thought she had enough to handle, and I knew Pop wouldn't want to spend money on glasses."

Shocked by Jonah's crippling politeness, I wrote out a lengthy note explaining the situation to his Aunt Ida. I hoped she would find it reassuring. "I'm telling your aunt she needs to take you somewhere to buy some glasses before school starts. Do you know whether they have an optometrist in Bent's Fort?" Jonah shrugged. I rolled my eyes at my own stupidity. "Of course you wouldn't. If no one in your family wears glasses and you can't see the blasted signs, how could you know?" I folded the note over and handed it to him, along with the copy of Sir Gawain, a blank copybook, and the magnifying glass. "I'll ask around and find out, so you don't have to waste a trip. In the meantime, use the glass to start copying out Sir Gawain line for line. You'll need to work on your penmanship too, I'm sure. It should give you good practice since you already know the story by heart. Copy out the first thousand or so words. When you're done, bring them back to me and we'll discuss how you can improve."

I've never seen a student so eager to have a copying assignment in my entire career! Jonah wrapped his big arms around me in a bear hug, lifting me off the ground. Then he tore off toward his horse. He galloped home bursting with the news that he wasn't stupid after all, just nearly blind. Which is really sad, if I think about it; the fact that even Jonah's mother, before she died, never did anything to help him with his vision. I have no doubt Jonah will end up being one of my best students now he's been given this little boost of confidence. Sometimes that's all it takes for a child—someone to care. That's the best part about being a teacher, in my opinion. The ability to be that person for someone else.

After Jonah left, I spent the rest of last night uneventfully planning lessons. I've used the better part of today filling out paperwork for the steady stream of parents who stopped by to sign their students up for school. It appears my little trip to church yesterday worked. Even if they aren't willing to give up their chosen pews, the parents of Auraria seem quite ready to hand over their children to my tutelage. I'm hoping that means they're enthusiastic for their children to begin their education, and not that they'd prefer to have them away from the house and out from underfoot. We shall see.

Regardless, when the benches are done, we should have seating capacity for up to fifty pupils. Getting three dozen signed up on the first day is really encouraging. I haven't yet tried the Ute or Navajo villages nearby to see if they have any children who might be interested in an American-style education. That is half the purpose of why I'm here. If I can get as good of a response from those families, I should have a full school by September! Maybe even enough to send for a second teacher! That would be wonderful, not having to manage alone.

Glancing at my little rose-gold watch as the sun set, it was already past eight o'clock. If I wanted a meal from the saloon, I knew I had better hustle. Locking up the schoolhouse, I hurried down and managed to get the last plate of corned beef and cabbage for the evening boxed to take back to the schoolhouse. When I got there, a familiar horse was tied up next to Cressida.

"Cawdor!" I exclaimed, excited to share my triumph of enrollment as I saw him walking around the corner of the building. "Guess how many students I picked up on the first day?"

Then, I stopped. Something was clearly wrong. "Mae, we need to go inside," he said. "I have to tell you something very important." I started to ask what had happened, but he waved me off. "Not here. Wait until we get inside. No offense, but you're pretty loud. I don't want anyone to hear."

Overlooking the remark about my volume, which everyone always chastises me about, I quickly unlocked the door and let us both inside. Cawdor insisted I lock it behind us. He seated himself in the back center of the room on a pile of lumber between the chalkboard and stove, so as to be difficult to see from the windows. Wondering what all the secrecy was about, I sat my dinner box down and joined him.

"What I am about to tell you, you cannot tell a soul until the official announcement is made. Agreed?" I consented, and Cawdor continued.

"There's been an attack at the mine. Four men were killed. All white miners associated with the Russell Company. One of them was a banker here in town."

"Oh my God," I exhaled, remembering my realization with Jonah. "Was one of them named Mooney? Fat, curly-haired fellow? Always drunk?"

He eyed me suspiciously. "Yes. He was the bank's partner overseeing their investment in Russell's operation. There's a rumor it was an Indian attack, but no one's been able to find the bodies. A lot of blood, and items belonging to the four men missing were found at the encampment, but nothing else. Not a trace. They're going to have a special meeting of the town council tomorrow night about what the next steps should be. They will decide whether I am to be sent as a liaison between the Russell company and the town to meet with the Ute, Navajo, Cheyenne, and Arapaho leaders."

"Do you think it could have been one of the local tribes?" I asked.

"No," Cawdor replied. "Most likely I think it was a rival mining group. A lot of people are starting to come out here. Now that word has gotten back East, many are desperate to be the first to stake their claims. How desperate they are remains to be seen. Enough to kill four men and make it look like they disappeared?" He shrugged, "Maybe. I've known a lot of men in my lifetime who wouldn't think twice about killing to make a fortune."

"What happens if the Russell Company blames the Indians anyway? Without any proof? Will there be..." Cawdor cut me off, shook his head, and rose to go.

"That's what I'm afraid of," he said. "Russell's company has been itching to get their hands on the land, but the tribal council isn't budging. They know there's a lot of gold there too, they just don't have the financial backing or the equipment to extract it. But the entrance *is* on Ute land, and there's no telling how far or deep into other tribal lands the vein might extend. Legally, Russell can't just take it. He has to negotiate a deal and pay them their share, however much that is that they finally agree to. Unless..."

It was my turn to interrupt. "Unless he has some reason to prove they are all bloodthirsty killers. He would be able to justify attacking to force them off the land. After that, Russell and his men could just move in and take it all for themselves."

"And the military would back them up." Cawdor said, pacing back and forth across the floor. "Which is why I had to get back here and tell you as quickly as I could. If we can't get this situation straightened out soon, and without the whole town knowing about it, I'm afraid you're going to have a really tough time. Getting Auraria parents to believe their children should be shoulder to shoulder in this room with native children whose parents might be dangerous murderers would be impossible."

Exchanging goodbyes, Cawdor rushed off. He vowed to return tomorrow to help with getting our construction projects started. I settled down to my corned beef and cabbage, which was cold.

What Cawdor said about the murders makes sense, in light of my dream. I've always been interested in Spiritualism, both real and as an exposer of fakes. It seems only natural to me that, now that I am out here in the unspoiled air, something as tragic as a quadruple homicide would resonate in my second sight. It also makes sense my mind would interpret such a resonant signal as being the product of inhuman beasts, as I attempted to come to grips with witnessing the horrific event from afar. Although I am comforted by this new revelation, which seems to point back toward my mind's use of spiritual symbols as a coping mechanism, I am more disturbed by what might happen as a result of the killings.

Will the white families in Auraria, all of whom have some kind of connection to the Russell mining mission, withdraw their children from the school if I continue with the rest of my plan to try to recruit native children? Or will they perform some other kind of silent, stonewalling protest? That is what they did around the secret of Jonah's mother's death. A history of circling the wagons to protect their own financial interests precedes them.

Only time will tell. Perhaps the only good news to come from today is that one thing is certain. Jonah Mooney won't have to live in fear of his father ever again.

August 17, 1858

True to his promise, Cawdor arrived bright and early this morning as I was preparing my eggs and toast. Claiming he'd already eaten, he refused my offer of coffee. He waited patiently, studying the furniture plans, as I finished mine. While I was putting the breakfast things away, I heard the heavy hoof beats of another horse galloping up. Then, a thundering series of bangs on the door.

"What on Earth?" exclaimed Cawdor, dropping the plans. However, I was not surprised to see who it was when I let him in.

"Howdy, Miss Ulrich!" said Jonah. He fell through the entryway, tripping over a small crate of nails I'd been using as a doorstop. Righting himself, he tipped his hat to Cawdor, who glanced over at me in disbelief.

"Seamus Mooney's boy," Cawdor said, extending his hand for Jonah to shake. To me, he gave a quick glance with a clear meaning. *Say nothing.* "Good to see you again. Are you planning on coming to school here with Miss Ulrich?"

"Already started," beamed Jonah, pulling the copy book out of his back pocket. "I've already finished them first thousand words, Miss Ulrich. Stayed up all night, and got them done. What's next?"

"Well..." I said, glancing around the room. "I can give you another assignment this evening. For the moment, how are you at carpentry?"

"Aw, real good!" Jonah said. "I can build all kinds of things. I hung around with Pop's handyman, Mr. McEntire, a bunch. What do you need? Fence? Sawhorses?"

"Ever made any benches?" Cawdor asked.

"No sir, but I can probably figure it out. Do you got any plans?"

Cawdor handed the plans to Jonah, who held them right at the end of his nose. The paper rustled from the closeness of his breath as he spoke.

"Aw, these ain't that complicated. The way they're joining them makes a lot of extra cuts, with all that dovetailing. Simple nailing would be easier. I can help you put them together that way, and they'll be just as sturdy, but maybe not as fancy. How fast do you need them?"

"School starts September 1st," I said. Jonah whistled, pushing his hat back on his head like an old man. "Plus, I also have to put together a desk downstairs, and some kind of bed for the loft, so I'm at least off the floor when it gets cold. It's a lot of work. And remember..." I said, pointing at Jonah jokingly. "I'm going to lose my foreman for at least 8-10 days while he goes to see the optometrist."

"Yep, yep, yep," Jonah said, surveying the room. Then he stopped, my comment about the optometrist finally registering. "Aw, we won't worry about that part for a while, Miss Ulrich. Uncle Sam said to tell you there is an optometrist he knows in Bent's, but since he's not going to be down there again 'til October, those glasses will have to wait. So, I've got plenty of time to get the work done."

"No, I'm afraid that won't do," I said. "I can find other help for the benches, but you're going to have glasses before September, even if I have to take you there myself."

"Actually," said Cawdor, "I'm heading that way later this week. Have to talk to the tribal council for that thing we discussed. I'm coming right back. I'd be happy to have him ride along with me." Cawdor gestured to Jonah for his opinion, to which he surprised me by being more reluctant than I'd anticipated.

"Well, thank you Mr. Cawdor, but there's so much to get done here," Jonah said, looking around the room again. "I mean, a bed and a desk, that'll take at least one full day by itself. And the benches... the longest part is the sawing and fitting. After that, they just join together pretty quick, like a fence. All the measuring and cutting though, that could take several days."

"How long would it take one woman," I asked, "to do all of the measuring and cutting by herself with the proper instructions?"

"At least a week," said Cawdor, catching my drift. "We could do the harder parts together today, that bed and desk, and leave you with the materials and instructions to cut up the wood for the benches while we're gone. That is," his green eyes twinkled at me, "if you're not afraid of messing up your hands."

"Please," I replied, holding up my hands. "No one is going to be interested in looking at these for at least a year. I think I can afford to buy a pot of callus cream to get them back smooth by then."

"Alright," Cawdor slapped Jonah on the back. "You heard the lady. Let's get to it. We can get those first two pieces knocked out by dinnertime. Then help her mark everything off to work on while we're away getting your glasses. How's that sound?"

Jonah looked as if he didn't know what to do. He kept glancing back and forth between Cawdor and me as if we were speaking some foreign language. Clearly, he wasn't used to adults treating him as if he was someone sensible enough to be listened to, let alone collaborated with.

Hoping to give him a task so that he had a little time to recover, I asked, "Jonah, do you think Mr. McEntire has any sawhorses we could borrow? Could you go ask while we lay everything out to get started?" Jonah stammered something like a *yes*, and stumbled out the door and down the steps, before galloping away on Sir Gawain at top speed.

Cawdor grinned at me. The old, pointy-toothed grin. "I think you just made that boy's day. Possibly his year."

"Hopefully, his lifetime," I said, sighing and picking up the plans. "I'm sure you know all about his family?"

"Of course," replied Cawdor, coming closer to look over my shoulder. I could feel the warmth of his body brush beside me. He wasn't as gaunt as he had been before the hunt. The muscles of his chest were more pronounced and his angular face was filled out more attractively. Cawdor reached for the plans and turned away. "It's the worst kept secret in town. Jonah's a good boy. Considering his situation, that's nothing short of a miracle. How'd you meet him?"

"Church," I said, to which Cawdor cackled loudly. "What?" I continued. "I'm recruiting students. It was a professional necessity."

"I bet," he replied, wryly. "Are you planning to try visiting the Ute and Navajo villages too? For recruitment?"

"Of course," I said, slightly indignant. "I believe it would serve all my students to learn how to get along with one another in one classroom. We're all new here, right? Except for the Indians? Perhaps this could be a fresh start where we finally get it right."

"Mmm hmm," Cawdor murmured, not looking up from the plans. "You're a dreamer, Mae Ulrich. May you always dream." He gestured broadly toward the ceiling and the sky above it, in a mocking way. "In the meantime, would you like to come to the Auraria town council meeting tonight? You might not grasp all the ins and outs of local politics, but I can fill you in. I think it will give you quite a few," here Cawdor paused, squinting, "important insights as to the real state of white and native relations around these parts. For future reference in your student recruiting efforts, of course."

"Of course," I replied, snippily snatching the plans back. I didn't care for his condescending manner. Did he think I don't *know* that white settlers and natives don't get along? Pfft! Why did he think I took the job?

"Perhaps all they need is a little re-education on what it means to be an American."

"Oh, don't worry," Cawdor said, as we heard the heavy hoofbeats of Sir Gawain approaching again. "Out here, you'll learn everything you need to know about what it *really* means to be an American."

August 18, 1858

Today, I have two kinds of news—good and bad.

Good news is that, after the diligent efforts of Jonah, Cawdor, and myself yesterday, I am now sleeping on a freshly built "real" bed and writing on a "real" desk for the first time since leaving Bent's Fort. We made a lot of headway on the student seating too. All that remains is for me to mark and saw the wood into pieces for the benches. Cawdor and Jonah will finish the nailing and gluing after they come back.

Bad news is that, after last night's town council meeting, it seems convincing the families of white and native students to be in the same room with one another might be much more difficult than previously thought.

After we'd finished our construction activities for the day, I changed into a fresh dress and rode down with Cawdor to the council meeting. It was held in the courthouse next to the jail. Cawdor advised it was best we entered from separate ways, so I "didn't receive any negative associations" by being seen with him. Normally, I would think this was complete balderdash. But given the fact I've only been here a few days and already ascertained I am the only unmarried woman over eighteen in town, it was probably for the best.

The meeting itself, if you could call it that, was a disaster. In fact, it was more of a brawl. At least, in the second phase. There was a first phase, in which some kiss-up local government officials proposed changing the name of Auraria to Denver, to honor of the local territorial governor. That part was extremely boring. Next, someone else stood up and said something about how Auraria should keep its current name in honor of a gold mining town of the same name in Georgia, and why that name was superior. Then, a lot of bickering back and forth ensued about which sites would be better or worse for the planning of streets. At which time I totally lost interest. The ins and outs of city planning have never held much appeal for me.

Finally, it was time to address the killings at the mine. Since it was at last Cawdor's turn to speak on behalf of the native tribes in the area, my ears pricked up. To my knowledge (or at least according to what I had "seen" within the metaphorical context of my dream) Cawdor gave a fairly accurate account of how the men died. In short, they were attacked by a group of unknown assailants and had not been seen or heard from again. Their tools were abandoned in place, and there was no evidence of any gold being stolen.

After much murmuring and speculation, a tall, slender man in an embroidered waistcoat stood up. I recognized him from the group of men with whom Julia Holmes had been holding court back at Bent's Fort. Introducing himself as Lawrence, he spoke in a formal tone. "I would like to go on record as saying the Lawrence Party had no part in these killings whatsoever. We are encamped a little further down in the Dry Creek area. We have seen no bands of Indians moving near either mining operation. Nevertheless, I have heard tell of a band of eighty to a hundred men who claimed to be miners heading out this way. They robbed and killed the shopkeeper of a general store on the Smoky Hill Route recently. I wouldn't put it past a few in that group to have been the culprits. People are getting desperate now that gold's been struck. But," he pointed a finger at Jonah's Aunt Ida, who was taking down meeting notes, "make sure the record states the Lawrence Party had nothing to do with it and we do not stand behind any implication of the native tribes in the area either." Clearing his throat with a few satisfied dry coughs after having spoken his piece, Lawrence sat down.

The room buzzed with rumors. This time the speculation was wilder. The most disturbing story I heard was about a couple of men called the Blue Brothers. They ate a man they'd been traveling with after being stranded without food on the way out to the mines. Considering that was just one of several cannibalism accounts I've heard since starting my journey, I'd have to agree with Lawrence's assertion that things are becoming desperate. It's especially troubling, considering the area has scarcely a hundred people in it!

My conjecture as to what wild things might yet come was interrupted by the hems and haws of Green Russell. He spoke up next, in a Georgia accent as thick and greasy as half-melted butter. "I appreciate your concern, Mr. Lawrence. Even if I do wonder why you are keeping your eyes so closely glued on my operation that you seem to be aware of all comings and goings there. The fact of the matter is that I'm now down by three men, which brings the remaining number of my party to ten. Lawrence, I am not accusing you or your men of anything. I think you are a civilized and sensible fellow. When the time comes for us to talk through the business of whose claims are to end once we've figured out the true lay of this vein of gold we both have our noses to, we'll be able to do it. *However...*" he leaned on the word as he moved out from the pew in which he had been sitting.

Stepping into the center aisle, he fluffed himself up like a preacher about to address a congregation. "I do not believe this was a random act of violence perpetrated by a random gang of cannibals." Russell whiffled his fingers through the air. On each stubby digit, I could see a gold ring. "No sir. I believe this was a deliberate act by the local native tribesmen to intimidate us to the negotiation table. It's extortion. Give us our share when we ask for it and we will continue to allow you to work your mines on *our lands.*" Here, Russell raised his hands to indicate mock quotation marks. "*But I've got news for them.*" He bared down on each word with force, punctuating them with jabs of his bejeweled index finger.

Scanning the crowd for Cawdor, Russell found him. His accent growing thicker and louder with agitation, Russell yelled over the crowd. "You go back, Cawdor, and tell all these chiefs whoever-they-are that this is the United States of America. When *real* Americans stake their claim on the soil of an *American* territory, it is *ours!* There *ain't* no runnin' us off, and there *ain't* no negotiation. Ain't none of them Indians really from 'round here. They're all moved here from somewhere else we done run 'em off from. So, in my opinion, they can just *keep on runnin'.*"

Cawdor sat watching his uncle fume with an almost deathlike stillness. He did not rise when Russell spoke. Instead, Cawdor said simply from his seat, "Mr. Russell, you are just as aware as I am the Utes have been in this area for thousands of years. So have the Navajo. The Cheyenne and Arapaho, although nomadic, have considered these lands part of their hunting grounds for almost as long. So these *are* their lands. And there *will* be a negotiation, or we *will* go to court over it. All the way to the Supreme Court if we have to."

Russell burst out in a fit of laughter so hard that tears ran down his face. Mopping them away with his pocket square, he shook the cloth at Cawdor and then gestured to the crowd. "Listen to this one, will you! He should know better than anybody what happens when Indians try to take their case to the Supreme Court about who land belongs to when there's gold under it! *Boy*, the Supreme Court not only gave the Cherokees' gold to the Great State of Georgia, but then they called in the Army. Then, the Army pushed those Cherokee off that land nearly all the way out here! Why else in God's name do you think we'd all be here right now?"

He gestured back to the pew filled with his fellow Georgians, some white, but others either pure Cherokee or mixed. Russell's laughing fit was over. His face began to flush to a dark crimson. "Some of your people have wised up and decided to join me for what I say is their fair share. And if all the other Indians around here want to get anything out of this mine, then they'd better give up on all this high-handed horseshit of sending their little negotiator out here to try to work me over." Russell put his hands on his hips, displaying two long-barreled pistols with pearl grips. The belt circling his broad midsection was spiked with silver bullets. "Because *boy,* I know who *you* are, and I know who *they* are. But even more than that, I know this is *my* turn. Goddamn it! *Mine*! And there ain't but *one* way all this is gonna work out."

Russell stood sweating and glaring at Cawdor, waiting for him to respond. Cawdor stared at his uncle for a long time. Finally, Cawdor put on his hat and walked toward the back door.

"Ain't you gonna say nothin'?" Russell jeered.

"What is there to say?" shrugged Cawdor. "When you have made it so clear the negotiations are over." Then, he smiled at Russell. That long-toothed, sly smile, and left.

Afterward, there was a period of intense chatter. The remaining crowd voiced a generalized acceptance that Russell's men had indeed been murdered by Indians. They claimed everyone needed to be especially vigilant, because who knew what might happen next. Then the meeting settled back into boring talk of grain supplies for the coming winter, the new stagecoach road one of Russell's cousins from back East was building, and other matters about which I had no knowledge or care. At the earliest moment in which I could leave without attracting suspicion, I snuck out the back door. Cawdor was waiting for me. He was already seated on Troy's back, clearly in a hurry to leave. Swinging up onto Cressida, I followed him onto the road leading south out of town.

"I'm going back tonight to tell the elders' council there isn't any use trying to pursue the negotiations further. Russell isn't going to listen. We're going to have to retain legal counsel, and we need to do it fast. If we don't file suit to stop Russell's operation before winter hits," Cawdor looked out over the horizon, "this whole valley will be filled with thousands more just like him come spring. We'll have lost our chance."

"As much as I hate to say it, isn't Russell right though? About Indians going to Court? The Cherokee didn't win in the end. They were pushed off their land and their gold was taken. *The end.* You told me that yourself. There has to be another way." I insisted.

Cawdor swallowed heavily and the muscles of his jaw tightened. "Yes, there is another way. It won't stop them forever though. Nothing will. You and I both know that. They just keep coming, and coming, and coming, and they take, and they take, and they take. We've already been pushed from sea to shining sea. Pretty soon, we're going to run out of unwanted parts of America for them to push us on to. There's only one thing left to do now."

"You have to push back," I said. "I know it's going to sound stupid and presumptuous, because I know there's no way I can ever feel it as deeply as you do, but *I do* feel it. Just as sure as old fishermen know when there is a storm coming, I can feel it. Almost as clearly as if I'm seeing it before it happens. Like that dream I was telling you about before..."

Cawdor pulled Troy up short and looked at me. "I have to tell you something. I don't like lying to anyone, but to you especially, and a half truth is as bad as a lie. That dream you had." He paused, clearly struggling with himself about what to say next. "I had that dream too. The one we talked about in the cave. Only, no, that's not right either. Damn it!" Cawdor wheeled Troy around in frustration. The horse pawed the ground. He could clearly sense Cawdor's anxiety building. "Come here!" Cawdor pointed for me to pull Cressida up right beside him. "Now, look at me. Really, really look hard. Then close your eyes and tell me what you see."

I did as he instructed. I looked straight into his pale green eyes, and I saw them begin to glow. A soft golden light at first. Then brighter and brighter, until it was almost painful, like staring into polished brass turned to reflect the sun. I had to shut my eyes. When I did, I saw it! The world of my dreams. Only I wasn't watching it from my own perspective, as I had been in my sleep. I was watching it through the eyes of the wolf. My wolf! My wolf who was...

"It's you! You are my..."

Cawdor looked so happy that he could almost cry. "You've finally got it! Everything that you have dreamed, I have dreamed. What you are seeing is what I see. Do you understand what that means?" He quickly answered himself. "Don't tell me. All I need to know is that you know. And now I do too. Once you've seen it—really seen it—you can't deny it. There is only one possible explanation."

"But that's madness!"

Cawdor grinned, "The only madness in the world is denying what you know to be true. And this is the truth. Trust it, Mae. Trust your dreams. All of them. Every part is true."

And with that, Cawdor rode away, leaving me to ponder the truth.

Which keeps pointing me back to one impossible, yet undeniable, direction.

What I am dreaming are not my own dreams. They are Cawdor's thoughts.

Also, somehow, my thoughts are written in some kind of spiritual metaphor.

Cawdor is my wolf, and my wolf is me.

August 19, 1858

T his morning, Cawdor took Jonah with him to the tribal council meeting. Afterward, they'll continue onto Bent's Fort and have some glasses made for Jonah before school begins. Jonah is of course thrilled to have the attention. Cawdor seems to have taken a liking to the boy as well. Good thing, since when I asked Jonah whether he'd asked his aunt and uncle if they were okay with him going on a week's journey with someone they didn't know, he just shrugged. He said it wouldn't matter. They never cared when he came or went.

I find this incredibly sad. Not only because Jonah's such a sweet young man, but also because his real parents did the same thing. Sad, and a little bit dangerous. As much as I hate to admit it, there is some legitimacy to his aunt and uncle's worry that Jonah might grow up to be as violent as his father. The resentment smoldering beneath his almost-too-eager-to-please demeanor could easily burst into a wildfire of rage if left unchecked. At Jonah's size and strength, it could be deadly.

After they left, I pondered how best to approach the tribal leaders myself, in hopes of winning over a few native students. Cawdor advised against it completely. However, half of my reason for coming out to the far side of the world was to create an environment in which the children of both natives and settlers could come together in the same classroom. I feel as if I have to try. I'm thinking Friday might be a good time. It's not quite a half day ride to the Ute village from here. It's the closest; the Arapaho and Navajo are each a day or so farther South. If I left early in the morning, I could return by nightfall. The effort will give me at least some insights as to how my offer of Western education will be received.

For most of the afternoon, I have been measuring and marking boards. I plan to begin cutting them tomorrow. Hopefully, everything will be ready to nail together by the time Cawdor and Jonah return. Going by the old saying "measure twice and cut once," I figure if I measured all of them this evening in the afternoon light and then again in the morning light, I'd be doubly sure of my calculations and can cut with confidence. At least, that's what I've convinced myself. Having never constructed anything larger than a birdhouse before, my carpentry skills are limited.

Last, out of sheer restlessness tonight, I finally opened the letter from Dr. Wheeler. Although I sent a wire saying I had arrived safely, he never answered. I thought that was unusual, considering he had written to me twice already in an effort to ascertain whether or not I was still okay, given his nightmares. Unfortunately, after I opened it, I wished I had responded sooner. It appears the good doctor has gone quite mad with the idea that some terrible harm is soon to befall me, even now that I have reached the relative safety of Auraria. Here are the contents of his letter:

Dear Miss Ulrich,

If my calculations are correct, by now you should have reached your destination. Even though in my previous communication, I had stated I was willing to wait until a reasonable time had passed for you to arrive in Auraria, and then to send word back to me in St. Louis that you were safe, I find myself unable to wait any longer. I have packed my trunk for an extended journey. I will be leaving tomorrow by overland stage heading in your direction. My plan is to ride the stage line as far as it will take me, and then continue by wagon until I reach you.

The dreams of which I wrote to you previously have become even more graphic and disturbing. At the risk of frightening you with every excruciating detail, I will suffice it to say I am no longer able to sleep at night at all. Every time I doze off for even a second, the image of you amidst the flames jolts me back awake. After consulting again with Miss Jilpa regarding the situation, she told me this meant the fate prescribed for you in my dreams was solidifying into greater certainty by the day. Thus, I have no choice but to act. I am so despondent from insomnia, I am of no use to my patients or anyone else here, otherwise.

I have no idea what I will do after my arrival. Since it is unlikely a new boomtown will have an abundance of doctors, I shan't want for employment. St. Louis has been ruined with me for a long time now. I've been needing a change of scenery. Perhaps it's two birds with one stone. Regardless, I will arrive in about a month. If all that results from my journey is seeing you safe and the satisfaction of my mind that this was all just a bad dream, then we can share a good laugh about it at my expense.

    Your friend always,

    Ernest

The breeziness of his closing puzzled me. *Your friend!* Bah! Who did he think he was fooling in trying to be nonchalant in his motivations for following me? At least one of two things were true from the contents of his letter. Ernest might be truly terrified I was in grave peril and no assurances I could give him would persuade him otherwise. The other possibility was that he had become infatuated with me. If so, he may have created this as an excuse to create a situation in which he could appear to be my rescuer. According to my usual assessment, that the truth is usually somewhere between two extremes, I've decided it's a little of each. Dr. Wheeler—Ernest—is both intrigued by me and concerned enough for my well-being to cast aside his well-appointed life in St. Louis and rush out here to see what I am doing.

I don't know whether to be flattered by this circumstance or appalled at his presumptiveness. The letter has no internal date. Given the normal time of exchange for mail, I would say I could expect to see him within the week. By then, all this unpleasantness about the missing miners should be settled. I will be well into my first school term. Hopefully, that will be enough to satisfy Ernest that I am capable of managing my own affairs—and that includes whatever I am to do with him, whenever he finally arrives.

August 20, 1858

V isited the Ute village today. To be honest, I am concerned it was a completely wasted trip. The few who spoke enough English to know what I was offering literally turned up their noses at the idea. Even those who grudgingly took one of the pamphlets I gave them immediately tossed them away the moment my back was turned. Only one young lady, Chipeta, who must have been the one Penny spoke of and admired so, seemed truly engaged. Despite her interest, several older women who saw us speaking scowled at us the entire time. The mindset among most of them is that allowing their children to participate in a Western style of education and learning English would result in abandonment of their own culture. They fear the youth would be forced to assimilate to white ways. I can see the truth in their resistance. Nothing we Americans have done so far to "improve" the lives of natives by bringing them into our culture, such as it is, appears to have benefitted them in any way I can discern.

The big question, if I want to win them over as students, is how do I get them to see the value in educating themselves according to our methods? That is a question for which I do not have an easy answer. Until I do though, I have plenty to keep me occupied with cutting and sawing. Perhaps as I am sweating that out over the next few days, an idea will come to me.

If not, I will ask Cawdor when he returns. Maybe he has better ideas. I know he thought it was a lost cause before he left. However, if he's had some positive results after consulting with the council of elders, then he might be in a more hopeful state of mind.

August 21, 1858

S awing, sawing, all day long. Nothing exciting to report. My hand is so stiff that I can barely hold the pen. Wish we had an apothecary near here. I'd give anything to be able to buy some numbing salve.

August 22, 1858

S till sawing. Trying to think of something constructive to do with all this sawdust rather than throwing it away. Seems a shame to waste so much of it, especially considering it probably contains equal parts of my sweat to the wood. I'm contemplating making some over-large pillows to prop up together in a sort of low armchair formation. This would involve some fairly heavy duty sewing, so it will have to wait until my fingers have healed a bit. My hands look truly wretched. It finally dawned on me today that I should have been wearing gloves the whole time, but it's too late. Both paws are already ragged with blisters. I will face my students with scabby hands on the first day, I'm afraid. But perhaps that's a good thing. It will show them how devoted I am to the task of being their teacher. With any luck, that will inspire them to reciprocate those efforts by dedicating themselves to serious study of their subjects. *Pfft...* who am I kidding! They're children, and children never think of such things!

August 23, 1858

E ureka! Finished all the sawing today around noon. I celebrated by taking the evening off. As luck would have it, who should come riding into town but Brandy and Penny! Penny was overjoyed as usual to see me. She lit up like candles at Christmas when I showed her around the schoolhouse. During dinner at the saloon, I told them both about the success I had in getting the settlers' families to sign up after church, and the utter failure I'd had with the Utes.

"Oh, you just don't know how to ask them the right way!" Penny exclaimed. "Mama and I can go and talk to them again, can't we Mama? Mama can convince anyone to do anything."

"Almost," Brandy said, resisting the urge to correct her daughter's manners. The girl was speaking through a mouthful of shepherd's pie. "Although it might be more difficult than usual after what happened at the mines. Has anything else gone on? Any retaliation by the folks around here?"

"Not yet," I replied, "Cawdor has gone to the tribal council to speak with the Ute, Navajo, and Arapaho leaders all at once, to see if they have any insights as to who might have killed those men. He knows they're not responsible, but he wants to make sure he does everything he can to preserve negotiations about sharing the profits. Once gold starts being extracted, things could get ugly."

Brandy snorted disbelievingly. She swirled the last of her wine in the glass, and drained it in a long swallow. "Good luck with that! There's no way Green Russell is sharing any of that gold with anyone. Not the Indians, nor this new Lawrence Party that's come into town. No one." She leaned forward and whispered across the table. "The only question I'm wondering about is whether he's willing to kill again for it. Indians or even his own men."

"Wait, what do you mean by *again*?" I whispered back, leaning in closely so that no one in the busy saloon could hear. "You don't think Russell staged the whole thing, do you? Killed some of his own men he might have thought were causing trouble or stealing, and then blamed it on the Indians?"

Brandy straightened and poured herself another glass of wine, the remainder in the bottle we had shared. "It's common knowledge that Russell has pulled stunts like this before. Surely you noticed that horrific display of power we passed on the way into town? Yes, all those poor men were convicted of stealing from the mines, but it was a sham. What kind of court allows the aggrieved party to serve on the jury? Or to carry out the orders for their execution? Especially in a town with no real judge or law enforcement whatsoever?"

She motioned for one of the waiters to carry away our empty plates. "The longer Russell continues to make progress in the mines, the richer he becomes. And the richer he becomes, the more he can persuade people that anything he says is the gospel truth. So, until someone else comes along to push him out of power, what he says goes. Until now, he's been content to give some semblance of legality to the whole thing, but he's getting impatient. If Russell doesn't make a bigger strike and declare his full rights over it before the snow falls, he'll lose his chance to be the top man in town. And he knows it. News is already out. Every prospector in America will descend on this place like a plague of locusts in spring. The only thing stopping them is the weather. Once heavy snow comes in around the end of October, everything stops."

Brandy seemed as if she wanted to say more, but she plastered on her professional smile instead as the waiter cleared our places. "We can talk about the long-term prospects of this tomorrow. I've got to give the girls and my carpenters some instructions in the morning. I should be able to ride out with you to the Ute village in the afternoon. Perhaps we can make a bit more headway as a team effort." Brandy looked down at my hands, and clucked disapprovingly. "Clearly, you need some help. What happened?"

"Sawing," I replied. "Cawdor and Jonah are going to help me finish putting together the student benches when they return from Bent's Fort in a few days. Cawdor said it would be best if I got the measuring and sawing part done on my own while they were gone."

Brandy snuffled something that sounded like, "how convenient." Penny capped the remark with a noise between a squeak and a snort.

"You mean Jonah the Whale is coming to school too?" Penny asked, clearly amused. "I didn't know he could read!"

"As a matter of fact," I corrected, slightly taken aback at Penny's derision, "Jonah is a perfectly bright young man. He just has a vision problem that has impeded his ability to progress in his studies."

"Well, just don't let him sit by me!" Penny exclaimed.

"Why not?"

"Cause he's always grinning at me and trying to talk. I hate it. He's so awkward and gets all tongue-tied. It's like trying to talk to a bear."

"Perhaps he gets tongue-tied because he fancies you," suggested Brandy, chiding her daughter. Penny elbowed her mother in the ribs and scrunched up her nose.

"Eww... that's awful. He's such a big clumsy oaf. Not handsome at all. I mean, his uncle is rich and his father was too. He might get his father's money, which would make him *less* awful. But he's still..." Penny trailed off, sighing and shaking her head.

"How superficial of you, Penny!" I mocked. "Considering whether to care for a fellow simply because of his potential monetary worth. Especially at your age. You're not even old enough to be courting yet."

"I don't find it superficial at all," replied Brandy, raising an eyebrow. "I think it's very practical. It's never too early for a girl to be mindful of the financial aspects of any potential relationship. It's the only way to secure her future."

"Well, not the *only* way," I said.

"Not every woman can flit about the world as you do, Mae Ulrich. Making the most of what gifts we have been given in beauty and charm while we are young and able is the only way for most of us to survive." Her attention diverted to the door, Brandy set down her empty glass. She stepped away from the table, motioning for Penny to follow. As she crossed the floor, I spotted Green Russell among the party that had just entered. Greeting them with her most professional smile, my stomach knotted as I saw Penny copy the exact same expression.

Though I am grateful as always for Brandy's guidance and willingness to help me in this very different land, I cannot help but disagree with her judgment at times. I understand that she did what she had to do to reach prosperity in her life. Though now she has money and influence beyond any other woman here, why does she continue to pander to men whom she knows to be of poor character—or even possibly murderers?

At what point does a woman cease being a victim of the circumstances into which she was born, and become instead part of the problem?

August 24, 1858

I hate that I was so quick to judge Brandy in the previous entry. Perhaps it was the wine. True to her word of last night, she and Penny met me just after lunch and rode down to the Ute village. Unlike my initial encounter with them, which was merely tolerant and stand-offish, the Utes greeted Brandy like an old friend. Knowing some of their language helped, of course. As usual, I remain in awe of the ease with which Brandy is able to communicate with anyone.

It was apparent that Penny had many friends in the village too. They chattered with excitement. When Penny pointed at me every now and then, they nodded enthusiastically. I suppose she was also trying to build up their anticipation for the enterprise. By the time we left, Brandy handed me a list of a dozen Ute children whose parents had agreed to allow them to come to school. Scanning the list, I couldn't say any of their names. On the ride back to town, Penny and she both giggled as they corrected my attempts at pronunciation. I took notes.

"Is there any kind of Ute dictionary or phonetic guide I could order?" I asked. "I know I can't learn their language in a week, but I want to look like I'm trying. I think they would appreciate that."

Brandy screwed up her face at me. "The only native language with a written dictionary I know of is Cherokee. It might help you some with Russell's miners. Most of them are at least part Cherokee. As far as I know though, they didn't bring any children with them. They're mostly grown men. Being from Georgia, they already speak English. Well... almost." She paused, giggling. "They speak Southern English. I suppose you'll communicate just as well with them as any ordinary person can with Southerners."

Along the way, Brandy informed me the way the Utes had decided their children would attend school is for one or two of the adults to escort the children over in the morning, have their lessons in the afternoon, and then ride back in the evenings.

"But that means they'll only get half a day of lessons," I complained.

"Isn't that better than nothing?" Brandy sighed. "The only way I convinced them to come was to tell them you would teach the white settlers' children in the mornings, and them in the afternoon. The elders are a little skeptical of an English-speaking school to begin with, but they realize it's important for the children to learn the language if they are going to be living cheek to jowl with them as Auraria grows. Their greater concern was that they don't want their children having to share space with the settlers' children socially. They are afraid the white children will teach them bad manners. Ute children are very respectful of their elders. The Utes don't like what they've seen of the white children in the area. They think they're too rowdy."

Blame it on my complete lack of cultural awareness, but I had never even considered the possibility that the native parents would think the white children might be a bad influence on their own children. I had only considered it from the other way around.

"I guess I can rework the schedule," I said. "All the children are at such different educational levels. Perhaps I will have to do something more like individual tutoring."

"That's the kind of education most of them have had. It's what I've done my whole life," suggested Penny. "You'll probably get a better result because it's what they're used to."

On the way back to town, we chatted about the best way to change my lesson plans. Penny helped a lot, since she knew the children better than her mother. Though her judgments about many of them were harsh, they were probably accurate. Given Penny's input, what I think is best is to put them into three general groups. Settlers' children who can't read and need to be taught that first. Next, settlers' children who can read and need individual instruction on various subjects. Then, native Ute children, none of whom can read English except Chipeta. I will probably end up tutoring her individually.

I'm sure this initial attempt at categorization will change as soon as I meet them. At least I have all the students I can handle at present, and I can shift my efforts from recruiting back to planning. With about three dozen students, all of whom will need something slightly different in their instruction, I'm certainly going to have my work cut out for me.

August 25, 1858

Had another dream about my gray wolf last night, which is to say I dreamed of Cawdor hunting. Still have not figured out the true nature of our spiritual connection, or the full extent of why it manifests itself visually in my dreams as this wolf metaphor. Though, it is comforting now to know that is all it is.

In the dream, I saw him moving stealthily through the tall grass. The soft shafts of it swayed overhead as he crept upon a herd of elk. Through his eyes, I could feel the urgent hunger as he scanned the herd, singling out an elderly bull on which to pounce. Soundlessly, save for the rush of grass that fell before his feet, I felt him surge forward. He leapt for the elk's throat and clamped onto it with his powerful jaws. The momentum of his body carried him forward. With a terrific ripping sound, he tore its neck open. The old bull elk fell to his knees as arterial blood sprayed out like a fan. The herd took off bellowing, abandoning the bull to his fate. The wolf stepped away from his kill and waited for the elk to stop breathing before he moved in to eat. He tore the hide away to expose the fresh meat. Thrusting his nose skyward, the gray wolf let out a mournful wail. It was answered by half a dozen others. Having alerted his pack to the kill, the gray wolf dug into his prey. He ripped out the elk's still-warm heart and swallowed it whole. Having eaten his fill by the time the rest of the pack arrived, my gray wolf separated from them. He lay down in the grass, rolling back and forth for a good back scratch before trotting away.

I wonder if my dreams of the gray wolf representing Cawdor will continue like this. As a symbol of his spirit. Or if I will ever see him in his true form when he is away.

August 28, 1858

Cawdor and Jonah rode back into town today. Jonah was wearing a new pair of silver-rimmed spectacles. Although they looked a bit small on his face, they have already helped both his reading and his co-ordination considerably. He managed to make it through an entire day of assisting Cawdor and me in assembling the benches without tripping over a single thing.

As for Cawdor himself, he's acting strangely guarded again. This I've come to realize is one of his many mercurial moods. I asked him how the elk hunt went, and whether he'd brought anything back. He looked at me as if I'd asked him why he didn't fly through the sky and bring back a piece of the moon.

"Why would I need to bring anything back when I've already eaten?" he asked.

I could tell the question irritated him.

"Well, for later, I mean."

"There is never any left over. Even if there were, it wouldn't be any good," Cawdor looked at me puzzled, as if I were missing something that should be completely apparent. Not wanting to feel stupid, I changed the subject.

"Did you make any progress with the tribal council?"

"Nope," Cawdor said, shaking his head. "Unless you count them reaffirming what they've been saying for months now. They demand at least a fifty-fifty split of the proceeds from the mines between Russell's company and whatever tribe's lands they run underneath. In Russell's case, that would be the Utes. With this new Lawrence group, it seems like it's going to be the Arapaho and Navajo, depending on how far the vein of the strike stretches."

"What did they say about the miners? Do they know anything?"

"They know everything, but they're not saying much," Cawdor replied, suddenly getting cagey again. "Only thing they will admit is that their tribesmen had nothing to do with it."

"If it wasn't them, and they know who did it, then aren't they afraid they'll be next?"

Giving me an exasperated look, Cawdor sighed. "The tribes have nothing to fear from these mon... these men. They'll do what they have to do to make Russell's party move along. Hopefully it will all be over soon, and another group will come in who are more willing to engage in reasonable negotiations."

I studied his expression. "You almost said a different word. What was it?"

"No, I didn't," he replied testily. He shook the nail box, and started toward the door. "Need to go get some more."

"Wait," I caught Cawdor by the arm. "You almost said *monster*. I heard you. There's nothing wrong with calling a murderer a monster. What makes me curious is why you stopped yourself from saying it. The Utes know who it was, don't they? You just can't tell me. Because you feel like you can't trust me, for some reason."

"I don't trust anyone," Cawdor barked, snatching his arm away. "Especially someone who claims to be so smart, yet she's unwilling to see the truth when it's right in front of her face. *Think, Mae!*" With that, he stormed out the front door of the school, letting it slam behind him.

I started to follow, but Jonah stopped me. "I'd leave him alone, if I were you. Mister Cawdor is an alright fella, but he gets that way sometimes. 'Specially when he gets frustrated."

I collapsed onto one of the completed benches next to Jonah. "I know there's something Cawdor believes I should know already, but I don't. I thought I had it figured out, but I don't."

"Yeah, I know," replied Jonah. "The wolf dreams. We talked about them a little bit. I have them too, sometimes. Ever since my mom died. Cawdor said he knew about mine too, but he couldn't tell me what they were either. He says when the time comes, I'll find out for myself."

"When the time comes?" I blustered, even more confused by the knowledge that Jonah was plagued by wolf dreams too. "Well, when is that going to be, I wonder? Whenever Cawdor decides? No. If all three of us are having these same violent dreams, I want to know why. Today. I'm going to make him tell me when he comes back."

I didn't get the chance. When Cawdor returned from the general store with the nail box still empty, his whole countenance had changed. Something was wrong.

"There's going to be a raid on the Ute village. Russell's men. Tonight. I have to go."

Setting the box down, Cawdor gathered his things and ran outside to saddle Troy. Once he was seated, he looked down at me harshly. His piercing green eyes glowed as they had before, when he had explained to me... what exactly?

"For once, Mae, *pay attention!*" Cawdor growled, deflecting my demands for more information. "Don't *analyze*, just *watch!* With an open mind. And *feel!* If you really concentrate on what's happening, you'll see it tonight in your dreams. Then you'll know everything." Cawdor took off, shouting a final order over his shoulder. "And don't follow me!"

I looked at Jonah, who was standing gape-mouthed behind me on the porch. "What was all that about?"

"I'm not sure, but I'm going to find out." I told him. "Let's finish this bench first, and then I'll buy you dinner. You don't think your aunt and uncle will miss you?"

"Haven't even gone home to show them my glasses yet," Jonah said. "They think I'm still out with Cawdor, I guess, if they've thought about me at all."

"Good," I said. "You're coming out to the Ute village with me tonight. I think it's time we both learned the truth about whatever it is that Cawdor refuses to tell us."

August 29, 1858

I s it possible I have been sleepwalking through life?

I feel I must have been. My waking consciousness seems to have become completely divorced from reality. Or perhaps, it is the other way around, and I have only been fully awake in my dreams. Given what Jonah and I witnessed last night, that appears to be the case.

After Cawdor left in such a hurry yesterday afternoon, we finished nailing together the last of the benches. Attempting casual conversation at first, inevitably we came around to the topic of our dreams. Jonah explained that he began to have wolf dreams a few months ago, just after his mother's murder. Other than a shift in perspective that proved we were experiencing the same events in collective consciousness, albeit from slightly different perspectives, we determined our dreams concerned the same occurrences. Jonah had even seen his father's death, to which he expressed the same chilling level of nonchalance that I have come to expect. I have yet to decide whether this indicates an unusual level of resilience for someone so young, or something darker.

"My father was a very bad man," Jonah said flatly, never missing a beat with his hammer. "He cheated people at the bank. He browbeat the miners who worked for him and Russell, and he killed my mother. He would have killed me too if I hadn't always been sharp enough to stay out of his way. There just ain't no good in some people. Some people, there ain't no choice left but to kill them. And if this wolf or these monsters, whatever they are, did it... well then, I ain't so afraid of them. They saw someone who needed killing and they made it happen. That makes 'em okay in my book."

Then, quick as a wink, Jonah brightened, and asked what he could have for dinner. I told him anything he wanted. This ended up being a plate of venison ribs, potato salad, and two large slices of chocolate cake at the saloon. The cake was exceptionally good. I managed a slice of it with a whiskey and soda. Unlike my companion, who seemed to be excited at the prospect of what the night would reveal, I was filled with dread and lost my appetite.

We went to the Ute village by a hunting path Jonah knew, not along the main road. "If there's going to be a raid," he said, "they'll come out the main road, to make a big show of power. If we want to be able to watch and not be seen, we should come around the back of the ridge. Tie the horses down behind the hill, and then walk up quietly to look over."

"You sound like you've done this before." I said. "Spying on the Utes."

"It's not spying," Jonah shrugged. "It's observing. They're interesting. The way they do everyday things. The ways they communicate with one another, hardly saying any words. Like everyone already knows what to do all the time. I like watching people like that. Just to understand how they are when no one thinks they are watching."

"You'd make an excellent scientist," I said. "Or a doctor. Most medical diagnoses and building theories are all about observation."

"Maybe," Jonah replied, considering the idea. "I just don't like all that sitting still. I like to be moving. I get restless and kind of trapped feeling when I can't be outside."

"Perhaps a veterinarian or naturalist then," I corrected myself. We continued to chat along the way to the village. I was surprised at how quickly the three hours went by. If there is something more sinister lurking in the boy's psyche, it certainly doesn't inhibit Jonah's conversational abilities. He could charm paint off of a wall when he chooses.

Arriving at the base of the overlook, we tied our horses as Jonah suggested, and crept up to the ridge. Our timing was perfect. The sun had just set. Below us we could see the two dozen or so smaller family lodges in a circle around the central meeting one. The usual buzz of activity was nonexistent.

"Cawdor must have warned them already," I whispered to Jonah. "They're probably waiting for the raiders inside."

"Yes, I have," came a voice from behind me that I did not expect. I froze, because I recognized it instantly. Cawdor! As I turned, I heard a second voice I recognized, but I couldn't see either of them anywhere.

"What are *they* doing here?" demanded Nascha in an accusatory tone. "I thought you told them not to follow!"

"I did!" Cawdor snapped back at her. Then, Cawdor stepped out from behind the sawbrush where he had been concealed. He was completely naked.

As I watched, the sinewy muscles of his chest and abdomen began to quiver. Sweat coursed down his face. Stretching his long arms to the sky, they quickly covered themselves in silvery gray fur, from the tips of his fingers to his feet. Falling forward onto all fours, his entire body shook as it expanded rapidly to almost twice its size. Within a matter of seconds, I stood face to face with the great gray wolf of my dreams.

"What do you think of me now?" Cawdor growled, his green eyes flashing. "Am I real enough for you? Or will you rationalize this away as just another dream?"

I had no time to answer, as Nascha and half a dozen other women emerged from the underbrush. They were also naked. Their perfect bodies glistened with sweat in the summer moonlight as they transformed. Only, they were not wolves. They were something else entirely. Their beautiful faces contorted into the grotesque, snaggle-toothed bear-creatures of my nightmares, with massive racks of antlers like elk. Their lanky limbs were like those of giant wolves, but reddish brown instead of Cawdor's silver gray. Instead of human hands or wolf paws, each arm ended in long claws that looked like massive eagle talons.

As they stood arrayed in a V-shaped flank around us, I could hear the hoofbeats of Russell's raiding party coming up the main road. Without a sound, the beast women flew past. Diving with unbelievable swiftness off the edge of the cliff, they sailed down into the valley on unseen wings. The wolf who was Cawdor let out a long, mournful howl, and took off on all fours, racing down the snaky trail of the cliffside. Hearing the call of the wolf, the Utes ran out of their lodges and leapt onto the backs of their horses. Fanning out into a curve around the front of the village, I could see the Utes themselves would be the second wall of defense against the raiding party. They charged after the monsters into the valley.

Their first volley of fire was met with an ear-splitting cacophony of otherworldly shrieking as the flying beasts bore down on the raiding party. All of Russell's men and the settlers in the first wave were knocked off their horses. Within seconds their screams filled the air. The beasts tore the flesh from their bodies. Some of the second wave of raiders pulled up so abruptly that several fell off their horses and were trampled. Others, seeing their fellows ravaged by the beasts, tried to turn back in retreat. The Utes descended on them, shooting and stabbing. Many more fell as the beasts continued the attack, shredding their bodies to pulp. I saw Cawdor in his wolf dashing in and out among Utes and beasts, leaping to snatch the fleeing raiders from their horses. Another group of Utes, who emerged with spears, finished off the raiders who lay sprawled on the ground. It was over in minutes. The last few would-be raiders fled before even reaching the edge of the village. Cawdor's wolf howled again. Both the Utes and beasts ceased the frenzy of their actions, and assembled in a circle before the meeting house. Their long cry of victory arose from the valley.

Jonah rolled over from where he peered over the edge of the ridge. For the first time since I'd met him, he seemed unable to speak. His black eyes were wide with shock. Finally, he whispered. "They let some of them get away. Why?"

"So they can go back to tell Russell and his bunch who they're dealing with," I mumbled, also dumbstruck. Jonah squinted down at the mass of bodies scattered in the valley. The Utes were dragging the dead raiders into a row near the trail leading into the village.

"They'll be back," said a familiar voice, causing both of us to look around. Neither Cawdor's wolf nor Nascha and her beasts were anywhere to be seen. From somewhere near us, the voice—Cawdor's voice—laughed. "I am here and not here. Physically far away, but spiritually, right beside you. Such as it is with the mind of the pack."

Glancing at Jonah, I could tell he heard Cawdor's voice too as it continued. "The time is near for each of you to come into your wolf, as we say. Not yet, but soon. As it always is, you will hear the call before you feel the pain that will bring about your transformation. Now that you know what is true and what is inside you, a choice must be made as to what kind of creature you are. As the legend goes, the wolf you become is the wolf you feed."

Then, Cawdor's voice was gone. Though I could see nothing different, I could feel his presence had left us as clearly as I could feel the light behind my eyelids when the moon emerged from behind a cloud.

Far removed from the almost jovial conversation of our early evening, Jonah and I rode back to Auraria in the total silence of a breezeless midnight. Tomorrow or the next day, of course, news will come of what happened to the raiding party. The Utes would be blamed, I felt certain, for their alleged aggression, even though they'd been defending themselves from attack. What would happen next remained a mystery. Auraria was a small town. At least half of its men lay dead in a row by the village trail. Another raid was not possible, but as Brandy had opined, Green Russell was a man willing to stop at nothing, even murder. Russell was the driving force behind the night's raid. Now that it had been thwarted, who knew what retaliation he might plan next to protect his fortune?

As we rode, a second set of worries began to surface from the shadows of my brain. Cawdor was a wolf. Not just a symbolic wolf in my dreams, as I tried to rationalize the idea when he first shared his visions with me, but an actual, flesh-and-blood *wolf man*. The *loup garou* of my grand-père's nightmare tales. I saw him physically transform, right before my eyes. I also saw him attack and kill several men. How am I to reconcile that with the kindness Cawdor has shown to me and to Jonah? What did that mean he would be willing to do to ensure the tribes received their fair share from the mines? Was he just as much of a monster as his uncle?

Over and over, the words of Cawdor's spirit wolf floated through my consciousness. Nascha witnessed them too, weeks ago, as she told me her story on the prairie when we made our crossing. In my mind's eye, I visualized her beast also, and those of her sisters, but they had been beasts of a very different kind than Cawdor's. Beasts of strange and unnatural combinations. Whereas Cawdor's wolf was intimidating from its intensity, I had never truly felt afraid of or repulsed by it. But Nascha's... whatever that thing was... it wasn't only inhuman. It was uncanny. A creature not of mere ferocity when riled, but undiluted rage. Pure hatred wrought into flesh and fur. A Wendigo.

The wolf you become is the wolf you feed, both had said.

My question is what kind of food does it take to become which kind?

And even more importantly, where does the wolf end and the monster begin?

August 31, 1858

It's been two full days, and there has been no response, insofar as anyone is willing to talk about, to the settlers' disastrous raid on the Ute village. Cawdor has also been missing, which is not unusual except that I have had no dreams of him either. Neither has Jonah. We've discussed the matter several times in-between his reading lessons. Even Brandy's saloon has been strangely quiet. The whole town seems to have rolled up like a scroll.

"They do that here," Brandy said, as we had a quiet dinner together tonight. "Just like when Jonah's mother was killed and those Indian miners were hanged. The first town ordinance of Auraria seems to be that no one shall speak about anything wrong in Auraria."

"Doesn't that make you even more nervous though?" I asked. I swirled the contents of my whiskey and soda around mindlessly in the glass. It had been hard for me to eat or even to drink much to relax these past couple of days. I've been too on edge.

"Hmm..." Brandy replied, sipping her wine thoughtfully with no trouble at all. "Yes and no. It's ruined business for a while. Everyone's afraid to get out. The Utes are generally peaceful people. Since it seems the Utes have gotten the upper hand on them, I don't really see Russell or any of the rest rushing out to do anything to retaliate. They're much more likely to regroup over the winter and huddle around their gold mine with their tails tucked firmly between their legs."

"But the rumors going around about the way the raiders were killed," I insisted. "Those beasts or whatever the survivors claimed they saw weren't Utes. What do you make of those?" For some reason, I didn't feel comfortable telling Brandy about what Jonah and I had seen, or that we had been there. Even though we were close enough to have dinner together several times a week, the fact that Brandy was still willing to keep regular company with Green Russell and his men made me unable to trust her fully with any important information.

"Eh... probably just the usual boogeymen, like we've talked about before," Brandy answered dismissively. "All those tales from the Navajo and the other tribes. Skinwalkers and Wendigo and such. Just things to scare children and to try to explain the unexplainable. Have you asked Nascha about any of it? She's the expert, or so she claims. She tells that tall tale about her mother being one. You remember, right?"

"Yes, I remember," I said, recalling how Brandy cautioned me against believing Nascha's story that her mother had become a Wendigo. "I also remember you told me Nascha was the Skinwalker because she and the other women ate parts of the Spaniards."

Brandy laughed, her too-rehearsed, professional laugh. "I told you that was the right *story*, if Nascha had been telling it correctly. That's what I had heard from Gad when he was drunk and telling some other men. They were making fun of him for letting his wife run around as she pleased. All of it is just a twist upon a twist of a story upon a story. They're all spinners of tales. Who knows what the truth really is? So long as their fear mongering doesn't interfere with business too long, who cares?"

"I care," I said softly, under my breath. "Because that's how legends are made."

"Legends of what?" Penny asked, wandering out onto the porch to join us.

"The legend of the little girl who grew up to be queen of the world," said Brandy. Her whole countenance brightened at her daughter's entrance. "Do you have everything ready for your first day of school tomorrow, princess?"

"I think so," replied Penny, settling down into the chair between us, and self-consciously smoothing the silk of her dress. Since I'd last seen her in Bent's Fort, Penny had started dressing noticeably different. More mature and ladylike. She'd even begun coloring her face most days, and putting her hair up in an attempt at some of the current styles. However, her wiry red curls failed to cooperate, springing out of their pins at odd angles of their own accord. Brandy was greatly amused by her efforts, but it concerned me. I didn't like the thought of Penny flouncing around the saloon all day, looking older than her age. It seemed to be an invitation for trouble. "Who all is going to be there?" Penny asked.

"Well, I've got about twenty settlers' children and a dozen Utes signed up," I said.

"I wouldn't count on that many attending," Brandy remarked. "In fact, I'd be surprised if any of the town kids showed up at all. People are so scared." She took another thoughtful sip of her wine. "Don't know about the Utes though. Could go either way. Might encourage them to take a more active presence in town, or might cause them to stay home too, not wanting to rile anything up."

"I bet Jonah the Whale wouldn't miss it for the world. He's already hanging around there all the time anyway," quipped Penny, patting an unruly curl back into place primly.

"How observant of you to monitor his comings and goings," I answered, testing her. "Might the revelation that Jonah is not in fact as stupid and clumsy as you first gave him credit for have piqued your interest? I have it on good information directly from the source that he does indeed fancy you."

"No, he's still a whale," Penny replied. She wrinkled her nose in a girlish way I found oddly reassuring, given her current preoccupation with appearing grown-up. "It's just boring around here with no one to talk to and nothing to do."

As I left, I reassured Penny that the unfortunate situation of her boredom would be remedied tomorrow as soon as we had our first lessons. Walking home tonight, I have to admit I am a bit apprehensive that attendance will be low to begin with, considering how subdued the town has been. The only way to know for sure is to wake up tomorrow and put on a brave face for whatever comes.

September 1, 1858

A lthough I wouldn't call the first day of my school a complete failure, because a dozen Ute children showed up for the afternoon session, I was very disappointed in the lack of turnout from the Auraria settlement. Out of the twenty who enrolled, precisely two showed up: Jonah and Penny. Upon seeing that her admirer was the only other Auraria student present when school commenced at eight, Penny had to be persuaded not to leave. Once she'd settled into the front bench opposite from Jonah and became engaged in the morning's lessons though, I knew I had gained her interest in staying.

Since they are the same age and of similar levels of intellect, I have put the two of them on the same course of study. A half hour each of mathematics, natural science, literature and rhetoric, then we end the morning with history and geography. We eat lunch together, and work on music and sketching until the Ute children arrive for the afternoon session. The two of them have self-selected their art form. Penny already plays the violin, or "fiddle" as she calls it. Revealing a talent heretofore unbeknownst to me, Jonah is quite good at sketching. On the first day, Penny was less than plussed by his offer to draw her playing the fiddle. Jonah settled for working on a remarkably accurate rendition of Sir Gawain instead. He tries, poor thing!

I allowed them to stay through the afternoon if they liked. Jonah, unsurprisingly, jumped at the chance. He's always game for anything that keeps him out of his aunt and uncle's house. Penny declined, once she saw her friend Chipeta was not among the party who arrived shortly after one o'clock. "They're just babies," Penny scoffed, gathering her things together as she left for the day. "I'm past all that."

In a way, Penny was accurate in her assessment. All the Ute children who came were between the ages of six and ten. That made my job easier. I could easily fit them into two groups: those who spoke a little bit of English, but didn't yet read it, and those who neither spoke nor read the language. Fortunately, the Utes had the presence of mind to send along two interpreters, both women, to assist in their lessons. One was a sort of grandmotherly figure whom I had not met before, named Chenoa, and the other was Nascha. Neither woman wore her native dress, nor did the children. All were attired simply in the Western fashion, with shirts and denim pants on the boys and printed dresses in light cotton fabrics for the girls.

"You didn't have to change what you were wearing," I said to Chenoa as she helped me get the students situated with their primers and slates.

"The council thought it was best for them to know the full life," Chenoa replied. "What it feels like to be one of you. So when they come home, they will know the differences between the two worlds. When they are older, they can decide which one they'd rather belong to."

I thought that was a very astute assessment of this type of education. It truly does represent a difference between worlds. Not only in spheres of thought, but dress and action.

Throughout the afternoon, the Ute children remained attentive, if a bit squirmy. It was clear they were trying their best, but were unaccustomed to having to sit and listen for so long. They kept glancing around too, as if evaluating how they measured up against one another in this strange new environment. I could tell Jonah was just as entertained as I was in watching them see a completely average day at school unfold for the first time. However, a sharp glance from Chenoa was all it took, and any whispering or movement ceased, at least for a while. By the end of the afternoon, I saw what the Ute elders had been concerned about: the danger of their children learning bad habits from the settlers' children. It is impossible for a child to know how to make fun of a teacher or disregard a lesson if all one has ever known is the discipline of being attentive and respectful.

Nascha didn't say a word to me during the entire afternoon's lessons, until it was time for everyone to leave. As they were packing up their things and getting ready for the hour's ride back to the village, she motioned for me to follow her outside.

"I suppose you know why I am here?" Nascha began.

"Because you're so excited to help out the children with their education?" I offered, sarcastically. She winced and ignored my attempt at humor.

"No, I can't stand children. Too noisy. Like being trapped around a flock of geese that can't fly. But I know the importance of keeping them safe. The elders sent me as their guard, for reasons I'm sure you know." Nascha looked at me pointedly with her intense, steely eyes. It was painful to hold her gaze for long, so I glanced away.

"Yes, I am well aware," I said, hoping she would to continue.

"I know you want to ask about the other night," Nascha offered. "So, ask. Cawdor believes you should know the truth. That is good enough for me."

I decided that simplicity was best. "I know what Cawdor is, I think. You and those other women though. You're different. Physically, and..." I motioned across my face.

"In every possible way," Nascha finished. "When a person comes into his or her wolf, what they are inside can be seen on the outside. If a person is filled merely with pain, then they usually become what Cawdor is. A wolf in spirit, prepared to defend himself, if necessary, but without the pure hatred that it takes to turn one mad enough to kill on the offensive. And not just to kill, but to dominate—to consume—to find joy and power in regaining what has been taken and more. To attempt to fill the unfillable depth of a soul lost into the blackness." As she described this, Nascha's silver eyes shone with a white-hot intensity. I could not look at them. But I had to know the rest, so I pressed her further.

"What do you call it? This thing you are?" I was careful not to say "monster," but Nascha sensed what I meant anyway.

"This *monster*," she leaned on the word, the tips of her two long eye teeth just visible in her amusement at my reluctance. "It is okay to say it. I know it, and I celebrate what I am. The reason I did not tell you before and claimed it was my mother instead, is that in a way, it's true. In coming into my monster, I have become my own mother. By eating the flesh of my enemies, I have been reborn into eternal life. I have the spirit of the wolf, yes. The need to protect myself and my pack. But what I am is more than that. I do not *feel* rage. I *am* rage. Pain has shaped me into a spear of vengeance. I am known by many names. In white culture some would oversimplify and say werewolf or *loup garou*, but that is only half correct. The Native wolf spirit is more complicated than those in the West. There are different..." she searched for the word, "layers, one might say, of humanity that remain resonant within us. For someone like Cawdor, who knew what love and acceptance felt like, before the incident that brought out their wolf, they are able to maintain a level of restraint. Those wolf spirits walk the bridge between animal and man. They can still feel for others, and keep part of their humanity. Then, there are those like myself, for whom the mark of human kindness never made as indelible an imprint as that of the wolf when it was called forth. For those like me... the Skinwalkers, the Wendigo, there is almost nothing left of our human form. It is uncomfortable even to stand here speaking to you as a human, when living as my monster is so much more natural."

"And that's why you are away from home so much then. From Gad. Is that why you never had children?" I asked.

"Yes," Nascha answered. "That is the most tragic part of being a Skinwalker. One's human skin becomes harder and harder to wear over time. Finally, we have to shed it and become nothing but the monster. However, what we receive in exchange, the power of eternal life and the total absence of fear from any living creature, is more than worth it."

"But you must have some degree of compassion left," I insisted. "Otherwise, why would you be here? Helping the tribe protect its children."

Nascha nodded, "Because this is my last stop. The transformation from human to Skinwalker is not immediate. It builds over time. Fresh wrongs, fresh blood justices meted out, gradually push us to the point where it is no longer about vengeance at all. It becomes merely killing and the hunger for killing. Raw animal power. The law of life. Anyone who starts as a wolf spirit can become a Wendigo. A bite of this one here, another of that one there, until finally all that one lives for is the consumption of flesh. Do you know how long it has taken me to get here? Has anyone told you?"

I shook my head *no*.

"Over a hundred years," Nascha said. "The Spaniards who burnt my village, attacked my mother and me... they lived during the time of the American Revolution. I was once in the place where Émile Ulrich lived was when he awakened into his wolf. Years later, I was where Cawdor is now. Over time, with all the other things that I've seen and done, the monster inside me slowly grew. The wolf that I was changed, until now I am almost past return. It will not be much longer. This last battle, I believe, will be the end."

"Wait," I said, startled, "My grand-père? He was a... what you are?"

"Not quite," Nascha said. "He was a werewolf. He kept tight rein on his wolf. Émile Ulrich's transformation happened during the Revolution. I'm sure he never spoke of it. Most soldiers who are also men of feeling cannot talk about it. When that rage was unleashed, all wolves can sense the history of other wolves. We can feel what happened before in their lives too, through the universal instinct of the pack. However, we can only remember specifically what has happened after the wolf within has been awakened."

Nascha paused here to let it sink in. "As one ages, it's harder and harder to control. Did your grandfather spend a lot of time in the woods by himself? Away from people?"

"Yes, on his dairy farm. Weeks at a time, as he got older," I said, marveling. "When I went to visit him, we went hunting together. He told me all these stories about the *loup garou* from France. Things that happened when he was a boy."

Nascha nodded. "He saw the wolf within you too, as I do now. That was his way of telling you without actually saying the words. We're not allowed, you see, to reveal the mysteries of the pack. To do so is punishable by death. The pack must protect its secrets, and every person must find the way to their wolf alone."

Suddenly, Cawdor's reticence to make me realize what he was washed over me like a flood, along with one final question. "Then why are you able to tell me now?"

"As I said before," Nascha replied, beginning to walk away as Chenoa and Jonah came out and helped the children up onto their horses. "My time is growing short. Only a few more kills, and the transformation will be complete. And then," she made a motion across her throat, "no one can touch me. But your choices may be different."

Nascha swung up onto her horse. "You were right, Mae. It's not just which wolf you feed... but how much, and for how long."

Nascha smiled, the tips of her eye teeth showing again. "Of course, the kind of animal you were to begin with is another factor to consider. No one really knows that but you." She looked slowly from me to Jonah, then she turned and rode away.

September 5, 1858

T his week has gone by in such a blur, I haven't had much any time to reconsider my ominous discussion with Nascha. I've spent hours scrambling to rework my lessons once again for the individual interests of Penny and Jonah, and to accommodate the needs of my Ute students. On a more personal note, I've also been presented with a dilemma I've never experienced before. Somehow, I have attracted the unsolicited attention of two gentlemen at the same time. First, Ernest—Dr. Wheeler—arrived yesterday completely out of the blue, so I've been wrestling with what to think about his proposition. Then tonight, Cawdor reappeared to unshroud some of the mystery behind his evasiveness over the last few weeks. Strangely, it was only partly to do with his wolf. More on that later.

I hate to admit it, but seeing Ernest ride up in his tweed jacket and spectacles filled me with a sense of nostalgia. Part of me longs for the normalcy of my former life, in which everything was always in apple pie order. After we'd greeted one another, Ernest wasted no time to tell me what he had seen in his dreams that compelled him to follow me. Wary of being overheard, Ernest insisted we ride out into the prairie, out of earshot of town, before he began.

"The nightmares are always the same," Ernest said, "Sometimes over and over again in one night. There is never any sound to them—only images. Looking across the main street, I can see an angry mob circling around the schoolhouse. They are brandishing their fists and chanting. Their backs are to me. It is nighttime. The snow is thick on the ground, almost to the tops of their boots. An old Indian woman is standing in the door, yelling at the men. From somewhere I cannot see, a shot is fired that hits her square in the chest. She staggers back into the schoolhouse, where she collapses. I assume she is dead. After she falls, several of them rush forward with torches and bundles of straw for tinder. They light the schoolhouse afire. There must be kerosene or something in the straw. It goes up immediately. In only a few minutes the whole thing is ablaze. Native children begin jumping out of the upstairs window in a panic. Some make it and run a few yards, only to be caught, while others land awkwardly and try to crawl away, crying in the snow. They are snatched up by the men. Regardless, their fates are the same as they are all apprehended. Then, there are these—I don't know what to call them—beasts of some kind, that rush out and begin attacking the men who are seizing the children. At last, I see you come to the window. You throw out some kind of big cushion-looking thing, and are urging the rest of the children to jump for it. They run with their mouths wide open, their faces streaming with tears. There is more shooting. Some of the beasts lay dead in the snow. At least, I think they do. Seconds after I watch them die, it's as if they all disappear."

Ernest paused a moment, motioning his hands to suggest their assumption into the ether. He'd unbuttoned his vest, and his shirt was soaked with nervous sweat. "That's the part where I recognize it must be a dream. Where would they have gone, those beasts? Before that, it's all so immediate. As if I'm right there watching, but can't do anything. After that, the dream continues. I see you then leap out of the window. You hit the cushion, fall down, and start crawling toward your horse," he nodded at Cressida. "A gang of men grab you and throw you to the ground. They try to roll you over and... " Ernest winced at what he didn't want to say. "Try to harm you in a very personal way. You are kicking and fighting so much that they give up. The one sitting on top of you smacks you hard across the face with the butt of his pistol. You fall back, not moving anymore. They bind your hands and feet like a dead animal. With another rope, they tie you to drag behind one of their horses."

"What happens then?" I asked, morbidly fascinated with the tale of my demise.

"I don't know. It always goes black after that. I can't see anything else." Ernest shook his head. "Do you see now why I had to come out here? Or do you think I'm crazy?"

"I don't think you're crazy," I said. "I think you're seeing something which might be a premonition." I looked at him with what I hoped was reassurance. "Since it hasn't happened yet, then there's still time for the future to be changed."

"I was hoping you'd say that," Ernest replied. "That's what I've been thinking about on the way out here to see you. Mae, you have an open mind and a curious heart. You're not jealous or self-righteous. You're just as you are, and I... I think I love that about you." Ernest swallowed hard and snatched off his glasses. He swabbed them with his handkerchief so he didn't have to look at me as he spoke. "And well, I'm... I'm thinking about making a new start of it. Back East, all these new industrial millionaires are building enormous mansions. Cottages, they call them, up and down the New England coast. Some are having their families live there year-round and there are calls for private physicians. I've applied for several positions of that sort, and..." At that point, he seemed almost gasping for air. "I thought if there was a demand for private doctors then there must be an equal need for private tutors for their children. So, I thought you might," he coughed uncomfortably. Glancing at me for a response, he nervously concluded, "Might want to come with me and have a go at it."

The tension between us was thick as soup. "A go at it," I repeated.

"Yes," Ernest replied, quickly and awkwardly. "With me. There. Teaching. And such."

"And such," I said again slowly. I had never been proposed to before, and I wasn't really sure this was it either. He'd done it so obliquely. "As your..."

"Well, not right away," Ernest stammered. "I mean, we could work for different families. Get to know one another a bit more. And then maybe..." again, his words failed him.

"I see," I said. "What if I'm happy where I am?"

This response shocked him. "How can you possibly be happy here? There's nothing!"

"You're correct," I said. "There is nothing, and I am unhappy. I had unrealistic expectations about what I might be able to accomplish. Those have already proven to be foolhardy." I hadn't been ready to admit it until that moment, but it was true.

This rallied his courage once more. "Then why the devil would you stay?"

"Because this was my choice, and I'm not done with it yet," I replied, more testily than I intended to sound.

"How long will it take? I've told you I'm willing to wait here as long as..."

I stopped him. "Don't be so ready to abandon your plans, Ernest. I think you should go East. Make a fresh start as you've said. It would do you good. Given all you've been through in St. Louis, it was right for you to leave there. For now, though, my place is here."

"But the dreams," Ernest continued. Again, I interrupted him.

"I thank you deeply for sharing them with me. I know they must have caused you a great deal of distress. I feel your need to warn me about them was genuine. Even though possibly also inspired in part by a sense of emotional anguish that I might be slipping away. I will be more careful, I assure you, because of them. However, until I have finished what I intend to accomplish here, I'm afraid you will either have to wait for my answer or move on."

Ernest muttered something along the lines of "I'll wait," under his breath like a scolded child. I could tell he was still heartened I had not rejected him outright, even through his pouting.

The ride back was filled with amicable banter, if somewhat forced. We managed to make it through dinner at the saloon with a rather stimulating discussion about the connections between Spiritualism and the psyche without bringing up the unwieldy topic of personal affections again. Yet, the other part of our earlier conversation hung over the evening like a cloud. We talked around it in theoretical terms like two circling hawks. I left our dinner that evening with two opposite sensations. One of genuine comfort, at having found a real friend if not exactly the perfect romantic companion, and another of genuine fear. Since if I were to accept Ernest's story about his dreams as the truth, and to believe that they were indeed some kind of psychic premonition, then I had a great deal to be concerned about.

The next evening, I was once again returning from dinner at the saloon. (An aside: Is that another part of the reason why I have almost no students from town, I wonder? Do their prim mothers not approve of how many meals I take in Brandy's establishment?) I found Cawdor waiting for me. He was sitting on the schoolhouse steps, and he was drunk. Not quite as drunk as I'd first seen him, but nearly.

"Lo!"

"Hello," I said, breezing past him. I could smell the whiskey sweating off his skin. When I turned to shut the door, he stood in the frame, preventing me from closing it. Then, he kissed me. It lasted for a long while. His lips were soft and sweet with the liquor, and his kiss was tender and sincere.

"What was that for?" I asked, and he stepped inside.

"'Cause I wanted to."

"Really?" I asked. "Why are you only nice when you're drinking?"

"Easier."

"I see," I said. Cawdor watched me, swaying lightly back and forth, but saying nothing. "Did you have something to tell me?"

"Yep. Wanted to 'splain."

"About..." I knew very well what it was about. I was hoping he'd say it.

"'Bout the other night. Sorry I didn't have no clothes on."

"That was the least of my concerns."

We both laughed. Cawdor stepped closer and reached up, brushing his hand through my hair at the temple. "Didn't mean for you to see none of the rest of it neither. Not that way. But now that you know," he massaged the side of my head slightly. "What do you think?"

"I haven't decided yet. I'm still considering it."

This seemed to satisfy him. Cawdor kissed me again. As he pulled back, the familiar wolffish smile came across his face. "I heard you talkin' to that other feller."

I didn't have to ask how he'd heard me. "As I said, I'm still considering *all* of it."

"Carefully considerin' the whole situation, that's good, that's good," he nodded. "It's a big decision, this. Really, really big. You're smart to..." Cawdor paused to hiccup, "to take your time. Did you talk to Nascha? She said she spoke to you 'bout it."

"Yes, I did."

"Well, she probably didn't tell you *all* of it," Cawdor gestured broadly. He was even drunker than he appeared at first glance. "See... there's always a stoppin' place." He held up his open palm. "For everthin'. A stoppin' place for gettin' back at what you really hate." He brought his palm back down and punched his fist into it with a loud smack, ground it around, then relaxed. "And a stoppin' place for what you really..." Cawdor took a step towards me, "really..." another step, "really want."

His green eyes flashed into mine. Not a blinding light, but a beckoning one, like the sunlight outside a schoolroom window on a warm spring day. "If you really wanted to be like me, I could show you how to find it," he whispered. He was so close that I could feel our lips touch again as he formed the words.

"The stopping place."

We closed our eyes and stood together like that for a long time. Breathing in and out in unison. Finally, Cawdor crossed out to the door and left, saying nothing more.

And so that is where I am this evening. Will I go back East with Ernest, or will I stay in the West with Cawdor? And become... what, exactly? In either place?

I pride myself on being an honest person in matters of the heart. Yet honestly, I don't have the slightest clue which one to choose. But I do wonder... isn't there some third option? One in which I choose my own destination?

September 10, 1858

B randy had a very definite opinion about my new potential romantic entanglements. This was no surprise. Brandy has an opinion
about everything.

"Which one is he?" Brandy asked. She peered around the saloon in
a more obvious way than I would have liked, after I told her about
Ernest and his almost-proposal. Making an effort not to point with
my finger, but instead by turning a breadstick sideways to indicate his
location, I directed her attention to Ernest. He was sitting at a table
conversing with Jonah's Uncle Sam, the banker, and a few other men
I didn't recognize. Ernest was sitting with his back to us.

"Not a complete tragedy," Brandy said, appraising him. "Too short
for my taste, but he's in shape and doesn't appear to show any signs
of going bald, even if he is a ginger." Ernest turned and put his arm
over the side of the chair, allowing us to see him in profile. "He'll
probably have a double-chin if he puts on weight when he gets older.
But that nose!" Brandy giggled. "Let's just hope you have only boys.
Any girl with a nose like that would be downright vulgar." She pulled
her fingers down into a cone to indicate Ernest's long, pointed nose.

"What makes you so certain we'd have children?"

"Oh, honey, doctors always have a passel of kids!" Brandy cackled.
"There'd be nothing left of you after popping out five or six of the little
heathens. It's why first wives are always so paunchy and die early. They're
just worn out." She took another sip of her claret and concluded the
appraisal. "Still, he's definitely suitable. And you may be right. Given his
past, he might not want children, which would be a blessing for you. Life's
always better as a second wife. Not only might you avoid children, but

you'll also inherit his later career money. That's when they always have the most."

"Don't you find it just a bit unnerving though, that he assumes so much?" I probed. "I mean, we only spoke that one evening at length. Then he had all those bizarre dreams and came all the way out here. It's hundreds of miles!"

Brandy pondered this. "Men will say anything to try to appear like a protector, it's true. But you say too he really believes in all this mumbo jumbo spiritual whatever-you-call-it. Can't be many other sensible, educated women besides yourself who do. At least, in the polite circles in which he moves. Perhaps he is truly that smitten to find a lady who doesn't suppose he's insane. Which brings me back to my point. A man will say almost anything to a woman to seem strong. From what you've told me about his previous life and that wretched first fiancée in St. Louis, it's very possible that Ernest viewed you as a friend during your initial meeting. Only later, as he pondered how much less crazy you were than she, even though you still cottoned to all his other bizarre goings on, did it dawn on him that you might be the one who got away. So out here he came at a gallop, with his wild premonition story. Ready to whisk you off your feet."

"So, you think it's a lie then, about the dreams?"

"I think his infatuation with you is very genuine," Brandy said. "But yes, I believe the dreams are probably just a line to fish you in."

I settled back in my chair, processing this somewhat clouded view of the situation. "Okay, what about his proposal? Do you think that's just a crock too?"

"Oh, no. I believe that's for real. If I were you, I'd take him up on it," she answered curtly. "Get the hell out of here and go back East. Especially since he's willing to escort you there without marriage first. It's like he's your ticket back to civilization. When you arrive at the station, you can scope out all the other prospects before you make up your mind. Personally, I could never figure out why you came here in the first place. If my family had an established bar and cheese company in Portland, I'd be up there running it right now."

"We're two very different people, I guess," I replied, folding my napkin into smaller and smaller triangles on the table as the waiter cleared our plates away. "Here's the biggest problem I have with it. I don't love Ernest. How could I? We've only spent time around one another for two actual days. Yes, I agree that the school idea of mine was a disaster. It's probably not going to work out, given the circumstances. But it's not as if my trip out here has been a total waste. I've seen a part of the country and met people whom I'd have never known existed otherwise. And that's meaningful." I sat the folded napkin triangle on the table pointing skyward like an arrow. "So, I'd kind of like to stay and see it through. Just until the end of the school year."

Brandy smiled. Not her toothy, professional smile, but with just one side of her mouth twisted up into a half-frown. "By meaningful interactions with other people, I take it you mean a certain Cherokee trading man whom everyone in town has taken note of hanging around the school and engaging in a little free handyman work?"

"It's not like that," I said, more defensively than I intended. "We haven't done anything."

"But you've been thinking about it," Brandy mimed a contemplative pose. "Pined for it," she mocked a tragic heroine gazing up at the stars. "*Desired it*," she raised an eyebrow as the sidelong professional smile returned.

I nodded slowly to myself. "Yes. Yes, in fact I have."

"Well, you're a fool," Brandy said, dismissing me with a wave of one hand and beckoning to a group of men entering the saloon with the other. Russell's men, with him in the lead. Green Russell ignored Brandy as if she were a passing bird and headed straight for the table with Dr. Wheeler and Jonah's uncle. Brandy leaned down and whispered venomously in my ear. "I've spent my entire life trying to gain and hold the attention of men with some modicum of money and social standing without one shred of success. Yet here you are, with a fish on the line and you're about to cut him loose with the hook in his mouth, all for a shark you've seen out on the horizon. Clearly, there are many lessons they do not teach women in college about how to survive."

With that, our amicable council was broken. Brandy turned on her professional smile full power and left the table. She wormed her way into the seat between Russell and Ernest, who looked hopefully over for me to join them. Brandy even gave a halfhearted wave of welcome in appeasement, although I knew she was still fuming about our conversation. I pointed at my watch and declined, gathering my things and stepping out into the chilly night air alone. Although I did not remain so for long. I heard hurried footsteps behind me. A voice called out, somewhat self-consciously at the prospect of being overheard.

"Mae, wait! I would like to walk you home so we have the chance to..." here, Ernest stopped, with usual hesitant awkwardness. "To talk over again what I asked you the other day. Have you given it any more thought?"

"Yes, Ernest, a great deal," which was true. I had. Even though I didn't trust my feelings enough to share them. No use in breaking a fellow's heart when you're not absolutely certain. He looked disturbingly hopeful. "I just need more time. As you know, the school isn't going very well so far, but I do have a year contract."

"If that's the only problem you perceive, the contract and waiting out the year, well that's no problem at all," replied Ernest, beaming. "I've been talking over the prospect of opening an office here with Sam Krause. He's the banker I was having dinner with. Krause says he knows you through his nephew Jonah. He agreed with my proposal that Auraria needs a doctor. He is willing to finance an office for me, fully furnished with all the equipment I'd need, at a lower than usual rate. That way, we can stay here through the winter, get to know one another better, and I can still work. When the spring comes, and all the wildcatters start pouring into town, I'm certain I would have no trouble recruiting a newly graduated doctor to take my place so we could go back East."

I have to admit I was impressed at how thoroughly Ernest had planned it all. Impressed, and a little sad. He's a very nice man. Also, as Brandy said, other than being a bit short, which doesn't bother me, and having somewhat of a more prominent nose than is usually desirable on a fellow, Ernest is not terrible looking. Men with ginger hair can be cute in a way. Clearly too, he is smitten with me... and still...

"I appreciate all your consideration Ernest, I really do," I told him. "But I can't in good conscience give you an unequivocal answer when I'm not completely certain. I'm sorry."

His exuberance deflated a bit. However, he was willing to take encouragement wherever he might find it, I could tell. "That is perfectly understandable. We have all the time in the world." Ernest left me with a slight spring in his step that indicated he felt progress had been made. I hope I didn't give him too positive of an impression about his prospects. My intention is to let him down easily and gradually over time. Because I do believe in my heart he's a genuinely good fellow—just not the right one for me.

Stepping into the moon-darkened schoolhouse, I trod upon a letter lying on the floor. Someone had doubtlessly slipped it under the door. Without opening it, and even though the envelope bore no markings other than my name, in an ornate and many-flourished hand, I knew who it was from.

Mae,
Meet me in the morning at daybreak, on the cliff overlooking the Ute village. I'd like to ride out to the mines so I can show you something.
JC

As usual, vague and mysterious. Folding the letter and going upstairs to work on piecing the canvas together for my sawdust-filled floor pillow, I wondered if that wasn't part of the appeal. Too big of a part. Once a mystery is revealed, the result is often less than appealing.

September 11, 1858

The stillest place in the world is the desert just before daybreak. I learned this when I rode up to meet Cawdor alone at the ridge above the Ute village. Having grown up in a seaside city, if I wanted to experience quiet time alone, I could always go out to the coast. I was used to the constant roll of the waves as being a peaceful sort of backdrop for my thoughts. Thus, the total silence of the early morning desert felt unnatural. Like the tension in the air just before the first massive burst of thunder announcing a storm. Rather than finding solace in the stillness, I found myself constantly looking over my shoulder. If not for the comfort of solid contact with Cressie's saddle beneath me, I would have surely turned back. The stillness was so eerie, I felt as if I had somehow entered another world entirely.

Seeing Cawdor slouched in Troy's saddle, waiting for me as promised, was reassuring. I was also happy to see that he was sober, and had bothered to dress smarter than his usual rumpled mass of fabric that passed for clothes. New boots, a jacket with real trousers, not denim, and I could swear he'd actually pressed his shirt!

"Don't you look sharp today!" I complimented him.

"Thought you'd appreciate the effort," Cawdor said. "Since it occurred to me you'd never seen me in anything other than my riding clothes and, *ahem...* the Other."

"I do," I replied, intentionally avoiding engagement with what he meant by the "Other" comment. "So, what did you bring me out here to see?"

"We'll get to it," Cawdor replied, overly casual in tone. "I'd like to explain a few more things, at least as much as I can. Maybe correct whatever notions Nascha's been filling your head with. She can get carried away sometimes. I thought you might want to hear a bit of a different perspective. That way you'll really know what it means to be someone like me."

My response to this was what I hoped was a thoughtful sounding *hmm*, to encourage him to explain.

Cawdor took a deep breath, stretched to adjust himself into a slightly rearranged slouch in his saddle, and began.

"As I told you before, Momma did all she could to raise me right. At least, according to what she thought I needed to know. Her theatrical friends helped out a lot too. Even though my father had died, I didn't want for other men to look up to in his place, or for her affection. Until Momma got sick, I never wanted for anything really. Food, nice clothes, plenty of opportunities for education and entertainment. Growing up as I did, I think that helped me later on to control the *Other*, if you know what I mean."

I gave another hopefully supportive *mmm hmm* as he continued.

"In fact, until I came out here, I'd really never had anything particularly bad happen in my life. Besides my father's death, which I was too young to remember, and Momma's illness. I had so long to get used to the idea of her dying that the shock was not too great. As a result, I'd have to say my Otherness has been what Christians might call a blessing. I was sick with tuberculosis when Uncle Russell abandoned me in this desert. Having nursed Momma in close contact as I had been for so long, it was inevitable I would catch it at some point. I would have died from it too. Since the only real injustices I'd ever faced before I came into this Nature were those, it's easy to maintain the self-control needed to make the most of it. To wield the power without letting it consume who I still am inside of it."

He pulled back on the reins to slow Troy's pace slightly. He came into step with me on Cressie as the path widened into the road. "Nascha probably didn't tell you that, did she? That being what I am doesn't necessarily mean you will inevitably become what she is. Self-control is a good part of it, yes. But that's all relative. It matters where you start from too."

Although Cawdor did not ask the question directly, I knew he meant for me to share my story with him as well. It occurred to me as I told him about my family and my old home in Maine how strange it was that I'd not done so before. Back East, I could never stop talking about my family. Out here, I hadn't said a peep about them to a living soul other than Brandy and Penny. When I finished, he seemed satisfied with my account.

"I think you'd be fine with it," Cawdor said nonchalantly. His demeanor was the same as if I were choosing a new home or some equally mundane long-term commitment, rather than a change in physical and spiritual form. "The choice is yours to make really. If what you've just described was completely honest, I don't see any reason why you shouldn't be able to have full control of it, like I do. Might even enjoy it some. I have. It's very freeing, the wild abandonment of it. The total absence of fear."

"Yes, Nascha told me about that part," I said. Feeling what he was hinting at, I realized for the first time that our purported mission of showing me the mine might actually be an afterthought. The opportunity to have this conversation alone might be the real goal. "Would it have to be so? That I would need to change. For *us* to be a *we*, I mean?"

"It's safer that way," Cawdor said. "Certain bursts of emotion are harder to control. I have found there are various activities," he glanced over at me sideways to gauge my reaction, "that, because of their intensity in feeling, sometimes provokes the appearance of the Other when it is not particularly appropriate. Not trying to be indelicate, but that's the way it is. Drinking helps dampen it down, which is why I hope you'll excuse certain aspects of our encounter the other night. And all the other times you've seen me pretty skunked as well. It's easy enough to talk about out here in the daylight, riding apart from one another like this. When I'd only recently come back from hunting, and had a long time out there to think about the prospect of us being together though..." Cawdor readjusted his hat and reset his gaze on the horizon. "It was safer for me to be heavily anesthetized."

"Oh," I breathed. "I understand. So, what Brandy said about..."

He snickered. "Brandy's always thought I was queer because every time I'm out somewhere, I'm always drunk and don't ask for nothing from the girls. What she don't know is that if I weren't intentionally shitfaced and barely able to function every time I was in the saloon, somebody could get seriously hurt from me... expressing my emotions."

"However, if your chosen companion were also... an Other," I responded carefully. "Then, everything would be okay. I follow you. But why not someone like Nascha? Or one of the other women. Why me?"

"They're all too mean!" Cawdor exclaimed. "They've gone past the point where they're not like what I am anymore. Not really. I'm sure she gave you an earful about all that. Plus, Nascha's married. I like Gad, even though he's a poor sort of sap for hanging onto all that for so long. Must be something else to it for them. Because if their marriage were *really* real, Gad wouldn't be alive by now." He snickered again. "Maybe that's a new avenue of gossip for Brandy to explore."

I ignored the disturbing mental image that his remarks about Nascha and Gad conjured. "What about the other part? Why me?"

"Don't know," Cawdor said. He glanced sideways at me again from underneath the brim of his hat, his wolfish grin taking over his face. "You ain't much to look at, and pretty stupid to boot. Ain't like we'd ever have a thing to talk about, you knowing nothing about the theater and all. Not to mention being too weak to put together your own furniture."

"You're an absolute ass!" I said, swatting at him playfully. He dodged away, galloping ahead and then wheeling Troy into a circle around me. He was very happy to have gotten out of such a serious conversation without having to say a single thing even remotely complementary.

"There it is, down there," Cawdor called, pointing down into the valley. Trotting up behind him, I could see the riverbed. Miners had set the sluice gates all along it to trap sediment for panning. Following it up toward the source, I recognized the open mouth of the mine from my dreams.

"That's where they had the..."

Cawdor finished my sentence for me.

"Cave in, yep." He steered Troy down the trail into the camp. "They could likely have made the big strike this summer, if not for that. But they dug into it too quickly, without putting in the proper support. Greedy, as usual. Trying to get too much too fast, that's always Uncle Russell's way. I heard that's what cost him the silver mine in California. Same thing. Got a decent amount of silver out of it though. Enough to get started on this operation once he'd gotten wind of it, but he lost a bunch of men there too."

"Were they your folks? The men who died?"

"Sort of," Cawdor said, twisting this way and that in the saddle to maintain his balance as Troy picked his way down the steep, rocky slope. "Some of them were related to Momma in a roundabout way, I suppose, being Cherokee from the same general tribe. Russell's wife is too. We weren't ever close, since Momma and I were sort of exiled in Savannah. I knew of them only from what Momma told me before she died. Even then, they weren't too friendly. The ones who stuck by Uncle Russell were just about as bad as he is. All about the money. Nothing else matters. Not who's an Indian and who's not, or who lives or who dies. This ain't their land anyway. Not like it is with tribes who are from around here. Eastern Cherokee have already been pushed all the way across the country from anything that was really theirs to begin with. We ain't got nothin' left to lose at this point."

He spat into the dirt at the entrance to the mine. On some of the rocks, I could still glimpse faint traces of blood from the massacre I'd seen in my dreams. I shuddered. "Why isn't anyone else here? Aren't there supposed to be guards or something?"

Cawdor hopped down from Troy's back and tied him to a scrub pine nearby. "All gone to town. It is Saturday, you know. Everybody just got paid last night. Probably gone to Brandy's establishment, if I had my best guess." He winked at me, and my heart turned a flip. "Except the two left to guard. I paid them off. They're probably enjoying their drink by themselves elsewhere, I reckon."

"What did you give them?"

"Eh, nugget of gold each. They're easy enough to find, laying around and in the riverbed if you watch for them closely. Fortunately, I have excellent eyesight." Cawdor's green eyes sparkled in the sun. "Wanna come inside and see? It's safe enough, the parts we'll be going to."

He motioned for me to follow. Lighting a couple of kerosene lanterns, Cawdor handed one to me as we went inside. I'd never seen anything else like it in my life. After the entrance, everything before me was intensely black. I could see the silhouettes of the support beams and ladders leaned up against the walls, but it was already so dark they were merely shadows. Cawdor could sense my apprehension moving forward, and took me by the hand. After we'd gone about a hundred yards, the tunnel made a sharp curve to the left, and the comforting light of the entryway eclipsed into the void.

"Look right over here," he said, guiding my hand. Feeling along the wall, I touched many cold, sharp edges. Moving my lantern closer, I could see my palm was on a wall of pure gold.

"Oh my God!"

"Shhhh..." Cawdor hissed. "Not so loud. You'll make the bats swarm." He gestured to the ceiling. In the light of his lantern, I could see scores of sleeping bats.

I turned back to the golden wall, and began feeling around. Everywhere I showed my lantern was gold and more gold. As the tunnel went on, it seemed there was no end to it. The vein of gold went straight down into the center of the Earth. "What's down there?" I whispered, pointing further down the mineshaft.

Cawdor shrugged. "More gold, I guess. And sooner or later, who knows? Maybe the Devil. Although some might say he's already come up from out of there and is walking among us. I tend to think so sometimes."

"How much do you think it's worth?" I asked, swinging my lantern from side to side.

"Nobody knows," Cawdor shrugged. "Even Uncle Russell. Although he and Mooney were trying their best to guess. They wanted to make a somewhat believable lowball offer to the Utes. That is, before negotiations broke down, which Russell chooses to believe is his excuse just to take it all for nothing. It's gonna turn out to be the biggest strike since California in '49, I think."

"I can see why people would be tempted to steal it," I said. Glancing down at the floor, every loose pebble sparkled in the lamplight. I picked up a nugget the size of my fist. It was immensely heavy. "It would be so easy just to take one and put it in your pocket."

Cawdor grinned his wolfish smile at me. "Try it."

I put the nugget into the pocket of my dress, but I knew it was too heavy as I carefully loosened my fingers. Hearing the threads begin to pop, I took it back out again. "Oh, I see. You'd have to have a thick bag. Leather or something sturdier."

"And don't forget, this is the only strike for hundreds of miles producing nuggets of that size. Try trotting down to Sam Krause's bank, or Bent's Fort, or Hell... all the way back to Kansas. See if you don't run into a lot of difficult questions when you tried to exchange it. You have to remember everybody out here working the mine knows everybody else. If anybody tried to steal, they'd better get a good running start. Uncle Russell would have someone on their tail before they could buy a stagecoach ticket out of town."

"And then he'd try to hang them for it," I said, remembering the still-rotting bodies of the native men on the way into town.

"Probably. Although those miners who were executed weren't really stealing. Didn't find more than a few little flakes of gold on them, and those could have been planted. I was at their so-called trial. They were Utes. A group the local tribe sent down to spy while they picked up work so they could see how much gold was down there. Knowledge gives them better negotiation leverage for land deals. Russell doesn't want them to know of course, and wouldn't likely have hired them if he'd suspected initially. All Indians look the same to men like him though, and he needed cheap labor. It was much easier to say they'd been regular men in his employ who were stealing from the company. Believable and easy to rationalize to any townspeople who might call his ethics into question after a same day trial and execution."

"Why didn't the tribe do something to defend them?" I asked.

Cawdor gave me a sort of dumbfounded stare. "You've been teaching their children for a couple of weeks, have you not? What English they're able to speak is about the equivalent of what their parents know too. They were given no opportunity to offer a defense, and they wouldn't have been able to articulate clearly what happened even if they had been. Which brings me to another point..." he said, taking me by the hand again to lead me out of the mine. "You've got to be careful with what you say and do at the school. Not a soul in town, except maybe Jonah and Penny, appreciate what you're trying there. Teaching the Ute children to read and write in English. Being able to communicate clearly, in some people's eyes, makes it more difficult for them to be taken advantage of. Many of the settlers consider that to be a threatening prospect to everything they're trying to build up so that they can take over."

I winced at my own naivety. How could I have been so blind? The reason why no white settlers' children, besides Penny and Jonah, who were both outcasts, came to my school wasn't just that their parents didn't want them to be taught in the same room with Indian children. Those people didn't want Indian children taught *at all*. To keep them ignorant was to keep them humbled and vulnerable. Easier for them to be taken advantage of.

"So that's why they all signed up in droves, but then no one came?" I asked, as we rounded the bend and started upward into the light at the mouth of the mine shaft.

"Yep," Cawdor replied. "I hate to say it, but you have our two favorite big-mouths to thank for that. Once Jonah and Penny spilled the beans to the other children in town that you also planned to invite native children, that effectively ended any prospect you might have had to grow a school for the settlers' young'uns here."

"Then I'd already failed before I even got started," I said. I turned off the fuel to my lantern and placed it back on the hook as we stepped outside. "In order to continue to grow the school and get my contract renewed for next year, I have to be able to report back to Hartford that I've recruited and retained at least fifty students by year's end. I'll never be able to do that with just the children from the Ute village. There simply aren't enough."

"Nope," Cawdor said, replacing his own lantern on its peg. He untied Troy from the branch.

"Then what in Hell am I going to do?" I despaired.

"Leave," Cawdor replied simply. "That's what I'm doing. Dr. Wheeler ain't the only one who's got the means to go back East. Just because a man don't like to flash his money around don't mean he ain't got none. That only causes trouble."

Chalk it up to my own prejudices, but I have to admit I didn't think Cawdor had two nickels to rub together, given the sloppy way he dressed. "Where would you go? And how did you..."

"Get the money?" he asked. Fishing down into the top of his new boot, he pulled out a nugget the size of a quarter. "Eh... I take a little bit every time I have a chance to get down there. You'd be surprised at how often night guards fall asleep drunk." Cawdor smiled softly. A close-lipped smile, the tips of his eye teeth just barely visible. "Why, any kind of wild creature could just slip in and out past them with one of these in his mouth pretty much any time."

I had to know. "How much have you got?"

"Such noisiness about my financial state is unbecoming," Cawdor tutted. "If I didn't know you already as a lady and a scholar, I might think you were an average *gold-digger*." His eyes twinkled at the joke. He stuck the nugget back down in his boot. "If you must know, it's more than enough that I'll never have to work again once I leave here. As for where I'm going, that is yet to be determined. I might be swayed."

"Swayed by what?"

"Not by what, but by whom," he leaned in to kiss me lightly on the temple, and then turned to mount Troy. Untying Cressie, I followed suit.

"Aren't you worried you'll get caught? Or that Russell will figure out once you've gone?"

"Nah, that's why I'm waiting here and trying to help broker this deal with him and the Utes. I'm telling Russell I'm taking a cut of the Utes share, so he'll think *that's* where it came from. The tribal elders know I'm not accepting payment though. I told them I've already been taking my part, one little piece at a time. That was how I won them to trust me as the negotiator, by showing them some of the nuggets I'd already pilfered and making it clear I'd go in there and help them get back all I could steal. We had a really good laugh about it at the council meeting."

"What's in it for you, though? Why keep trying to help the Utes, when you've already got what you need and Russell's such a tough nut to crack?"

"All I want is the satisfaction of seeing Uncle Russell's face," Cawdor replied, his expression growing hard. "Not only when he's told *no* by an Indian, but when the Indian telling him is *me*. The one whose father was killed when people like him couldn't push him off his land. I want to push *him* off for a change. All the way back down to Georgia, where he belongs. Where there ain't nothin' left for him to steal, because bigger thieves than him have already taken it."

On the ride back from the mine, we spoke about more cheerful things. Mostly about places that each of us had been and wouldn't mind living. I found he'd never been to New England, let alone outside of the United States. I suggested we must go in the spring, as that was the best time. Then possibly move across the pond to England and some of Europe before we fully made up our minds. Cawdor was intrigued by the details of my journeys. I have no doubts he will make a most engaging traveling companion due to his inquisitive nature.

When we reached the schoolhouse once more, there was a notice secured by a small nail to my door. In formal, all-capital printed letters, it read:

MISS ULRICH:
THE TOWN OF AURARIA REQUESTS AN AUDIENCE WITH YOU AT AN EMERGENCY MEETING OF OUR COUNCIL TO-MORROW EVENING AT 7 O'CLOCK, IMMEDIATELY FOLLOW-ING SUNDAY SERVICES. PLEASE BRING YOUR STUDENT ROS-TER AND BE PREPARED TO RESPOND TO QUESTIONING.
SINCERELY,
AURARIA TOWN COUNCIL

"What kind of questioning?" I asked. Cawdor took the letter from my hand. He scanned it quickly.

"Like what I've been telling you about," Cawdor said, tossing the notice away. It caught in the evening breeze and blew into the street. "Apparently, they've decided to make a public spectacle of shaming you into kicking all the Ute children out of school. Then, they'll probably want you to devote your attention to educating their own little nightmares."

"Well, I'll just not go," I replied huffily. "The Institute at Hartford has a strict policy of not denying entry to any students who present themselves as willing and able to attend."

"Tell that to those poor fellas," Cawdor replied, pointing down to the end of the road, where the ragged remains of five native men still hung on the gallows, twisting in the wind.

September 12, 1858

S unday's town council meeting left me with no doubt in my mind that it will be impossible to continue my plan for integrating the children of natives and settlers. I have already written to the Institute in Hartford regarding the situation. I requested advice on whether I am to continue to finish out the school year with just the native students, plus Penny and Jonah, or if it would be more prudent to resign. I plan to post the letter first thing Monday. Since it is about six weeks for the post to run between here and Hartford, I hope to receive a response by Christmas.

The meeting itself was hostile, not only to the concept of an integrated school, but also directly toward me as an individual. The thinly veiled animosities I have felt from the women in town since arriving bubbled up as well. Quite a few snide remarks were made regarding my character and fitness to teach. The general consensus was that an unmarried woman of my age who was willing to travel so far from home alone must have *something* wrong with her.

Ultimately, the outcome was that I am to immediately cease and desist from engaging in the tutelage of white settlers' children in the company of natives. When I mentioned the fact that only two white children had bothered to show up at all, and that they were already separated into the morning session, whereas the Ute children did not arrive until after lunch, they seemed nonplussed. While the council itself never said so outright, the intention was clear. They want me to dismiss the Ute children permanently, so that their own children can have the entire day. Of course, only Green Russell was bold enough to say it explicitly. Although he is clearly the town blowhard in addition to its richest citizen, his message was supported by all.

As I left, no one would look me in the eye.

"What did you expect?" asked Cawdor, who had been waiting for me at the schoolhouse. He had not attended the meeting, based upon the assumption his presence would only further exacerbate the situation.

"I expected to perhaps find a few people who were willing to listen to reason," I answered in exasperation. "I mean, this is a new part of the country. A chance at a new world." I sat down beside him on one of the student benches, where Cawdor reclined with his legs propped up. "Aren't these prospectors supposed to come from all over? It wouldn't have been difficult in New England to find a few with more liberal views, especially amongst the abolitionist community. Why aren't there any abolitionists in this town?"

Cawdor uncrossed his legs and leaned forward to face me. "Because if you haven't noticed, the majority of these miners in Auraria are from Georgia. Southerners. A lot of these new Western townspeople are. They've already seen the writing on the wall. The South is bleeding capital, and a war is certainly coming back East. A war they don't have a prayer of winning. So, they're moving elsewhere to re-secure and reinvest their assets. I'm sure you've read about all the struggles these past few years with cotton production down there. Land's plumb near worn out. All those big plantations won't be able to sustain themselves more than a few years longer. Once that goes kaput, their whole world will fall apart. War or no war, the end is coming. Everyone smart down South knows it, so they're leaving. That's why Russell is here in the first place. You ought to have heard him talk years ago, on the way out here. He knows the days of plantations with hundreds of slaves to work the fields is almost over, and it's time to move on. Just because he's smart enough to realize that doesn't mean he isn't vicious. Most of the others in town feel the same as him. They're just too well-mannered to say so."

Cawdor was right, as usual. Thinking about it, I could see their prejudices laid plain. "So, you're saying I should just give up and go back to Maine?"

"Not necessarily," he replied. "There are other places in the world besides Maine where I believe that your abilities would be valued, if given the right introduction."

"Really," I scoffed. "Like where? Europe? I do speak French and bits of German. Perhaps I could..." Cawdor broke in.

"I was talking about coming to live with me," he said. "Among one of the tribes. You've seen my place with the Utes. I also have friends among the Navajo, Pawnee, and Arapaho. They're standoffish at first, but they're also wise to the changes that are coming. The leaders realize it's only a matter of time—spring really—before the valley floods with wave upon wave of these wildcatters. By then, it will be essential for them to know the language of their enemies so they will be able to deal with them. If not fairly, at least with equal understanding."

"You're suggesting that we," I gestured between the two of us, started to say "marry," then corrected myself, "come together and go live among the natives?"

My face must have appeared shocked at the suggestion, because Cawdor laughed. "What? The great emissary between cultures has never considered life among those whom she seeks to educate?" He made a *tsking* sound and continued, "Mae, I'm surprised at you. Yes, I agree it's not the easiest life to someone who's accustomed to the comforts and convenience of cities, but I think you would find it quite intriguing. And I didn't mean we were to stay forever. The urgency of their need for bettering communication will have arrived by summer along with all the wagons emblazoned, *Pike's Peak or Bust*. It's quite a different experience, I assure you, but not an unpleasant one. Gave me a completely new perspective on things. We could try it for a while. If you find that you miss city life, we can always go back East with the fall." Cawdor slapped his hands on his thighs and rose, stretching his long arms over the classroom. "After all, this is supposed to be America, right? Isn't the freedom to go anywhere we want and do whatever we choose the whole point of this great experiment?"

I agreed on all counts. And I do find the prospect of teaching native people whilst living among them intriguing and energizing after these worrisome past few months, as well as extremely freeing. I could teach anything I wanted. I would be going, as my favorite passage of Thoreau says, "to live deliberately. To front only the essential facts of life, and see if I could not learn what it had to teach, and not, when I came to die, discover that I had not lived."

Isn't that what we all want when we die? To be remembered as someone who really and truly lived?

September 26, 1858

I feel as if I should make some explanation for my absence from these pages. For the past two weeks, I have been waging a war of attrition against declining attendance from my Ute students. Although I made no mention to them of my discouraging meeting with the town council, ever since the Monday following it, I have lost students steadily. At present, fewer than half a dozen remain, and even they appear distracted. Their initial interest in the enterprise is certainly diminished. I have no other causes to blame other than the fact they have either been told directly or have sensed they are unwelcome. As an educator, it pains me deeply.

What am I to do? I have turned over and over in my mind Cawdor's suggestion that I go with him to live among the Utes, but that would mean completely abandoning my post here. When we do go back East, or anywhere else eventually, what kind of reference would the Institute be able to give regarding my capacity to teach? I can hear that grim Headmaster already. *She used to be an excellent teacher, but for some reason she went off her rocker when she went West, quit her job, and joined an Indian tribe. Not sure why—take your chances!* The fact that the citizens of Auraria were hostile to my methods would not help matters much either, since few schools are willing to accept such a rule-breaker. Strangely, even though we in education preach free-thinking, in practicality, it is primarily the conformists who secure gainful employment.

Additionally, I am troubled by Penny's absence from the classroom. I've pleaded with her to return several times. Penny seems to miss our time together, but her mother keeps blocking my messages. It seems that, as eager as Brandy is for her daughter to receive an education, she is not willing to risk raising the hackles of the men in town who provide her income by allowing her daughter to continue studying with Auraria's social pariah.

Speaking of being lost, I continue to drop hints the weight of anvils on Dr. Wheeler that I am not interested in returning his affections. Alas, they are to no avail. He has hung out a shingle for his doctor's office in one of the new buildings just down the way. Ernest must not have enough patients to occupy his idle hours, because I swear he watches at the window in the evenings for my students to leave so he can time his walk home perfectly to match mine as I depart for dinner. I know it must sound contradictory for me to support the idea of Penny potentially finding a liberal doctor to marry in the future whilst I am ignoring the affections of one at present. Ernest is surely a gentleman of that mold. He's charming, without being cloying, in a sort of stumbling intellectual way. We are certainly never at a loss for stimulating conversation, given our mutual interests in Spiritualism and other subjects. It's just that, for some reason, I don't feel for him in *that* way. The way that I feel for Cawdor, I mean.

Jonah cracked me up the other day. For even he has noticed that Dr. Wheeler appears to be waging a losing battle for my affections. "Women," Jonah said, shaking his head as if at not quite fourteen he had even an inkling of knowledge on the subject. "Always want what they can't have." Poor thing is referring, of course, to Penny. She continues to dodge his attempts at engaging her interest as much as I avoid Dr. Wheeler's.

"Isn't Penny the only girl around your age whom you really know, though?" I asked him, as Jonah sat pouring out his woes to me one afternoon. "You can't judge all of us by just the one. Plus, you're both very young. Perhaps someday she'll change her mind."

Jonah heaved a heavy sigh. "Only seems to get worse as they get older though. Look at you. You're like the best old lady I know—no offense..." He added quickly, noting my surprise at being called old outright. "But you don't give a fig about that poor Dr. Wheeler who follows you around."

"On the contrary, I do give a fig," I replied, shuffling the papers together that I had been correcting for him and handing them back. "Dr. Wheeler is a very nice man, and I enjoy his company as a friend and colleague. He will make someone an excellent husband and his children a perfect father. It's just I'm not that person. I want something different."

"You want to be with Mr. Cawdor," Jonah agreed. "I know, I know. I can see the way you get all sparkled up when he's around. But why? He ain't nothin' special. Not really."

"To me, he is very special," I said primly, hoping to end the topic by getting up to put on my coat. The last thing I wanted on a Saturday afternoon is to have a lengthy conversation about my romantic interests with a thirteen-year-old. However, I could hardly help it. Jonah has a tendency of making the conversation veer in that direction. As if by examining my life as a kind of specimen, he could solve the question of human affection like it was a scientific problem.

"Is it because he is... what he is?" Jonah asked. "What we saw? Is that what makes him so special? That he's different, and strong so he can protect you maybe?"

I paused in mid-wrap of my scarf. Jonah and I had spoken of Cawdor's transformation, and that of the women with him on the night of the attack, in hesitant suggestions over the past few weeks. Jonah knew we could not speak of it openly, for fear of retaliation by the pack against Cawdor. He also knew Cawdor and I shared dreams, and that some of his dreams overlapped with ours, albeit from a different perspective. Yet Jonah's connection of my greater level of interest in Cawdor with our shared dreams and *Otherness* as we called it, since we couldn't say the true name, was of his own deduction.

I tend to agree with his rationale. "Perhaps that's it, I hadn't thought of it that way."

"Is that what makes it happen then?" Jonah asked, pushing his glasses up where they'd slid down his large, wide nose. "Why a girl chooses one fella over another? They have to be the same in the ways that both of them are different?"

"I think that's one of the things, yes. Also, I think it helps if they sort of fill in the gaps for one another," I explained. "Where one is weak, the other is strong, and vice versa. It never seems to go well when the both of them are too much alike."

Jonah's face turned very serious, as if he were studying the situation intently. "You and Dr. Wheeler are too much alike in your own strengths to like each other. However, you and Mr. Cawdor are just different enough. I get it. So, do you think if I could show Penny that I was really strong, but not in the ways she is, and different, but in a likeable way, then that might do the trick?"

"Jonah," I sighed, as we left for dinner. "You're trying to apply logic to a situation where logic simply has no place. Love is the most illogical thing man has ever invented." He seemed downcast during our walk down to the other end of town. Thankfully, he perked up when found out the saloon was serving barbecued pork, which was his favorite.

As I stood fumbling around in my shoulder bag on the porch for some money before we entered, Jonah hugged me. A big bear hug that would have toppled me over if I had been more unsteady on my feet. I wasn't expecting it. "Thanks for being like my mother," he said. "For listening, I mean. No one else ever listens to a word I say. But I have a lot of them. Words."

That he does. About a myriad of topics, now that he reads constantly. After dinner, as I watched him walk back to his aunt and uncle's house in the early chill of evening, I knew Jonah Mooney was going to be all right, despite all that's happened to him. Inside, at least. It's sad though. Given the fact he's a big, clumsy, boy who talks too much, it's unlikely that he'd ever find anyone else to listen.

Hopefully, I'm wrong though.

The world would do well to hear someone as thoughtful as Jonah is at his age.

How many thirteen-year-olds would be both smart enough to attempt to fathom logic from love, and sensitive enough to accept the answer when they failed?

Only one whom I have met. A prodigy of a strangely unfathomable kind of alchemy.

October 3, 1858

I've given up on going to church altogether. Every time I attempt, it's like this impenetrable phalanx of hoop skirts prevents me from entering. After nearly three months in town, I still can't even find a pew without someone pushing me to move along. It's almost comical, this game of musical chairs they play in which I'm always the odd woman out. Even though this morning I'd redoubled my efforts at giving all appearances of being a model citizen in hopes of getting into good graces with the mothers of town, the heavy curtain of their unspoken prejudice seems to have been drawn against me forever.

Nevertheless, when I returned to the schoolhouse this morning after failing even to hear the sermon because I refused to tolerate sitting on the porch again like a naughty child, Cawdor was waiting for me. We had spoken about the prospect of my attending the meeting of the intertribal council, which was in the evening. It was in support of that visit I had tried one last time this morning to gain an audience after church with the mothers of my potential students. I had hoped to bring some kind of olive branch to the tribal council meeting as an overture of goodwill. Alas, it was to no avail.

"Well, I can't guarantee the elders will welcome you with open arms either," explained Cawdor, as we rode out to the Ute village. "But since I'm bringing you, I can guarantee you'll at least have a seat in the circle and be allowed to speak your piece."

Turns out, he was right. The elders' council began at dusk, after an excellent meal of smoked buffalo, mashed sweet potatoes, corn with spicy peppers, and fry bread. As we milled about, I could see from the differences in their dress and speech that members of several different tribes were present. The fact that my remaining Ute students recognized me and rushed up to chatter excitedly about why I was there helped to defrost a bit of the conversational chill with which the meal had begun. Some of their mothers even came up to introduce themselves, with the help of Chenoa and Nascha, who were also there. They were really helpful, considering that Cawdor split off to go sit with some men as soon as we arrived. I didn't see him again until the council convened.

Once we'd settled down into the council meeting itself, I immediately noticed a difference in the way that business was conducted in comparison to the practices of the Auraria Town Council and others in Maine that I had attended in my past life. Although one youngish looking man opened the discussion, it wasn't readily apparent which one was in charge. I recognized Gad sitting by Nascha, but none of the others. Cawdor, who by this time was translating bits and pieces for me in whispers, explained the preferred method was for speaking authority to travel around the circle of elders once, so that everyone had a chance to voice their concerns. Then there would be a sort of group discussion by everyone regarding what was to be done.

When my time came to speak in the circle, I told them about the idea Cawdor and I were considering, that I would like to come to live with him in the Ute village to teach English to their children, with their permission. Some of them understood my request, but others had to wait for Cawdor to translate the message. He did this very adeptly into Ute. After Cawdor finished, Nascha added something quickly in the other languages, besides what I had said.

"She's telling them you have the support of her and the other women of her group," Cawdor whispered in my ear. "Her endorsement carries a lot of weight around here. Every man in these tribes is scared to death of her." Glancing at the expressions on the faces of the other men in the circle as Nascha spoke, I knew Cawdor was right. They were hanging on her every word and nodding almost in unison. What she had told me about the greatest benefit of what she had become was true. Their attention was rapt, and their fear of her judgment palpable. No one else who spoke in the council meeting garnered so much deference.

Many other matters were discussed, as the talks continued around the circle. Cawdor narrated the highlights to me at the conclusion of each elder's remarks. Most were worried about the failed raid on the Ute village, and the fact that no retaliatory action had been taken yet by Russell or any of Auraria's men. They all knew it was coming, but none of the intelligence they'd attempted to gain either through direct contact or spying had given any clues. This made them nervous. Of secondary concern were the negotiations about how to properly divide proceeds from the mines, which had completely stalled in recent weeks. I could feel tensions were mounting. Cawdor continuously had to answer questions directed to him out of turn in the circle. The intensity of the debate among some of the elders grew more heated. Finally, the one who had opened the council pointed at me, then to Nascha, and without knowing precisely what words he spoke, I knew he was insisting both of us leave.

Once we were outside, I must have looked disturbed. "Don't worry," Nascha said. "It always gets like that toward the end of the council. Most of the elders feel as if they have to put up a show of arguing against any point that wasn't theirs to begin with, so they can concede in the end without looking like they've lost face. A lot of the back and forth is just posturing. Each flexing their power by pushing against one another." She shrugged with indifference, "Could be as big as this mining deal or as small as arranging which tribe will host the next council meeting. Doesn't matter, they're all very proud and like to go back to their people with the ability to talk about having won some points. It's how they hold onto people's respect."

We waited for another hour or so. I could hear the volume and pace of their speeches continue to grow louder and faster. At last I recognized both Gad and Cawdor calling out something that sounded like *esat tsanh* several times, which I took to mean something like "stop" or "listen," because everything got quieter. They each said something else quickly, and then all was silent. When the talking began again, only the first man, whom they called Ouray, spoke for a long time. I think he was the moderator.

"They're getting ready to vote," said Nascha. Then, sure enough, I could hear again what I took to be the *aye's* and *nay's* of whatever they were voting on in the circle. Several minutes later, they all filed out of the main lodge, chatting amongst themselves as usual. As they passed by me, a few of them gave me a slow nod, saying something that sounded like *yaateeh* and *osiyo*. I interpreted along with their gestures to indicate that meant *welcome*.

"Congratulations," said Cawdor, smiling and more relaxed than I had seen him in a long time. "You've been officially invited to come to the village and tutor the Utes whenever you're ready. Not just the children. A lot of the adults want to learn too."

"Was it that much of a struggle?" I asked, worried the debate indicated resistance similar to what I had experienced in Auraria.

"Naw," replied Cawdor. "Biggest concern was who would get to have you first. Navajo would like you to consider coming down to their village near Bent's Fort too, as soon as possible. They figure the gold rush settlers will move there next. They want everyone to be prepared."

"I told them you could both stay with us, in one of the apartments above the saloon," said Gad. "We agreed you'd stay where you are through the winter to teach as much as you could here. If you're still willing after spring thaw, you can move on to work with the Navajo. Then, we'll see what happens. The Arapaho were also interested, and perhaps the Apache after that. Since the next tribe's turn will be during the summer months when everyone is less stationary, we decided to wait and decide that at a later time. After everyone knows what the world is going to look like when this new gold rush hits."

I was slightly taken aback that so much had been decided about my fate without my even being in the room. I had expected a lot of talking, but for things to move more slowly, like everything else in my academic life. "What about the school in Auraria? What will I tell the Institute back in Hartford?"

Cawdor took my hand, pulling me close to his side. "You can take time to figure that out and start whenever you're ready. There are two apartments over Gad's place, so you can have one to yourself, or one with me." He paused and then added, "If you're interested in having me."

I'm certain that I stammered around in some dreadfully awkward way before I finally replied *yes*, I was interested in having him. By the time I got to it, Cawdor looked pale and Gad was chuckling at him. "Close call, my friend," Gad said, slapping Cawdor on the back. "Easier to sell her on leaving an entire civilization than taking you on."

After we'd both recovered from these revelations, Nascha was impatient to know what had been decided about the mining negotiations and what was being done in preparation for the counterattack. Everyone felt it was inevitable.

"Ouray wants us to keep waiting. Be patient," replied Gad. Nascha scowled at him disapprovingly as he continued. "I think he's right. We have absolutely nothing to gain by continuing to stir up hostility with Russell and his men. If we take our time and let the next wave of miners rush in with the spring, they'll get rid of Russell for us and save us the blame. It's possible at least some among this next group will be more reasonable and willing to strike a deal. Ouray's going to be the new Chief very soon, without question. His marriage to Chipeta in the spring will solidify the alliances among tribes. All the elders support him. As for retaliation, Russell should know he has neither moral justification, nor the men to support it. Too many have already died. Many of the Cherokee he brought out here have already left, hoping to beat the winter back home to Georgia. All Russell can do is hunker down in Auraria and wait to try and cheat any newcomers as they arrive. His time as king of the territory is coming to an end, whether he's willing to admit it or not."

Nascha shook her head in disgust. "Russell's not hunkering down. He's coiling up, like a snake. And being a snake, he'll strike at the weakest spot when he feels cornered. To suppose he won't is our greatest weakness. What do you think, Cawdor? You know more than anyone what Russell is capable of."

Cawdor dropped my hand and crossed his arms defensively to Nascha. There was a flash of something like electricity between them. "Of course I do. But I believe what the council decided is true. No matter how wicked his intentions might be, Uncle Russell knows a counterattack is futile right now. He has, what, fewer than a dozen men left? All his other supporters are just a bunch of townspeople who are far too afraid to take up arms against people they perceive to be bloodthirsty savages. How much of a threat could they be?"

"You'd be surprised," I said. Nascha fixed her owl-like gaze upon me, "what men are capable of when they feel cornered. I wouldn't put anything past Russell. Or most of the rest of them either. There's something uncanny about those people. I've felt it ever since I learned how quiet they kept the murder of Jonah's mother. I don't know what it is, but I agree with Nascha. They're capable of anything."

"Listen to these women," said Gad. He had disappeared when Nascha began talking and returned with a bottle of whiskey and a handful of tin mugs. He popped the cork on the bottle and poured each of us a drought. "Always worrying about something. Let's enjoy what we've decided tonight. Mae is becoming one of us!" Gad wiggled his mug in front of me, suggesting a toast. Gad, Cawdor, and I clinked our mugs together.

Not Nascha though. She looked down into her mug as if it were filled with worms.

"That's the problem with all of you," Nascha said, swallowing the whiskey in one slug and dropping her mug into the dust. She gazed up at us. "None of you remember anything. I have the opposite problem."

Her eyes gleamed like liquid mercury. "The problem with me is that I remember *everything*."

October 9, 1858

E ven though I am writing this, as the words flow through my fingers onto the page, I marvel in wretched bewilderment that such a thing could have happened to me. Yet, I must record it, if for no other reason than to get the facts down before my mind blocks them out in an attempt to save my sanity. My entire life, I see now, has been lived in the protective shade of mostly honorable people, with generally honest, if sometimes self-serving, intentions. However, what happened yesterday has changed everything I know. Now, I am divorced from the world, because I have found the world has divorced itself from humanity.

Friday began inauspiciously enough. Jonah and I had our morning lesson. Then he went over to Ernest's office, as has become their custom. Over the past few weeks, Ernest has been allowing Jonah to work in the afternoons as his assistant, compounding medicines and such. It's been a beneficial relationship for them both, and it is more constructive for Jonah to be learning a profession than roaming the prairie. Plus, it gave Ernest a companion who wasn't me. How foolish I was to think dodging Dr. Wheeler's intentions was my greatest concern! But no more of that now. I must force myself to write down the rest of what happened here.

It snowed all day. Several inches had already accumulated. The sky remained filled with heavy clouds, from which a few light flakes still drifted down. Darkness had fallen when, as Chenoa and I were helping the children organize their things to depart, I heard shouting outside. Nudging aside the woolen blanket I'd put around the door jamb to stop the drafts, I peeped through the crack. There, I saw a large crowd gathered. I recognized the faces of most of the men in town, and a good number of the women. Some of them called my name, in drunken, leering voices, along with various uncouth epithets referring to my native students. Shutting the door again, I called Chenoa to look. Unfortunately, Nascha had not come that day, nor any other day over the past week. She had gone hunting with the other women of her pack and Cawdor. They were hoping to eat well before the snow rolled in.

"What do they want?" I asked Chenoa.

Chenoa's normally placid face knotted with anger as she squinted out the crack in the door. Slamming it shut, she replied, "I have seen mobs like these before. We need to distract them here in the front so that the children can get out the back." Chenoa called the children to her. Saying something very rapidly in Ute that I didn't understand, their heads bobbed in unison. One little girl began to cry. Chenoa took her by the shoulders, speaking to her very sternly. The girl's tears stopped suddenly. She looked shocked. When Chenoa let go of her, she hastily stepped sideways and took her brother's hand, squeezing it hard. After giving a few more instructions, Chenoa shooed them off to the back door, where they waited, watching her tensely.

"What did you tell them?" I asked, peering around the curtains. The mob was now beginning to spread, encircling the schoolhouse. Jonah's uncle, Sam Krause, was walking around the growing circle with a bucket of something into which each were dipping sticks wrapped in rags. I didn't have to wonder long what it was. Green Russell followed behind Krause holding an extremely large fiery torch. As Russell touched each person's brand, it burst into flame.

Hearing the kerosene catch, Chenoa pushed past me and threw the door open. She let out a string of what I barely recognized as insults in Ute. The crowd jeered and booed at her. For a second, she turned her head to yell over her shoulder to the children, who scrambled for the back door. That's when it happened, and everything started to move extremely fast.

There was a loud crack of a rifle. The next thing I knew, Chenoa lay bleeding just inside the doorway, shot through the heart. The deep red pool of her blood spread rapidly across the floorboards. She twitched for a moment and then lay still. I stared at her lifeless body in disbelief. In an instant, I understood what was happening. We were living out the world of Ernest's worst nightmares, albeit slightly changed due to the unpredictability of natural human reactions. Even worse, there was almost nothing I could do to stop it.

The children, who had tried to run out the back door, slammed it shut as a volley of shots followed them from that direction. They ran screaming to me, snapping me back into my senses. Unable to shut the front door because Chenoa's lifeless body blocked it, I herded them upstairs to my loft as quickly as I could. They huddled together, crouched on the floor as I looked down from the window facing the street, to see two people come running from opposite directions.

Being only a few buildings away, Ernest got there first. He went straight up to Krause and knocked the bucket of kerosene out of his hand. The liquid inside it splashed over both men. Krause, recovering first, hit Ernest with his flaming torch and jumped back. Ernest cried out in shock as he caught on fire. He stumbled blindly backwards into the snow, where he rolled over and over. The crowd jeered at him. As Ernest attempted to put himself out, those nearest began kicking and stomping at him mercilessly. Krause, undaunted by this atrocity he had caused, picked up a second bucket of kerosene and walked up to the front porch of the schoolhouse. Several other men followed suit. At Russell's signal, they put their torches to bundles of straw they'd pushed against the walls. The fire caught at once, racing up the dry timber sides of the schoolhouse like lightning.

By this time, Brandy had run down the street from the saloon, screaming and waving her arms. On the saloon's porch down the street, I could see several of her girls wrestling with a struggling Penny. She was trying her best to break free and follow her mother. As the fire climbed beneath us, I saw Brandy make a beeline for Russell and slap him hard. Faster than a snake, Russell struck back, whipping Brandy hard across the face with the long silver barrel of his pistol. The smack of its collision with her jaw was audible above the roar of the crowd and the fire. From the way it cast off to one side, I could tell that her jaw was broken. Brandy sprang for Russell anyway, but he was too fast for her. Shooting from the hip, Russell put several shots through her chest and midsection. Brandy's innards sprayed out of her back as she fell forward into a bloody heap on the ground.

Seeing this, Penny screamed and escaped from the women holding her back. She ran up the street wailing, with the rest of the women chasing after her. They were quickly grabbed and restrained by some of the miners whom I recognized as Russell's remaining men. Russell yelled at Krause to tie them up. Binding the women and Penny hand and foot, they threw them like logs into the wagon from which they had taken the buckets of kerosene. They lay struggling and crying out, but unable to escape.

Just as they finished and returned to join the circle, I saw an enormous horse and rider flash down the street. Wielding a large ax on a long, curved handle, I saw Jonah bear down on his Uncle Krause. Jonah split the man wide open, from the top of his head down his neck and into his chest. The ax stuck for a moment until Jonah wrenched it free with a ripping sound. The crowd pushed back as he wheeled his horse. Holding the ax high above his head, Jonah charged forward again toward Russell. Whipping the gun from his side holster yet again, Russell shot Jonah off his horse. Terrified, Sir Gawain took off, the horse fleeing for his life in the direction of the Ute village. Jonah struggled to his feet, cradling his right arm and yelling for Penny. He was immediately set upon by several other men. The whole row tumbled over, brawling in the snow.

By this time, the fire was visible through the ladder hole, and I could feel its hot breath licking up through floorboards beneath us. Realizing we only had a few minutes before the whole thing went up, I had to choose. Put the children out the window and let them take their chances to escape the murderous mob, or allow all of us to burn to death in the loft. I grabbed the heavy, leather-bound volume of Shakespeare's collected works from beside my bed and used it to break out the window. Kicking out the last remnants of glass brought a new volley of shots from below. I urged the children to lay flat. It was difficult, because the floor was now almost the temperature of coals. Glancing around for something to break their fall as they jumped, I knew that my corn shuck mattress was too large to fit through the window, but the reading cushions I'd made from the sawdust and canvas could be squeezed through. Crawling across the floor, I dragged them back to the broken window and pushed them through the opening. More shots followed.

Understanding my intentions, the oldest boy who had tried to comfort his sister pulled himself free from her grasp and peered over the window sill. He motioned to me that he thought he could make the jump. As I watched, he slipped smooth as a mole out the window. When he hit the cushion, he curled up into a ball. The momentum carried him rolling into the street, where he regained his footing and took off running. He'd only gone a few steps, though, before someone shot him in the back. He fell face down. As the snow grew red around him, I sank to the floor with my back to the wall. Realization crept over me that we might not make it out alive. The five remaining children stared at me with wide-open eyes, too scared even to scream.

What was left? I thought, scanning the loft for some other way out. There was none. The children were now standing because the floor was too hot. The cracks between the floorboards glowed like lava. I had only one choice left, and I had to make it quickly. I yanked the white slip off my bed pillow and waved it out the window. A couple of shots, but as they ceased, I raised myself up and leaned out the window.

"I know it's me you're after," I called out. "If you'll let the children leave unharmed, I'll come down and you can do what you like with me." A cheer went up from below. Gathering the children, I told them they were to wait until they saw me stand and be taken, and then make the jump afterward as best they could. Taking one last glance around the loft, I spied this journal, which I tucked into the deepest pocket of my skirts and buttoned shut. Then, I climbed out the window, took a deep breath as I gauged the distance to land on the cushion, and jumped.

If I had been thinking clearly, I would have taken my boots off first. Perhaps that would have spared me the broken feet. Though their heels were very low, the impact of leaping from the second floor drove my wooden boot heels through the leather bottoms and into the heel bones of both my feet, cracking them. Calcaneus, they are called, as I have learned from Ernest whilst I lay here immobilized and writing, with both of my feet bandaged tightly.

Nevertheless, the pain that shot up through my feet and legs after I hit the ground caused me to stumble and fall, whereupon my attackers swarmed. Binding me, they looped another longer rope through the one around my wrists and dragged me over to my horse. There, I was hoisted onto Cressie's back like a slain deer, and tied once again with hand to foot crossways of the saddle, around her midsection.

With the pain beginning to blacken the periphery of my vision, I watched as the little girl who had cried first tentatively crept out the window. She jumped, as I'd instructed. However, she missed her intended mark of the sawdust cushions and fell forward onto all fours. Her little arms bowed in a way that her shoulders must have dislocated. She collapsed, sobbing into the snow. Jonah's Aunt Ida grabbed her by the legs and pulled her off to the side. Screaming like a dying rabbit, she lay there shaking as the other children bobbed up and down in front of the window, equally scared of the fire and the drop.

What happened next is somewhat of a blur. Most of what I know about it I've learned from Cawdor. At some point, I blacked completely out with pain. The last memories I have are seeing the angry hoard scatter as Cawdor, Nascha, and her Wendigo women charged. Fearing the beasts, the mob dropped their torches and scrambled away, taking the wagon of female captives and the injured Jonah with them. More concerned with the Ute children, Nascha and the others sailed past the loft window, snatching them one by one. Nascha herself picked up the girl with the broken arms. Cawdor managed to get Ernest onto his back. Cressida had been herded along among them, apparently with me unconscious and still tied to her back.

They brought us here to the Ute village. Ernest is severely burned and slashed from head to foot, most likely with several broken ribs. He is swathed in bandages that cover the damage to the sides of his face and torso. Yet, he remained cognizant enough through the whole ordeal to recall his treatment. Ernest told me one of the medicine men of the tribe had washed and dressed his wounds. Then, he'd given Ernest some type of pain remedy he did not recognize, which made it almost bearable. Both the little girl's shoulders had indeed been dislocated but not broken. She lay sleeping next to me in another bed. Her arms were swaddled close to her sides with her hands crossed over her chest so their repositioning would hold. Since there were no means to set my heel bones properly, I had merely been splinted to keep me immobilized until someone could sneak in to retrieve Ernest's instruments from his office. From what Cawdor told me, the school and all my things are ashes. Russell has chosen to place blame for both the burning of the school and the deaths surrounding it on Jonah.

"Why him?" I asked. "If he wanted an excuse to get rid of the Utes, then he could just point a finger at the tribe."

"That would be too big a lie even for Uncle Russell to tell," Cawdor replied. "What with Chenoa and her grandson dead and her granddaughter seriously injured, he knows there would be further retaliation if he tried to blame them. It would be too insulting. Chenoa was a beloved grandmother of the tribe. The boy and girl are her only grandchildren. They'd never stand for it. Plus, I think he's going to lose a lot of support amongst the townspeople themselves for shooting Brandy. That was cruelty even they can't ignore. If Brandy's girls were free, I'm sure there would already be some kind of internal rebellion brewing."

"So where are they?" I continued, the words feeling thick through a medicinal haze. "Where's Penny? And Jonah?"

"The wagon carrying the women was seen heading toward the mining camp. We know they were hauled away, but they haven't been seen since. Jonah is locked up in the back room of the church. Word is he will be tried on Sunday at sunset. After which, I'm sure he will be found guilty of all crimes and immediately hanged," Cawdor said.

"They can't hang Jonah. He's just a boy! Plus, he only killed his uncle to try to save us!" I replied indignantly, trying to sit up but finding it difficult. Whatever I'd been given for pain made my arm muscles numb. "How are they going to explain the murders of Chenoa and her grandson? Everyone saw them get shot before Jonah arrived. What happened their bodies?"

"Having no evidence didn't stop them from hanging those native men," said Cawdor darkly. "My best guess is Russell will call Jonah's Aunt Ida to testify the boy was a sullen and difficult. She'll claim he has dangerous tendencies that everyone in town knows he could have inherited from his father. Jonah's mother's murder is the worst kept secret in town, so it will be easy to believe the son is a killer too. They might spin it that he was possibly insane enough to have fixated on you too, so that when he found out you'd decided to leave town, he chose to vent his anger by burning the school. In a town where everyone knows everything about everyone else, it's easy to twist intentions. As for Chenoa and her grandson, it would be simple for them to say she attacked them first or the boy leapt out of that window armed. Not to try to escape, but to attack them for revenge. His father, Chenoa's son, is one of those hanging in the road."

"I didn't know that," I said, lying down flat on my back. I was astonished I'd never put two and two together. The Ute village wasn't that large. Of course some of my students must have been related to the men who were executed. It made perfect sense then, why Chenoa had come to guard them. Her grandchildren were her only remaining family. I'm ashamed to say I never asked. Perhaps Chenoa hadn't wanted the stigma to attach itself to her or the children. Perhaps she hadn't trusted me enough to confide in me. Now, I will never know.

Cawdor sensed my feeling of helplessness. "There is, however, something we can do. Nascha doesn't like it. She says we should only take care of our own. Yet, the council was against her. They believe as I do that Jonah is on our side, and the boy deserves to be saved for trying to help them. To do that, we'll need you."

"Anything," I said. "Anything I can do to help Jonah. He's... he's like," I could hardly get the words out. "He's like my son."

"Then the decision should be easy," Cawdor said decisively. "It's time you came into your wolf."

October 10, 1858

This morning, I finally understood what my beloved Walt Whitman meant when he wrote, "I cannot be awake, for nothing looks to me as it did before, or else I am awake for the first time, and all before has been a mean sleep."

In my new life as a wolf, I know the world around me must be the same, but I see it differently now. A dazzling array of colors and shades. And the smells! To know not only the scent of grass, but the soil that birthed it, the rain that nourished it, and the beasts of the land and air that have traversed it! Far beyond the five senses too, I have gained a certain sixth one. I only felt tremblings of it before, in periods of deep meditation. Now, even as I lie fully at rest, on the verge between sleep and wakefulness, I can feel shivers of the earth under my paws, and know a herd of bison is passing by miles away. Or a breeze wafting through the air ruffles my fur, and I know before looking skyward that a hawk sails above me. With each breath, I inhale the richness of the earth, the life and death wheeling around me every second. As I exhale, I understand all is as it should be, for wickedness has its place too as the left hand of righteousness. I am not within the circle, casting it protectively about me, but rather, I am one with the circle itself, integral to its living magic.

Last night, after the palliative herbs had numbed the throbbing pain in my feet and ankles enough to sit upon a horse when lifted into the saddle, I accompanied Cawdor on the long ride back to the cave in the desert. The one with all the wolf prints in a circle on the walls, where he had awakened into this new world. Carrying me inside, for I couldn't walk on my broken feet, Cawdor sat me down gently and explained the wonderful mysteries of this life. Then, he asked whether I was ready. I agreed. I was tired of the pains and disappointments, but most of all the helplessness to do anything about them. Those things came with mortal life because of who I was and what society expected of me. I say these things in the past tense, because I no longer feel the restricting pull of any of these bonds. Instead, it is as Nascha and Cawdor have described. In my wolf, I am free.

We slept through most of the day. When we awakened at dusk, Cawdor lay curled in his gray wolf form, watching me. The first sensation I felt was the throbbing of my feet and ankles, because the numbing herbs had worn off. I winced in pain. He made a soft whimper, patting his paws at me, and lightly caressing the side of my face. As I met his green twinkling gaze, I could hear Cawdor's voice in my head, although I did not see his wolf speak. He asked if I was ready, and if so, to hold out my arm. I did. Taking it in his powerful jaws, Cawdor nipped with his incisors, so only a small part of the skin on the inside of my forearm caught between them. He bit down, and I felt a sharp, stinging pinch. He tore away a tiny piece of my flesh about the size of a dime. Cawdor swallowed, and then began to lick the small, bleeding spot on my arm as an animal would lick a wound. Miraculously, the bleeding stopped in an instant. I looked down to see the wound had already scabbed over.

That's when I began to feel it. A tingling warmth radiated first through to the ends of the fingertips on my right hand, which turned into a long, slender paw covered in jet black fur as I watched. Then, as it traveled up my arm, I could feel my bones lengthening. The tension stretched out of my muscles as if I were recovering from a sprain. Gaining momentum, within less than a minute, my whole body shook with it. I could feel my chest cavity expanding as the buttons of my dress burst open. As the tremors finished coursing through my legs, I yelped in pain. I could feel the crushed bones of my feet and ankles grinding back together in their proper places. Then, they stretched out into the angular shape of a wolf's hind legs. The wave of pain was gone in seconds. As I grew, the seams along the back and shoulders of my dress popped. I reached around with my elongated muzzle and finished tearing off the dress with my teeth. I turned my shaggy head this way and that, circling my tail and curiously lifting my paws up one at a time to examine them.

Cawdor stood waving his tail, watching me. "You are just as beautiful in your wolf." He said, in unspoken words. He nuzzled up against me affectionately. Bumping his nose under my right front leg, I lifted it up.

Although all my visible fur was black, the spot on my forearm where he had bitten me was silvery gray. It was the color of his coat.

"A new wolf always carries the mark of the one who made her," Cawdor said, winking at me in a way that was very non-wolf-like. "So that you'll never forget me." His tail gave a few more swishes, and then he bounded out of the cave.

We stood on the steamboat rock as the last shadows of daylight faded over the horizon. When the next wave of thoughts passed between us, they were less like words but more like pulses. I knew instinctively he was asking me to follow him. Racing over the prairie, I ran faster than I had ever before as a human. As fast as a horse at full gallop, or maybe faster. It had not snowed as much there as it had in town a few miles north. After a couple of miles, the desert space passed into sea of dry autumn prairie grass, and our pace slowed. Cawdor crouched down on all fours behind a scrub pine. As our eyes met, I did so too. We sat waiting, breathing quietly in unison, for hours.

Finally, I could feel the same tingling sensation from my transformation begin again. From the tips of my ears, it spread rippling down my spine. I heard hoof beats approaching. The realization flashed across my consciousness that I was hearing elk walking, when I had never known such a sound existed. Each step they took on the crackling frost-dead prairie grass was as loud as that of a horse's hoof on cobble-stone. Cawdor and I lay down flat on our bellies behind the dead sawgrass.

Then, we saw them. A herd of at least two score, with a large racked bull elk following in the rear. His hair was completely gray. I could tell from the wide spread of his antlers that he was very old. His gait had a little hitch in it. He stepped mincingly, putting his back left foot down only when the herd came to a complete stop. Even then, he propped just the tip of his hoof on the ground for balance. Thoughts crackled back and forth between Cawdor and me, as we registered what this meant for our prospects. Exchanging the briefest of glances for reassurance of position, we pounced!

I went for the old bull elk's neck, and Cawdor the flank of his sore leg. Hitting him together, we knocked the elk over. The rest of the herd scattered, bleating in terror. Readjusting my grip as the bull struggled, I sank my teeth into his jugular and felt the hot rush of his blood flood into my mouth. Swallowing again and again in great gulps, the warmth of his life filled me from the inside out. As I lay next to him, with my jaws closed around his throat, the bull's whole life flashed through my mind's eye.

I smelled the flowers of his first spring as he frolicked with his twin sister while his mother watched. Next, I felt the heat of the chase for his first cow a few summers later. This was followed by the horror with which he fled a group of hunters. He saw many of his herd fall, leaving him as the dominant bull, though he had been merely one of the herd before. Last, my back left foot shot through with a spasm of pain when I felt him slip on a mountain trail. His hoof was caught in a crevice between two rocks until he twisted it out in a panic, snapping the tendons. He thought he would die there. However, his herd waited on their patriarch patiently for several weeks, until the chill of oncoming winter pushed them forward. He followed in the rear, too proud to let any of the younger bulls see him limping. All these things I felt as the fountain of his blood subsided. Letting go of him, all I could think of was *thank you. Thank you for this life you have lived, and have now given to me so I may live also*. At last, the old bull elk closed his eyes and lay still.

Cawdor and I ate our fill of him, organs first. Then we each tore off a hindquarter to drag back to the cave.

When we'd returned, I asked Cawdor in our unspoken language how long I would stay in my wolf like this. He replied I could return to human form at any time.

"As long as you hunt as we have done tonight, within the natural order and not for human-kind, your wolf will always be a part of yourself that you control. For that is in accordance with the law of life. The hunter and hunted move in an endless circle, which fulfills them both and is sound and good. Unfortunately, you too will live only until your time has passed. You will die, as a human dies, all in due time. It is the proper order of things. Only by casting away both what is human and natural, as Nascha and her sisters have done, can you gain immortality. But I ask you, what is that immortality worth? Is it not enough to feel the sun on your face and enjoy the mystery that keeps birds in the air, without having to live long enough to know the answer to every unfathomable question? As you already understand, the answer is never as satisfying as the wondering. That is the true cost of absolute power. Yes, there is an absence of fear, but fear is what makes us know we are alive. Having all the power, all the knowledge, and no self-preservative fear leaves nothing satisfying within life itself. All that remains is a hunger that never ceases. The unrelenting ouroboros of discontent."

Speaking thus, I watched as Cawdor's fur receded and his limbs shrank to their slightly-more than human proportions. Although I did not look to see it, I could feel my own human form returning as well. We sat naked on the blanket which had initially covered us as we'd fallen asleep in the early morning. "Is it not enough," Cawdor concluded, "to live simply as we are? Walking this line between life and death; however precarious it might be?"

"Yes," I replied, tracing my hand along the outline of his jaw and pressing my lips to his as we came together. "It is more than enough."

October 12, 1858

Cawdor and I returned to the village today. Although we'd planned to stay in the desert longer to give me more time to get used to the transition into my new life, I insisted we go back because I had another nightmare. Nascha met us on the trail. It appears that Ernest, Nascha, and her sisters shared this vision too. Though still not able to travel, Ernest was bursting to warn me about it as well. I am concerned both by the dream's contents, and that Cawdor did not share it with us. His absence from it, given the subject matter, is disturbing.

In the vision, we all see Jonah convicted of the murder of his uncle and the burning of the school. He was immediately taken out to the scaffold where the five native men's bodies still hung. As they were stringing him up, a violent melee erupted involving Russell's men, the townspeople, the natives, and us—the Others. None of us saw the outcome of it, for the nightmare stops at the moment the fighting begins.

Further, two Ute scouts have confirmed what Cawdor suspected was true two nights ago. Jonah's trial, such as it shall be, will be held on Friday. The projected outcome, of course, is that he will be sentenced to die as a scapegoat. His conviction will save Russell from having to provoke an attack on the village or risk his business interests before the full force of winter hits.

Penny and the women who worked at Brandy's saloon are being held at the mining camp, in some sort of cage like dogs. The rumor is they will be brought back for Jonah's trial. They will be given the choice of either corroborating Russell's version of the facts in exchange for their freedom, or being blamed as accomplices and hanged along with Jonah.

The native council has met and there are groups of warriors from each of the affiliated tribes on their way. Under direction from Chief Ouray, they will not accompany us into Auraria for the trial, but instead remain stationed on the ridge above the Ute village so they can observe the proceedings. The elders have officially decided the protection of a young white man is not an issue of tribal concern. However, the fallout that may result afterwards, if Jonah's captors are emboldened by his execution enough to proceed with a second raid on Ute village, is. They wanted to know the outcome immediately so they could prepare their defense.

Nascha and her sisters have agreed to accompany Cawdor and myself to Jonah's trial. I wondered about her unexplained interest in Jonah's welfare, until I realized it had nothing to do with Jonah at all. Nascha and her Wendigo women know, as do Ernest and I, that some sort of violent attack will be the only way to rescue Jonah from the gallows.

If that is the case, it may be the self-described last battle on their path to permanent transformation into Wendigos, which means total abandonment of their human forms. Having seen what they are capable of even in their current state, I'm somewhat scared to think what the cost of accepting their help might be when only their Otherness remains.

Last, I get the sensation Nascha is hiding something from me. Now that I have come fully into my wolf and I am party to the collective thoughts of the pack, I keep catching glimpses of something being worried over repeatedly in her mind. It concerns Penny, the women from Brandy's saloon who are being held captive, and also Chenoa's granddaughter, who still lies in bed mending her two dislocated shoulders.

Every time I attempt to engage those thoughts and probe deeper, it's like some sort of mental door slams shut. Nascha's consciousness turns to other benign topics. Though I've asked Cawdor about these visions, he claims to be sensing nothing, which makes me all the more uneasy.

I wish I'd come into awareness of my full wolf consciousness earlier. If so, I might have the ability to figure out how to break through such tightly closed doors of perception.

October 15, 1858

How can the life of one young man be worth that of so many other people?

That is what I lie awake pondering tonight. Rest eludes me while I listen to Jonah slowly breathing, sleeping the sleep of which only those who are bone-tired are capable. Jonah is in many ways an exceptional boy, but I cannot help but wonder selfishly if it would have been better for him to have died instead of Cawdor. What can become of a fellow like Jonah, who will be forced to go through life with only one arm? And what will become of me, with no life's companion to guide me in living the ways of the wolf?

This morning, Cawdor and I rode into town, bundled in long, heavy woolen traveling cloaks. He rode Troy, as usual. I was on Cressida, leading Jonah's horse Sir Gawain by my side. Nascha and her sisters arrived separately, so they would not cause attention by transforming in front of the crowd. Instead, they would be prepared to attack on signal after Jonah was on the scaffold.

The plan was for Cawdor and me to remain concealed in our cloaks and in our human forms through Jonah's poor excuse for a trial. Then we would transform and create a distraction near the scaffold as his sentence was being proclaimed. We agreed that Green Russell would not miss the chance to place final blame on his scapegoat personally in a public forum, and that would be our best chance to attack. Cawdor's role was to go immediately for Russell. Once Russell was down, we felt certain there would be mass confusion. During that, Nascha and her sisters would take would attack townspeople who had taken part in burning the school. Then they were to carry Penny and Brandy's girls to safety. My part was to watch carefully and do whatever was necessary to prevent Jonah from falling through the fatal drop. Then, get him on his horse and out of there as quickly as possible.

It would have worked, if not for two unforeseen circumstances.

The trial was moved from the smaller courthouse building to the church, in order to accommodate a crowd that seemed to include the entire town. We watched as Jonah's Aunt Ida, crying crocodile tears, falsely proclaimed that Jonah had always been a bad seed, prone to disobedience and violence just like his father. Ida Krause claimed she and Jonah's Uncle Sam had tried everything to bring him under hand. During her testimony, Cawdor whispered to me that Mrs. Krause had already sold the assets from her husband's bank to a speculator who'd come out West with the Lawrence Party. She planned to leave with her children on the next stage-coach heading East on Monday.

Then, one by one, the women from Brandy's saloon, along with Penny, were led in to testify. From their appearance, one would have thought they were the criminals. They looked like they'd been fighting for their lives while awaiting trial. Though they weren't shackled, they walked like doomed prisoners chained hand to foot, in halting, shuffling steps. The previously comely features of each lady were obliterated by the evidence of what could only have been savage beatings. Every one of their faces were swollen with broken noses and bruises. Their torn dresses were covered with stiff smears of dried blood. Penny, who entered last, had two black eyes. When she spoke, I could see her front teeth had been knocked out. Even worse was the look in Penny's eyes. A hollowed out, empty gaze that scanned the interior of the church nervously, but seemed to take in nothing. From the crude whisperings among the mining crowd gathered inside, I understood Penny and the women had been made victims during their captivity to what my mother had called "the worst instincts of men".

Nevertheless, almost all gave testimony claiming to have been eyewit-nesses to Jonah's killing of his uncle in cold blood. The saloon girls also lied and said they had seen Jonah kill Brandy too. Despite the fact most of the adults in the room had seen Russell murder his paramour, they murmured in assent to this false testimony. Only Penny, when asked to avow that Jonah had murdered her mother, remained silent. This was interpreted by Russell, who presided over the trial in the unique dual role of victim and judge, as merely a sign of the girl's trauma at having seen her mother killed. I expected Penny to protest, but her once spiky temperament had been beaten out of her. She just sat sobbing, her labored breathing whistling out through her broken teeth, until she was led away.

The murders of Chenoa and her grandson were never mentioned. Though I had braced myself to see their bodies displayed on the scaffold, I saw no evidence of them anywhere. Nor did I see the remains of the man who had been Chenoa's son, or any of the five other native men who had been left to hang for months. It was as if their existences had been completely erased.

At last, Jonah was brought forward to give his testimony. His right arm, the one in which he had been shot by Russell, was bare. The flesh swelled tight and red with infection. I surmised normal handcuffs would not fit round Jonah's wrists; that was the only somewhat humane explanation for the way in which he was being restrained, with a thick leather collar around his neck. Men walked both in front of and behind him, each holding onto a length of chain welded to the collar. From the flush in his face and the way he staggered from side to side as he walked, I could tell Jonah had a very high fever. Sitting down with a guard on either side of him, Jonah swooned in his chair and had to be propped up. Though he repeatedly declared his innocence and pointed to Russell and others with his good arm, his speech was often rambling and incoherent amidst the fog of his fever. The jurors, through Russell's guidance from the church pulpit, were led to believe this was due to Jonah having a complete mental breakdown after his murderous rampage.

The jury, all miners who worked for Russell, deliberated while openly chatting for all to hear. They reached their verdict of *Guilty* in under fifteen minutes. They wasted no time in leading Jonah to the scaffold. Only a single noose dangled there, made of very thick rope to accommodate a boy already larger than most men. The witnesses stood in a row to the right of the trapdoor in the middle, while Russell stood to its left. Jonah was walked to the center, the noose placed around his neck, and the chained collar removed.

Through his fever haze, I saw Jonah scanning the gathering of onlookers for something. Following his gaze to where it rested, I saw where I had left Sir Gawain and our horses untied near the post office. Recognizing Sir Gawain, Jonah's dark eyes flashed. Then, he turned his head ever so slightly in my direction. Instinctively somehow, he knew I was there. A weak grin played at the corners of his mouth as he caught me looking at him. Very slowly, he blinked once.

After the trial, Cawdor and I transformed behind the church, which was beside the scaffold. Still wearing our cloaks to conceal ourselves as best we could in our wolves, we slunk around to hide behind the church's woodpile. Then, I noticed the glowing silver eyes of Nascha and her sisters peering out hungrily from the shadows cast by the scaffold. They were positioned directly underneath where Penny and Brandy's girls stood, which I registered as suspicious. If their part in the plan was to attack the crowd from behind to increase the level of panic and distraction, then why were they in front?

Russell had already begun his sentencing proclamation, so it was too late to say anything. Cawdor and I waited patiently behind the woodpile. As he completed his recitation of lies, Russell asked Jonah whether he had any last words. Jonah coughed, and replied in a husky whisper, "Just three."

Cawdor glanced over at me and crouched, readying to pounce. I did the same. Russell asked snarkily whether the words were "Help me, Jesus."

Jonah didn't even look at him. His fever-bright eyes flashed with recognition straight past the back of the crowd as he yelled. "Sir Gawain, *now!*"

Many things happened at once. First, I saw Jonah's horse Sir Gawain come barreling through the throng, trampling every person between him and his stricken master with his enormous hooves. The guard holding the pull for the trapdoor froze, mouth open as he watched the great horse crush men into the dirt. Russell pushed the guard out of the way, and he released the rope. As the trap door swung open, Cawdor pounced on Russell, his jaws closing around his throat. I didn't see what happened next, as I sprang forward. Diving under the scaffold, I thrust my body between Jonah's feet and the ground. Above me, I heard multiple shots, then a series of screams as Nascha and her sisters leapt from their place of concealment and onto the platform. They grabbed not Russell's men, but Brandy's girls and Penny!

All these things only half-registered as I felt the heavy weight of Jonah's feet hit my back. "Grab the rope!" I cried, as Jonah scrambled frantically to keep his footing on the slope of my spine. There was a sway of his weight to the left as he caught hold of the rope, then the pressure lifted as Jonah flexed the considerable muscle of his left arm enough to pull himself out of the hole. When I jumped up through the platform, Jonah stood panting and in shock, still clutching the rope.

There, I saw Cawdor lying motionless on his right side behind Russell. Cawdor was in his human body. Three holes poured blood out of his back. Not wanting to believe what I knew was true, I circled slowly, nuzzling Cawdor and desperately wishing for him to move.

"Get away from me, you Devil!" Russell screamed. He had one hand pressed against the side of his neck. His flesh had been ripped away from the quivering muscle beneath and bled profusely. Russell tried to shoot, but all that came out of his silver pistol were a series of sharp snaps as he pulled the trigger over and over. Frustrated, he threw the gun at me. It bounced off my shoulder and went skidding across the platform. I snarled and pounced. Russell scrambled like a crab backwards until he fell off the back of the scaffold and took off running.

When I turned back to where Cawdor had lain, his body was gone. Kneeling by the spot where he had fallen, I ran my tongue over the wood planking. Not a spot of blood remained. The only thing I felt were three indentations, which upon closer inspection contained three silver slugs from Russell's gun.

I wanted to cry, but my body would not allow the release. All that came out was a series of dry gasping heaves that made the edges of my vision go black. I came out of my wolf and back into human form, shaking like a rabbit drawn up into a ball. Realizing my nakedness, I asked that Jonah close his eyes while I trembled down the stairs to fetch my cloak. Wrapped tightly in it again, but still shivering both from the snow beneath my feet and the shock of what had happened, I somehow managed to get Jonah untied.

The street was empty, save for the dead who had been trampled by Sir Gawain. The horse picked his way gingerly toward us, making gentle whinnying sounds. He seemed to sense his master's illness, and nudged up close beside him. Jonah was able to mount him from the scaffold, which was good, because I don't think I could have helped him up onto his horse in my state. Calling my horse and Cawdor's to us, I mounted Cressida and stroked Troy's mane. Cawdor's horse knew something was terribly wrong too. Attempting to comfort him helped me. At least, it made me able to cry as we rode past the charred remains of the schoolhouse and into the cold desert. Every door and window was shuttered. The town had rolled up like a scroll once more.

Jonah remained uncharacteristically quiet. I figured the rush of energy that hit him had worn off. As I watched, I could see he was crying. "Penny," he said, in a tremulous voice. "They took her."

"Nascha and her sisters?" I asked. I was still working through the trauma of Cawdor's death and hadn't thought much more about Nascha or the women. I assumed they'd helped the women to escape like we planned. I had not seen their bodies among the dead. "Yes, they were supposed to get them away as quickly as possible. Did you see where they went?"

"Yes, well... no," Jonah stammered, grasping for words through a haze of pain that muddled his thoughts as well as his speech. "Nascha and the others bit them, and they changed. Into the things... the things we saw. And then they all flew away. Over that way." Jonah pointed weakly toward the Ute village. A shiver ran over me as I realized what he meant.

Nascha and her sisters hadn't come to help rescue Jonah at all. Nor were they truly interested in revenge against Russell and his men for killing Chenoa and her grandson. Somehow, they had sensed the pain and fear felt by women who were abused at the mining camp and knew they could twist it into rage. For them, it hadn't been a rescue. It was a recruitment, which meant that twice as many vengeful Wendigo were heading straight for the Ute village.

"Can you ride any faster?" I asked Jonah. He nodded sleepily and nudged Sir Gawain lightly in the ribs. The horse, feeling his master sway dangerously backward in the saddle, trotted only a few steps faster before slowing down to his original pace.

I did not urge Jonah to try any harder. I was in no hurry to see what I was terrified we would find in the village.

October 16, 1858

When we arrived late that evening, it had already happened. Chenoa's granddaughter was their initial target. However, when Nascha's bite failed to transform her as it had the other women, the girl bled out almost instantly. Enraged, they rampaged through the village, killing as many as they could reach before sailing into the night.

"I don't think we'll see them again," explained Chief Ouray, when I asked if he was afraid of another attack. "Their transformation is complete, and their numbers are high enough now to take anything else they want. They had no particular animosity toward us. The only reason for the massacre was that Nascha couldn't have the last girl she wanted. Once her rage over that was unleashed, they took enough blood to satisfy her and left."

"I don't understand. Why couldn't she transform Chenoa's granddaughter like Penny and the women from Brandy's saloon?"

"Because her soul wasn't hard enough yet to go straight from human to Wendigo," Chipeta explained. "She was just a little girl who had lost her family and suffered a terrible accident. Through the love and support they had given her before and what she would have continued to receive from the tribe in their absence, she would have recovered. Her arms would have healed. Yes, she would have become tougher and more bitter, perhaps enough to come into her wolf easily as she became older. To go from human to wolf is to let go of inhibitions, and let the untamed spirit take over. Yet the spirit itself remains. However, to move from human to Wendigo requires an absence—a total void. The spirit must already have been driven out, past the point of healing, or the hatred of the Wendigo will not fit."

Chipeta ground her palms together hard, indicating the struggle. "Pure rage takes up too much spiritual space. So, there is a fight inside the person, between their natural human spirit and this... absence of one. And it always ends the same." She released her hands and spread her fingers skyward. "The good spirit is released from its torment, from this struggle with the Wendigo who would consume it. That person's spirit dies so the monster can live forever."

"And so Penny too..."

Chipeta stopped me, and closed her hands around mine. Her caramel-colored eyes were warm and sad.

"I have known Penny ever since she first came here. She was a strong, intelligent girl. But there was no hope for her. Her mother... I do not like to speak ill of the dead, but her mother did her no favors by staying here. Brandy had enough money to free herself from the life she led before she ever left California. But she was greedy, and they both paid for it with their lives. There was only one way Penny's life, and her mother's life, could have ended. Penny had already witnessed so many bad things that, when the miners attacked her, it pushed out the last part of her true spirit. The Wendigo could sense that, and that is why they were able to take her. It doesn't seem fair, I know, but almost nothing in life is. The measure of each of us is how we choose to confront that unfairness."

"Which wolf we feed," I said, watching Jonah sleep. He'd been given a sedative and was resting. Ernest and I had discussed at length what was to be done about the boy and his rotten arm before he'd taken his laudanum for the evening. Ernest had hated to take it again, given his past with the drug, but it was the only way he'd been able to sleep through the pain of his burns.

"Jonah will die soon if it doesn't come off," Ernest said bluntly. "Problem is, I can't do it." He held up his bandaged hands. "Even when these burns heal, I'm afraid I will never be able to perform surgery again. Too much tissue damage. And my face..." Ernest trailed off. I knew what he meant though. What patient, especially one already experiencing medical trauma, would be willing to trust a physician who looked like a fire-ravaged monster?

"How much time do we have?" I asked him. "Could I get Jonah to Bent's Fort and a doctor there?"

"He won't last," Ernest replied. "He'll be lucky to make it until morning. An emergency amputation would be his only hope." He studied me closely from between the folds of bandages that swaddled his face. "How strong are you? Not just physically, but your constitution? I could instruct you how to..." I stopped him.

"There is another way," I said. Then I did what no wolf is supposed to do, unless she is offering another human a choice to become one of us. I shared with him our secrets.

Thus, Ernest and I have agreed. Tomorrow at sunrise, if Jonah is still alive, I will help them both come into their wolves.

October 17, 1858

I t is done.

This morning at first light, I explained to Jonah what Ernest and I thought was best. As I sat next to him, I could feel the heat of his fever rising off of his skin like roasted meat straight out of an oven. Although too weak then to speak, Jonah managed the slightest perceptible *mmm hmm*, when I asked him if he understood what was about to happen and whether he was ready. Then, I changed out of my human clothes and wrapped the long woolen cloak around me again, so as not to frighten any of the Ute people who might see me moving from one lodge to the next. Chief Ouray had thought it best we performed the transformations alone inside the main lodge meeting hall, which was the largest building in the village. That way, if anything went wrong, no one would know.

When Jonah saw me pull back the hood of my cloak, our eyes met for a moment. I felt certain at last we had made the right decision. His eyes, still clouded with pain, glittered like black diamonds, eager for the relief that the change would offer. His good left arm lay on top of the buffalo robe covering him. I took the smallest nip of skin from the pale white flesh inside of his left forearm, swallowing it down and licking the blood clean from the spot as we both waited with our eyes closed.

Across my mind's eye, I saw a panorama of Jonah's memories. First, he played with blocks on the wooden floor of his parents' kitchen, until his father came stomping in, drunkenly tripping over one. The man kicked both the blocks and Jonah across the room. Then, I felt the panicked beating of his heart as Jonah wrested himself from his father's grasp and ran as fast as he could for the woods. The vision slowed a bit then, as I could feel the glow of happier memories. Jonah in a stand of pines near a stream, in what must have been a favorite spot, conversing with birds and squirrels, and gently coaxing a young fawn to eat from his hand. The day of his mother's murder was there too, and the pain of it seared like lightning through my consciousness. Not long afterward was the happiness Jonah felt on the days that he taught Sir Gawain riding tricks, the horse enjoying their companionship as much as the boy. Near the end, I felt his heartbeat go wild again, not with fear, but with hope and excitement. I saw myself telling Jonah he wasn't stupid, he just needed glasses.

As this final intense memory passed, the heat of the fever coming from his injuries intensified. Jonah's entire body shook with tremors. His arms and legs lengthened, and I could see a covering of solid white fur sprouting all over him. The raw swollen wound of his right arm healed in an instant. Yet, Jonah did not stop, as I had done, at roughly twice the size of a normal person. Instead, he kept growing larger and larger. When he finally rolled over onto all four paws, I realized Jonah could not fully stand up within the meeting hall where his body had lain. In his wolf, he was the size of an elephant.

Jonah looked down at his massive white paws, the size of parlor chairs, with wondering eyes, and then up at the ceiling. The tips of his ears grazed the rafters as he sniffed with nervous curiosity. I could hear his thoughts. Jonah worried he had ruined everything somehow because he he was too big to fit through the door. I tried to reassure him nothing was amiss and that he should lie down. Then, I went to fetch Chief Ouray.

Furrowing his brow and shaking his head as I explained what had happened, Ouray said, "This cannot be. The Great White Wolf is not a native?"

Chipeta, however, seemed to comprehend what had happened. "It makes sense," she rationalized. "The one who was sent to build a bridge between worlds would have to come from the world that seeks to dominate. Otherwise, why would those with whom he seeks to make amends ever agree to cross the bridge with him?"

Chief Ouray accepted this explanation, and asked to see Jonah. Once he had done so, immediately Ouray fell down upon one knee, whispering a prayer in his native Ute language. Chipeta told me he'd said something along the lines of *Great Spirit, forgive me for questioning your wisdom.*

For his part, Jonah looked uneasy with all the attention. I tried to comfort him, so he would not worry. Jonah lay down with his gigantic, shaggy head on his paws and his tail wrapped around him. I followed Chief Ouray and Chipeta outside and then into another smaller lodge nearby, where they were already speaking hurriedly in hushed tones.

"I accept it is the Great Spirit's will for this boy to be his manifest," Ouray said to me. "Given that though, are you certain the doctor is still the right one to guide him? Wouldn't he better learn the ways of our tribe and how to protect them if he were to remain here with us?"

"Ernest is a good man with an open heart," I reassured Chief Ouray. "He has already promised he will be everything a father should be for a young man. Jonah doesn't just need a father figure, but he also needs a proper education back East. He's never known anything but cruelty here from his own people. If he is to be the Great Negotiator between worlds, Jonah must learn how to speak to white men who are worth speaking to. Those who would be willing to listen to reason and who might have a real interest in changing things."

"But what if he goes the other way?" Ouray replied, his brow furrowing again. "What if they teach him to be manipulative as they are, and they bend his power so his will is no longer his own?"

Chipeta took Ouray's hands in hers. "The Great Spirit would not have chosen him if that were possible. Jonah is a kind and curious boy. Intelligent and rational. Much wiser than grown men twice his age. Have faith that when the time comes, Jonah will choose the right path."

Ouray's response to Chipeta's urging was lost to me, as a loud commotion had begun outside. A loud cracking sound came from the direction of the meeting house, like trees falling in a storm. Rushing out, I saw the entire village gathered around Jonah. They were chattering nervously. The meeting house in which Jonah had been transformed was sitting off to the side of him. The frame had been pushed up out of the ground. Jonah stood on his hind legs at his full height, which must have been over twelve feet tall. Yet, he wagged his tail cautiously from side to side like an uncertain pup. Seeing my surprise, Jonah's explanation flashed through my brain.

"I was just thinking how much I wanted to be able to stand up and get out, and then the whole thing just moved!" Jonah bent down with pleading eyes, as a dog might when hoping to avoid being scolded. Still in my wolf, I went over and brushed my much smaller muzzle along the side of his massive one reassuringly, which heartened him some. I looked over at the meeting house. It appeared to be on the verge of collapse.

"Can you put it back?" I thought to Jonah.

"I'll try," Jonah thought back. He stepped carefully out of the now-empty space where the meeting house had been. His black diamond eyes, such a sharp contrast against his sparkling white fur, focused solidly on the building. The meeting house began to shake, and then slowly dragged itself back where it had originally stood. Then, as if pushing corks into bottles, the exterior staves slid into the ground. The structure resettled itself into place without a single crack in the adobe walls. The assembled villagers watched in hushed silence until it was done. They broke out in a mixture of prayers and cheers afterward. I saw Chipeta exchange glances with Ouray, whose normally austere face had relaxed into a relieved smile.

Jonah wagged his tail again and yawned, his huge jaws opening wide. "I'm tired," he said. "That took a lot of effort."

"I'm sure it did," I replied, giving him an encouraging bump under the chin with the top of my head. "You're just coming down from that fever too. Why don't you go over that ridge there and lie down. Think of something calming. The change back should happen naturally. And take this," I pulled down a blanket drying on a line nearby from someone's wash and dropped it at his feet. Jonah picked it up in his mouth, licking his lips awkwardly, as he tasted the wool. "You'll need it to cover yourself when you transform back. When you're rested and ready, we can work on Ernest later this afternoon."

Jonah trotted off as instructed. I went back to my lodge, came out of my wolf, redressed, and went to see Ernest. When he asked how it went, I laughed and told him we'd gotten more than expected. Explaining the Utes thought Jonah was the white spirit wolf of legend they'd been waiting for, Ernest was less surprised than I thought he would be.

"I always knew Jonah was special," Ernest replied, wincing from the pain of his burns as he propped himself up. "So what do you think? Do you think I'm still up to the task?"

"Of course! Jonah admires you very much. Why are you having doubts?"

Ernest's bandaged hands smoothed the coverlet. "Not about Jonah. We get along perfectly, and I've always wanted a son. I just wonder what my wolf will be like? Both of yours seems to reflect what you were inside. I'm afraid there's just not enough in there for me to have that kind of power. Do you know what I mean? Whether I have *the stuff*?"

"Ernest, the only reason you were injured," I said, indicating his bandages, "Was because you had *the stuff*. You came out here to save me. Then you took my telling you *no* like a man, and we're still friends. Real friends. Probably the only other friend I have right now, other than Jonah. You confronted those men without a weapon. If you hadn't nearly been burnt to a crisp, I'm sure you'd have been right out there with Cawdor and me during Jonah's rescue. Of course you have *the stuff*."

A mixture of emotions passed through Ernest's clear blue eyes, some of relief and others of doubt. He stared down at the covers again. "I'm honored that you regard me so highly. As your best friend. I don't have another one of those either. And that you think well enough of me to be in charge of Jonah. But do you believe that we..." after all he'd been through, Ernest still couldn't get the words out. "We could ever be what we talked about before? If I am back whole again once I come into my wolf?"

"I still can't answer that," I replied. For I knew I could not lie to him, especially after he became part of the pack. He would know my thoughts, the same as Cawdor had. So I decided to tell him the truth. "I cared so much for Cawdor. I loved him. As we spoke before, I need time. Time to think about who I am now, especially since everything has changed so quickly. What remains after I've been forced to become something totally different than what I was."

Ernest met my eyes again. "I don't think you're any different at all. More of who you were to begin with, perhaps, but nothing's changed in your essence. Not really, except perhaps confidence, which I think the both of us needed a hefty dose." Ernest gave a little half cough, and continued. "But I understand. God, more than anyone, I should understand what it means to lose someone suddenly, shouldn't I? Especially when she—he..." Ernest shook his head as he corrected himself, "was your first choice. Take all the time you need in the world. If at the end your answer is still no, then I can take it. I'm a big boy." His forehead lifted where his eyebrows had been. "Big enough to realize that keeping your best friend is the most important thing in the world."

"Well, you'll always have that from me, I promise."

I left Ernest to rest until that evening, when Jonah came riding back up on Sir Gawain. He looked like his old self again, whole and without fever. Not wanting to cause further commotion, we agreed that Ernest's transformation should take place on the bluff overlooking the village. Since many of the Utes had seen us and were not afraid, I asked a group of Ouray's men to carry Ernest up to the overlook in a wagon. They left without being asked as Jonah and I approached them in our wolves, knowing we desired to be alone.

Before they left, they'd unwrapped Ernest as I'd instructed, so that the full extent of his injuries were visible. As Ernest sat in just his underwear on a blanket in the back of the wagon, tears welled up in my eyes. His entire torso was covered in an oozing crust where the fire had ravaged him. Ernest's chest, palms, and face were the color and texture of raw meat. In some places, almost no skin was left. As I met his bright blue eyes, I felt the desperation there. He could not live that way. The transformation had to work, or Ernest would kill himself.

Jonah stepped up to him. Looking for a spot of skin on his forearm to take for the transformation, but seeing none, he looked nervously at Ernest. "Here," Ernest said, grimacing as he lifted his charred arm across the remains of his chest, revealing the intact strip of pale freckled flesh just above his elbow on his triceps. Using just his front two incisors, which were still the size of playing cards, Jonah took the nip of flesh that was needed and swallowed it. Ernest squeezed his eyes together tightly, his face twisting in pain as Jonah placed his tongue over the spot to stop the bleeding.

The transformation was nothing short of miraculous. As his bones began to lengthen, I watched as Ernest's skin regenerated first, recovering his raw flesh. The large pointed nose that dominated his face straightened into a long, thin muzzle. Next, his fur, mixed red and gray like his human hair, came in over it, save for a large patch of white on his lower jaw, throat, chest, and the insides of his arms. All the places where the fire had burnt away his human skin. His ruined hands became two white stockinged paws. Ernest marveled at them as the transformation was completed. All in all, he looked something like a very large fox.

"A red wolf!" Ernest exclaimed, enthusiastically circling his tail as he examined himself from head to toe. "I should have known!"

We spent some time together comparing what it felt like for each of us, but I could tell that Ernest, for all of his excitement, was just as exhausted as Jonah had been. We agreed we should all re-transform and rest for a few hours. We'd reconvene at midnight for our first hunt together. Jonah trotted off happily. As Ernest turned to me, his expression was concerned. I heard his worried thoughts that, back in his human form, his body would still be a mass of scars. Without speaking, I knew he wanted to be left alone to see what would result, so I followed Jonah back to the village.

Turns out, we needn't have worried. Ernest took a long time to calm down so he could concentrate and return to human form. Tentatively, he walked to a pool from a nearby stream to view his reflection. I was elated when I sensed the relief flash through his mind as he caught the first glimpse of his face in the water. So eager was he to display to us that his entire upper body had been restored to its original state that Ernest walked all the way back from the ridge barefoot in human form. It took him over an hour. The blanket from the wagon swathed around his lower half trailed in the dust behind him. He staggered like a man in a daze. As Ernest went off to rest in one of the lodges, I felt more thoughts pass between him and Jonah. Remnants of the bond of common memory they had forged during Ernest's transformation.

I'm sorry all those other boys made fun of you when you were little, calling you speckled trout face. That was really mean.

A trout's face is better than no face, but I appreciate the sympathy. I've never been so grateful to see this old freckled mug in my life! Ernest returned, clearly still giddy from it all.

Later that evening, once we'd all transformed back into our wolves, I took them hunting. We tracked down a herd of elk grazing nearby. Jonah spooked them, by revealing himself too early, so we had to wait until almost sunrise before finding another old bull that was easy to pull down. Their reaction to feeling the rush of memories course through the elk as the last of his blood ebbed out was the same as mine had been. Pure gratitude for the miracle of knowledge this other life had given us.

October 18, 1858

Wolves can travel faster than horses, and for longer distances. We bade farewell to the tribe early this morning and made it to Bent's Fort by midafternoon.

Finding a lawyer to draw up the necessary papers for Jonah's joint guardianship arrangement between Ernest and me was no trouble at all. Lawyers at a loss for employment can always be found at the kind of bar that serves alcohol. There were two at Gad's saloon, so we chose the soberer one and had it done in an hour. First, I had the lawyer write out a deed of transfer for Grand-père Ulrich's dairy farm to Jonah, with Ernest and myself as co-conservators until Jonah came of age. Then, in the sealed letter I wrote to accompany the transfer, I thanked my uncles for maintaining the property in my absence. Also, I reassured them that since I had no plans to return East any time soon, I had sold a half interest in the property to Dr. Wheeler and his son, who were allowed to live there indefinitely until my return.

Grand-père Ulrich's cabin is solid and well-isolated by the surrounding forest. I have no doubt it will be the perfect place for Ernest and Jonah to hunt and become accustomed to their wolf forms without fear of detection. After all, I suppose that's why my grand-père built it in the first place. Although Ernest still plans to look for a position as a private physician somewhere, we all agreed Newport society was no place for werewolves.

Jonah and Ernest are staying at Gad's place tonight, but I've already said goodbye. In the morning, they'll begin their journey back East. I may follow them in the spring or summer. By then, I should be ready once again for human company. Perhaps.

For now though, I prefer to live alone. To enjoy the silence of my own thoughts among the trees and canyons, and later, to head further West.

That's one of the things I'd hoped to do when I first came out here, to see California and maybe even go all the way up the coast to Alaskan territories. Now that I have the freedom to go anywhere I choose, completely alone, I want to see the whole of America before we Americans have time to ruin it all. Maybe when I'm done, I'll be ready to come back and become part of the productive human world. Maybe.

This evening, I sat by a fire in the cave Cawdor and I shared, studying the names written on the walls in all their languages. Afterward, I walked around in my human form, staring at the pawprints left by other wolves in the higher circle on the wall. Try as I might, I could not identify which ones might be Cawdor's. Even after I changed into my wolf and put my own prints into their place in the circle, I could not have told any difference between the marks I'd left and all the others if I hadn't put them there myself. Perhaps it is better that way, though. For each wolf not to be remembered alone, but for all of us to be indistinguishably immortalized together, as a pack.

Or as my dear Walt put it, as part of the infinite poem that is America.

Tomorrow, when I say farewell to this place, I am putting my diary in a little crevice I've found up near the steamboat rock. Since I plan to do all of my traveling this winter season as a wolf, I have no way of carrying it, and I do not want it to be lost. At least, not forever. If something should happen to me, and I am not able to return for it, then I think someone should stumble upon it eventually. But if not, then perhaps that was how it was meant to be after all.

For anyone lucky enough to happen upon this little volume, and who seeks to find out what happened to me, I leave you this advice regarding my whereabouts:

> *I bequeath myself to the dirt, to grow from the grass I love;*
> *If you want me again, look for me under your boot soles.*
> *You will hardly know who I am, or what I mean;*
> *But I shall be good health to you nevertheless,*
> *And filter and fiber your blood.*
> *Failing to fetch me at first, keep encouraged;*
> *Missing me one place, search another;*
> *I stop somewhere, waiting for you.*

Acknowledgements

Writing a novel is a sport that is certainly more of a marathon than a sprint. Publishing four novels in one year is an epic odyssey.

Now that it is complete, I would like to acknowledge the four individuals who have been by my side along this journey: my editor, Raigan Nickle, my cover designer, Marta Obucina, my beloved partner in life and perennial first reader, Andrew, and my cat and favorite confidante, Jim.

Next, I would like to express my appreciation for all of my history teachers who instilled in me a love of the many mysteries of worlds long ago, if not necessarily far away: Lantry Brandon of East Elementary School, Dean Green of Cullman Middle School, Rebecca Reeves of Cullman High School, and also Dr. Larry Nelson, Dr. Mary McDaniel, and Dr. Thomas Ott of the University of North Alabama.

Additionally, I would like to thank all of the students whom I have had the honor to teach over the past twenty years. Truly, I had a wonderful time and learned more than I ever expected. Hopefully, you did too.

Finally, I am infinitely grateful to all of the Native American storytellers and teachers from the past, present, and future. Without you, there can be no genuine history of America.

About the Author

Vivian Catfield is the pen name of Dr. Candace Ursula Grissom. She holds a PhD in English from Middle Tennessee State University, an MFA in Creative Writing from Sewanee: The University of the South, and a BS in Music Business, also from MTSU, among other degrees. Born in North Alabama, she lived in Murfreesboro, Tennessee for many years. Currently, she resides in Cincinnati, Ohio with her partner Andrew and her cat Jim Nightshade. Outside of literature, her interests include acting, exploring haunted history, and spending time outdoors. Wolves We Feed is her fourth novel. If you enjoyed it, please consider checking out her first three novels, Keys in the Dust, Looking Glass Theory, and Prophet of Eden Park.

Also by Vivian Catfield

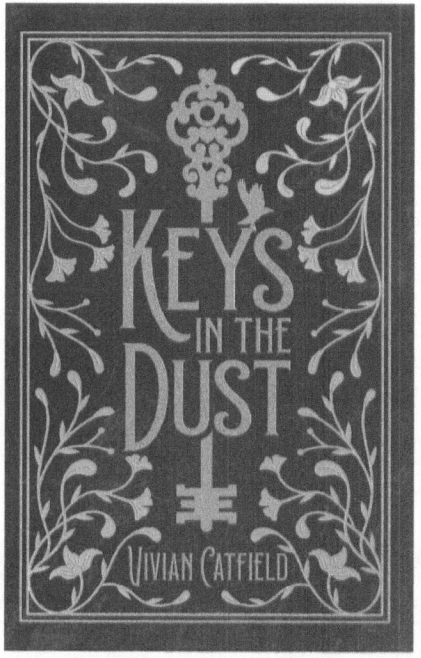

What if one silver key could unlock your power—and your destiny?

Willow Todd never expected a mysterious key to lead her to Rookes College, a hidden school of elemental witchcraft on an island shrouded in a magickal glamor. As a Spirit witch, Willow enters a world of natural magick, sisterhood, and ancient traditions—where students bond with animal familiars and harness the power of Earth, Air, Fire, Water, and Spirit. But Rookes isn't just a sanctuary. A deadly hurricane is coming, threatening to destroy both the island and the balance of the Otherworld. Guided by mentors inspired by historical heroines, Willow and her coven must raise a Cone of Power to defend their home. As Willow's magickal gifts awaken, so does her connection to Elliott—a mysterious Spirit witch with a broken past. Together, they'll discover that love, nature, and unity may be the most powerful magick of all.

Also by Vivian Catfield

What would you change if you could live your life over again?

Following her husband's death, Nora Hewitt seeks a new beginning by opening an interior design firm in Wilmington, North Carolina. However, Nora's entrepreneurial dreams are shattered after she acquires a set of haunted mirrors. Eerie, inexplicable events lead her to befriend a ghost hunter, revealing a forgotten world beyond the glass. When her sister vanishes, Nora must confront her family's tragic history: secret paranormal experiments, her father's alleged suicide, and her husband's mysterious death. Guided by restless spirits, including a past-life lover, Nora races to save her sister, while embracing her power as a woman alone.

Also by Vivian Catfield

Who can you trust after finding out that your beloved was a liar?

Grieving her husband Ethan's murder, private detective Shiloh Foley finds two dead women in Eden Park. The investigation reveals a shocking secret: Ethan, a Cincinnati police officer, knew about the cover-up of a horrific sexual abuse scandal at his elite local prep school. Now, the victim seeks revenge as the Prophet of Eden Park, building a cult in the city's abandoned subway tunnels to systematically terrorize and eliminate his attackers. With a team of unlikely allies, including a nun, a teacher, a social worker, and her assistant, Shiloh struggles against family betrayal and fights political corruption to uncover the truth as she races to stop the Prophet's deadly plan before it's too late.